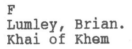

# KHAI OF KHEM

# KHAI
# OF
# KHEM

# BRIAN
# LUMLEY

 A TOM DOHERTY ASSOCIATES BOOK · NEW YORK

This is a work of fiction. All the characters and events portrayed in this novel are either fictitious or are used fictitiously.

KHAI OF KHEM

First published in the United States as *Khai of Ancient Khem* in 1981 by Berkley Books, New York

This book is printed on acid-free paper.

Map by Mark Stein Studios

A Tor Book
Published by Tom Doherty Associates, LLC
175 Fifth Avenue
New York, NY 10010

www.tor.com

Tor® is a registered trademark of
Tom Doherty Associates, LLC.

Library of Congress Cataloging-in-Publication Data

Lumley, Brian.
    Khai of Khem / Brian Lumley.—1st Tor ed.
        p. cm.
    ISBN 0-765-31047-3
    EAN 978-0765-31047-7

    1. Immortalism—Fiction. 2. Time Travel—Fiction.
3. Weapons—Fiction. 4. Egypt—Fiction. I. Title.

PR6062.U45K46 2004
823'.914—dc22

                                        2004048043

First Tor Edition: October 2004

Printed in the United States of America

0  9  8  7  6  5  4  3  2  1

for
M. Evelyn Hartley,
who had a great
deal to
do with it

# CONTENTS

# CONTENTS

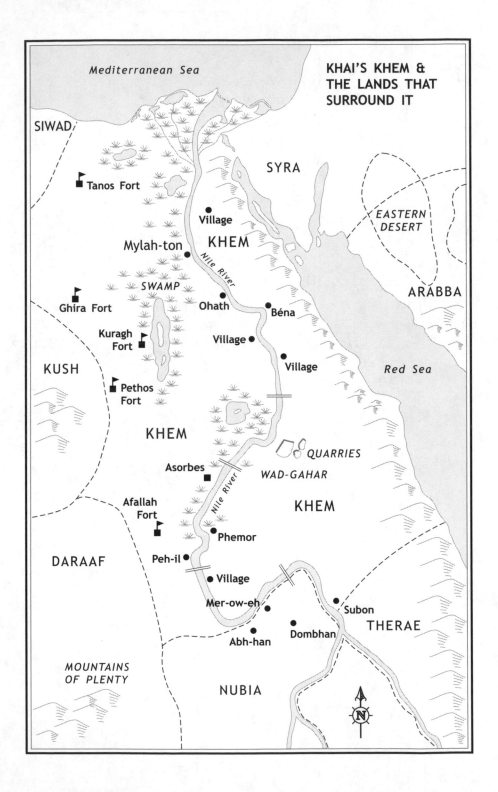

KHAI'S KHEM &
THE LANDS THAT
SURROUND IT

Mediterranean Sea

SIWAD

SYRA

Tanos Fort

Village

KHEM

EASTERN
DESERT

Mylah-ton

ARABBA

SWAMP

Ghira Fort

Ohath

Béna

Kuragh
Fort

Village

KUSH

Village

Red Sea

Pethos
Fort

KHEM

QUARRIES

Asorbes

WAD-GAHAR

Afallah
Fort

KHEM

Phemor

Peh-il

DARAAF

Village

Mer-ow-eh

Subon

Dombhan

THERAE

Abh-han

MOUNTAINS
OF PLENTY

NUBIA

N

# part
# ONE

# I

# AT THE POOL OF YITH-SHESH

Ashtarta—dark-eyed, raven-haired Ashtarta, with skin of a pure, light-olive complexion—knelt by the Holy Pool of Yith-Shesh in a cave high in the foothills of the Gilf Kebir Plateau. The pool, which did not contain water but a thick liquid seeped at the dark of the moon from a crack in the floor of the cave, was black as Ashtarta's huge, slanting eyes and still as her face. Its surface, like her outward appearance, was calm . . . for the present.

But beneath that surface . . .

Mirrored in the pool, the queen's face stared back at her with eyes in which the shiny jet of the pupils was almost indistinguishable from the flawless ebony of the irises. Her eyelashes, painted blue, were long and curving; and above them her thin eyebrows, which like her hair were so black as to be near-blue, tapered to the point where they almost touched the square-cut fringe that decked her brow. At the back of her head and at its sides, falling so as to cover her small flat ears, her hair looked almost metallic in its lacquered sheen. Parted at the nape of her neck, it was drawn forward over her shoulders and caught together again with a clasp of crimson gems in the hollow of her long neck; from where it fell in a wide flat band to be cut square just above her navel. Her nose, small and straight, was perfect in its symmetry and given to a haughty lift; when tiny nostrils would show dark, tear-shaped and occasionally flaring. Her chin was small but square and firm, and it too could tilt warningly when Ashtarta was angry.

The facial features at which she gazed—her own—were utterly beautiful, classic as those of another woman whose face would grace the pages of text-books thousands of years in the future; but Nefertiti would be a Queen of Khem (or Egypt, as Khem would become before Nefertiti's time) while Ashtarta was a Candace of Kush. And Khem and Kush were enemies poles apart, had been so for hundreds of years and would continue to be until one was finally destroyed—or until both were swept away by time and the ravages of war.

It was because of the present war between Khem and Kush that Ashtarta was here in the cave, kneeling by the side of the black Pool of Yith-Shesh. Her army, under command of the generals Khai Ibizin and Manek Thotak, had gone down from the Gilf Kebir into Khem, to the waters of the Nile itself to strike at the very heart of the Pharaoh Khasathut's kingdom. They had laid seige on the massively walled slave-city Asorbes—whose center was Khasathut's future tomb, a great pyramid forty years in the building and almost ready now to receive his mummy when at last the tyrant died—and by now the Candace should have received news of their victory.

Could it be, she wondered, that the Pharaoh's wizards and necromancers had turned her army back? Surely not. And yet she had seen enough in the five years of her reign to know better than to discount such an idea out of hand. That was why she was here now, waiting for Imthra, the mage who had promised her a vision. But Imthra was old now and could not climb the mountain of the pool as fast as he used to. It seemed to Ashtarta that she had been waiting for him for a long time. Now, as finally she heard the wheezing rattle of the old magician's breath and the shuffle of his sandaled feet, she looked up.

The old man, whose flowing white hair and long white beard seemed to burn golden as they trapped the mid-afternoon sun before the shadow of the cave's mouth fell over him, shuffled at last into his sovereign's presence. The golden glyphs of his wide-sleeved, black mage's robe continued to glow even in the gloom of the cool cave, while a redder light burned through the holes in a tiny firepot which hung from his wrist on a leather thong; and as his ancient eyes grew accustomed to the dimness, so they saw Ashtarta where she kneeled at the edge of the pool.

He saw her and held his breath. For frail with years as he was and most of the fire burned out of him—indeed, and the Candace the great grand-daughter of his own long-dead brother—nevertheless her beauty was such as to lend even his old heart wings. It was a beauty, he thought, which might wake the very dead.

She wore a clinging scarlet sheath of a shift with one clasp at her left shoulder. Her arms, neck and right breast were bare. But however simply attired, her beauty seemed almost immortal to the old man; like a perfect pearl in the dark flesh of an oyster, so Ashtarta stood out in the gloom of the cave. She looked more a goddess than a mere queen, thought Imthra, except that he no longer believed in the old deities. No, for they were dead as the recently green Sahara, mocked at, spat upon and murdered by Khasathut's black cruelties, destroyed by his necromancers and wizards.

Imthra prostrated himself, ancient joints creaking as he went down on one knee, then to all fours in the dust of the cave's floor. Ashtarta made no attempt to stop him. It would be pointless. Too late now to protest a love, loyalty and devotion that spanned eighty years, which the old magician had given Ashtarta, her father and his father before him.

He touched his head to the floor and she put her hand on his white locks. "Up, father," she said, "and let's be at the seeing. It seems to me that if all were well we should surely have heard from Khai and Manek by now."

"Aye, Candace, you could well be right," he answered, kneeling beside her at the pool's edge. "But I must warn you that the Pool of Yith-Shesh is no longer the bright crystal it once was. Its pictures may no longer wholly be trusted, and their meanings are often obscure."

"Still," she told him, "we shall see what we shall see."

They turned to the shiny black surface of the pool and Imthra flicked upon it the contents of a small leather pouch. Then, beckoning the queen back a little from the pool, he commenced an invocation handed down immemorially from his magician ancestors. Strange and alien the cadence of his old voice, and weird the energies that soon began to fill the air of the cave.

Then, at the height of his chanting, he began to whirl the firepot by its thong about his head. Soon it issued a scented smoke, at sight of which Imthra caught the jar in his free hand and unstoppered its perforated top. Done with his invocation and as its echoes died away to be replaced by an eery wind that filled the cave, the old man stretched out a trembling hand and tipped the glowing contents of the small vessel onto the surface of the pool.

# II

## THE DREAMS IN
## THE POOL

At once the pool caught fire, burning with a lambent blue light formed of a million tiny flickering flames that danced on the dark surface and turned it a luminous blue. The herbal substances that Imthra had scattered on the pool burned, issuing heady, scented fumes that immediately assailed Ashtarta's and the mage's own senses.

There where they kneeled amidst softly flickering shadows, the minds of the old man and the young queen suddenly reeled—whirling chaotically for the space of a half-dozen heartbeats—then steadying as the little flames began to die on the surface of Yith-Shesh's pool. And as the flames flickered and died, so the play of blue fires upon the dark mirror surface seemed to form moving pictures.

The two sighed as one, leaning forward the better to read the message of the flames. They looked and . . . they saw. And as the rising fumes thickened in the cave, at last Imthra and Ashtarta succumbed— just as the old mage had known they would— falling into drugged dreams of ethereal figures and formless phantoms. . . .

"Candace, majesty, please wake up! And you, magician—you, Imthra—rouse yourself!"

"What? Who is this?" mumbled the old man, shaken awake at last by none-too-gentle hands. He looked up from the cave's floor and saw a young warrior kneeling beside him. The youth wore the insignia of a charioteer, but his left arm was in a sling. That was why he had not gone with the army three months ago, down from the mountains to do battle with Khasathut's troops in the valley of the Nile.

"Wake up, Imthra. It is I, Harek Ihris. Up, old man, and bring the queen awake. A rider comes, two or three hours away. The mirrors signal his coming."

"What? A rider? A messenger!" Assisted by Harek Ihris, the old man sat up. The queen, too, awakened by their excited voices, stirred herself.

"Candace," Imthra wheezed, "a rider comes from Asorbes, from the battleground. Doubtless he brings news. The mirrors foretell his coming, which will be in a few hours' time. At the onset of night, then he will be here."

Ashtarta stood up and Harek Ihris assisted Imthra to his feet. They passed out of the cave into the cool air of early evening. Low in the western sky hung the ball of the sun, and away to the east something flashed briefly, brightly, reflecting the golden glow of the slowly sinking orb.

"See," said Imthra, pointing a trembling finger. "The mirrors of our watchers speak to us with Re's own voice."

"Re is a god of Khem, old man," the Candace sharply retorted, frowning. "And we are children of Kush. The sun is the sun, no more a god than the so-called 'sacred' crocodiles that the Pharaoh's people also worship."

"Just so, Queen," the old magician mumbled his agreement, though deep inside he felt that there would always be a godliness about the blazing solar furnace. He turned to Harek Ihris. "You go on ahead, young man. We will follow in our time. We have things to talk about."

As the young soldier started off quickly down the steep mountain path, Ashtarta called after him: "And when the rider comes, make sure he knows that he is to be brought straight to my tent. And let there be meat and wine ready. . . ."

An hour later, as they neared the foot of the mountain—more a high, steep foothill than a mountain proper—finally Ashtarta and Imthra found time to talk. Until then they had saved their breath, assisting each other in those places where the path was at its steepest or its surface loose and treacherous. Now, as the slope gentled toward the tents of the encampment, which lay about a pool surrounded by trees, palms and green shrubs, Imthra asked: "Did you see anything, daughter, in the black crystal Pool of Yith-Shesh?"

She looked at him and frowned, then nodded. "Yes, I saw something— many things. But they were to me a nonsense. Come, Imthra, you are the magician. What did *you* see in the pool?"

"Candace, I—" He hesitated, then quickly went on: "But as I have explained, often the pool's pictures lie, or at best they present an obscure or confused—"

"You saw evil, is that it?"

Imthra looked down at his sandaled feet and appeared to pick his way most carefully. "I saw . . . something. Its meaning may not be easy to explain. Therefore do not ask me, Ashtarta, for my vision would only disturb you—perhaps unnecessarily. Young eyes, however, often see far more clearly than old ones. What did *your* eyes see in the Pool of Yith-Shesh?"

For all that she was young, Ashtarta was wise. She did not press the magician for an answer but told him instead of her own visions. "I saw carts without oxen, without horses, moving fast as the stars that fall from the sky," she began, her great slanted eyes filling with wonder. "The carts carried many people, all dressed in a strange and wondrous garb. I saw great birds that served these people, carrying them in their bellies without eating them; and ships that went without sails on the ocean, which were as long as the side of Khasathut's pyramid! Aye, and I saw vast encampments greater by far than all of Kush and Khem camped together, with dwellings of stone taller than mountains and teeming with peoples of all kinds and colors in their millions. Then—"

She turned quickly, catching Imthra off guard, her troubled eyes searching his face. "Then I saw the general Khai, my future husband, who came to me as a boy out of Khem. Did you, too, see Khai, Imthra?"

"Khai? Khai the general? The Warlord?" He did his best to look surprised.

"Do you know of any other?" She peered at him suspiciously through silk-shuttered eyes, like a cat at the cautious pattering of a mouse.

"No, Candace, of course not," Imthra mumbled. "And no," he lied, "I did not see Khai in the Pool of Yith-Shesh. My visions were of no consequence compared with yours. Now please continue, daughter," he urged. "Go on, tell me what else you saw. Tell me of Khai the general."

For a moment longer, the Candace peered into Imthra's lined old face. Then she relaxed and said: "There is little more to tell. He had wings; he stood on a green mountain in a wild, craggy and alien land; he flew. Then . . . something swooped on him out of the sky like a great hawk. He crashed to the ground. After that I saw no more."

They were walking now through tufts of spiky, coarse grass between the tents. Directly in front of them, beside the springfed oasis pool, Ashtarta's large, pavilion-like tent stood scarlet and gold in the last rays of the sun as it sank down between twin peaks. Silhouetted against the tent, whose color merged with that of her dress, Ashtarta's flesh seemed almost green, exotically beautiful.

A handmaiden at the tent's entrance bowed low and kissed the hand that the queen held out to her. Before entering, Ashtarta turned to where Imthra had paused. "When the messenger comes, you will bring him to me?"

"Of course, Candace." Bowing, the old magician began to back away.

"And Imthra—"

"Majesty?"

"While we are waiting, perhaps you would give some thought to the meaning of my vision?"

"Majesty," he bowed his obedience.

"And to the meaning of your own—" she continued, piercing him through with her gaze, "whatever it was. . . ."

As the queen turned from him and entered into the scented luxury of her tent, Imthra bowed one last time, shivering as he felt the first chill of evening creeping into his old bones. He should consider the meaning of his vision, should he? Little need of that when the messenger, who would be here soon enough, would doubtless be able to explain it for him. And not, he was sure, to his liking.

So the old man turned away from Ashtarta's tent and made for his own less sumptuous apartment, a low, black affair with four poles, numerous silver symbols sewn into the walls, and black tassels hanging from each corner. He supposed he might look into his shewstone; there might just be something to see in there, but he doubted it. His eyes were of little use now for the scrying of mysteries, and his mind not much better. As for the vision he had seen in the pool: what interpretation could he possibly place on it except the obvious one?

He had seen Khai, yes. He had seen him stretched flat on his back on a bed of funerary black, with baleful blue fumes rising from seven encircling censers while chanting wizards in strangely horned, pschent-like headdress performed an ancient rite. It was a ceremony old as time itself, come down from predawn days before Khem and Kush, Therae and Nubia, before ever the first tribes of the hills and valleys came from the East and the South to settle in and around the valley of the Nile. The time-lost ice-priests of primordial Khrissa had known it and the long-headed Lords of Lemuria—whose alien blood, it was rumored, ran even now in the veins of Khem's pharaohs— and it had been practiced, too, in legended Ardlanthys.

And Imthra had known the ceremony immediately, even though it was not practiced by the people of Kush. He had recognized it despite certain basic anomalies, despite one highly peculiar circumstance. It was that rite with which the Khemites sent the *ka* of a dead person winging on its way into the next world—except that from the slow rise and fall of Khai's chest, Imthra had known that the young general was not yet dead!

# III

# ΜΑΝΕΚ ΤΗΟΤΑΚ

Almost two hundred miles away and a few miles west of the Nile—beyond vast, blasted areas of savannah, marshland and forest, where all the trees were now flattened down or snapped off at their bases and the grass was blackened stubble—there the Pharaoh Khasathut had built Asorbes, his titan-walled city and stronghold.

The heart of the city was a golden pyramid, almost complete now, whose base covered twenty-three acres. Built of fifteen million tons of yellow stone, it towered to a height of almost six hundred feet. In a later age, its tumbled and scattered blocks of vastly-hewn limestone would be floated almost three hundred miles downriver and utilized in building the lesser monument which one day men would call the "great" pyramid, ranking it as one of the Seven Wonders of the Ancient World. Khasathut's pyramid itself would not survive the ages, no, but if it had then surely it must be the first of all such wonders.

Central in all the lands of the Pharaoh—which until recently had consisted of the entire Nile Delta and Valley from the Mediterranean to the fourth cataract, and from the Red Sea to the swamps, forests and savannahs of the west—Asorbes stood huge and until now impregnable. Khasathut had used the crocodile-infested swamps as a buffer against the resurgent mountain tribes of Kush, whose people in their thousands he had once enslaved for the building and maintenance of his fortress city and pyramid tomb, a task which had absorbed him and destroyed them for years untold. There were few Kushite slaves in Asorbes now, for they had refused to breed for the Pharaoh and their blood had finally run out; but it had been the blood of a proud and fierce race and the Kings and Candaces of Kush would never rest until the agonized ghosts of their people no longer cried out for red revenge.

Now the savannahs were razed to naked earth, the forests laid waste and the swamps magically dried up from the city's west wall as far as the eye could see. Now, too, half of the army of Kush laid triumphant siege on the city and awaited orders from Ashtarta; and yet there was no rejoicing among the grim warriors without the walls. In the hour of his triumph the general Khai had been kidnapped, taken by the enemy and smuggled away into Asorbes by the black wizards of Khem. His fellow general, Manek Thotak, had bargained with Khasathut for Khai's life, and the Pharaoh's terms had been a truce in exchange for the young general's freedom. A truce, and the withdrawal of Ashtarta's army from Khem's ravished territories.

Manek Thotak, acting on his own initiative, had accepted these terms; but when Khai was lowered from the walls of Asorbes into the hands of his men, then it was seen that he was stricken with a strange malady. He was not dead, but it was as if he were.

Nevertheless, the Pharaoh had honored his part of the agreement, however deviously, and so Manek Thotak immediately ordered the withdrawal of Kush's army; and knowing of Ashtarta's love for Khai, he made preparations for the stricken general's immediate return to Kush. Manek had overestimated his authority, however, with those tribes previously under Khai's control, especially his Nubians. The chiefs of his *impis* refused to lift the siege but determined instead to wait outside the city's massive walls for Ashtarta's decision.

Doubtless the Candace would feel obliged to accept the terms arranged by Manek Thotak, but if she did not . . . Khai Ibizin's legions would wait here, beneath the walls of Asorbes, until word came back to them from the queen herself. If that word was peace—then, however, reluctantly, they would leave.

But if it was war . . .

Many miles beyond the dried-out swamps and shattered forests, hurrying westward, Manek Thotak led fifty men across a shriveled wasteland which recently was a sweeping savannah. He rode in a chariot alongside one of his lieutenants, while to the rear his men rode ponies and kept watch over a central cart in which, on a pile of soft furs and linens, the waxen form of Khai Ibizin bounced without injury as the cart sped over rough ground.

Manek had left his eighty thousand warriors in a temporary camp a mile or so inside the dead forest's border, within a clearing of sundered, shattered trees. There he had led them—many of them crowded into horsedrawn carts, a few riding in two-man chariots, the rest on foot or seated two-astride the backs of sturdy hill ponies—and there he had bade them wait. Then, setting off with his fifty men and the cart containing Khai, Manek had sent a lone rider on ahead to warn of his coming and to prepare the Candace for a great shock. The war with Khem was all but won, but the general Khai was lost.

Manek had known well enough not to leave his regiments camped too close to the general Khai's troops, for that would surely have caused unnecessary problems. The armies were, after all, gathered together from three separate nations comprised of many different tribes; and it was bad enough to have Khai's men refuse his authority in the matter of the siege without further exacerbating matters. His own troops would not take kindly to the fact that Khai's men had seen fit to ignore his orders. Since many of these little kings were recent rivals, they might well turn upon each other in his absence; and so he moved his regiments to their present location.

During that move, they had trampled a front two-and-a-half miles wide, with flanks half a mile deep. Now, by comparison, Manek felt almost naked. His fifty men seemed like a mere handful; this despite the fact that he knew there was nothing this side of the Nile which could possibly threaten him. All of these lands now belonged to the Candace, should she desire them. But Manek believed she would honor his arrangements with the Pharaoh. She was an honorable woman and must surely see that if he had not come to some agreement with Khasathut, then Khai Ibizin would now be dead.

As it was, the general Khai lived—if such a condition could properly be called life—but he could no more command Ashtarta's armies than could a puling babe. More to the point, he was no longer a contender for the Queen's hand, no longer a threat to Manek Thotak's own ambitions.

Manek ordered his driver to rein back until the cart carrying Khai drew up alongside. He looked down at the stricken general and a frown creased his high brow beneath the rim of his bronze war helmet. "Aye, old rival," he said under his breath, "and now see what you have come to. . . . You were always her favorite and knew it, though I never guessed it and you never hinted. She loved both of us—but me as a brother. You—" he grated his teeth and ordered his driver to speed on ahead once more, "—you she loved as a man, for your pale skin, your fair hair. And how well will she love you now, I wonder, with your slack mouth and vacant, staring eyes?"

"I see from the set of your jaw, Lord," said Manek's driver, "your pain at seeing the general Khai lying so still. What ails him, I wonder? Is it some disease contracted in the Pharaoh's cells within Asorbes' walls—or is it some device of Khasathut's black magicians?"

"Why do you ask me?" Manek rounded on him. "Are there not enough problems without your search for more? Leave the general Khai be. What can be done for him will be done. Concern yourself with your driving. I'm sore from the night's ride. Never have I suffered such a bruising!"

"My Lord, I only—"

"Be quiet!" ordered Manek. "And look," he changed the subject, "did I not see the flash of a mirror from the hills just then?"

"Aye, Lord. The mirrors have been talking for an hour or more. Since the rising of the sun. In a little while, within the hour, we will reach the camp of the Candace. Even now she awaits your coming with the general Khai, for our horseman carried your word to her last night, since when she has not slept but waited for you. The mirrors have told all of this, but you have not been watching. Your mind has been busy with more important things and so you have not seen the mirrors talking or read their messages."

"Aye, you are right." Manek saw little point in denying it. "My mind has been with the general Khai. He was a warrior among warriors."

"He surely was, Lord, even if he was a Khemite! Will there be a cure for him, do you think?"

"I think not!" Manek harshly answered. Then, seeing the surprised look on his driver's face, he added: "What use to bolster false hopes? You can see him there and know he lies as one dead. Indeed, he *is* dying. But if the doctors of Kush can save him, then he will be saved. Now let it be, my friend, and concentrate on your driving. Take me home to the hills of Kush. To Kush . . . and to the Queen who waits there."

# IV

## IN THE QUEEN'S TENT

It was early afternoon. All through the morning Manek Thotak had been questioned by the Candace—almost to the point of interrogation—and to little or no avail. The three royal physicians had attended Khai on his couch in Ashtarta's tent, and as a man had proclaimed him poisoned and on the brink of death. One of them, Hathon-al, had said he thought it just possible that the general was possessed of demons, and that perhaps they could be let out by boring a small hole in his head.

Trepanning was an operation with which Hathon-al was acquainted; his father had performed a similar exorcism on a young woman some thirty years ago. Because of the intervening years, however, he was not completely sure of the postures and incantations; but still he was perfectly willing to try. He would use only the most beneficent postures, and his brother physicians might care to join him in the utterance of their favorite and most curative incantations.

Ashtarta, who like her father before her had little faith in the healing magic of the physicians, had ordered them out of her tent. Theirs was a mixture of magic and science not at all to the Queen's liking. She could accept magic for its own sake—indeed, she had ample proof of the efficacy of many forms of the mystic arts—but she suspected that the doctors were mere amateurs in occult matters. All well and good that they should mend broken bones and sew up gashes, but when the soul itself was injured . . . ? The true mages, on the other hand, had earned Ashtarta's respect in more ways than one; and now, acting on Imthra's advice, she called them to her tent.

There were seven of them in all, their number signifying the Seven Mystic Arts of the Ancient Ones—those mighty God-magicians who came from the stars with all knowledge at a time lost in the world's dim and terrible infancy—and it was as a direct result of the incredible efforts of the seven that the balance of the war with Khem had swung in Ashtarta's favor, when their magic had stemmed dark forces which had changed the face of Africa for thousands of years to come and which, but for them, had perhaps blasted the whole world forever!

At the onset of Kush's latest offensive the seven had gone into the most inaccessible regions of the Gilf Kebir, and there they had remained in a secret place, using their long-range magic whenever the armies of Kush most needed their aid. Now a dozen riders were out looking for them, with orders to bring them to the Candace at once; and while she waited for their arrival, which might not be for several days, Ashtarta questioned Imthra about their powers.

These were *Alkhemy* (the old man explained), which did not originate in Khem at all but had been old when the Nile was a mere streamlet; *Fascination,* or hypnotism; *Necromancy,* or communication with the dead; *Pyromancy* and the control of elemental fires; *Oneiromancy,* or the interpretation of dreams; *Elementalism,* the control of the elementals of air, earth and water; and finally *Mentalism,* the use of the mind as a physical power. All of these arts were embodied in the seven mages to one degree or another; and Imthra himself, having been a student of the Ancient Wisdom all of his long life, understood something of them all.

As Imthra's interpretation of the arts of the seven grew more complicated and detailed, the general Manek Thotak sat on his chair and listened intently. Though sunken-eyed, the young general seemed very alert for a man who must by now be greatly in need of sleep, and plainly he was absorbing all that was being said. This almost anxious interest of his did not go unnoticed by Ashtarta, who put it down to the fact that Manek shared her own great concern for Khai Ibizin's well-being. And yet . . . she had been far from satisfied with Manek's version of Khai's misadventures, and even less satisfied with the truce he had arranged with the Pharaoh.

Now, as Imthra began to define the powers of mentalism—which in a later age would be known variously as telepathy, telekinesis, levitation and so on, and grouped under ESP in general—she put up a hand to stop him. She, too, was very tired, and Imthra's droning voice was making her even more so.

"Later, later," she told the old man. "For the moment I would speak again with the general."

"Ashtarta," Manek immediately responded, straightening up in his chair and granting himself the familiarity of first-name terms, "I feel I must offend you by my presence. The dust and grime of travel are still on me. I am unwashed and uncouth. Perhaps if I were to—"

"You do not offend," she cut him off, "nor have you ever. But indeed I am sure that your weariness has dulled your mind and tongue, for still I find the things you have told me unsatisfactory. Explain to me once more, if you will, how the general Khai comes to be in his present condition. Leave nothing out, for the future of all Khem—if indeed the Land of the Pharaoh has a future—surely lies in the balance."

The three of them were seated about the body of Khai where he lay as one dead upon his couch, and now Imthra sighed and leaned back in his chair, steepling his fingers on his chest and relaxing for the moment. In her present mood, the Candace was most demanding. He had suffered her angry ranting, her furious, frustrated sobbing and impatient questioning, for some hours. Now it was Manek Thotak's turn once more and Imthra was glad to be off the hook.

As of yet, the Candace seemed to have forgotten that she had ordered him to provide interpretations of their dreams at the Pool of Yith-Shesh, for which he was grateful. While her dream had been very difficult to understand and probably full of symbolism, his own had been fairly easy; but he knew that if he told it to Ashtarta, and if he so much as hinted at its meaning as he suspected it, then that she would be heartbroken. Better first to let the seven mages see Khai, and then to tell them of that ominous vision glimpsed in the flames of the cavern pool.

So, while Imthra sat and wrapped himself tiredly in his own thoughts, Ashtarta prompted her general again, saying: "Well, Manek? I am waiting."

"Majesty," he answered, "I've already told you everything there is to—"

"Tell me again, and do not sigh at me. How was Khai taken?" She reached down and laid her hand on the stricken man's cheek.

For a moment Manek looked as if he might rebel, but then he shrugged and turned his eyes down. Rather than let the Candace see the anger in his eyes, he stared at the precious furs where they lay on the white sand floor. Plainly Ashtarta found fault with his handling of the affair; perhaps she even blamed him for Khai's condition. Nor was he blameless.

"We were camped outside the walls of Asorbes," he began after a moment's pause. "Having defeated the Khemites wherever we met them, our armies were tired and needed their rest. Our tents were some four or five miles from the city. We had some meat, for Pharaoh's herdsmen had not been able to gather in all of the cattle before we surrounded the city. Indeed, we took a pair of young boys as they were herding, but they were mere children and so we let them go.

"So we ate and rested, and Pharaoh's necromancers sent their blight against us, which I have already described. On the following night, when we went to parley with the Khemish commanders, then Khai was taken. As to how it came about—" he shook his head. "It seems impossible now that we could be such fools. We suspected nothing. The wonder is that I, too, was not taken; and—"

"Aye, tell me about that," she broke in on him. "Tell me how Khai was taken, kidnapped, while you yourself—"

"Majesty! Majesty!" A handmaiden entered the tent unbidden, plainly confused and flustered. She approached nervously, bowing low. "Majesty, the wise men are here. They have come, as bidden—but the horsemen are not yet returned. The wise men say that . . . that they *knew* you desired their presence—and so they have come!"

# V

# KHAI'S SICKNESS

Evening was creeping in when Manek Thotak was awakened by one of his men. Ashtarta had sent him out of her tent upon the arrival of the seven mages so that she could be alone with them. Imthra had been allowed to stay, even though his own talents were as nothing compared with those of the seven. Manek, too, would have preferred to stay, but he was a warrior and had nothing to offer where the occult arts were concerned. The Candace had told him that she would call for him when she was ready, or when she had news. Now, having come to some decision or other based on whatever the seven had told her, she wanted to see him.

It was not without some trepidation that Manek prepared himself, splashing his face with water from a jar, combing his beard and making of his appearance what he could before leaving his little makeshift tent and heading for Ashtarta's marquee. He was chiefly worried about the mages and their conclusions. Not so long ago, he might scornfully have dismissed the feasibility of magic in any shape or form; and certainly he would rather place his trust in a strong arm and a keen blade than rub shoulders with wizards, conjurers and old mummers like Imthra. Lately, however, he had seen more than enough of injurious magic to make him change his mind, and he now knew that without the seven mages the war with Khem could never have been won.

Their powers were so completely . . . inexplicable—so much more than human. Why, rumor had it that like Khasathut and the five Pharaohs before him, these seven mages were descended from the Ancient Ones themselves! That was why (or so the fable went) they were so *different* from ordinary men. Nor were their differences confined to fantastic powers alone. . . .

Manek had seen the seven arrive as he left Ashtarta's tent, and they struck him now as forcefully as the first time he had seen them. A stranger crowd he could never wish to meet. They were gathered from the seven lands on Khem's borders: from Siwad, Kush, Daraaf, Nubia, Therae, Arabba and Syra, and yet in many ways they were as like as locust beans in a pod. Alike in that they were all very old, and yet sprightly and keen-minded in their old age. Alike in their bearing, which was proud and upright; alike, too, in the hugeness of their heads. All of which set them aside almost as a different species. But then, if they were indeed descended from the Ancient Ones, surely that was only to be expected.

Entering the marquee of the Candace, Manek bowed before her and turned to the seven mages. Though he had not seen them since the commencement of the latest hostilities, he knew well enough the part they had played in the destruction of the Pharaoh's armies. He saluted each one in turn, acknowledging his own and Kush's debt, and those of the lands of Siwad and Nubia. He kept his eyes averted from theirs as best he could, however, while yet scrutinizing them and attempting to gauge their mood and degree of penetration of Khai's condition.

But no, they were utterly inscrutable, particularly the yellow man. Had they arrived at any decision at all, Manek wondered? Certainly they had taken enough time over their deliberations. Again he let his eyes flicker quickly over the faces of the seven where they stood in their long white robes, arms folded on their chests, along one side of the tent.

Manek knew none of their names but easily recognized their origins. From left to right they were the yellow mage, from a land far to the east but recently an oracle in Arabba; the pale, long-bearded Theraean mage; the black, frizzy-haired Nubian from his country's southern forests; a leathery, spindly mage from the swampy borderlands of Siwad; a sure-footed, keen-eyed brown mage from the mountain regions of Daraaf; a wind-carved, sun-scorched Syran from the hot eastern shores of the Great Sea; and finally Kush's own hermit-mage, a wanderer of the hills, valleys and plains to the west. And here they were all gathered to council Ashtarta, come to her in her hour of need. Looking again at those seven huge heads, Manek Thotak felt a shudder run up his spine as he wondered at the workings of such great brains.

"General Manek," came the Queen's voice, drawing his attention, "you appear quite pale. Is something amiss?"

"Nothing, Majesty, except—I worry for the general Khai."

She nodded. "We all do, and with good cause."

Looking at her where she stood beside the stricken man, Manek saw the strain in her face, the great depth of the shadows under her young eyes. He crossed to Khai's couch and looked down at him, then again faced the Candace. For a moment they stared into each other's eyes.

"General," quavered old Imthra, breaking the spell. He shuffled forward out of a shadowed area of the tent. "General, Khai Ibizin is not sick—not as we understand sickness. Indeed, the physicians could never help him, for his malady is quite outside their realm. However, I was shown a vision at the Pool of Yith-Shesh, and my reading of this vision has now been confirmed by the seven mages. There is a chance, of course, that we are all wrong, in which case there is no helping the general Khai. If we are right, however—"

"Then?" Manek prompted the old man, his mouth suddenly dry and tasteless as he waited for Imthra to continue.

"Then we will need a volunteer for a perilous mission."

"A mission?"

"Aye, Manek," the sweet voice of the Candace, husky with emotion, rejoined the conversation. "You have known Khai since he came to us out of Khem. You have been rivals at the games, warriors fighting side by side, friends and generals together. You know him as well as any man knows him. Would you offer yourself now for this special task?"

"I . . . I would do anything you wish of me, Majesty, you know that. But what is this mission you speak of?"

"May we explain, Majesty?" The new voice, which belonged to the yellow mage, was a rustle of leaves, a mere wisp of sound. And now, as one man, the seven stepped forward, moving to form a circle around the still figure on the couch, enclosing Imthra, Manek and the Candace also.

The yellow mage positioned himself directly opposite Manek Thotak. Then, turning his great head to look at the Candace, his slanted eyes bright in the lamplight, he said: "With your permission, Majesty?"

"Please go on," she said at once. "Time is wasting."

Now the nodding heads of the seven all seemed to lean inwards, closing on Manek Thotak like the petals of some carnivorous bloom about an insect. The yellow mage said to him, "The Pharaoh's wizards have taken Khai Ibizin's soul. They have performed the death rite of the nobility over him— while yet he lived! They have sent his *ka* down the centuries, to inhabit the body of another yet unborn."

Manek stared into the eyes of the yellow mage and said, "And how may I help?"

"We are not completely familiar with this rite," the whispering voice continued, "for it is an evil thing that the Pharaoh's wizards have done, in keeping with their evil natures. Still, we believe we may be able to duplicate their dark handiwork." Now the great heads leaned closer still.

"We wish to send your *ka* on Khai's trail, also to be reborn in some far future, and we wish you to find him and bring him back. That is your mission, Manek Thotak, and if it is not done soon then surely will this mortal body of Khai's turn into a shriveled husk. Without his soul, the general will soon die. You are the ideal choice, for you have known him well and will surely recognize him when you find him."

Manek's throat was now completely dry, his tongue glued to the roof of his mouth. His eyes went from those of the yellow man to his six strange colleagues, and from them to Ashtarta.

"Do this for me, Manek," she said, "and you may name your own reward."

Now he found his voice. "Candace, you must know that I would claim the richest prize of all?"

For a moment her eyes widened, but in a little while she answered: "If you so desire, Manek, aye. I have thought for some time that you were an ambitious man. Is it love for me which prompts you, I wonder, or do you simply desire the throne of Kush?" She held up a hand to quiet him before he could answer. "No matter. As you must know by now, my heart was ever Khai's. And . . . if he were to die I should not want to live. To know he is alive, here, in *this* world, even though he can never be mine—there is no price I would not pay. Would you still want me for your queen on terms such as these?"

"On any terms, Ashtarta."

"Then you accept?" Hope lifted her voice.

"I will undertake this mission, aye. And when I return—with or without Khai's soul—then you promise to make me your king?"

She cast her eyes down, nodding in agreement, then looked him straight in the eye. "I do, Manek. And if knowing it pleases you, I think there are few men in Kush would make better kings."

"Manek," said Imthra, shuffling closer, his voice sharper than ever the general remembered it. "Not when you return but if! You understand, of course, there is no guarantee that you *will* return? No man can say what awaits you in your next life. The perils may well be extreme. . . ."

# VI

# TIME CAPSULE

"How will it be done, and when?" Manek asked. "I have an army camped where the forests of Khem once stood, and Khai's thousands wait outside the walls of Asorbes. Though they have their own chiefs with them, still they cannot be expected to wait forever. Who will carry your word to them, Ashtarta, and what will that word be? Without their generals the armies are a rabble, and—"

"If all goes well," Imthra broke in, "then the armies will not wait long for their generals. So long as Khai's army surrounds the walls of Asorbes, the Pharaoh stays within. Let him wait! Only the seven mages may answer the rest of your questions."

The Nubian mage came forward, his voice a deep rumble as he said, "You must put your faith in us, Manek Thotak. We shall perform the rite at dawn, with the rising of the sun—or, if things should go amiss, it may be repeated with the sun's setting. All should be well, however." His great brown eyes stared into Manek's. "I am the Mage of Fascination. I shall come to you with the dawn and bring you here, to Ashtarta's marquee. I will put you to sleep and impress upon your mind the importance of your quest, that in your new life you shall remember and go about the task set you." And the Nubian stepped back into line with his brother mages.

To Imthra, the yellow mage said, "There is the matter of a reminder."

"Ah, yes!" Imthra replied, and he turned to

Ashtarta. "Candace, when Manek finds Khai in his future incarnation, he will need something to quicken in him the true essence of Khai. The *ka* will of course belong to Khai, but *our* Khai will be asleep. There will have to be something to shock him awake!"

Ashtarta tried to understand him, frowned, shook her head. "What is required?"

Imthra looked at the seven mages. The yellow mage had picked up a face-mask of beaten gold from where it lay on a soft cushion. It was in the image of Ashtarta, a funerary device prepared on her orders against the possibility of her armies being defeated by those of the Pharaoh. She had vowed that in such an event and rather than being hunted down and taken alive, she would kill herself in a secret cavern tomb in the mountains. Dying, she would place the mask over her face. As her body decayed still she would wear the golden mask, going into the next world as beautiful as she had been in this one.

"Your mask, Queen!" Imthra exclaimed. "It would seem the ideal instrument."

"My mask? But how may we send a solid thing such as my mask to follow Khai's *ka* down the years? I do not understand."

Imthra smiled, his old face wrinkling like ancient leather. "We will not send the mask anywhere, Candace, but merely enclose it in a box of hard wood and bury it. Only I shall know of its hiding place, myself and one other. The other will be Manek Thotak. When his *ka* alights in the future world he will remember the mask—the Mage of Fascination will see to that—and recover it. When he finds Khai, and when Khai sees the mask—"

"—It will trigger his awakening!" Ashtarta finished. "Good! But—"

"Majesty?"

"Let there be more than merely the mask. See—" she pointed at the stricken general's recumbent form, at his right hand. "He wears a ring. He wore it as a boy and it has never left his finger. See how deeply it indents the flesh? His father gave it to him. Remove it now."

A physician was sent for. He arrived, applied oils to the middle digit of Khai's right hand and slid the heavy gold band loose from flesh which was permanently grooved. The Ankh relief on the ring's face gleamed dully in the light of the lamps.

"It is fitting," said Imthra. "As a boy he was a Khemite. The people of Khem believe that the looped cross protects. Since the ring has failed Khai in this life, let us pray it serves him better in the next."

"Manek," Ashtarta turned to the silent general and held out her hand. "Let me have your ring."

Without a word, Manek removed his silver ring and gave it to her. She gave both rings to Imthra, saying: "Let these things be buried under cover of darkness, tonight. Go now, Imthra, Manek, and mark well the place. Then return by a winding route. Tomorrow as the sun rises, there will be the ceremony. And then—"

Her gaze seemed to burn as she turned it upon the yellow mage. "How long?"

The mage steepled his long fingers and stared at them for a moment. "If all goes well, Candace," he whispered, "the transition will be immediate. However far Khai Ibizin's spirit has journeyed, and however far Manek Thotak must follow—even in the matter of Manek's recovering these buried things and his searching out of Khai—time is of no importance. For when the *kas* of the twain return they will be drawn back to this place, this time. The ceremony will take place and Manek will be seen to wax as one dead, even as the general Khai. Then, if all goes well, both shall awaken, renewed, restored!"

"If all goes well," she repeated him, her voice trembling, her painted eyes close to tears. "So many uncertainties. But what can go wrong? Tell me."

He shook his great head. "We have not done this before, my child, and—"

"And ignorance is dangerous—is that it?"

"Candace, we have this one chance to make Khai Ibizin well, to give him back his *ka* and make him a whole man. If we fail—" Sadly he shook his head.

Ashtarta turned to Imthra. "Wise one, go now. Do what must be done."

The old magician faced Manek Thotak and it seemed to the latter that the ancient's eyes were suddenly veiled. "Come, Lord Manek," Imthra said, leading him from the tent and out into the evening's dusk. "We go to find a place. And then you must get your sleep."

"Sleep, old man? I think not," Manek replied. "After we have buried the mask and rings, I must be riding. The village of Thon Emahl lies not far to the west, above the heights of Dah-bhas."

"That is so," Imthra agreed, "but what do you want there?"

"Thon was killed when we clashed with Pharaoh's army in the grasslands, and him without a son to carry on his name. His widow does not know—not yet."

"And you yourself ride to tell her?"

Manek nodded. "I do . . . and to spend the night! She is a beautiful woman, Imthra, with neither family nor children. And I have been too long away from the women of Kush. Before she knew Thon, she knew me; aye, and I would have wed her if I did not desire the throne."

The old man started, but before he could speak Manek caught his arm. "Listen, old one. If I do not survive this wizard's quest, will you see to it that the widow of Thon Emahl has my things, all I possess? If there is issue—" he shrugged. "Thon Emahl will have been the father. He saw his wife recently."

"We all hope and pray that you do return, Manek," said Imthra.

"Do you?" Manek turned on him with a snarl. "Do *you,* Imthra? I was of the opinion that Khai was your favorite! Or perhaps that is why you pray for my return—so that Khai will also be returned? Well, no matter. If I do return, I myself shall see to the woman's needs. I can find a husband for her from among my men. . . ."

"Why do you do this thing, Manek?" Imthra asked. "And why tonight, of all nights, when the Candace has promised herself to you?"

"What?" Manek returned. "Do you believe that? No, old man, she has promised me the throne of Kush, nothing more. She would be my Queen, yes, but never my woman. Why do I ride to Thon Emahl's widow? Look up there, at the bright and starry skies of Kush. Tomorrow I go to seek my destiny in a new world, Imthra, and I may never see these skies again. That is all well and good. But tonight . . . tonight I intend to leave something of myself in *this* world. Now do you understand?"

For answer, Imthra tugged his arm free of the other's grasp. "Come," he said. "We must be about our work. And you had better ensure that you are here when the Nubian mage comes looking for you before the dawn. . . ."

When the first pale flush of morning showed as a haze of gray mist on the eastern horizon, then the Mage of Fascination found Manek Thotak, haggard and chilled, where he crouched by the embers of an open fire. Together they went to Ashtarta's tent, where certain preparations had already been made. All was still except for the phantom drift of dark figures on the camp's perimeter, the night watch about their duties. Although the war was almost at an end, its lessons would not die an easy death.

In Ashtarta's tent, the Nubian lay Manek down on a second couch set apart from the general Khai's. He propped Manek's head on a cushion and then, by the light of a hanging brazier, began to make intricate passes before his face. As he did so, he uttered a long list of sonorous, languorous words. Manek did not recognize the meaning of these words—if indeed they had a meaning—but nevertheless, he found them very lulling. In any event he was tired, and it was not unpleasant to simply lie here and listen to the black wizard's low incantations.

The Nubian's hands seemed full of rings, golden bands that caught the glow of the brazier and threw it into Manek's eyes. Without realizing it, the general found himself closing his eyes against this glittering coruscation, and as he did so the mage's low-spoken gibberish took on a more readily recognizable form. Now he was telling Manek what he must do in his next incarnation, repeating over and over a list of careful instructions, demanding utmost obedience, indelibly imprinting his subject's mind. . . .

Somewhere, as the glow in the east increased and the brazier's fire dulled to a sullen glow, a cock crowed.

The Nubian straightened up, went to one of the partitioned areas of the marquee and drew the curtains back. There his six colleagues waited, all seated cross-legged in a circle. Their instruments of magic lay close at hand: bronze censers, golden wands, high-domed wizard's caps and capes embroidered with golden glyphs. Imthra was with them, but sat apart from them in a chair.

As the seven mages silently took their paraphernalia to set it up about the silent form of Manek Thotak, so Imthra left the marquee and went to the tent of Ashtarta's handmaidens which stood nearby. Moments later, he led the Candace, her eyes still full of sleep, back to her marquee.

Now the eastern horizon was aglow with subdued light and soon the sun's disk would show its golden rim above the edge of the world.

Ashtarta's heart quickened and the roots of her raven hair prickled as she followed Imthra into the incense-scented cavern of her royal tent. . . .

# part
# TWO

# I

# THE DREAM LOVERS

He was lying on a bed of rich furs in a room whose walls were huge sheets of purple linen. Above, glowing golden through the thin linen ceiling, a bloated moon slowly slid across the night sky. A brazier burned, sputtering slowly, emitting puffs of incensed, mildly narcotic smoke. If not for a warm current of air from beyond the bead curtain of the entrance, which brought pine sweet mountain air to the room, the atmosphere would be heavy with these heady fumes.

Used to the dark, his eyes wandered about the room. Close to the thickly piled furs where he lay, an old and intricately carved camphorwood chest from the east lay open, spilling flashing jewelry on a floor of pure white sand. The walls had pockets sewn into their lower edges which, filled with sand, anchored them firmly to the floor. He knew that this room was but a segment of the greater whole, which itself was a great summer tent, a royal dwelling-place. That it was summer was obvious: the heat welling from—from everywhere—would be suffocating were it not for the breeze from outside. The night was young, however, and it would grow cooler as the night grew older. Toward dawn it would be quite cold.

He had bathed earlier (he seemed to remember that), in a cold mountain pool beneath a waterfall, but he was uncertain how he came to be here on this bed of fine furs, with flickering, brazier-cast shadows leaping on the linen walls and glowing on his tanned, hard-muscled warrior's body. It bothered him mildly that he could not remember his name or his coming to this place, but he was drowsy and his eyelids were heavy, and it seemed a great bother to have to worry about or concentrate upon anything but the pleasure of simply lying here.

If only it weren't so hot!

Ah, but the heat had come with the *Khamsín* blowing from the great western deserts beyond the land of the Hyrksos, that scorpion wind of madness that dried up men's brains and drove them to monstrous excesses. He made a mental note that tomorrow—or the day after, he could not remember for certain—when his polyglot army went into battle, then that he would do well to wait for the hot breath of the *Khamsín* before striking.

Before striking at what, at whom? Once again he was at a loss to say. He could not remember. Perhaps it was the *Khamsín* which had stolen his memory, making his mind weary. And was it also the *Khamsín,* he wondered, which had driven her to invite him to her tent, whose husband he would be when the war was done? He hoped not. But in any case, the scorpion wind was gone now, flown down into the valley of the river to deposit its furnace heat in the lands of the enemy. And here he was in her tent, having crawled beneath its colored walls until he found the purple of her bedroom.

Ah, now he was remembering!

*Her* tent, yes, the tent of the woman whose bed he now lay upon. . . . But who was she? And why must he sneak like a thief in the night, who was a great general in the army of . . . whom? Slowly, he shook his head. He had only remembered her after hearing, tinkling from somewhere beyond many walls of linen, the voices of her handmaidens.

Handmaidens?

She was royal, then. And he was to be her husband. And she had bade him come, but not in at the door for that would be to shame her, whose pride was fierce. . . .

She must surely have finished with her bathing by now. What was she doing and why were they all laughing? Did she have a confidant among the girls, he wondered, who already knew that he was here? Did they all know? Well, what of it? He was who he was, and—

And *who* was he?

"Who am I?" he asked himself in a whisper, frowning. Before he could begin to seek for an answer, there came a flitting shadow, an outline seen in silhouette against a linen wall; then, the rustle of a bead curtain as a figure stepped through it into the room.

He had not known what to expect . . . but certainly it was not this. She was dressed—no, she had been dressed—in a sheet that wrapped her from head to toe; but now, on entering the bedroom and seeing him lying on her bed, she had discarded it, stepping from its folds naked as the day she was born. The purple of the walls and gold of the fire in the brazier were reflected from her skin, which shone with scented oil. Slippery as a fish she looked, sinuous as a snake. And like a snake's, her half-shuttered eyes were hypnotic as she began to dance, hardly ever leaving his own eyes for all her body's rapidly mounting gyrations and sensuous undulations.

Somewhere, as she danced, a drum seemed to take up the beat and now she matched its pulse. Perspiration began to mingle with the oil on her body until she gleamed with droplets of colored light like some queen of ancient magic. Spinning, her feet sent the white sand of the floor flying as she whirled round the heaped furs where he lay watching her. Her body was sweet and glistening, shapely and firm. A girl's body, narrow-waisted and round in the hip, with breasts thrown out now by the speed of her spin and dark nipples erect in the passion of her dance. For this was a nuptial dance old as the nation itself, the dance a bride performs for her man before she gives herself to him on the bridal bed.

As she whirled closer, he reached for her, his pulse pounding with that of the unseen drum, catching her wrist and pulling her off balance. He could not hold her for every inch of her body was oiled; but even as she slipped from his grasp, she tripped and fell panting, breasts heaving from her exertions and round thighs agleam with oil so heavily applied that it stained the furs beneath her body. Fully roused, he kneeled over her, his skin pale by comparison, his now harsh breathing matching hers in its passion.

Suddenly, seeing him poised, panic or fear flashed in her eyes. Where the heat of the *Khamsín* had burned in her veins, now chill mountain streams ran, taking the fire from her blood. A cooling breeze, rising up from nowhere, set the walls billowing and caused the brazier to sputter and its flames to burn a little lower.

She made to swing her legs past him, but he caught her knees and moved in quickly between them. Arching her back for purchase, she tried to wriggle backwards across the furs. Cruelly, he gripped the soft flesh of her thighs, drawing her to him. She sobbed and beat at his face, her shoulders on the furs but her lower body held up by the strength of his arms. Now he threw an arm under her supple body, his other hand seeking her breasts. Lifting her higher, he lowered his head and kissed her belly, his tongue finding the hollow of her navel and tasting the oil gathered there.

And abruptly she stopped fighting him. Beneath the fingers of his free hand, he felt her nipples stiffen. He lifted his head from her belly and looked at her. Her own head had fallen back onto the furs, where her shoulders took the weight of her upper body; and gradually he felt her weight lift from his arm as, one at a time, she drew back her feet to tuck them under her thighs.

He leaned back momentarily, reached out both hands now to her breasts. Her breath came in harsh gasps as she began to move her head from side to side, faster and faster. And although the hot wind from hell was long gone, still the *Khamsín* seemed to have taken her back into its spell. His eyes went to her gleaming belly, to the dark, tightly-curled mass of hair where her legs came together. Like a strange, sentient orchid, slowly her body opened for him, moist, hot and inviting. He gave a choked cry to match her moaning, and—

—*And started awake!*

The alarm! The damned alarm!

His arm sought the clamoring, clattering alarm-clock, swept it from its position on the small table beside his bed, sent it flying across the room to bounce off the wall and fall, still ringing, to the floor. With the action, pain shot through his body and he felt again the brace that held his neck rigid. Sweat bathed him from head to foot and his bedclothes were a tumbled mound on the floor beside his bed, thrown there by his dreaming struggles.

And already his dream was receding, as it always did, fading into mists of subconscious mind. "No!" he cried out, then cursed and fell limply back onto his pillows. "God *damn*!"

Her name . . . if only he could remember her name! But no, he had not even known it in his dream, so how might he now hope to remember it in the waking world? She was gone, and the dream too, returning to wherever it is that dreams are born.

Outside, the morning traffic rumbled in London's streets, and the tent of Paul Arnott's temptress was suddenly thousands of miles away. Thousands of miles and thousands of years away, lost in unknown abysses of space and time. . . .

# II

# PAUL ARNOTT OF LONDON

Wilfred Sommers made his way from the hospital reception and enquiry area through double swinging doors and down a corridor lined with children's wards. He passed through a second set of doors out into the hospital gardens, where he followed a path between a landscaped clump of shrubs and a rock outcrop toward the gymnasium. The latter was the physiotherapy center where Paul Arnott, the man Sommers sought, was half-heartedly complying with his doctor's orders that he help toward his own rehabilitation.

Sommers entered the gymnasium complex, made his way past a small pool where handicapped children swam under the careful guidance of specialist nurses, through one more door and into a room of wall-bars, weighted pulleys and all sorts of similar therapeutic apparatus. There, lying on his back on a rubber mat, Paul Arnott pumped small dumbbells, one in each hand, grimacing as his efforts put strain on his neck and back. His neck was braced front and rear by a sort of girdle affair which was laced up one side. It sat stiff and uncomfortable on his chest. Looking up at Sommers, Arnott nodded a painful welcome.

"Physiotherapy?" Sommers grinned.

"What?" Arnott grimaced again. "Good heavens, no—*uh!*—Wilf!" He slowly pumped his weights. "I'm—*uh!*—a masochist, didn't you know? Anyway, what brings you here?"

"Two things," Sommers laughed. "First, it's

been a week or two since I last dropped in, and—" he paused.

"And?"

"And I've brought something to show you." The smile passed from Sommers's face as swiftly as it had come.

"Oh?" Arnott prompted. "Well, then, why so hesitant about it? Show me."

Sommers nodded. "Put down those weights and sit up."

"Hmm? All right." Arnott gritted his teeth and forced himself upright. Bending at the waist, he allowed the dumbbells to thump down onto the rubber mat. "I have to admit, they were starting to get a bit heavy," he said ruefully. Then he looked quizzically at his visitor. "All right, what's your big surprise?"

For a moment Sommers said nothing, just stood and looked down at his friend. For all that Paul Arnott was an Englishman of a long line of Englishmen, no one meeting him for the first time could help mistaking him for a "foreigner." Even knowing him as he did, Sommers still occasionally regarded him that way. His looks were proud, hawkish, dark . . . Arabic. A man of the sands, a chief of wandering desert tribes, the son of a sheik, perhaps, or an educated emissary of the new, oil-rich Middle East—but surely not an Englishman.

He was English, however, and quite well-to-do; but much more important where Sommers was concerned, they shared a common interest. Along with the fact that they were both fairly young men, their mutual interest was the one thing they did share, for in everything else they might almost be opposites.

But in the three years of their acquaintance, a mutual fascination with Egyptology had made of them firm friends. Wilfred Sommers, following in the footsteps of his famous Egyptologist father, Sir George Sommers, was by profession an archeologist specializing in the Nile Valley; by contrast Paul Arnott was an "amateur" Egyptologist, albeit the most amazingly knowledgeable and controversial amateur one could possibly imagine. Certain of his theories concerning Ancient Egypt were, to say the very least, "unorthodox."

"Well?" Arnott prompted his visitor again, staring up at him.

"Paul—now I mean this," Sommers said. "I'm not joking at all. This thing might shock you."

Arnott's eyes searched the other's face, then went to the large manila envelope he carried. "Is that it?"

Sommers nodded. "It is."

"What's in it?"

"Just a photograph."

"A photograph is going to shock me?"

"It might. Certainly it will fascinate you." Sommers handed the envelope over. "There you are, see for yourself."

Arnott opened the envelope's flap and pulled out a colored photograph.

Sommers watched his face as he studied the picture, a photograph o
tifully worked funerary mask in glowing gold. At first Arnott's face p
surprise—a little shock—then astonishment and disbelief. His mou
open and he turned his gaze once more upon his visitor.

"Paul?" Sommers crouched down and gripped the other's shoulder. "What
is it?"

"Sh'tarra!" Arnott finally gasped.

"What? What did you say, Paul?"

"I said—" Arnott shook his head. His eyes were very wide, misted almost.
For a moment, they seemed to shine on another place, another time. Then
they cleared. "I said . . . Sh'tarra!"

"Is that a name, a place?"

"I . . . it's a name," and again he shook his head. "Wilf, where did you get
this?"

"You've noticed the likeness, obviously."

"Likeness? To Julie, you mean? My God, man, I'd have to be blind not to
notice it!" He made to get to his feet and Sommers helped him. "And yet—"

"Yes?"

Again Arnott seemed to gaze into space and time. "It wasn't just the likeness that stopped me. I don't know what it was, really." He shrugged half-
apologetically. "Give me a hand, will you?"

He wore tracksuit trousers. Now, with Sommers's assistance, he began to
struggle into the jacket. Holding the jacket for him, his friend considered
Arnott's remarkable powers of recuperation (his accident had been a very bad
one) and thought back on what he knew of the man, particularly of those
unconventional "theories" of his.

For instance: Arnott shared the Russian magus Gurdjieff's belief in an
unrecorded, sophisticated pre-dynastic civilization which was as ancient to
the Ancient Egyptians as they themselves were to the Greeks; and his firm
conviction, without a shred of hard evidence, that indeed Egypt was the forgotten source of all Man's wisdom, must surely place him alongside the most
exotic or esoteric of theosophists and half-baked cultists and their apostles.
And yet, Sommers knew that Paul Arnott was no crank.

His education and background alone were such as to preclude any sugges-
tion of irresponsible quirkiness; his instinctive and deep knowledge of the
accepted areas of his subject fully demonstrated his credibility as an authority;
Sir George himself had made him a standing offer of work in the field based
on his own estimation of the man's ability, and accepted Egyptologists of
more than merely perfunctory note had found occasion to seek his advice as
an expert. All of which only served to highlight those areas where Arnott's
beliefs were less than orthodox.

He himself insisted upon his purely amateur status—no, not even that, he professed himself to have merely "an interest" in Ancient Egypt—but certain so-called "masters" in the field would give their eyeteeth to be able to learn those things which Paul Arnott seemed instinctively to know. He had his detractors, of course, and if he had ever attempted to project himself as a professional, then these would certainly have made profit of those peculiar anomalies in his reasoning concerning a much earlier Egypt.

Sommers could readily understand why. . . .

# III

# MEMORIES OUT OF TIME

For example: Arnott was emphatic in his belief that the wheel had not been developed as a work tool but as a true wheel for use in conveyances and vehicles of war, specifically the chariot. Its war use, he said, must have preceded any domestic application by many centuries, though certainly it had been lost to Egypt's armies by the time of the Hyrksos invasions.

He agreed that the entire area now falling within the boundaries of the Sahara, including all of Egypt and lands adjacent, had once been a green and fertile belt as recently as 7,000 years BC, but disagreed with current concepts which relied upon gradually changing weather conditions and declining rain patterns to account for the rapid encroachment of the deserts. According to Arnott, the dessication of the land had occurred much more speedily than that—in a matter of weeks or even days—when vast herds of elephants, ponies, buffalo, hippos, perhaps even *Bos primigenius* had been surprised by the sun no less rapidly than the Siberian mammoth, equally mysteriously, had once fallen prey to the ice.

He argued that the iron sword had not been introduced into the Nile Valley by invaders, but that they had simply *re*-introduced it. The use of iron in weapons had arisen in Egypt or a bordering land and had spread outwards; the original center had somehow "lost" the art of forging iron; and the iron sword had finally come back again thousands of years later with blood and fire and the black thunder of war.

The pyramids (according to Arnott) were not merely fantastic tombs, but were all examples or inferior copies of an earlier monument long ago destroyed or lost in vast *ergs* of drifted sand. He had it that the "original" Egyptians—or rather their rulers, Pharaohs of conjectural lineage—had built their pyramids for an entirely different reason, in imitation of something which had stood there in an even older epoch.

And in this last example, Arnott's themes seemed inescapably to link him with the theosophists, with "sensation seekers," and with the authors of the current spate of lucrative but wildly speculative and romantic books dealing with primordial incursions from outer space. For he made no bones at all about his belief that indeed the source of Egypt's ancient wisdom was the stars. The first pyramid had not been built in Egypt at all—it had *landed* there!

Thinking back on these things as they left the gymnasium complex together, Sommers was brought back to the present when Arnott repeated his earlier question:

"The photograph, Wilf—where did you get it?"

"Hmm? Oh, sorry, my mind was wandering. I took the photograph myself, yesterday, at the museum. I'm on my way back there right now, if you're interested."

"*If* I'm interested, Wilf? Try to stop me coming back with you!"

They walked out of the room together and along the side of the swimming pool. The pool was empty now and Sommers's voice echoed as he said: "I'll be glad to have you along. It's been some time since the Old Man has seen you. But are you entirely free to come and go here? Don't you have to book yourself out or something?"

"No, I've been back at the flat since yesterday morning, but I'm still to report in here daily for my sessions. In another fortnight I'll have this dammed thing off my neck, and then—"

"Then back to risking that same silly neck hang-gliding, I suppose?"

"You know, Wilf, if they had only known how to go about it, men could have been flying hang-gliders ten thousand years ago. The materials were all at hand—rough and ready, certainly, but available."

"Is this the start of another Ancient Wisdom theory, Paul?"

Arnott shook his head. "No, but in any case, I think I'm finished with hang-gliding. I've thought about it, but—oh, I don't know. Perhaps the accident soured me. Julie . . . you know."

Sommers knew. Three months earlier Arnott had been flying at Glenshee in the Grampians. Julie had been a novice pilot. On the day in question Arnott had forbidden her to fly; the winds were blustery, the landing site awkward, the rocks far too sharp. She had waited until he was airborne and had then launched herself after him. He saw her—the way her badly-rigged kite was about to fold up—and he put himself beneath her to break her fall. She killed herself and almost took him with her.

"Paul, I'm sorry," Sommers said. "I didn't mean to—"

"Of course not, I know that. But let's drop it now. . . . About the mask," he changed the subject. "Where did it come from? How did you get your hands on it?"

"The damnedest thing," Sommers answered. "It was brought in by an Egyptian!"

"An Egyptian?"

"A fellow who works for a travel agency in Cairo, yes. Apparently he's a bit of an archeologist in his spare time, a treasure hunter at any rate, and he dug the thing up on a lone expedition to—"

"To the Gilf Kebir!" Arnott finished it for him.

They were just passing out through the hospital's main doors and into suburban London's streets. Sommers caught at the other's arm. "Paul, how did you know that? How could you *possibly* know?"

"How did I know?" Arnott shook his head, looked dazed. Worriedly, he said: "I . . . it was a guess."

"A guess?" Sommers's amazement showed. "Don't make me laugh. Why, you'd have to be telepathic! I mean, of all the God-forsaken places—"

"I tell you it was a guess!" Arnott snapped, his naturally dark features strangely pale. "As soon as I saw the thing I . . . I thought of it as coming out of Kush."

"Kush?" Again there was amazement in Sommers's voice. "But Kush lay south of Egypt, Paul, not to the west!" They crossed the pavement to where Sommers's car stood at the curb.

"It did in your ancient world, Wilf, but not in mine," Arnott answered; and again it was as if his eyes shone on distant scenes. "The Kushites did move south later, yes, but originally their land lay to the west of Khem, and its strongholds were in the Gilf Kebir. . . ."

"And of course you have proof of all this?"

"No," Arnott grinned sheepishly, seeming to come back down to earth. "It's just another one of my 'crazy' theories!"

"You and your theories," Sommers shook his head and held open the door of his car until Arnott was comfortable inside. He climbed into the driver's seat and started the engine. Out of the corner of his eye he could see that a worried frown had appeared on the other's face, that deep lines of concentration furrowed his brow.

"Paul, are you sure you're well enough to be out of the hospital? I mean, quite apart from your broken neck and busted ribs, you took a bad knock on the head, and—"

"No, I'm fine, Wilf. It's just that when I saw your photograph . . . it was like . . . I seemed to, well, *remember* things."

"Things like Sh'tarra?"

"Sh'tarra? Yes. I saw the likeness to Julie, of course, but the face on that mask—it was the face of Sh'tarra. It was her face."

"But who is Sh'tarra, Paul, and when did you know her?"

Arnott looked at him, looked through him. He shook his head. "How could I have known her, Wilf? That mask is eight or nine thousand years old. And don't ask me how I know that, either."

Somehow he managed a weak laugh. "Blame it on my crazy theories, if you like, Wilf. Why not? Just another of Paul Arnott's nutty notions. . . ." In another moment, his voice went deadly serious. "But crazy or not, I'll tell you something. The woman whose face is on that mask, that's Sh'tarra—and I've been waiting for her all my life!"

# IV

# ARNOTT'S STORY

"Wilf," said Arnott as the other guided the car out into light traffic, "I'd like to tell you about... about myself. Your father already knows most of my story. I once had a drink with him and I loosened up sufficiently to explain a thing or two—a few of my 'theories,' a dream or two—things that have been with me as long as I can remember. We talked of this and that and—oh, everything. He draws things out of a man, your father."

"Yes, Sir George is a wise old man, Paul," Sommers answered. "He accepts you, and that's good enough for me. He once told me that I'd do well to listen to you—that I might learn a lot—that you were the oddest collection of contradictions in human form it had ever been his good fortune to encounter. After that... you may believe I'll listen to whatever you have to say."

Arnott nodded. "Your father flatters me. But I suppose he's right; I'm sure enough a strange one, and that's the truth." He settled himself more comfortably in his seat. "Do you believe in destiny, Wilf?"

"I suppose I do," Sommers answered. "But it's for great men, Paul. For kings and generals—not for ordinary men."

"Oh? It's funny, but I've always felt that destiny was just around the corner for me. Is that strange? Oh, I know I've been a wastrel and ne'er-do-well to some, philanderer and fool to others—but ever since I was a small boy, I've felt that something was beckoning me. It beckoned and I sought it out. I've climbed mountains with the best of them, but destiny wasn't up there. I went with Adrian Argyle to look for old Atlantis in the Aegean. He didn't discover Atlantis and I didn't find destiny."

Sommers smiled. "Wanderlust is the word, Paul. You're not weird, you're just restless!"

"Restless? Yes, I suppose I am. I spent a year on a *Kibbutz* in Israel, two more on Hokkaido learning martial arts from the real experts, and I lived for a good twelve months in a so-called 'iron-age' pre-Viking settlement in Norway. Now tell me, if I wasn't searching for something that couldn't be found in the ordinary world, then just what the hell was I doing?"

"Getting ready for your clash with destiny, perhaps?" Sommers answered.

"Maybe," Arnott shrugged. "I'm not sure. I only know that when I was in Japan, it seemed all-important that I should turn myself into a fighting machine; and when we were isolated in that frozen fjord, the only thing that mattered was knowing how to cure skins and forge iron as it was first forged at the beginning of the iron age. But always, as soon as I achieved my aim—" he shrugged again and fell silent for a moment, then continued in a different vein:

"As for sports: when other kids were playing football or splashing around in the swimming pool, I was fooling about with archery and fencing, even medieval jousting! I've flown with the birds in a kite-frame of silk and aluminium; and I've donned fins and tanks of air to take me down to the bottom of the sea. But in all of these things, always destiny has given me the slip."

"Yes, you've done a good many things, Paul," Sommers agreed, "and you've certainly traveled a great deal, too. But why didn't you ever try Egypt?"

"Egypt?" Arnott frowned and shrugged again. "Perhaps I've been pursuing destiny on the one hand and avoiding it on the other—like a cat chasing its own tail." For a moment he mused silently, then:

"It's the one place—the one thing—that I've always feared," he admitted.

"You're afraid of Egypt?" Sommers laughed. "Now you really have lost me!"

"It's like a Shangri-la to me, Wilf, a Brigadoon!" Arnott turned in his seat to stare hard at his friend. "I've never been there, but I feel that I have. And I feel that *my* Egypt is still there. Not in this century, no, but in another time, another world. I feel—I've always felt—that I'm a sort of stranger here, in this century. And yet I've feared to go back, to visit Egypt now, today. I suppose I'm afraid of what I might find there."

"So you believe that your fancies aren't just daydreams after all but, well, memories of a sort?" Sommers glanced at him out of the corner of his eye.

"Something like that, yes," Arnott nodded. "I'm sure that your father guessed as much without ever asking. Of course, I've never told anyone else about it. I much prefer to be seen as an eccentric rather than a downright lunatic! But I'll tell you something: a few of those ideas of mine aren't nearly so crazy as they're cracked up to be."

Sommers knew what he meant. During a recent drought, a chariot wheel had been found in the clay banks of the Blue Nile at Wad Medani. Although it had been in a very poor state of preservation, it could still be seen to be different in construction from other Egyptian wheels. Also, while fragmentary artifacts found in the same clay were plainly bronze age Egyptian or Nubian, the hub of the wheel had been of iron! Iron? In a wheel come down from an era many thousands of years *before* the Hittites were allegedly the first to forge iron in Asia Minor? How could that be? Or . . . was Arnott right about a prehistoric wheel and a "bronze age" use of iron?

Then again, how could one take the man seriously? What of his rather more esoteric belief in visitors from outer space originating an Ancient Wisdom in pre-dynastic Egypt? Well, even in that area Arnott was not entirely alone in his thinking, though certainly his contemporaries were seen as charlatans and sensationalists. Sommers, for all that he must remain skeptical, could not help but remember an illustration Arnott had once drawn for Sir George. It was simply a picture of the *ankh,* the Egyptian symbol of generation; but alongside the conventional drawing Paul Arnott had drawn a second *ankh,* making it to look like something else entirely:

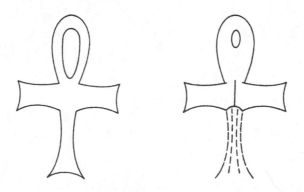

And what of the Egyptians themselves, the popular "Ancient" Egyptians as opposed to that earlier race of Arnott's convictions? What were the real origins of their belief that the Pharaoh was a "son" of the sun god and his representative on earth? And why did they believe that his body had to be enshrined in a great tomb, a pyramid, in order that he might ascend to the sky to become one with his father?

Why, if one's imagination were sufficiently fertile, it might almost appear that Arnott's—

"I'm accused of having been a wild one in my time," his friend's voice broke abruptly in on Sommers's mental wanderings, "and perhaps I have been. But if I was then it sprang from my neverending sense of frustration. Doing the things I've done—the dangerous things, the risky things—was my way of escaping, of running from the mundane side of life. Perhaps my mother's money spoiled me, I don't know, but it let me do what I wanted to do when I wanted to do it. Then, when I found Julie . . . she was the closest I've ever been to that dreamworld of mine, do you see? And yet it wasn't really Julie at all. It was just the way she looked."

"Like Sh'tarra, d'you mean?"

"Like Sh'tarra, yes. Like the face on that mask, that funerary mask from olden Kush. I have to see that mask, Wilf, hold it in my hands, feel it! The photograph brought things awake in me, raked over the embers, but I'm sure there are other memories that still lie dormant. I just have this feeling that the moment I lay my hands on that mask again—" And abruptly, he paused.

As the car drew to a halt at the curb outside the museum, the two men turned to stare at each other. They sat there like that, silently, for long moments. Then, with the slightest tremor in his voice, Sommers said what both of them were thinking:

"When you lay your hands on the mask 'again,' Paul?"

To which neither one of them had an answer. . . .

# V

# THE AWAKENING

The museum was a three-storied building standing central in an early Nineteenth Century street. Set back from the street proper, it stood close to the river, which could be seen from its higher windows. Its main entrance was through massive doors at the top of a flight of balustraded steps. Though one of these doors stood open, a sign clearly proclaimed the museum to be closed to the public for the afternoon. The last visitors had already left.

A museum of antiquities, the ground floor was filled with remnants of historic and prehistoric Britain; the first floor concerned itself with Ancient China, Mycenae, Peru, Crete and many other lands; but the second floor, where Sir George had his office and study, was the museum's center of greatest interest. For that topmost floor was a small corner of Old Egypt, trapped and immobilized here in London, where all the magic of that ancient land was concentrated into an almost tangible essence within four walls of comparatively modern stone.

Climbing the stairs close behind his friend, Arnott said: "Will I get a chance to meet your mysterious Egyptian? I'd certainly like to talk to him."

"That's already been arranged," Sommers answered. "He's staying in London for the time being."

"What's his name?"

"He calls himself Omar Dassam."

"And the Egyptian authorities simply let him

bring the mask out of Egypt and into England? Why did he seek out Sir George?"

Sommers coughed and answered, "He apparently *smuggled* the thing out! Being employed in the trade—as an agent for one of the big airlines— he had no difficulties. As to why he brought the mask to us—" he shrugged. "He says he 'guessed' we were the right ones to approach!"

Arnott frowned. "It all sounds too weird to be true. And what kind of a crazy trick was it to smuggle the thing out in the first place?"

They paused on the second floor landing facing a scaled-down three-dimensional model of Hatshepsut's Temple at Deir el Bahri. Sommers shrugged again. "I know," he agreed, "it is weird, isn't it? And I haven't told you everything."

The private section of the second floor, where Sommers's father had his office and study, lay at the west end of the building. Now, as they made their way down aisles of exhibits—between mummy-cases and man-sized models of Ancient Egyptian gods—Arnott asked: "Well, then, tell me the rest."

"When I came to see you," Sommers admitted, "it was chiefly to get you to come back here."

"You succeeded," said Arnott. "I would go to John-O'-Groats to see that mask."

"No," Sommers corrected him, "specifically, I wanted you to meet Omar. He . . . well, in a way, he's as big a bundle of mysteries as you are. My father will explain."

They passed through a door bearing the nameplate of Sommers's eminent father and through his office, then paused at a second door which would open into Sir George's study. Sommers knocked lightly and a voice from within said, "Come in."

"Paul," Sir George smiled, rising from his chair behind a desk that dwarfed his slight figure, "I'm delighted you could come." He extended his hand.

"How are you keeping, sir?" Arnott politely inquired, taking his hand in a firm grasp. "You certainly look well."

"Oh, I'm well enough, Paul—and all the better for seeing you. Moreover, I'm more than a little excited!" The professor was small, dapper, gray-haired and always nervously alert and full of a boundless energy. At this very moment, he seemed to sparkle with that excitement he had mentioned, and Arnott could only imagine that it had something to do with him.

"And so you're up on your feet and out and about at last," the elder Sommers continued. "And how do you feel?"

"I'll feel a lot better," Arnott grimaced ruefully, "when they take this damned straight-jacket off my neck! Wilfred has told me about your peculiar visitor, but he says there's more still to be told. Perhaps you'd like to enlighten me?"

"Ah!" the professor smiled again. "But I had hoped you might enlighten us!"

"I don't follow you."

"Sit down, Paul, sit down. Wilfred, get him a drink, will you? Paul, about this Egyptian, Omar Dassam. Does the name mean anything to you?"

"No, I never heard of him before. Why do you ask?"

"Well, I've spoken to him at some length, and to tell the truth—and quite apart from his accent and the obvious difference of character and background—it was much the same as talking to you!"

"How on earth do you mean?" Arnott frowned.

"When he talks about Egypt," the professor explained, "—about the prehistoric Egypt which predated the ancient land we study and try to understand—then he sounds just like you. It's almost as if you shared a common source of knowledge. . . . But listen, you don't have to take my word for it, you'll be able to talk to him yourself in a few minutes. He's on his way over here now. Meanwhile, what do you think of the mask?"

"The photograph? I'd much rather see the real thing."

The professor nodded and sat down in his chair. He opened a cupboard behind his desk, took out the large, heavy mask and placed it on the desktop where Arnott could see it. Arnott stood up immediately, took up the golden mask and held it up to the light from the window. He stared at it wide-eyed.

At that very moment, there came the sound of footsteps from the office beyond the closed door, followed by a knock and a guttural, muffled inquiry: "Sir George, are you in?"

"You see?" said the professor. "He's already here." In a louder voice he called out, "Come in, Omar, come in."

Arnott heard Sir George's words, heard the study door open and close behind his back, but he made no move. He remained as he was, as if frozen in that position, with the mask held up to the light. His eyes burned in its reflected glow.

"Ahem!" the professor coughed. "Wilfred, perhaps you'd do the honors?"

"Paul," came the younger Sommers's voice as if from a million miles away, breaking in on Arnott's rapt contemplation of the funerary mask, "this is Omar Dassam. Omar, Paul Arnott."

Now Arnott turned to gaze at the newcomer. Dark eyes stared into his own, a strong hand reached for his. The man was obviously Egyptian, sharing with Arnott a slim-hipped, broad-shouldered build. "How do you do?" he inquired, sensuous lips forming a curiously cautious smile.

Their hands met.

Dassam glanced down at the hand he held—and immediately snatched his own hand back.

"Wha—? What the devil—!" Arnott exclaimed, startled and angry.

The other carefully took hold of his hand again, pointed at the white groove that ran in a band round the middle finger. "That mark," he rasped. "Do you wear a ring?"

"No," Arnott answered. "The mark is a scar—I think. It's been there as long as I can remember."

Dassam released his hand, groped in a pocket, brought out two rings. One was silver and he placed it on a finger of his own hand. The other—large, golden, with an *ankh* relief—he gave to Arnott. "Try it on," he nodded eagerly, licking his lips, visibly held in the grip of unknown emotions.

Arnott stared at him a moment longer, then pushed the ring onto his finger. It sat in the groove of flesh as if grown there. Then—

The room seemed to reel!

To the two men freshly introduced, it was as if an earthquake had struck suddenly, silently in the heart of London, one whose shock they alone could feel. While the professor and his son looked on in amazement, Dassam and Arnott staggered and fell one against the other, held on for support, then straightened and gazed once more into each other's eyes. All was as it had been, except that now there was something new written on their faces.

Recognition. . . .

"Khai!" Dassam gasped, his voice choked, breaking as it gabbled something in a harsh, unknown tongue.

"Manek!" Arnott answered in that same tongue. "You, Manek Thotak!"

And in that long moment as the two stared, they seemed to look through their present forms to a time beyond—and they remembered . . . they remembered.

# part
# THREE

# I

# KHAI'S WORLD

The center of Khai's world was Asorbes, the Pharaoh Khasathut's fortress city. Asorbes stood a mile and a half square, built mainly of limestone, a little less than two miles from the west bank of the Nile. Indeed, the river was clearly visible from the top of the East Wall. Khai had been out of the city as a small child, down the river with his father almost as far as the Great Sea itself, but that journey was only a dim memory now. He did remember, however, that it had been a great adventure; how he had hunted imaginary beasts in the hills and quarries while his father prospected for the fine limestones of his craft.

Of Asorbes itself: Khai had long since explored most of the city at one time or another. He had been atop the massive walls, walking right round the city and back to his starting point all in a single morning. That, too, had been with his father, and Khai remembered how much it had tired the old man. And indeed, Harsin Ben Ibizin *was* old now. Khai was a child of his old age, conceived of an old man's seed in the womb of a younger wife.

Harsin Ben, because of his age, was lucky that no younger man had taken his place. He had his rivals, true, but it was also true that no other man in Asorbes or all of Khem had his skills as an architect. His greatest achievement—which stood him high in the favor of the Pharaoh and his councilors and guaranteed his continued employment well into the foreseeable future—was the great pyramid itself, Khasathut's massive monument, as yet unfinished but slowly nearing completion with each passing season.

Of necessity, Harsin Ben had to be at the pyramid's site almost every day, but that was the one aspect of his work which displeased him: the sight of those polyglot slaves whose life's blood stained (and not only figuratively) each single huge block of stone from which the pyramid was constructed. Khai, too, had found the sight of the myriad half-naked brown and verminous bodies that struggled, sweated, bled and died under the lash of Khasathut's overseers painful and offensive. Often, during his lone wanderings about the city, whenever he found the vast pyramid looming before him, he had paused to wonder why these people were forced to remain here in Asorbes when their homelands lay beyond Khem's farthest corners.

"Son," his father had once explained, "the Pharaoh has decreed that his pyramid will be built in his lifetime. He will be buried within the completed structure to await the second coming of his own kind, Gods from the stars who brought Khasathut's forebears here when the land was chaos. Because he knows that his time among mortal men is running out, he is in a hurry to see the work done. And so he takes slaves. Using Arabban slavers, he takes them from Therae, Nubia, Daraaf, Siwad and Syra—even from the hills of Kush, when he can get them. Aye, and the criminals of Khem, too—they also serve their sentences in the quarries and on the walls of the pyramid." And Khai's father had looked at him with wise eyes.

"I know what you are thinking, Khai, and even though your thoughts are deep and strange for a small boy, still I agree with them. You would not be my son if your thoughts were other than they are, for you are a kind boy, even as I am kind. But they are dangerous thoughts, my son, and must never be given voice, not in Khem. Console yourself as I do with this thought: your father only *designs* great monuments. He is not responsible for the way in which his masters choose to build them, or for the work-force they employ. . . ."

So it was that in all Khai's world, as in his father's, the one black spot was the great pyramid. The pyramid . . . and perhaps the ghetto, that sprawling huddle of low, crumbling piles and crooked, smelly streets where the slaves were quartered, where they lived out their lives and reared the next generation which, upon reaching the age of eight or nine years, would commence working on the pyramid in its turn. As for the rest of Asorbes—indeed throughout the entire lands of Khem, from the Mediterranean to the Nubian border and from Kush and Daraaf to the Red Sea—Khai's world was green and wonderful and teemed with life.

The river for most of its length harbored countless hippopotamuses and crocodiles, and in the forests the elephants and buffaloes were everywhere. Fishes proliferated in the Nile's waters and mollusks grew large and fat in the warm mud of its banks and in the lakes and marshes. Cattle not too far removed from ancestral *Bos primigenius* were herded in their thousands along with sheep and goats, and the savannahs were alive with antelopes, gazelles and wild pigs.

It was a land of plenty, where a whole range of wild asses, ostriches, giraffes, aardvarks and lions wandered the forests and plains at will, and countless myriads of other animals sported around the water holes and in the long grasses of the savannahs. Though the horse was almost unknown in Khem, Khai had seen a small number of those graceful creatures imported from Arabba and lands east; and he knew that in the mountains of Kush, fierce tribesmen tamed wild ponies, riding upon their naked backs and using them for haulage and other domestic tasks. He had often wondered what it must be like to ride upon the back of a fleet-footed horse. Why, a simple horse would be able to run rings about one of Khasathut's jewel-bedecked, lumbering ceremonial elephants!

Because of the number and variety of beasts and birds, Khem was a hunter's paradise. Khai's father had given him his first bow and quiver of arrows when he was not yet nine years old, and less than two years later, he had brought home a brace of fine geese shot in flight over the papyrus reeds on the banks of the Nile. On that occasion Khai had been in trouble, for he was only a small boy and he had returned home late, bedraggled and weary—and it was an exceptionally bad year for crocodiles. Several children and a number of adults too had been taken by the ugly reptiles, so that the city's councilors had offered a goldpiece for every Nile crocodile killed.

It was curious to think that in at least one province downriver the crocodile was deified in certain seasons and its hunting utterly forbidden, when that same year in Asorbes the tanners had amassed such a heap of hides that there would be no shortage for several years and sandals, belts and other leather and hide goods were at their very cheapest.

"If it were not for the fact that your own hide is so soft and white," Harsin Ben Ibizin had told his son, "and that you are the light of your mother's life, then I would flay you alive for being so late home! Here I and your poor mother have sat and waited, not knowing if you lived or lay dead in the belly of some great croc, and you straggle home covered in Nile mud, and only a pair of scrawny geese with which to redeem yourself! Are these supposed to be worth a day's waiting and worrying? You'll not do it again, Khai Ibizin, d'you hear?"

And Khai had gone to bed without his supper; but later his mother, Merayet, had sneaked in to him with bread and meat and a cup of sweet wine. "My fine hunter," she had called him, and had gone on to tell him that indeed his geese were excellent birds, glossy and fat. "We shall eat them tomorrow," she said, "roasted on spits in the garden, when we all come home from the Pharaoh's Procession."

The Royal Procession, yes! And this would be the first time that Khai had ever seen it. The splendid pomp and ceremony of Khasathut's quarterly parade, when the Pharaoh himself would appear to the people, to be praised and worshipped by them; when he would choose three more brides, as he did four times a year, to enter with him into the pyramid and the glory of matrimony with the great and omnipotent man-God. . . .

# II

# THE GOD-KING'S PARADE

With the first rays of the morning sun—whose golden disk had been a god long before Khasathut's many-times great-grandfather had become the first Pharaoh—the peoples of Khem were out in all their finery, thronging through the streets, squares and thoroughfares of Asorbes to gather at the base of the pyramid.

Arriving mid-morning with his parents, his older brother Adhan and his sister Namisha, Khai was astonished at the masses of color, the fantastic arrangements of flowers which adorned the sides of the great ramp, the thousands of pennants emblazoned with Khasathut's double-looped *ankh,* and the gold and ivory gleam of the Pharaoh's Black Guard where they stood single-ranked along the three edges of the pyramid's plateau-like eastern summit.

Wide ramps of packed earth had once wound in a rising square whorl about a towering central pillar which had formed the core of the pyramid. Pre-shaped blocks of stone had been pushed, dragged and hoisted up these ramps to be positioned on the inside, thus forming the inner mazes, chambers and outer walls of that mighty monument. The north, south and west faces were now almost complete; they lacked only their facing of fine white limestone and the layer of beaten gold with which Khasathut intended eventually to cover them.

The eastern face, however, with its great ramp that ran up to it for almost half a mile from the distantly looming East Wall, was still incomplete. At its top it formed a man-made plateau. There the ranks of the Black Guard stood at ease, as they had stood since early morning, their spears leaning outward over the city; behind them a great pinnacle of carved stone in the shape of a vast arrowhead towered almost half as high as the plateau again.

As noon approached and the sun drew near the zenith, the merchants collapsed their many stalls and bundled up their wares, the crowds drew back from the paved road that reached around the pyramid's base and along both sides of the great ramp, and there was sudden movement atop the high plateau of the east face. There, where the ramp merged with the lip of the plateau, the Black Guard had drawn aside; and now, with a blare of brazen trumpets, the rest of the guardsmen snapped to attention and lifted their spears in the royal salute. This was the moment for which Khai had been waiting, when Pharaoh would show himself to his people.

Khasathut—a man, and yet a god—descendant of those Great Gods from the sky who came in their golden pyramid when the tribes of Khem were mere savages and left their seed to take root in the fertile valley of the Nile. Legend had it that the first gods who grew from that seed were weak and died young, and that many generations passed before there grew to old age a Pharaoh of that alien stock. This was because the gods had mated with the daughters of mere men, which had severely weakened their blood. By the time the strain was strong again, most of the wisdom of the sky-gods had been lost forever, for none had lived long enough to learn it and pass it on. Thus, only the legends now remained. And now, with his own eyes, Khai was about to see one of those legends—or the sole surviving descendant of them—for himself.

The Ibizins had an excellent view of the entire affair. They were seated along with many other high-ranking personages and their families on cushioned chairs placed about marble tables on a dais high over the heads of Asorbes' less prominent citizens. Even so, they had to crane their necks to look up at the plateau's rim where the Pharaoh now appeared.

Khai, because he had been distracted by a distant trumpeting of elephants from somewhere to the rear of the pyramid, did not actually see the figure of the Pharaoh come into view—but he heard the sudden cessation of all mundane sounds, and then the concerted sigh that went up from many thousands of throats. Only then did Khai turn his widening eyes up to the incredible golden figure on the plateau high above.

Towering head and shoulders over the huge black guardsmen flanking him, Khasathut was massive! In a flowing robe of royal golden-yellow, the God-king stood at the head of the great ramp and looked out over Asorbes, over all Khem. He slowly turned his huge head to the south, as if looking far beyond the borders of Khem to the unseen sources of the Nile, then to the north, toward the Great Sea and beyond, and finally he faced east and inclined his head downward to gaze upon his people. So huge was Pharaoh that Khai fancied he could make out his features: radiant, benign and beautiful.

Then the awesome figure slowly held up its arms and its robe fell from incredibly broad shoulders; and again that mighty sigh, that gasp of wonder, went up from Khasathut's subjects. The sun was reflected dazzlingly from golden armor that covered his body and limbs, from a golden crown that sat upon his head, and thousands of eyes watered as they stared at a skirt embroidered with hundreds of glittering jewels.

"Why!" Khai thought out loud, his voice the merest whisper, "his arms and his thighs, they must be like trees!" He had seen huge Nubian wrestlers fighting bouts for their Khemite masters in the market squares, but even they would be dwarfed by the massive figure atop the ramp who now drew the crowd's amazed and adoring attention. And why shouldn't they adore him? His prosperity was Khem's prosperity, wasn't it? And if ever a man looked like a king, surely the Pharaoh was that man. And if a king could be a god, then most certainly was Khasathut the God-king himself!

And now the members of the Black Guard were replaced on the high plateau by the royal trumpeters, whose molten instruments blared out in unison once more to herald the commencement of Pharaoh's parade. As a bellowing of elephants answered the call of the trumpeters, so a huge throne was pushed forward from behind the great golden God-figure and Khasathut seated himself (rather stiffly, Khai thought). Then, with a vast swaying of trunks and a pounding of great gray limbs, the Pharaoh's two hundred elephants appeared from behind the pyramid, maneuvering along the base of the north face and down the paved road toward the foot of the ramp. Wearing horned helmets of bronze and armored about their great knees—driven by tiny, big-bellied pigmy riders who sat the mighty beasts bareback—the huge pachyderms were the most fearsome creatures that Khai had ever seen.

No sooner had the elephants passed the dais of the dignitaries than Khasathut's archers appeared, jogging in ranks of ten immediately in the wake of the beasts. Following the bowmen—who numbered no less than fifteen hundred—came the infantry, rank upon rank of them, all in tens. Sixty thousand men of Khem and thirty thousand from neighboring Syra, Arabba, Therae, Daraaf and Siwad trotted by in strict military precision; and indeed their numbers were such that they took almost an hour to pass. And each and every man of them carried a bronze sword and a shield of hide patterned with bronze studs.

Kush and Nubia were the only absentees; for while certainly there were Kushites among the Pharaoh's slaves, no man of Kush would ever volunteer to become a mercenary in Khasathut's army. No, rather death than that. The Kushites were wild and wilful, hill-dwellers in the main who preferred the freedom of the heights to the lowlands and the oppression of Khasathut's border patrols and his Arabban slavers. The God-king had sworn that one day he would see Kush overrun and crushed, but until that day he would have to be satisfied with his few Kushite slaves. And even the children of such were unruly and unreliable, and certainly they could never be trained for military service—not in the Pharaoh's army, at least.

As for Nubia: Pharaoh had his Black Guard, but none of them were of good birth. They were all the sons of slaves, chosen for their size and trained from birth to attend Pharaoh's every whim. If he so much as snapped his fingers in command, each and every last one of them would fling himself from the plateau. He was also supposed to have five thousand trained warriors—an *impi* of terrific fighting prowess—but these had been withdrawn by their king in Nubia six months ago (ostensibly to be trained in the jungles of their homeland) and their return was already overdue.

So the parade passed. The infantry was followed by a thousand specialist spearsmen and seven hundred marksmen with their slings; and finally there came the generals five-square: twenty-five massive military commanders, all carrying their individual banners of nation and regiment, pausing *en-masse* where Khasathut could see them from on high. They dipped their colors low three times before him, and in return he held out his left arm over them, saluting them. Then they snapped to attention and turned to follow the army along the base of the great ramp.

All of these men—well over one hundred thousand of them—and the elephants, too, they had all been mustered unseen to the west of the great pyramid, in the hugely sprawling barracks that housed them when they were not maneuvering. But now the military side of the day was almost done. Now there only remained the Choosing of the Brides, and finally the presentation to the Pharaoh of all personages of note. Then all would be done except for the feasting and drinking, by which time Khasathut would have retreated back into the pyramid's secret ways with his new wives.

By then, too, the Ibizins would have returned home, preferring to celebrate in the privacy of their own splendid house near the East Wall. Harsin Ben did not yet know it, but on this occasion he would have precious little to celebrate. . . .

# III

# THE GOD-KING COMMANDS

As soon as Pharaoh drew back from the lip of his aerie and passed out of view, then the common folk of Asorbes began to disperse and drift away from the vast central plaza of the great pyramid; for them the show was over. A few minutes passed while the crowd thinned, during which time a large number of hugely muscled, freshly-scrubbed and cleanly-robed slaves assembled in pairs from the neighboring streets carrying litters of light, ornately woven reed. A third slave bearing a large fan made up each litter's complement.

As the families of the city's dignitaries stepped down from their dais, so they were taken up one by one into the litters and borne up a great flight of steps that climbed the side of the ramp from its base to the rim of the plateau. When each personage had been safely deposited atop that man-made mountain, then his bearers would take up their empty litter and trot with it down the long ramp, so that soon a line of them could be seen scurrying like so many ants down the length of the elevated roadway.

Simultaneous with this activity, a string of specially canopied litters was being borne by the broad steps, and within the silk walls of these carrying-chairs were those girls whose beauty had been noted by Pharaoh's scouts during the preceding quarter. These were the twenty from which Khasathut would choose his three brides-to-be.

The Ibizins, too, stepped down from the dais and into their litters to be carried up the great stairway; and Khai, gazing out over the city as he was lifted ever higher, grew dizzy with the view and wondered how his mother fared, who shunned heights and dreaded what seemed to her an all-too-regular nightmare. At last, however, the entire family stood among dozens of friends on the plateau itself; and when the last of the lesser dignitaries—rich merchants, river-lords, foreign diplomats and governors of one sort or another—were safely brought up, then there came the ceremony of the Choosing of the Brides.

Seated upon his massive throne in the shadow of the towering wall behind him, Khasathut nodded as each of the twenty girls was paraded before him, and on three occasions he lifted up his right hand to signify that this particular girl pleased him greatly. Each of the three girls thus chosen went forward in turn, kneeled and kissed the jewel-encased feet of their husband to be, the God-king himself.

By now Khai had come to realize that Pharaoh was not necessarily the huge figure of a man he had thought him, for on closer inspection it could plainly be seen that his outward appearance was merely a facade, a manlike construction behind which the true Pharaoh discreetly avoided the doubtless corrupting gaze of merely mortal men. This was of course as it should be, for Pharaoh was no common man upon whom any other might look whenever he desired. Indeed, it was rumored among the more ignorant of his subjects that Khasathut's beauty was such as to blind any commoner who might catch sight of him unawares.

Now, as his three newly-chosen brides were led away into the pyramid through a massive arched entrance that loomed behind him—from which they would nevermore step forth into the sight of common folk—Pharaoh called to his Vizier, Anulep the high-priest, and bade him draw closer. Anulep, who until now had stood to one side with his arms folded across his chest, answered Pharaoh's call by falling to all fours, crawling to him and putting his head between his jeweled feet.

"Up, Anulep," Khasathut commanded. "Bring to me the first of my Lords that I may know them again. And bring them before me for my blessing, each in his turn with his family, that they may share equally in that glory which is mine alone to bestow."

As Anulep rose and approached the assembled dignitaries and their families, Khai stared at him in awe and amazement—and with something very much akin to fear or at least apprehension: The man was spectrally pale, tall and gaunt, with a long scrawny neck and a face and head utterly naked of hair. He looked like nothing so much as a vulture in human form, or at best a gray and ghastly Theraen embalmer; and Khai found himself wondering if the Vizier ever had grown eyebrows or eyelashes at all, or if he simply shaved them off each morning. From the look of the polished dome of his head, hair certainly had not grown there for many years.

Moreover, when Anulep smiled at the nobles and officials as he invited them to step forward, it could plainly be seen that he was toothless. These peculiarities or anomalies in the Vizier's physical appearance were only accentuated by his dress: a tubelike, almost funereal sleeve of black cloth which covered him from shoulders to feet, leaving his spindly arms bare except for wide golden bands clasped above his elbows. All taken into account, Khai believed that he never before had seen anyone looking so completely repulsive.

The first dignitary to be called forward was a Nubian diplomat who was due shortly to return to his homeland in the south. Relations with Nubia were cool at best, but diplomatic channels still functioned. Almost as tall as Anulep, the black official was well proportioned and endowed with a crest of frizzy hair which he wore like a crown. His bearing was proud, his robe a brilliant crimson, and in his nose he wore a huge diamond. He approached Pharaoh and stood before him at a discreet distance, then went gracefully to his knees and bowed his head.

"Up, black Lord," commanded Pharaoh in a voice which Khai found at once awesome and inhuman. It was an almost mechanical voice, loud as an echo in a vault, each word uttered with a *whoosh* reminiscent of the smelter's bellows, so that Khai thought that Khasathut's lungs must be made of leather and his throat of copper. Perhaps he really did fill his vast outer case after all!

As the Nubian rose effortlessly to his feet, so Pharaoh spoke to him again. "I see you are alone. Did your wife fear to cross Nubia's borders? Does she not know that Pharaoh protects his guests?"

"Most high Son of Re, of Heaven itself," the black ambassador answered, calm and completely unruffled. "Such are my duties that I deemed it unwise to take a wife. A traveler in distant lands and places cannot be a father to his children, and as a representative of king and country I am—"

"A dutiful man," Khasathut cut him short, "—if a trifle long-winded. Yes, I can see that. Very well, you may go. Convey my compliments to the young king. Perhaps N'jakka would deign to visit me in person one day? Perhaps, too, he will bring me back my *impi*?"

"The affairs of a king, Omnipotent One, are—"

"I know, I know!" Pharaoh testily boomed. "And what of the affairs of a God-king? Do you think they are any less? No matter. Perhaps one day I might *order* N'jakka to attend me. . . ." He let the threat hang in the air for a moment, then dismissed the ambassador with the merest twitch of his hand. "Go now—go!" he said, and turned his great face slowly away from him.

This was a bad start and the forty or so remaining dignitaries were immediately apprehensive; but as the audiences continued and Pharaoh appeared to regain his humor, so they began to relax. Khasathut next spoke to a hooded Theraen priest of Anubis, called to Asorbes to attend to the ritual interment of a deceased official; then to an aging governor of Peh-il, a southern river town; until at last Harsin Ben Ibizin and his family were called forward. All five took up positions at a respectful distance and the children dutifully waited until their parents kneeled and bowed their heads before they also prostrated themselves before the God-king.

"Up, all," commanded the Pharaoh in that awe-inspiring voice, and the younger Ibizins were quick to be on their feet and offering assistance to their elders.

"Harsin Ben," the Pharaoh continued after a long moment of silence, during which his great carved head ponderously scanned the five, "Re has blessed me with an architect of matchless skill, and he has blessed you with a family of rare and radiant beauty. You have one son who is fine, strong and clever—who studies, I believe, the science of numbers and assists you in your structural calculations?—and another whose appearance I find strangely becoming. The boy is not an albino?"

"No, Descended from the Sky, his coloring is natural," Harsin Ben answered.

"And yet unnatural to the point of beautiful," Khasathut commented; and his great head angled toward Khai. "Come forward, boy."

"Go to him," Harsin Ben hoarsely whispered. "Go now—hurry!"

Trembling, Khai stepped quickly forward, prostrated himself and placed his forehead between Pharaoh's feet.

"Up," Pharaoh commanded, and Khai obeyed. He stood up and gazed wide-eyed at the great carven face before and above him. Shaded as he and the figure of the Pharaoh were by the as yet incomplete crest of the pyramid, the boy was able to look upon Pharaoh without being dazzled by the glittering face-mask and jewel-crusted body-structure. Behind the eyeholes cut in the facemask, he could now make out the moist glint of real eyes, wide and staring, which seemed to regard him with a hideous intentness.

"What do you do, boy?" asked the Pharaoh, and the boom and *whoosh* of his voice made Khai jump.

"I . . . I go to school, Omnipotent One."

The great head nodded. "Of course you do. And what would you like to do?"

"I would be an archer in your army, Descended from the Sky," Khai answered without hesitation, regaining something of his composure.

"Ah? Good! Then you shall practice at least one day in five. That will be arranged." The great head lifted and looked beyond Khai. "Harsin Ben, come forward and bring your daughter."

The old man and his daughter obeyed, began to prostrate themselves alongside Khai until Pharaoh stopped them. "No, do not get down," he said. And now his huge head moved to gaze at Namisha.

Khai's sister was dressed in a long, pure white chemise cut away to reveal her small, pert left breast; but with her hair in ropes, for all that she felt like a woman of the world, still she looked more like a girl of fourteen than a young woman of seventeen years.

"Harsin Ben," came Pharaoh's voice again, but lower this time and thoughtful. "This daughter of yours is lovely. In four more years, she should be given the chance to become a royal bride!"

Namisha gasped and staggered a little as if she were suddenly giddy, and her father could not stop his hand from flying to his mouth.

"Pharaoh—" he stumbled over his words, "Re on Earth—I don't—I can't—"

"Do not thank me," Khasathut checked him. "Merely ensure that she comes to me unsullied. As for the boy: let him practice his archery and we will see. But in four years, then both of them come to me."

"Namisha . . . *and* the boy, Omnipotent One? But—"

"Yes, yes," Pharaoh nodded, "the boy, too. There are duties for just such a boy in the pyramid. You have built my house and tomb, Harsin Ben, and is it not fitting that your son shall dwell therein with me? My Vizier, Anulep, has served me well for many years. Perhaps the time draws near when he should groom another for his work. . . ."

"Descended from the Sky," Harsin Ben started again with a groan he could hardly suppress, "I—"

"You are overwhelmed, I know," the great head nodded. "But I will hear no more of it. It is decided. You may go."

# IV

## THE ARCHITECT'S APPRENTICE

The pall of gloom which fell over the Ibizin household from that time onward was almost tangible in its intensity. While Khai could not quite understand it, he could nevertheless trace its source back directly to the day of the Pharaoh's parade; and on several occasions when he came across his mother and father in the rooms of their house or in its grounds talking worriedly and in low tones, he would hear Khasathut's name mentioned and know that indeed Pharaoh was the root cause of the mysterious misery.

Namisha, withdrawing into herself completely, became almost a ghost in a matter of months. This was partly of her own volition, her reaction to Khasathut's awful interest in her, but in the main it was her poor father's doing; for he dared not disobey Pharaoh's commands, whose spies were everywhere and would certainly report any divergence from his instructions. That was why Harsin Ben had assigned one of his slaves to accompany Namisha wherever she went, and why she was no longer able to attend those parties she had so used to love. Now, with the fall of night, she must be safely home and under her father's roof.

On those one or two occasions when Khai had asked what was amiss, he had been immediately and unjustly rebuked and sent away, and even Adhan would not explain to him what was wrong. When finally it got through to him that his own and his sister's futures were the source of the distress, then he was even more confused. Surely his parents did not take seriously Pharaoh's joke that he might one day make Khai his Vizier, his right-hand man? And was it not the greatest of all compliments for a girl to be chosen as a prospective bride for the God-king? In any case, four years seemed like such a long time to Khai and he couldn't really see what all the fuss was about. Why, in four more years he would be nearly fifteen and almost a man! And surely he would then be able to choose for himself whether or not he should go to live in the pyramid.

Once, coming across his parents in the garden where they sat alone in muted conversation, he overheard what amounted to treason when his mother said that perhaps Pharaoh would not last four more years. Harsin Ben had compounded the crime by answering:

"Bah! Sick he may well be, wife, but his sickness is not of the body. Even if he were physically unwell, his physicians would keep him alive until I finish his pyramid, of that you can be certain. And if by some miracle he were to die—and how I have prayed for that—do you think they would let him *stay* dead? No, they would not! There are seven black and seven white mages in Khem and the lands around, and Pharaoh has called all of them that are black to him. He provides for them, and they for him. Even life, of a sort, they would provide if he were to die."

"Husband," she had answered in a frightened, gasping voice, "surely these stories we hear are only old wives' tales? Lies that Khasathut's enemies—"

"Do not deceive yourself, Merayet!" Harsin Ben had cut her short, his tone unaccustomedly sharp. "I know of a man who has seen men and women dancing in the pyramid's lower chambers. And their faces were black with death and their bodies full of worms, for they had been dead for months! The Pharaoh keeps Theraens in his house who mix black magic and the embalmer's art in proportions which produce total abomination. And that is not to mention his Dark Heptad of necromancers. . . . There is a room," he lowered his voice to a shaky whisper, "where the viscera of mummies still live and move in tubs of fluids, as if they were never removed from their dead owners' bodies!"

"Harsin Ben, how can you say these things to me?" Merayet had cried out. "How *can* you when you know that Namisha and Khai—"

"*Hush!*" her husband had quietened her, detecting an agitated rustling of leaves. "Khai?—is that you, boy? Come out of there!" And Khai had emerged from the shrubbery to be given a thorough telling off—which did nothing at all to quell his curiosity.

So it was that desiring to know more about these things he had heard whispered but fearing to approach the other members of his family, Khai finally turned to an outsider. Imthod Haphenid was Harsin Ben Ibizin's apprentice, a young man five or six years older then Khai whose father had been Harsin Ben's good friend for many years. On his deathbed three years earlier, old Thutmes Haphenid had asked the architect to take Imthod into his tutelage.

The youth would be heir to Thutmes's house and his wealth—enough to maintain a modest standard of living—and if in addition he took a trade, then perhaps he could make something of himself. Too weak for soldiering and having little aptitude for business, the youth seemed of little use for much else. But that was not to belittle Harsin Ben's field, on the contrary, for Imthod did have a good head for numbers, measurements and sketches; and so maybe Harsin Ben could teach him his arts and in so doing prepare him for a useful and constructive life.

Imthod was duly indentured and five days out of seven came to study under his new master. A sickly, unhandsome young man, he could usually be found in the old architect's workshop studying his sketches and plans, or examining his models of pyramids, temples and other great houses. That was where Khai, who had always found Imthod friendly enough in the past, eventually approached him with his problems and questions.

On the subject of the Pharaoh, however, Imthod was worse than useless; he knew only that Khasathut was the God-king and the most powerful man in the world. As for strange goings-on in the pyramid: the ways of kings were known to be strange, Imthod said, and those of gods even stranger. How then for a God-king whose forebears came down from the stars? And anyway, what was Khai's interest in the first place?

And so, instead of learning anything from his father's apprentice, Khai ended up telling him all that had transpired after the Royal Procession, even mentioning his parents' fears for himself and his sister and their doubts with regard to Pharaoh's beneficence and the well-being of those he took into the pyramid as his own. And here Imthod was most attentive, prompting Khai until he had picked every minor detail and morsel of information from the boy's memory. Finally, having learned all, he cautioned Khai against ever repeating his story, then made as if to return to his studies.

After Khai had left him, however, Imthod sat at his bench for a long time doing nothing, with his eyes narrowed and a frown etched deep into his forehead. Four years, the boy had said. Four years until Pharaoh claimed Namisha for a bride and took Khai off to be trained for duties in the pyramid. And Harsin Ben was opposed to Khasathut's plans, was he?

Imthod began to wonder how much he could learn from the old man in four years. A great deal, he suspected, if he really put his mind to it. But would it be sufficient to earn him the Pharaoh's royal seal of approval, to make him the next Grand Architect of the Pyramid in his master's place? For if Harsin Ben were found guilty of treason, why!—then there would be need for a new man to finish his great work.

Oh, there were other architects in Asorbes, to be sure—but none of them had served under Harsin Ben Ibizin, and none of them could possibly know his work as well as his own eager apprentice. The more Imthod thought about it, the more he could see the possibilities. In four more years, he would be a mature man, and if he handled the affair cleverly, he might possibly become the youngest of all Pharaoh's favored ones.

After all, what did Imthod care for the Ibizins? Nothing! That snotty Namisha with her nose always in the air; and the boy, Khai, so naive and stupid; and Harsin Ben himself, who was blind to genius when it stared him in the face! What was he anyway but an old man, an insufferable old man who was forever complaining about something or other—always going on about how a man might get away with building a faulty house or even an ugly temple, but never an imperfect pyramid—always grumbling about how tasteless and slipshod Imthod's work was.

Ah, but just suppose that the old fool really *was* building an imperfect pyramid? What if it could be shown that Harsin Ben deliberately schemed to sabotage Pharaoh's great tomb? With this last thought Imthod nodded and smiled a sick smile. Yes, he would show the old dodderer, and in the process elevate himself to a position of great power.

But not yet, not just yet. Four years would be time enough . . .

From that time on—as the weeks turned into months and life in the Ibizin household, while retaining little of its former harmony, nevertheless began to balance out—Harsin Ben found at least one change for the better. This was in Imthod Haphenid's progress in the field his father had chosen for him. It was as if the apprentice had turned over a new leaf and could no longer get enough of his master's teaching, which was a transition at once welcome and unexpected.

Perhaps it was because the old architect was so unhappy—with his daughter's gradual decline, with Khai's neglect of his schooling in favor of archery practice at the massive barracks behind the pyramid, unhappy with the whole generally bleak-looking future of his beloved family—that he took so much pleasure from the way his pupil now responded to his teaching. One of the old man's qualities which helped greatly in making him a good teacher lay in his never failing to give credit where it was due, and he often remarked that Imthod's emerging dedication must surely pay the young architect great dividends in the years to come.

Old Thutmes Haphenid had been right after all, it appeared, and Harsin Ben took additional pleasure in the fact that his friend's faith in his sickly son seemed at last to be bearing fruit. . . .

# V

# THE TIME DRAWS NIGH

Contrary to Khai's boyish beliefs and his mother's prayers, and despite his father's sleepless nights and his sister's almost total withdrawal into herself—which of late had seemed to manifest itself in secretiveness, furtive nocturnal absences from home and bouts of tearful self-pity—the four years passed all too quickly and the day of reckoning rapidly drew closer. During that time, several changes had taken place in the Ibizin household, each of them as a direct result of the Pharaoh's decree.

Khai's father no longer protested his son's desertion of more mundane lessons in order to attend the ranges of the barracks; indeed Harsin Ben now openly encouraged Khai's participation in target practice, for he secretly hoped that in the end the Pharaoh might be swayed toward letting Khai follow a military career as opposed to inducting him into the affairs of the pyramid. The lad's prowess as an archer had won him countless awards in competitions with other young aspirants to the Corps of Archers, carrying him to a peak of marksmanship which even his instructors found difficult to match.

As for Adhan: he had become an especially brilliant mathematician—exponent of a comparatively new science which went hand-in-hand with measurement and the arts of pyramid-building—and was now his father's chief adviser in the design and construction of Pharaoh's tomb, which rapidly neared completion. Two or three more years at the outside, and it would only remain to fill the pyramid's topmost cavities with thousands of tons of fine sand and to coat its vast exterior with a shining skin of gold. To these ends, the finest sands had already been brought from the shores of the Great Sea, transported and sifted, and as for the gold: Pharaoh had now commenced the stripping of all known goldmines in the Eastern Desert and the forests north of Nubia, and despite N'jakka's coolness, he had put out feelers into the heart of the Black Kingdom itself, demanding an annual tribute in large measures of raw gold.

But the four years had taken a terrible toll of Harsin Ben Ibizin. He had aged far more rapidly than advancing years might readily account for, and his hair and eyebrows were now white as fine bleached linens. More and more he had come to lean on his apprentice, Imthod Haphenid, depending upon him for the handling of all architectural tasks with the sole exception of the great pyramid itself, and not once had Imthod let him down. No, for the apprentice had become a master in his own right, and of all other architects in Asorbes, only Harsin Ben could now deem himself Imthod's peer.

And it was just as well that Imthod had been available to handle his master's lesser affairs (which after all provided the Ibizin family's daily bread), for in the last twelvemonth Harsin Ben had grown more and more vague and abstracted as the terror which hovered over his household threatened to descend and stifle all. Now, as the days narrowed down, the old architect was more distraught and concerned than ever. His concern had to do with a summons, the Royal Command, which Khasathut invariably issued to the families of his future brides advising them that their daughters were to take part in his parade of prospective chosen ones. That command had not yet arrived, nor yet any word of Khai's future as foretold four years earlier, so that Harsin Ben was at a loss to know which way to turn.

It was as if the Pharaoh had altogether forgotten those words he had spoken on that fateful day of the Royal Procession four years ago, or as if they had been merely a whim to be uttered and then put aside; but Harsin Ben could put little trust in that. And yet... perhaps there was hope after all. There had been fifteen Royal Processions since that time, and Pharaoh's Grand Architect had been present at every one of them. On several occasions, Khai or Namisha had been absent—ostensibly as a result of "illnesses," or of holidays taken out of the city at the homes of friends in Béna or Ohath; but in fact as a rather unsubtle subterfuge to keep them out of sight and hopefully out of mind—and while on these occasions Harsin Ben had been apprehensive, not once had Pharaoh or his aides commented upon the absence of the young Ibizins.

On the tenth day before this sixteenth Royal Procession was to take place, Harsin Ben had asked his eldest son Adhan for his opinion. Adhan had grown into a fine man now and had a wise head on his shoulders. Perhaps he might have something constructive to say on the matters currently worrying his father. On this occasion, however, Harsin Ben found his son reticent and evasive. When he asked what was wrong, Adhan had advised that he should speak to Imthod Haphenid. Perhaps he could learn something from his apprentice, Adhan said, for he had heard it rumored that Imthod was spending a lot of his spare time in the city's taverns with several of Pharaoh's spies. One of the latter was well known as a scout for the Pharaoh, seeking out especially lovely girls for the quarterly ceremony of bride-choosing. Perhaps Imthod would know for certain whether or not Namisha was to be one of the twenty prospective brides. . . .

Two days later, when Harsin Ben was unable to bear the suspense a moment longer, he called Imthod Haphenid into his study and broached the subject in as direct a fashion as he could find, speaking first of the apprentice's friendship with certain employees and confidants of the Pharaoh.

"It's true enough, master, that I've formed friendships within a certain group of men whose duties are deemed rather odd," Imthod told him, grown suddenly a little more pallid than usual. "But since they carry out those duties on the orders and on behalf of Pharaoh himself, and since—"

"Hold, Imthod," his master cautioned him, holding up a hand. "I don't mean to cross-examine you. You must surely know that? No, it's just that I'm worried about the Royal Procession. There's only a week left. You know of course that four years ago Namisha was chosen by Pharaoh for a place in his bridal parade—the *next* Parade, in just a week's time? Well, since you have friends among Khasathut's spies—I mean, among those men he employs to . . . to—"

"I know your meaning, master," Imthod answered, saving Harsin Ben from further embarrassment. "The only thing that puzzles me is how you came to discover that I was working for you in this way."

"Working for me?" the old architect frowned. "I don't—"

"You see," Imthod quickly continued, "I had hoped that perhaps my friendship with these men might go unobserved, for my plan was a shaky one at best. Obviously, I've not been as subtle as I tried to be, for if you have suspected me, then what of them whose innermost secrets I've sought to discover?"

"What?" Harsin Ben gasped, failing to grasp the other's meaning. "Can't you be more plain, Imthod?"

"Master, do you think I've not known your dismay that your family must be taken from you? Khai and Namisha taken into the pyramid, never to return to you? I've suspected it must be so for a long time, which was why I cultivated such strange friendships with men whose natures are so far from my own. And master—" he lowered his voice, became confidential, "I believe that at long last I have news for you—good news!"

"News? Speak up, man!" the old man hoarsely commanded. "What have you learned?"

"Ah, be patient, Harsin Ben," Imthod answered, calling his master by name for the first time. "First I had to mingle with these men and gain their confidence, and when finally I learned that Namisha was most certainly to be one of the twenty—that indeed she might well be chosen as one of Pharaoh's three new brides—then I took my very life in my hands and laughed at my informants!"

"You did what?" Harsin Ben was amazed. "Why would you do such a thing?"

"I laughed that Khasathut's advisers could be so reckless of their own positions as to allow Pharaoh to take so dull and dowdy a bride!"

"You did wh—" the old man could not believe his ears. "How dare—"

"Harsin Ben—master!—pray, hear me out. Do you not see my plan? For I had sown seeds of doubt in their minds, and now at last it appears that those seeds have taken root!"

"How do you mean? In what way?"

"Why, don't you see? Namisha is no longer a candidate for Pharaoh's bed. She has been struck from the list of twenty names. She will not be called upon to parade for Khasathut's choosing!"

"You have done this thing, Imthod?" Harsin Ben's astonishment was gradually giving way to joy. "But why did you not—"

"You have not heard all, Harsin Ben," his apprentice quickly cut him off. "About Khai—"

"Khai?" the old man was immediately apprehensive. "What of him?"

"He is not to go to the pyramid after all," Imthod smiled. "No, for he is to be an archer in Pharaoh's army."

Harsin Ben slowly shook his head in astonishment, in disbelief. "And is this, too, your doing, Imthod? It . . . it's like a dream! How could you possibly have worked this wonder?"

"I am only partly responsible," the apprentice replied. "Khai's amazing skill with bow and arrows has been his true salvation. I had only to speak my opinion in the right ear: that a lad with Khai's talent would be wasted as a lap dog in the pyramid. The rest seemed to come almost naturally."

"And yet you've made no mention of these things before," the old man frowned. "Why is that, Imthod Haphenid? Have I been such a tyrant that you could not confide in me?"

For a moment the apprentice seemed lost for words, but then he found his tongue. "No, no, Harsin Ben, not at all—but what if all my work had come to nothing in the end? What then? Should I raise up your hopes simply to dash them down again?"

"But when did you discover that all was well? How long have you known?"

Again Imthod seemed at a loss for an answer, but eventually he spluttered: "As recently as . . . as last night—but even so I would have said nothing had you not asked me. I did not wish it known that I . . . that—"

"That you have saved me and mine, Imthod Haphenid! And to think that your father had to beg me to take you as my apprentice. Man, I owe you everything!" And he took the other by the shoulders.

Immediately the apprentice shuddered and broke free. "You owe me nothing, Harsin Ben." He stood up. "You have been my master and you taught me all you knew. Now there is no better architect in all Asorbes—save you yourself. For this I thank you. Why, my prowess is not unknown . . . even in the pyramid!"

"In the pyramid?" Harsin Ben raised his white eyebrows.

"Aye, for last night I, too, was invited to appear before the Pharaoh when next his great procession takes place."

"Huh!" the old man grunted. "But that is a mixed blessing, Imthod. A very mixed blessing indeed. . . ."

When the apprentice had left him alone, Harsin Ben called Adhan out of a small adjacent room where he had been listening to all that was said. Taking hold of his forearm, his father frowned at his expression and asked: "Well, did you hear? Now what have you to say? Don't you understand, Adhan, it's all over! We're to stay just as we are: a whole family. And all thanks to Imthod. Who would have believed it?"

"Who indeed?" Adhan answered under his breath.

But his father heard him. "What do you mean?" Harsin Ben questioned, his voice trembling. "Is something wrong?"

"Nothing, nothing at all," Adhan was quick to answer. "It's all so sudden, that's all."

But as he, too, left Harsin Ben's study, he was glad that he had not told the old man the whole truth. For in fact there might very well be something wrong, something very wrong. . . .

Adhan had been busy checking on Imthod and had heard certain whispers of a very odd, indeed sinister nature. Nothing factual or proven for certain, not yet—rumors mainly—but strong rumors. And horrible ones. For it had been put about that when Imthod was not studying under Harsin Ben, then that he not only mingled with Pharaoh's spies but had himself become one of them. He spent his nights in company with the most dubious of characters, and what Adhan had discovered of them did not bear repeating.

For it was said that if a pretty girl's family desired to keep her off Pharaoh's list, this might well be arranged through Pharaoh's own agents—though not without payment. Large amounts of gold had been known to change hands, but on occasion the price was something entirely different.

Adhan had heard that if a girl was desperate enough, she might retain her freedom by giving herself for a night or two to one or another—and sometimes more than one—of Khasathut's spies.

And it was further rumored that Imthod had sometimes shared in this unholy bargaining of flesh . . . but that in itself was not what worried Adhan.

He was more worried about his sister—about where she was recently accustomed to going, secretly in the dead of night, through the streets of Asorbes. About her destination, yes, and about what she was doing when she got there.

And with whom?

On the evening before the Royal Procession, a messenger came with word from the pyramid, from the Pharaoh himself. Harsin Ben Ibizin was to ensure that his entire family *without exception* accompanied him to the Royal Procession, and thereafter that they appeared before Khasathut atop the now greatly reduced summit of the east face. The Pharaoh greatly desired to see—indeed he especially looked forward to seeing the Ibizin family in its entirety. . . .

# VI

# THE PHARAOH'S WRATH

The day seemed little different from that of any other Royal Procession, and up to a point it proceeded in a like fashion. There were differences, however, one of which lay in the ever-increasing height of the east-facing plateau, which was now such that the litter-bearing slaves were obliged to elevate their human charges in relays. Three months previously, after the last Royal Procession, a Nubian slave had actually collapsed while carrying a litter. Only the quick reactions of his co-bearer had avoided certain disaster, when the litter and its occupant—an important Arabban ambassador—might well have gone plunging down the great flight of steps, taking other nobles, litters and bearers with it.

The offending slave, already dying of a burst heart, had been put to the sword there and then on the steps and his carcass tossed over the side. The broken, sandpapered thing which eventually thumped to a halt at the foot of the great ramp had been unrecognizable as a human being, and the city's stray dogs had made very short work of it indeed. The unfortunate black's quick-thinking colleague, a Khemish thief half-way through a three-year sentence, was then congratulated, set free and sent home, rejoicing, to Peh-il.

With the memory of so recent a tragedy still fresh in her mind, Merayet's apprehension—as she was borne up in her litter to the now reduced but still vast area of the lofty plateau—was considerable; but it could not compare to the fear she had lived with for the last four years, which only recently had been relieved by Imthod Haphenid's revelations as retold to her by her husband, Harsin Ben. As for last night's peculiar summons: doubtless, this was to enable Khasathut himself to outline his altered plans, which in their original form would certainly have affected the whole family. And so as the hour of the audience approached, Harsin Ben and his family took their places among the other dignitaries on the plateau high over Asorbes and awaited the Pharaoh's pleasure.

Khai's father had already noted the presence of an extraordinary number of governors and high officials from the many towns and villages up and down the river, and he had not failed to take note of the rather perplexed and occasionally apprehensive glances which passed amongst them. On chatting with several acquaintances of old, he discovered that they had all been called to attend the procession and its subsequent ceremonies at extremely short notice, almost as if on an afterthought, and that they believed Pharaoh must have something of great importance to say to them.

The general consensus of opinion was that he wished them to give their active support to his military recruiting—greatly stepped-up in recent months on account of recurrent Kushite raids across the western border, which Khasathut had sworn to put down—by forming still more regiments from their own towns and provinces. While Harsin Ben had accepted this explanation readily enough, still he was uneasy. Certainly the number of troops taking part in the procession had been greatly reduced, as a result of Khasathut sending thousands of his warriors west of the river and to north and south, but since when did Pharaoh require the compliance of his governors before issuing his commands? Waiting with the rest of them for Khasathut to appear, the old architect found his mind darting in all sorts of gloomy and doom-fraught directions; but he was not to be kept in suspense for very much longer. . . .

As the last of the dignitaries were brought up to the plateau's summit, so eight huge black guardsmen appeared from the hollow, half-completed peak of the pyramid bearing a litter containing a throne with the massive, ornately-garbed figure of Pharaoh himself seated upon it. They lowered the litter to the stone surface of the plateau and prostrated themselves, then retired on all fours, crawling backward away from the spot where Pharaoh sat. When complete silence had settled over the high place, then the figure on the throne signaled that the ceremony of the bride-choosing should commence.

Khai was aware of his sister's trembling where she stood close to him as the twenty girls were paraded one at a time before the Pharaoh, and as he chose his three new brides she shuddered anew and tried to make herself just a fraction smaller. But when the choosing was over and the brides-to-be had been led away into the pyramid, then events began to take a much less orthodox turn.

First of all, the Black Guard turned out in its entirety to line the three precipitous rims of the plateau, all of them facing inward and forming a black wall to enclose the drama about to be enacted high over Asorbes. When they were in position, then Khasathut called for his Vizier, Anulep, to go to him. And here once again the assembled nobles were witnesses to an occurrence of extraordinary rarity, when Pharaoh impatiently cut short Anulep's usual obsequious approach and drew him close to whisper in his ear. Such a thing was hitherto unknown and could only be portent of even stranger things to come.

Now, as a ripple of speculation passed through the assembled personages, Anulep approached them and passed among them, seeking someone out. Straight to Harsin Ben Ibizin he came, and ignoring all others—governors, high officials and ambassadors alike—he ordered the aged architect to bring his family before the Pharaoh. Harsin Ben heard Anulep's command as in an echoing tunnel, a dream, a nightmare. Some dreadful premonition told him that all was not well, far from it. In some sort of dreadful slow-motion he led out his family before Pharaoh and prostrated himself with them, then stood up to hear the God-king's word; which came with its customary *whoosh* and roar:

"Harsin Ben Ibizin—Grand Architect of the Pyramid—have you any idea why you before all others assembled here have been called before me?"

Harsin Ben tried to speak but could not find his voice. In the end, he merely shook his head.

"Ah! Perhaps you do know after all," Pharaoh continued, "and the knowledge has dried up your throat. Very well, let me tell you. I am going to make an example of you."

"An . . . an example, Omnipotent One? I—"

"An example, yes. To all others who might foolishly think to use their positions of trust and power against me. You are a traitor, Harsin Ben Ibizin. I, Pharaoh, accuse you!"

Following immediately on his words, the Black Guard uttered a single concerted *"Waugh!"* and as one man took a pace forward.

"You . . . you *accuse,* Lord?" Harsin Ben staggered as his family clung to him in terror. "But—"

"Not only you, architect," came the *whoosh* of Khasathut's voice, "but also them that stand with you. Traitors all—with the sole exception of the boy, Khai. Only he has kept my ordinances faithfully." The great jewelled head turned slowly to gaze upon the Vizier. "Anulep, bring out the architect's drawings."

Harsin Ben gasped as he recognized his plans and saw them laid out on a table set before the Pharaoh. He took a pace forward, reaching out his now-palsied hands.

"Stay, Harsin Ben, and listen," Khasathut commanded. "For these plans of yours are at fault, and as such they clearly show your treachery!"

"At fault?" Harsin Ben gasped. "Omnipotent—"

"If my tomb was finished according to these drawings," Pharaoh whooshed and roared, "then it would not be capable of performing its final function: to channel sand down into the lower regions and bury that nethermost chamber where my immortal remains will lie until the return of my fathers from the sky. And if that entombment were not utterly complete, how then might I expect to survive the centuries which may yet elapse before the second coming?"

"Most High Lord, I—" the old man started to say, only to be cut short once again.

"And if this mortal form which houses my immortal *ka* were not preserved, why, then the gods themselves might not have the power to bring about my resurrection! You know these things well enough, Harsin Ben, and yet you deliberately planned to sabotage my plans for immortality!"

*"Waugh!"* came that awful cry from the throats of the Black Guard as they took a second pace forward.

"No, Descended from the Sky, it's a lie!" the old architect cried, breaking free of his fearful family and staggering forward. Anulep quickly placed himself between the Pharaoh and the old man, and the latter went down on his knees before him and clutched at his feet. "Vizier," he cried, "tell the Pharaoh he is mistaken! Why, my plans were checked by my own son, Adhan, and he is a master of measurements and numbers!"

*"Silence!"* roared Pharaoh. "You merely condemn yourself with your stuttered denials. Mistaken, am I? And your son Adhan the mathematician checked your plans, did he? Well then, come forward, Adhan, and gaze upon your father's plans. Come, I command you."

Visibly trembling in every limb and white as chalk, Adhan went forward as ordered and stared at the plans on the small table. His eyes, at first puzzled and frightened, gradually grew disbelieving, then angry. Color came back to his cheeks as he gazed up into Khasathut's mask-hidden eyes. "Pharaoh, I see the error—but it is not of my father's doing—nor yet mine. These plans have been tampered with, and by an expert!"

"Tampered with? And your father did not notice this . . . this forgery? And you, the great mathematician, you did not see it? Where have you both been, if not at work on my pyramid?"

"The work was well known to us, Omnipotent One," cried Adhan, "and we rarely needed to consult the plans. Be certain we would soon have discovered—"

"Be silent!" Pharaoh whooshed. "You both lie . . . you and your father both. The plans were tampered with, indeed! Well, they are not alone in that, it appears. Can you deny that your sister, too, has been 'tampered' with?" His great jeweled arm rose up slowly until his hand pointed at Namisha where she hugged her mother and sobbed. "You girl, come forward."

Namisha took two paces forward, then crumpled in a faint.

"See!" Pharaoh roared. "Her guilt is plain to see. Because of it, she cannot face me. She is defiled, Harsin Ben Ibizin, and I know the name of her defiler. *It is Adhan!*"

Adhan's mouth fell open where he stood at the table. He staggered and almost overturned the table at Khasathut's feet. His mouth opened and closed like that of a landed fish. "Pharaoh," he finally croaked, "these are lies—filthy lies!"

"Is Pharaoh then a *liar?*" the great voice blared out.

*"Waugh!"* roared the Black Guard, closing their ranks as they took a third step forward.

"Not you, Pharaoh, no!" cried Harsin Ben, his voice stronger now and thick with fury. "Your informants are the liars. All of these accusations—they are all cruel and false. Who is it?" he cried, wheeling about to stare at the crowded dignitaries, at their death-white faces, the caverns of their gaping mouths. "Who is it that falsely discredits and destroys me?" He turned back to Pharaoh, struggled past Anulep and stood beside Adhan at the table. "Can you really believe, Pharaoh, that my son would seduce his own sister?"

"I can believe—I *do* believe!" Pharaoh roared. "Yes, he has had incestuous relations with her, I have proof. There was a witness. I can produce him. The gods may mate with their own flesh, Harsin Ben, to keep the blood pure—but it is not for ordinary men to defile flesh which Pharaoh has named his own. I would have considered her for my bride, but now . . . ? You may be sure I would not accept any but the most damning evidence. Aye, and I have that evidence! I know the names of others who have had her, men I occasionally employ to test the eligibility of the women I chose for my brides. When these men approached your daughter, do you know what she did? *She gave herself to them!*"

*"Waugh!"* came another roar from the Black Guard, and yet again the shuffle and stamp of their sandaled feet.

Merayet, throwing herself down on the ground and slapping at her unconscious daughter's face, cried, "Namisha, daughter, tell the Pharaoh he wrongs you. Tell him you are a good girl and pure. Say it is so!"

"Corrupt!" Pharaoh cried, his voice a throbbing whistle of rage. "The whole family—all in this together." He lifted his hands up high. "You have been tried, Harsin Ben, and you are found wanting. Let your punishment stand as an example to others who would practice treachery and deceit upon the Pharaoh!"

*"Waugh!"* howled the Black Guard, and they swept across the plateau to engulf the Ibizins in a merciless crush of ebony bodies.

# VII

## HORROR ON HIGH

As eight of the huge blacks moved directly to Pharaoh's litter-throne and lifted it shoulder high, four more drew curving swords and took up positions about the elevated throne, facing outward and watching the remainder of their colleagues as they commenced to mete out preordained "punishments" to the Ibizin family.

While Harsin Ben, Adhan and Khai were grabbed and held immobile—forced to look on in helpless horror as they squirmed in the grip of members of the Black Guard—so the rest of the huge Nubians pounced upon Merayet where she sprawled beside Namisha. They dragged her away from the girl and stripped both of them, tossing torn fragments of fine linens all about.

When the women were completely naked, four of the blacks lifted Khai's mother up horizontally and held her with her arms and legs outstretched, forming a human cross. Namisha was lifted into the same position; and without more ado, coldly and apparently without lust, the Black Guard commenced to rape both mother and daughter—one awake and screaming, the other oblivious of her body's torment—relieving themselves into their spreadeagled bodies one after the other and from the standing position.

The whole hideous process was remarkably quick and efficient, with each man working for mere seconds before withdrawing to be replaced by the next in line. Semen quickly formed small pools where it dripped from the suspended bodies of the brutalized women; and as the fifteenth or sixteenth massive black took his turn with Merayet, so she gave one final shriek and lost consciousness. At that, the four who held her sat her up in mid-air, their hands supporting her beneath knees and armpits, until her naked body formed the shape of a chair.

They ran with her in that position to the east-facing rim of the plateau. There, at intervals along the rim, bronze measuring rods stuck up vertically from locating holes in the outer blocks of stone. Two of these had been filed needle sharp; and upon one of them, without pause, the blacks placed Merayet's body, ramming her down onto the rod until she sat on the very lip of the plateau with her legs dangling over the side. The rod came out, red and glistening, from a position near the top of her spine.

Namisha, too, was hurried over to the rim beside her mother, but as she was being lifted up above the second of the two sharpened rods, so she regained consciousness. One scream only she uttered, high and bubbling, as she was driven down onto that long, slender bronze fang. Her limbs flailed spastically for a split second as the rod's point slid out above her left breast, and then she was still.

Through all of this, the three male Ibizins had howled, wept and struggled like madmen in the grip of the huge Nubians. But now, summoning a crazed strength from some hitherto unsuspected well, Adhan threw off the men who held him and turning, drove a sandaled foot into the groin of one of them that held his father. As the guardsman doubled up in agonized amazement, Harsin Ben somehow struggled free of the other man and hurled himself toward Pharaoh.

Adhan, snatching a spear from an astonished guardsman, went in the opposite direction. He rushed at the crowd of terrified dignitaries, their wives and families, howling: "Where are you, traitor, fiend? Oh, I know you now. *You,* Imthod Haphenid, you and no other—you have done this thing! In order to advance your own lofty ambitions, you have destroyed us! Where are you, sickly slug of a man? For as heavenly Re is my witness—*I'll yet eat your rotten brain!*"

The officials, to this moment horrified spectators only and in no way personally involved, now found themselves trapped between a frothing maniac and the northern rim of the plateau. They scattered to left and right as Adhan drove through them, until Imthod was revealed where he had hidden behind them. Drained white and trembling, the former apprentice cringed on the very rim of eternity as Adhan aimed his spear.

"Seduced my own sister, did I?" Adhan screamed. "'Defiled' her, did I? I did not. But I now know who did!" He drew back his spear arm to make his throw, but then—

The spear was wrenched out of his hand from behind and a great black arm locked about his throat. He was dragged backward and hurled down onto the plateau's roof. A crowd of furious Nubians poised their spears and swords over him.

"No!" came the *whoosh* and roar of Pharaoh's voice. "Spare him—but see that he never fathers children. The Ibizin line is forever cursed and must not be perpetuated!"

Pinned down, Adhan could only shriek and froth at the mouth as his clothes were torn from him and one of the blacks took out a sharp, curved dagger. In another moment, his screams soared up the scale . . . then fragmented into sobbing and insane babbling as his captors, done with their grisly work, released him. On all fours, leaving a trail of blood, he crawled for the plateau's rim.

"No!" Pharaoh whooshed again. "He may not kill himself. Take him to the foot of the ramp and release him. Let him live . . . as a reminder."

As Adhan's mutilated body was dragged away toward the ramp, Pharaoh turned his attention to Harsin Ben. The old architect had actually managed to fight his way to the cordon of Nubian guardsmen around Khasathut's throne. There they had stopped him, gutting him as he vainly tried to overbalance the royal litter. Holding his entrails where they threatened to spill through his fingers, he now lay where he had fallen; and knowing that he was already a dead man, Harsin Ben gave vent to all his rage, agony and horror as he cursed Pharaoh with an unending stream of fevered maledictions.

For a few moments more Khasathut listened to the dying man, before lifting his arm to point toward the plateau's rim. Two members of the Black Guard lifted Harsin Ben up and ran to throw him, guts fluttering like rags behind him as he flew, over the plateau's rim into empty space. . . .

To fill the utter silence which followed, a chill wind blew up that keened across the plateau and made a twisting sand devil in front of Pharaoh's throne. Then Khai's sobbing sounded on the quivering air and the spell was broken.

Slowly Khasathut's masked head turned in Khai's direction. The boy was slumped between a pair of blacks, exhausted by his terrific struggling. His blond hair was plastered to his forehead and dripped perspiration; his white shirt and kilt were drenched and adhered to his body like wet rags.

"Anulep," said Pharaoh, his voice completely void of emotion. "Take the boy into the pyramid. Do whatever is necessary to prepare him for training, which is to commence as soon as practicable. You will be personally responsible for his training, and eventually he will relieve you of certain of your duties—which I have long considered to be excessive. You have three months. . . ."

For answer, the Vizier bowed his head. He beckoned to the guardsmen holding Khai and they followed him as he entered the loftier chambers of the pyramid through an arched entrance of carved stone to disappear into stark black shadow. Stumbling dazedly between the blacks, Khai turned his head once as he was half-carried under the archway. Staring back through eyes which were glazed dull with shock, he looked one last time upon a scene which burned his mind like drops of acid:

The naked, butchered carcasses of his mother and sister where they sat like gargoyles—no longer human beings but slaughtered animals—overlooking Asorbes through sightless eyes, transfixed and supported by crimson-tipped spines of bronze. . . .

# VIII

# INSIDE THE PYRAMID

Unlike the tombs and monuments of a later age, Khasathut's pyramid was not an almost solid mountain of stone, but a multi-storied maze of shafts, corridors and chambers whose total internal capacity was perhaps as great as two percent of the whole. That is to say that for every fifty cubic feet of solid stone, there was perhaps one of air or living-space. There were also sophisticated air-conditioning systems, with inlets and outlets through panels of perforated stone in the pyramid's outer skin, and a catchment system which provided the massive monument with its water.

Moreover, incorporated into the structure was a series of smooth-lined, near-vertical shafts which were designed to channel sand from the topmost quarter of the pyramid to its basement temples and living areas, including Pharaoh's subterranean tomb and the quarters of his entire Black Guard. When Khasathut was ready for his interment, his guardsmen would accompany him into darkness—entombed alive behind thousands of tons of sand.

Khai knew the layout of many of these rooms, passages, slipways and watercourses well; indeed, he had always been interested in his father's work and during the last seven or eight years had often clambered with him in and about the pyramid's levels as each was completed in its turn. His interest had extended to Harsin Ben's drawings and plans, so that he understood a great deal of the principles underlying the pyramid's construction; and as his stumbling feet moved him forward between the huge blacks—and despite the fact that he was close to exhaustion and closer to madness—still he recognized the ways he walked and knew that he was quickly descending into bowels of rock. The way was lighted by steadily burning flambeaux, causing shadows to leap on walls of stone, and as the party approached these blazing sources of light, Anulep's shadow crept along the walls until it fell upon Khai. Each time this happened, it caused a chill inside the boy which was at once dreadful and preternatural.

As they went, so the Vizier began to talk to Khai, his voice sepulchral as it echoed back from where he strode on ahead. "One learns fast in the pyramid, boy, or else one is lost. Your father built the pyramid, and so I expect you will learn all the faster. You will learn the pyramid's ways; its known, well-trodden ways, yes, and its secret ways, too . . . and its laws. Above all else, you will learn obedience to me, and through me obedience to Pharaoh.

"Pharaoh's life draws quickly to an end, moves ever closer to that final day when he will draw his last breath—at least until the return of his ancestors from the stars. Age will not have brought him down, even though he is older than most men. No, for while his body ages, his lusts and passions seem to grow greater. Ah!—and did you think that Pharaoh was beyond passion and lust? As he is greater than men, so his needs are more . . . demanding. Certain of your future duties will be concerned with Pharaoh's needs—closely concerned."

So Anulep's voice went on and on, echoing through the bowels of the pyramid and becoming almost hypnotic in its monotony. Against all natural laws, Khai was drawn back from the abyss by that voice, saved from what might otherwise have become a permanent withdrawal from a world grown far too monstrous for him. Much of what he was told escaped his understanding, but at least the Vizier's voice was a focal point, something to hang onto as his mind clawed its way back from the chasm of horror which threatened to engulf it.

In what seemed to Khai a very short time, they had descended to the more frequently used and inhabited levels of the pyramid—those which were closer to ground level, where cavernous temples and great halls loomed on every side and slaves, strangely-crowned priests and acolytes came and went in eerie silence by the light of oil- and resin-burning flambeaux—but Anulep and his party barely paused before plunging deeper still. Khai had time enough to glimpse huge golden idols and figures carved from white limestone, massive statues of gods with the bodies of men and the heads of birds and animals, huge basins of burning oil which illuminated grottoes of untold mystery, and the blackened mouths of vast flues where they opened high in darkly domed ceilings, before he was carried down into the nethermost vaults beneath.

Here in the very bowels of the earth, the air-conditioning was less effective—either that or the odors of the place were more difficult to dispel—and Khai's nose involuntarily wrinkled as certain particularly offensive smells were wafted to him. The light was much more subdued here and the shadows so much darker; and now there were strange sounds and furtive-seeming movements suggestive of esoteric industry. Approaching the entrance to a huge room where the light was somewhat brighter, Anulep bade the Nubian guardsmen wait outside and took Khai from them to lead him into the chamber. They paused just within the threshold where the high priest cautioned: "Wait! We can see all we need to see from here."

There, engaged in various alchemical activities about sunken stone vats whose contents bubbled and seethed with unpleasant sucking sounds, seven darkly-robed figures worked to the slow pace of their own low chanting, only pausing when they sensed the presence of Anulep and the boy. Seven pairs of eyes turned to stare luminously in the flickering gloom, until Anulep pulled on Khai's arm and drew him out of the chamber.

"We must not disturb them, boy," the high priest said, "for they are about Pharaoh's work, as they have been about it for more than twenty years. They are the Dark Heptad—the seven most powerful necromancers and wizards in all Khem and the lands around, and they seek that earthly immortality in which Pharaoh would clothe his eternal *ka*. If they fail him . . . then he must wait on the return of his ancestors from the stars. But if they succeed—ah!— then Pharaoh will live forever!

"I repeat: it is not age that ails him, boy, though indeed he waxes very old. No, it is the poisons within him. The poisons of his own blood, and of the Nile's blood, which is in him as it was in his earthly forebears. The great gods that came when the tribes were ignorant hoped to strengthen their blood by mixing it with the raw blood of men, but they were not successful. Khasathut is the last of his line. His seed is plentiful, indeed copious, but it does not take root. There will be no more Pharaohs with the blood of gods in them. Not until the second coming.

"That is another reason why Khasathut seeks immortality; so that ordinary men shall never occupy the great throne of Khem. And so the Dark Seven work for him as he desires, and as you shall see, they have had their successes . . . of a sort. Come—"

Now they passed along a rock-cut corridor to a room guarded by a gate of massive bronze bars. Anulep produced a key and turned it in the lock, then threw the gate open. While the two guards waited outside, showing an agitation and a fear which Khai noted even through his aching numbness of mind, Anulep led his charge into the dark chamber beyond the gate. As if their movements had stirred up something rotten, gusts of an evil fetor seemed to rise up stiflingly from the floor, so that Khai pinched his nostrils.

The place was lighted by a handful of tiny lamps placed at intervals along its length, and as Khai moved slowly over crumbling debris, his eyes grew more accustomed to the gloom. And suddenly he understood the stench of the place as he recognized it for what it was: a mortuary! The feet of corpses by the dozen stuck out from niches in the walls, and cadavers in various stages of disintegration lay in piles everywhere. Now Anulep took up one of the tiny lamps and held it close to a mound of bodies.

"Dead, eh, boy? Dead and falling into decay, returning to dust. Ah, but they have known the touch of the Dark Seven! They are not incorruptible, no—but neither are they wholly dead—not yet. Look!" And from a pocket he took a tiny golden whistle which he put to his lips. He blew a single note, an eerie, undulating note . . . and at once the air was full of a leathery creaking, the suffocating stink of death—and motion!

"Come!" the Vizier's voice fell to a whispering quaver as he hurried Khai back along the way they had come. "We cannot stay here now. These are the slaves of Nyarlathotep—whose very essence the Dark Seven invoked to perform their black magic, defying even Anubis himself—and as such, they are dangerous. See how they awaken?"

Outside in the corridor the high priest quickly locked the gate, and beyond its heavy bars gaunt and leathery figures began to stumble and flail about in the darkness while their stench welled out in ever-thickening clouds. Half-rotten fingers tore at the bars and fleshless skulls grinned and bobbed.

"I could make them dance for you if I so desired," the Vizier said, once more in control of himself, "but theirs is not dancing for eyes such as yours. It amuses the Pharaoh, of course, but he is not as other men. No, and this is not the kind of immortality he sought."

Even as he spoke, from somewhere up above there came the boom of a great gong. Looking up, Anulep remarked: "The afternoon is already one-third fled. Well, I have my duties, Khai Ibizin, and so we must hurry." He blew one more warbling note on his whistle and the stumbling things behind the bars instantly crumpled into their previous immobility.

Again Anulep took Khai's shrinking hand. "I have one more thing to show you," he continued. "A hiding place, a peephole, from which you shall soon gaze out upon rare and wonderful things—marvelous things, your very future—and then I will take you to your room." He held the boy's hand in his own bony claw and lowered his face to smile a ghastly, toothless smile; and Khai could not help but notice again the small, circular gape of his mouth.

"Ah?" the Vizier opened his eyes wide. "Don't you like my little empty mouth, then? A pity, for you yourself must visit the dentist in just a day or two." He nodded his skull of a head. "You will see why . . . tomorrow night. But now, can you walk? Or must the guardsmen drag you? Ah, the resilience of the young! I see you *can* walk. Come then, and hurry, hurry. . . ."

# part
# FOUR

# I

# THE NUPTIAL CHAMBER

It was now some thirty hours since Khai last saw Anulep. Thirty hours spent alone in his room three or four stories above the temples and living areas of the ground level, hanging onto his sanity as best he might while his mind turned over and over again those monstrous events which had so utterly destroyed his world. But the hideous pictures were no longer clear in the eye of his memory—they had become strangely and mercifully blurred—and the more he tried to concentrate on them the more indistinct they became. The mind soon forgets or obscures that which it cannot bear to contemplate. Anulep's instructions, on the other hand—those monotonously delivered, almost hypnotic orders he had given Khai before leaving him in his dimly-lighted cell of a room—had remained crystal clear. Khai's mind had been bruised, even wounded, but not irreparably crippled.

As for his physical condition: since his ordeal on the pyramid's east face, he had taken no food and had managed to snatch only a little sleep—catnaps from which he was invariably driven back to the waking world by shrieking nightmares—so that he was steadily growing weaker. It was not that he had been deprived of food, on the contrary, for slaves had brought food to him on three separate occasions . . . only to be sent away by one whose appetite seemed to have died within him. He was, however, a boy on the verge of manhood, with youth's almost boundless energy, and it would be a long time before privation completely incapacitated him.

So he waited for the appointed hour and the reverberating tones of a gong struck five times; and when at last that gong sounded, signifying the approach of the midnight hour, he almost automatically took up his small lamp, slipped from his room and made his way through deserted, cramped and cobwebby corridors of rock toward the secret place where Anulep had told him to conceal himself. Not once had it crossed Khai's mind to run away; as of yet he was simply too stunned to contemplate or even imagine doing anything of his own volition. He knew only that he must do as he was bidden or suffer the Pharaoh's wrath, and that the living god's wrath was terrible indeed!

This was just about the sum total of Khai's knowledge concerning Pharaoh, but on the other hand, his knowledge of the pyramid was not at all inconsiderable. No one but his father, so cruelly murdered, had been better informed on the subject of the pyramid's internal construction. No one, that is, except for the pyramid's dwellers, and even they had not gone where their duties did not require their presence. Thus, even in Khai's dazed condition and assisted by so feeble a light as that of his little stone lamp, still he was able to make his way swiftly and surely to the secret place.

Soon enough he found himself peering down into that crevice shown to him by Anulep, from which vantage point he was to watch the chosen maidens become brides of the Pharaoh. Anulep had told him that during the ceremony he must pay particular attention to those duties of the high priest which he himself would soon be called upon to perform; duties of a secret, personal and intimate nature in the service of the Pharaoh himself.

Despite his torpor of mental exhaustion, Khai found himself wondering just what these intimate duties might be, when it was common knowledge that no man's hand might ever fall upon the Pharaoh's person or even touch him. For the Pharaoh was a god, strange and cold by mortal—no, by *any*— standards, and divorced from the mundane ways of men. His ways must be strange indeed, thought Khai; and yet Anulep's duties, whatever they were, were soon to be transferred upon him? It was all so very hard to understand. . . .

Still and all, the high priest had told him that Khasathut found him pleasing in his sight, and perhaps taking Khai into his service was the God-king's way of balancing matters. Since he had been instrumental in the destruction of Khai's family, perhaps it was now his intention to atone by drawing the boy to his own bosom. But what, Khai wondered, was to become of Anulep when finally the time came for him to hand over his duties?

With thoughts such as these crowding each other in his shrinking and fearful mind, the boy lowered himself into the hole until his feet touched bottom. Straightening up, his head came just level with the floor of the passage above. He blew out his lamp where its flame now flickered before his face, then crouched down and searched for the peephole that Anulep had mentioned. And sure enough the peephole was there: an uncemented horizontal slot three inches long and a quarter-inch wide, giving Khai an almost completely unobstructed view of the chamber behind the limestone wall.

At this particular spot, the wall was at its thinnest, built of soft-grained slabs as opposed to massive blocks, so that Khai's angle of vision was a wide one. Now he forced himself to concentrate, giving his undivided attention to whatever was about to occur in the bridal chamber. First, however, he would acquaint himself with the chamber itself, a room of which he had no previous knowledge.

It was essentially bare, that room, containing only one or two items of furniture. The principal piece was a golden throne of small-seeming dimensions, with two tiny steps in front. A single lamp, standing on a slender pedestal in the center of the room, lighted the high-ceilinged, hexagonal chamber with a dully flickering glow that caused the throne to gleam and coruscate from the many precious stones set in its arms and headrest. The light from the lamp also reached the walls, highlighting their bas-reliefs with lines of black shadow that moved flowingly with the continual flickering of the flame.

These bas-reliefs immediately caught and held Khai's attention, for they were especially erotic in nature and showed coition between naked men and women and all manner of birds and beasts. Moving with the action of the lamp-cast shadows, the figures seemed so full of lustful life that Khai soon became aroused by the sight. Finally, fighting his excitement, he forced himself to look away.

His eyes found the dark mouths of twin passages where they entered like huge nostrils into the bridal chamber through the wall directly opposite his vantage point. Between these tunnels, the buttress of the inner wall supported a bracketed, unlighted torch. Peering round the room, Khai noted that similar flambeaux were set in the other walls, including, it seemed likely, the wall through which he even now gazed. If these torches were to be lighted, Khai would have to be careful that his eyes were not seen shining through the peephole.

For the time being, however, he might as well make himself comfortable. Wedging himself into position, Khai waited in darkness until he heard sounds echoing through the thin limestone wall from the chamber beyond. Then, gazing once again through his peephole, he was at last rewarded by the sight of Anulep leading three girls into the chamber from one of the passageways. The Pharaoh's high priest looked once, pointedly and with narrowed eyes, directly at the spot where Khai's own eyes stared back at him, and then he turned to the girls.

To each of the three Anulep gave a taper which they lighted from the lamp atop its pedestal. Then, as they went about the hexagonal room lighting the flambeaux, the Vizier bade them wait and strode from the room into the second passageway. He returned a few moments later with six members of the pyramid's Black Guard. The latter were dressed in leather sandals, red kilts and tall bronze helmets. On their wrists they wore wide golden bracelets, and they carried long, curving and wickedly sharp daggers in their black leather belts.

As for the girls: they were dressed in flowing, virgin-white robes, their features almost completely hidden behind gauzy veils. It was an odd sight, Khai thought: these small, slender female figures, two Khemish girls and one Nubian—a girl of high birth, Anulep had told him, stolen from her home-land by Arabban slavers in a secret raid—surrounded by vast and nightmarish walls of massively lewd limestone; and the Pharaoh's men: tall, black and powerfully muscled, their sharply filed teeth showing white behind thick, grinning lips. Frowning in the darkness of his hideaway, the boy felt the short hairs at the back of his neck rising in a sudden and nameless fear.

# II

# ENTER THE
# PHARAOH

Now the girls were led to one of the walls, a
guardsman at each shoulder, and there their arms
were lifted up and their wrists locked in manacles
above their heads. As this happened, Anulep, in a
voice soft and oily, explained to the girls that they
now symbolized total subjugation, offering themselves in abject bondage to Pharaoh, their Lord,
Master, God, and Husband-Extraordinary. None of
them seemed in the least concerned about being
manacled in this fashion, and as Khai peered at
their veiled faces he wondered what was going on
in their minds.

Were they terrified, he wondered, at this ceremony, where soon they would become the brides of
Khasathut and enter into his harem? If so, they did
not show it. Perhaps they had been made to inhale
the *hen'ay* fumes, of which Khem's high elite were
currently enamored and which it was rumored the
Pharaoh himself had introduced from lands
beyond the islands of the Sea-Peoples. The *hen'ay*
was a resin which when burned made sweet waking dreams for all who inhaled its heady smoke.
The magicians of Khem had used opiates for as
long as Khem had existed, but recently Pharaoh
had added several refinements of his own.

Of one thing Khai was certain: the maidens
would all be beautiful. Pharaoh's brides were
always beautiful, his entire harem, which by now
must be vast. Indeed, the pyramid must be a veritable beehive of queens. Khasathut had taken his first

trio of wives seven years previously, at the onset of his reign, and thereafter at regular quarterly intervals. Employing his considerable knowledge of mathematics while he waited for the midnight hour (at which time, according to Anulep, the Pharaoh would make his appearance), Khai determined the current strength of the harem. He calculated that since this was the third quarter of the seventh year, Khasathut now had a total of eighty-one wives!

Eighty-one wives? As far as Khai knew, no one had ever seen them and he wondered where they could all be. There were many rooms in the heart of the pyramid, no one knew better than he, but sufficient to house eighty-one wives? And who did their cooking? And where did they eat? For that matter, where did they bathe? The pyramid simply wasn't equipped for it. And wouldn't they expect a degree of privacy, as befitted the wives of a great ruler? Of course they would; but they would surely never find it in the pyramid. For all its size, the open spaces inside the vast monument were not unlimited. . . .

As he was puzzling over the problem, Khai heard the bronze gong sounding from deep within the pyramid. It was a sepulchral sound in these stony confines, whose echoes seemed to linger ominously; but its effect upon Khasathut's huge Nubian guardsmen was immediate. Before the echoes of that single note had died away, the great blacks had backed off from the manacled girls until they flanked the jeweled throne three to each side. There they stood rigidly to attention, filed teeth hidden now behind tight lips, while Anulep took up a position directly behind the throne. Tall man that he was, the high priest dwarfed the throne; but he, too, stood to attention while he waited for Pharaoh to enter.

Now Khai was more puzzled than ever, for it would seem that this tiny bejeweled chair was fully intended to represent Khasathut's royal seat. Why not a real, man-sized throne? Surely Pharaoh could never cram his massive frame into—

But there Khai's thoughts came to an abrupt, astonished end, for suddenly he saw something which could not possibly be. A figure had emerged from one of the passageways. A figure wearing Khasathut's long-headed crown and clad in his royal, golden-yellow robes, which in turn were embroidered with his double-looped cross, the *tai-ankh*. To all intents and purposes, this then must be the Pharaoh himself . . . but how could it be? The man (was it truly a man? Khai wondered) was barely five feet tall, grotesque and limping, quite alien in its lop-sided, crippled-insect movements.

The Pharaoh—or Pharaoh's exotic pet? An ape, perhaps? But no, it was no ape. It was indeed . . . Khasathut!

Khai knew it as soon as the creature spoke, recognizing the voice of this travesty immediately. Though less powerful than the magnified *whoosh* and gasping roar which Pharaoh's subjects were used to, the voice was nevertheless his. Quickly recovering from his shock, without giving himself time to ponder the meaning of what he was seeing, Khai looked closer. He now desired to see—to know—everything.

The features beneath the long crown were much the same as had been the old Pharaoh's. Khai had been only seven years old when Thanop'et died, but he remembered the previous ruler's face: the long jaw; small, round, piercing eyes—slit down the middle like a cat's—with their thin, straight eyebrows; the sharply sloping forehead whose line was carried on by the long, backward sloping crown. All of these features were visible in Thanop'et's son, Khasathut. There was something of his mother in him, too: her smallness, for one thing, and the paleness of her skin. . . .

How old would Khasathut be? His father had been immensely old: one hundred and fifteen years, it was rumored. Since Khasathut had been born before the old man was forty, he, too, must now be well advanced in years. Yet his actions—something in his ways—reminded Khai of a child: a very old, very powerful and malignant child.

There was nothing childlike about his awful voice, however; and now, as he moved forward with a swirling of his loose yellow robes across the stark and stony chamber, he commented on the girls. "Beautiful," he said to each one in turn, peering at their eyes above their veils as he passed before them. "Beautiful. Charming. Oh, yes, Anulep—I am well pleased!" But while Khasathut's comments were warm, his tone remained as cold as a deep, rock-cut tomb.

"The Pharaoh's pleasure is mine," Anulep intoned, bowing from the waist until his forehead touched the back of the throne.

Now the diminutive Pharaoh approached his throne—moving, Khai thought, almost like a Nile crab, sideways—and mounted the tiny steps to turn and seat himself facing the manacled girls. As he took his seat, Anulep straightened up, then bent momentarily to whisper something in Khasathut's ear. Khasathut uttered a weirdly baying laugh. His and the Vizier's eyes went back to the three girls.

By this time, the Nubian girl, whose white-gowned figure was flanked by the two smaller, golden-skinned Khemish girls, was beginning to take an interest in things. The three had quite obviously been drugged, for so far they had simply leaned against the wall with their arms made fast over their heads. The one closest to Khai where he crouched in darkness had even appeared to fall asleep, her head hanging limply against her arm.

They were all awake now, however, and by their uncomfortable movements, Khai judged them to be feeling the strain of their awkward positions. The blood must have completely drained from their hands and arms by now, and the drug was beginning to wear off. The black girl was recovering much faster than her white sisters and her eyes were large as they stared about the room. Finally those brown eyes of hers found Khasathut's where they stared back at her.

Pharaoh licked his pale, thin lips and stood up. He seemed to tremble as he stepped down from his throne and sidled across the floor to where the girls were chained to the wall. He went to the Nubian girl and stared up at her, his octopus eyes unblinking and his tongue constantly licking at his lips. Staring down at him, the girl's eyes seemed to reflect—disgust? terror?—as they focused on Pharaoh's own yellowish orbs.

"Beautiful," Pharaoh said. Khai took his eyes quickly from Khasathut and the girls to peer for a moment at Anulep and the guardsmen. They had not moved, seemed frozen as they gazed across the room, their attention unwaveringly upon Khasathut and what he was doing. Something was going to happen, Khai knew, and he returned his eyes to the yellow-clad form of the God-king. . . .

# III

# THE GOD-
# MONSTER

Khasathut had just reached up his left hand to remove the black girl's veil; and now the terror could plainly be seen in her flaring nostrils, her drawn face, the film of moisture on her black brow. He stared at her a moment longer, and his tongue was like that of a snake. It flickered in and out of his mouth, licking back and forth ceaselessly over his lips. Pharaoh's hand reached up again, fingers crooked, to catch at the neck of the girl's gown.

Watching, Khai held his breath. Clearly this was no ordinary ceremony . . . no ceremony at all but something terrible, a parody of whatever the boy had expected. And now the two girls flanking the Nubian bride were also watching, their faces turned inwards to follow Khasathut's every motion. He looked from one to the other of them, the vertical slits of his eyes unblinking, then turned his attention back to the black girl. His hand tightened on the material of her dress close to the hollow of her throat, then, swift as a striking cobra tore downward.

The fine linen ripped wide open as, with sudden frantic tearing motions, Pharaoh stripped the girl to her waist, pausing only when her gown hung in tatters. Now the sight of the half-naked girl seemed to incense Khasathut. He stepped back and stared at her for a long moment, the trembling of his body clearly visible through the folds of his yellow robe. The girl's large breasts were heaving as she began to writhe, fighting to tear her wrists free from the manacles that held them. Sweat glistened on her breasts and naked belly.

Again Khasathut uttered his baying laugh, more highly pitched and breathless than before and full of a weird excitement. He lifted his hand to his own neck and plucked out the bronze pin that held the folds of his royal robe in place. Freed, the robe fell about his feet, leaving him naked except for his crown, which he now removed and tossed down upon the floor. The Nubian girl at once ceased her struggling and her mouth fell open in sheer horror as she stared at the Pharaoh through bulging brown eyes.

Peering through his peephole, Khai too gasped with shock at sight of Khasathut naked. Not because the mere thought was blasphemous, which it surely was, but because the God-king was far more monstrously deformed and alien than ever the boy might have guessed. Until now his only visible limb had been his left arm and hand, which had seemed normal enough. Beneath the yellow robe, however, things were hideously different.

Indeed, the only thing that seemed normal about Khasathut was his penis. But even this, because it was the organ of a full-grown man and firmly erect, looked inordinately large and freakish on the shrivelled, twisted body of Pharaoh. His right arm was only half the size it should have been, with the elbow correctly placed but having a forearm no more than six inches long. The hand at the end of that freakish arm was a stump of webbed fingers that lay twisted across his breast.

His legs, too, were deformed, the right being several inches longer than the left, which accounted for his crablike walk. His body, with skin so smooth and pink it was almost translucent, was completely hairless; and between his shoulder blades there showed the taut mound of a small hump.

Worst of all, however, as if the list of loathsomeness were not already long enough, was Khasathut's head. That incredibly *long* head—like the skull of some ancient, evil bird—which sloped backward and carried on the sloping line of the forehead for at least a further fifteen inches. No wonder he wore the great crown!

In short, with all of his deformities, Pharaoh was a completely and utterly alien monster!

And now the monster stood up straight as he could and leaned forward. His crippled, webbed right hand fell forward almost of its own accord and for a moment caressed the Nubian girl's left breast, then caught and held her large, squarish nipple. Quick as thought, his good left hand, which still held the long bronze pin from his discarded robe, rose up to thrust the metal sliver lengthwise through the center of the girl's nipple and into her breast. Only the ball of the pin, which instantly turned red and began to drip blood, protruded: a scarlet berry on a black velvet background. It seemed that time stood still and for a split second nothing further happened. Then—

All three girls began to scream—screams of desperation, of all hope lost—and the black girl commenced a wildly agonized threshing, banging her head again and again on the solid wall behind her. And as their screams rang deafeningly loud in that hollow chamber of torture, so Khasathut clapped his good hand to his ear and bent his head until his right ear pressed against his shoulder. In this position, shutting out the sounds of their screaming, he staggered back across the stone floor and almost fell into his throne.

"Now—*now!*" he said, motioning to his blacks, directing them to commence some prearranged play. The huge Negroes leapt forward at Pharaoh's command, two of them clapping hands to the shrieking mouths of the Khemish girls where they flanked the now-unconscious Nubian. Khai, his eyes glued to the crack in the wall, would remember what next happened to his dying day. For the sight was such as to freeze him, so that however much he desired to look away he could not tear his eyes from that scene of absolute cruelty and horror.

The wall behind the black girl's head was now red with the blood that dripped from her fuzz of black hair. But for all that she was unconscious, still two of Khasathut's blacks pinioned her body while a third held her jaws open. As for the fourth and last, he reached into her mouth, took his curved, thin-bladed dagger and sliced out her tongue even as Khai began silently to gag and choke on bile in his secret niche.

By the time he had regained control of himself and once more pressed his watery eyes to the slot, all three of the girls were hanging unconscious from the wall, blood slopping from gaping jaws; and now the blacks tore away their red-spattered robes before turning to face Pharaoh.

Khai, too, turned his horrified gaze upon Khasathut where he sat naked upon his jeweled throne. Anulep had gone down on his knees before him, was shuffling toward him with his forehead touching the floor, his hands behind his back. He kept his hands there, Khai knew, because no man's hand might ever touch Pharaoh; for a mortal's hand to touch him would be to defile him.

And yet . . . could one possibly defile this monster? Khai doubted it.

Finally, Anulep's polished head rested on Khasathut's knees, and there the high priest paused. Ignoring him for a moment, Pharaoh said to his blacks: "Get on with it. Wake them!"

One of the massive guardsmen took out a small stone bottle from a pocket in his kilt. He unstoppered it and held it under the noses of the girls until they jerked their heads and regained consciousness. Only the Nubian girl failed to respond. Khai thought—he hoped—that she must already be dead. The other girls stirred weakly after their initial response, moving their heads from side to side and making awful gurgling noises. They continually spewed blood and bile.

Ignoring for a moment the black girl, the guardsmen formed two teams, three men to each of the flanking girls. They took out their knives and began to skin their victims, peeling down wide strips of skin from their necks to their waists until only the girls' faces and breasts stood out white against the welling red horror of their upper torsos. Mercifully, before the blacks were half finished, the girls were once more unconscious.

Khai, too, had momentarily passed out, and only the feel of the cold and abrasive wall against his fevered brow woke him as he slumped down in cramped darkness. Weakly wiping his mouth free of sickness and blinking his eyes to rid them of stinging tears, he straightened himself up again until his eyes came level with the peephole. He no longer looked at the girls, however—not at those dangling travesties of raw meat which had been girls, no—but at Pharaoh. He looked with horror, with fear, with hatred!

Boy that he was and quite helpless, nevertheless Khai vowed there and then that the Pharaoh, and Anulep—yes, and all of Pharaoh's guardsmen, too—they would pay! Someday, somehow. They would pay for his family, for these poor tortured girls, for all Khem enslaved by this deformed creature that the people called a god! He looked, he glared his hatred out through the crack in the wall, a hatred so raw and red that his very vision was blurred with its passion.

Dimly, he was aware of Anulep's head moving slowly up and down between Pharaoh's thighs, and of Khasathut's left hand tapping out the time on the high priest's head. As if from a million miles away, he heard Pharaoh's panted command that the guardsmen should finish it, and in the very corner of his eye he saw knives flash, saw bellies open from crotches to rib cages as viscera poured out steaming upon the bloodied floor. He was aware of all of these things, but primarily he saw Khasathut's face.

That hideous face whose octopus eyes bulged as their owner tapped faster and faster upon the high priest's bobbing head, until suddenly Khasathut uttered a shrill scream and jerked spastically in his jeweled chair. Now his legs gripped Anulep's waist and his good hand clutched at the high priest's head, which had become almost a blur of motion. For a moment longer it lasted, then—

With a second shriek the Pharaoh drew back his legs, placed his feet on Anulep's shoulders and thrust the man away from him. As the Vizier sprawled on the stone floor, his hands still clasped in position behind his back, Khai saw the distended knob of Pharaoh's penis throbbing and discharging a few last drops of yellow slime. Then once again the boy was violently ill; but it was more the sight he saw with his mind's eye than the depravity of the actual scene which sickened him. He had simply remembered the way Anulep had smiled at him—the Vizier's toothless, circular smile—and the fact that tomorrow he himself was to visit the dentist!

# IV

## PLOT FOR FREEDOM

Of the rest, of whatever else passed in that hidden chamber of horrors deep in the heart of the great pyramid, Khai saw nothing at all. For when the blacks carried Khasathut's sexually expended, naked figure out of the hexagonal room in his jeweled throne, and long before they returned with Anulep to commence the cleaning-up of the place, he had already flown. Possibly that was as well, for as yet he knew nothing of the pyramid's deepest horrors and had not even questioned the reason why Pharaoh's blacks had filed teeth. . . .

But a flame had sparked in Khai's breast, the red flame of revenge, and his one desire now was to live to grow into a man—a great warrior—and then, somehow, one day, to drag Pharaoh down and destroy him. Just exactly how he might achieve this he did not know, but certainly he could do nothing here. Since there was nowhere in Asorbes for him to hide, perhaps no hiding place in all of Khem, then obviously he must flee Khem. First, however, he must escape from the pyramid.

Already a plan had formed in Khai's mind, a wild and daring plan but by no means impossible. It would be sheerest folly to try to escape through the lower labyrinths and out into the city via the pyramid's ground-floor entrances; any one of Pharaoh's hundreds of guardsmen might see him and take him to Anulep. Doubtless, orders had already been given to that effect: that if he tried to escape he must be brought back. Well then, by what other route might he make his escape?

For anyone else the task might have seemed impossible, but to Khai, whose father had built the vast monument and shown him many of its secrets, it was not even improbable; though certainly it would be very dangerous. As he hurried back to his tiny cell of a room through the inky blackness of the cramped corridors that formed the pyramid's interlocking mazes, he worried at the problem until the solution was crystal clear.

By the time he regained his room and struck flint to his tiny lamp, he knew exactly what he must do. The tools of his escape were to hand—a pair of woven rush mats on the floor, and the pallet he had been given for a bed—so that without more ado he formed these into a tight cylindrical bundle which he strapped lengthwise to his back.

Five years ago, Harsin Ben Ibizin had shown his son the Pharaoh's water supply and how it worked: the system of huge exterior surfaces of stone high in the pyramid's faces which sluiced droplets of condensation into narrowing watercourses that flowed in turn into brick pipes within the pyramid, where they descended steeply to the cisterns of the lower levels. Each single drop of moisture which formed on mighty sloping surfaces eventually found its way to the pyramid's kitchens, its bathrooms and ablutions. And Khai had been allowed to climb up to one of these watercourses until he had peeped out from a height of over four hundred feet to gaze in awe across the rooftops of Asorbes.

At that time, Khai had thought to ask his father if it would be possible to slide down the steeply sloping outside wall from such an inlet. Oh, most surely it would, Harsin Ben Ibizin had replied—if one had the hide of a hippo! Otherwise the stone, however fine-grained and smooth it might appear, would strip away flesh from bones like a huge file. Indeed, of those many workers who had fallen from the monument during the long years of its construction, many had slid down the sloping faces to the bottom, but none of them had survived.

Khai remembered his father's words to this very day. Well, he did not have the hide of a hippo, but he did have these rush mats and a linen pallet full of shredded straw. Also, if he could divert a little water from the mouth of the inlet and down the sloping face, perhaps that would lubricate his way to excellent effect. For a moment, as he retraced his steps by the light of his tiny lamp to a place where a narrow chimneylike flue appeared in the ceiling over his head, Khai was so afraid that he almost abandoned his plan there and then. But only for a moment. Death was far more to his liking than the life he would be forced to lead if he remained here.

And so he climbed into the flue and wound his way upward, pushing his lamp before him and placing it in whichever niches he could find while he used his hands and feet for climbing. It was not a hard climb but seemed interminable, just as it had five years ago. Hand and footholds were plentiful, a stairway almost, designed to give maximum assistance to any workman called upon to inspect the watercourse up above; and there were places where Khai could actually pause and rest, sitting on tiny ledges while his feet dangled into the black throat of the flue.

So he progressed, and within an hour of leaving his room he crept over the lip of the chimney and felt a cool breeze blowing from ahead. Rounding an awkward bend, he saw the stars of night set in a jet sky, and a moment later, his light sputtered and was blown out. Crawling on all fours with his head occasionally scraping against the low ceiling, Khai felt the rim of the brick pipe that descended into the bowels of the pyramid. Beyond the pipe, he followed the channel of the gutter that fed it with water and was pleased when his hands felt a trickling of cool liquid. So efficient was the system that water began to collect and flow soon after the sun went down, the flow increasing all through the night until, with the dawn, the gutters and pipes would be veritable rivers and waterfalls in miniature. Khai knew he must be gone long before then, however, and so hurried forward, eager now to put his plan into operation.

At last, he reached the end of the inspection tunnel where it narrowed to a circular opening high in the pyramid's sloping face. From here he looked out, as he had done five years ago, on the sleeping city of Asorbes. He had emerged on the south face and to his left could see the night-shining Nile wandering down from its vastly distant sources. The moon was thin-horned and gave little light, which was just as well. The air he breathed was full of familiar odors, of fires and cooking and spices, and other smells which seemed wafted to him from lands beyond. Lands of mystery and adventure.

Although there were nine such water-inlets—three to each face except the incomplete east face which overlooked the Nile and faced the rising sun-god, Re, reborn each day—the boy had deliberately chosen this one, set central in the south face. He had done so for a number of reasons. He knew there was a massive pile of soft sand at the base of the monument at this spot, soon to be used for filling in a disused subterranean vault; he knew also that the southern quarter of the city housed the vast majority of slaves of foreign origin— Nubians and Siwadis, a few Theraens, Syrans and Kushites—and that Pharaoh's guards and patrolmen rarely entered such areas at dead of night; and furthermore, beyond the slave quarters and close to the city's south wall, there dwelled his father's old friend Arkhenos. Arkhenos of Subon, a fortress city on the Khem-Therae-Nubia border. If anyone could help him flee the city, he was sure that Arkhenos would be the one. . . .

# V

## ESCAPE FROM THE PYRAMID

Cupping his hands at the limestone lip where the dripping water gathered, Khai spent almost an hour diverting the steadily increasing rivulet down the pyramid's exterior face. When he could see the thin moonlight reflected in a silvery path that reached almost to the ground far below, then he knew he was ready. Quickly, he soaked his pallet and rush mats in what little water had escaped his hands to fill the gutter, then tied the bundle at its corners so that the mats lay beneath the pallet.

Now he pushed the entire contraption out through the water inlet, holding on to it and edging forward until he sat on the lip of the inlet with his legs outside. Then he pulled the reinforced pallet up under himself until he could hook his sandaled feet into the forward corners while his hands grasped the knots slightly to his rear. In this position, with his head and shoulders slightly raised, he once more bumped and edged his body forward until, in one hair-raising moment, he felt his backside bump over the lip of the inlet onto the sloping surface of the outside face.

At first, it seemed that he was stuck there, immobile, but then, with a jerk and a slither, he felt the stone begin to slip by beneath him and almost immediately he started to gather speed. In the space of a few heartbeats, it was as if a wind blew upon him, though he knew the air was almost completely still. Then, too, his sled began to rotate, so that in a moment, he was riding side-on and could feel the pallet beginning to buck beneath him, threatening to spill him. A moment more and he was speeding backwards down the steep wall, then rotating the other way until he was back in his original position.

Feeling the pallet bucking again, he lay his head and shoulders back to flatten his profile and watched the stars overhead turning as he continued to rotate. And all the time he accelerated and the wind blew more wildly upon him, showering his face with rush fragments from the disintegrating mats as he thundered down the side of the pyramid, until he smelled smouldering linen and knew that his pallet must soon burst into flames!

Rotating faster and faster, while the stars above seemed to form a vast heavenly wheel, Khai felt a hideous sickness welling inside and closed his eyes. In another moment, the pallet bucked wildly and Khai guessed that he had reached the lower part of the pyramid, where his diverted stream of water had petered out. Again the battered, disintegrating sled bucked and rose up beneath him, this time leaping free of the stone face and tumbling over and over in mid-air.

Now he clung desperately to his smoldering pallet, his eyes tightly shut, expecting at every moment to feel the bite of the pyramid's stone face. Instead, he was dashed down in soft sand made hard by his rate of descent.

Mercifully, he had landed on the outward sloping side of the sandpile with the remains of his pallet still beneath him, breaking his fall. Wildly, he rolled and bounced, still falling and now completely out of control, but by the time he reached bottom, his speed was greatly reduced. At last, with a jolt that knocked the last remaining ounce of air out of him, he came to a halt on firm ground.

His first thought was to be up on his feet and feeling to see if anything was broken; but even the act of sitting up made him feel dizzy and sick, so that for the moment he lay still. Eventually, when the roaring had gone out of his head and the stars had steadied in the sky, he propped himself up on one elbow, gazing about at night's black shadows and wondering if his escape had been witnessed. It was unlikely, he knew, for the south face overlooked only the slave quarters, but nonetheless he could not stay here.

He forced himself to his feet and staggered for a moment while once more the night sky seemed to revolve. Then, crouching low and heading south, he ran as fast as he could over rough and pitted earth. In a matter of minutes he had left the shadow of the pyramid behind and the jagged silhouettes of the tumble-down slave quarters loomed ahead. At last Khai began to breathe more freely and he had to repress a mad urge to shout for joy. He was free of the pyramid, free—at least for the moment—of the Pharaoh, and in his freedom his heart soared like that of a small bird.

His mind was so full of plans that its thinking was no longer completely lucid, so that soon only the wild joy of freedom remained, and a natural directional instinct which took him straight through the heart of the rambling slave quarters. Part of his mental fatigue sprang from the fact that his stomach was empty, had been empty for much too long, and the rest of it was rooted in the mind-wrenching horror of his recent experiences, which surely would have stunned far more mature minds than Khai's.

Now the low, dark brick buildings had closed in on him and he trotted silently through winding alleys awash with filth and crawling with vermin. In all Asorbes, this was the one region where sanitation had been allowed to fall so drastically into disrepair, so that the sewers situated immediately beneath the streets functioned poorly and the water supply was just as unsafe as was its continuity uncertain. An eerie, unnatural silence shrouded the place, whose stillness was such that the patter of Khai's feet sounded clearly audible in his fear-sensitized ears.

He must by now be in the center of this region from which, through countless generations, the Pharaohs had drawn their polyglot work-force of menials and laborers. Just how much blood, he wondered, had these people given to raise Khasathut's monument to the sky? And with his thoughts returned morbidly to the pyramid once more, Khai paused in his running to cast an anxious glance back at that monstrous moonlit tomb whose silhouette loomed over the rooftops. One day, he promised himself, he would see that now-hated symbol of perverted power reduced to tumbled ruins. But for now—

He turned his face to the south once more—and ran straight into the arms of a huge black man!

# VI

## KING OF SLAVES

"Oh? And what's this?" the great black rumbled, holding Khai's head and turning it until the moonlight shone on his pale face. "A boy, running in the night streets with the rats? Aye, and a boy with meat on his bones at that. No slave's son this one, I'll warrant, but the well-fed pup of some bitch of Khem! Who are you, boy?"

At first Khai had thought himself caught by one of Pharaoh's black guardsmen, but now he could see that his captor wore only the threadbare rags of a slave and that he bore the ankh brand on his forehead. "Let me go," he gasped, wriggling and squirming, trying desperately to free himself from the man's grasp. "Let me go!"

"And where would you be going, young master? Hasn't your father warned you against entering the slave quarter at night?" The black man's voice was full of a wry cynicism, as if he already knew the answers to his questions and much more.

"I'm on my way to the house of Arkhenos of Subon," Khai answered, trying his best to sound affronted and failing miserably. "I decided to take a short-cut."

"A short-cut, indeed!" Again the black peered into Khai's face, a grim smile playing at the corners of his thick-lipped mouth. "And why, I wonder, did I see you pausing to shiver and tremble and look back over your shoulder—as if you feared that perhaps you were followed? Hardly the act of a boy brave enough to enter the slave quarter late at night, eh? And how is it you come from the direction of the pyramid?—but then, why shouldn't you. After all, it was your father built the thing!"

Khai shrank back in shock and astonishment, unable to believe his own ears. Had Anulep already discovered his absence, then, alerting all of Asorbes to keep watch for him? Were people already searching for him in the city? It did not seem possible. And yet, how else could this black slave know of him?

The Nubian chuckled as if reading his mind. "It's in your eyes, lad," he said, "written all over your face. Damn me, but you're a poor liar! Oh, I know you all right, Khai Ibizin, and I know of you. Didn't I spend a whole week building a wall around your father's garden? Ah, I see you remember me now."

Khai's mouth had fallen open. He did indeed remember the man. He and one other slave had been given the task of constructing a many-arched wall around the perimeter of the garden, so as to partially seclude it from the view of tradesmen coming into the courtyard. They had been tasked by virtue of their skill at stoneworking. It was a job which could have been completed in two or three days, but Harsin Ben Ibizin had gone very easy on the slaves and had made sure that they got their rest and were well-fed.

"Yes," the black continued, "you surely know me now. Well, I've been waiting for you since first I noticed you preparing your escape route."

"What?" Khai gasped again. "But how could you possibly have seen—" he began.

"Look!" the other commanded, cutting him off, forcibly turning his head in huge hands until the boy's eyes stared back the way he had come. At first, he saw only the littered street, the crumbling walls, huddled buildings and black shadows. Then his eyes went above and beyond these to the looming man-made mountain that was Khasathut's pyramid.

"The south face," said the black man by way of explanation. "It's in shadow now, but when the moon was on it—why!—at first I thought that the pyramid wept! It was the water that gave you away, Khai, the water you used to make your slide smooth and cool. It crept down the south face like a little silver river, like the tears of the moon!"

"But if you saw it," Khai gasped, "then perhaps—"

"Others?" The Nubian shook his head. "A few slaves, perhaps, but they would most likely come to me before doing anything or telling anyone else. As Pharaoh is the king of Khem, I, Adonda Gomba, am king of the slaves. You were wise, Khai, in choosing the south face, for it overlooks the slave quarter and little else."

The boy nodded. "I know. But you said you knew who I was before you saw me. How could you have known?"

"You're not the first one to run from the pyramid, boy. But you're one of the first to make it. Oh, you're not out of the fire yet, not by a long shot. But at least you've made a good start. As to how I knew it was you: you were the pyramid's most recent prisoner, and one of the youngest. Only a boy would have dared such a wild escape, and it would have to be a boy who knew the pyramid's innards better than his own." He shrugged. "Who else could it have been?"

Khai said nothing, and eventually Adonda Gomba continued:

"Well, boy, and things have gone badly for you, eh?"

Khai could only hang his head and nod. "I . . . I've run away from the pyramid, yes. From the Pharaoh's high priest, Anulep. He . . . he is *horrible*! And Khasathut is a monster!"

"Oh? And you've only just learned that, have you?" Sarcasm dripped from the black's tongue.

"What will you do with me?" Khai asked, his eyes searching the streets and shadows, his mind racing to discover a way out of his predicament.

"That depends on you, boy," the other answered. "On what you want to do now that you've broken out. One thing is certain: you can't stay in Asorbes, and certainly not here in the slave quarter. And as for Arkhenos of Subon—a friend of your father?—why, his house is the first place they'll look for you!"

"You won't hand me over?" Khai could hardly believe his luck.

"Little fear of that," the other answered. "There are no rewards for slaves—especially black ones. No, I'll not take you in. But come, we're out in the open and that's not wise. While I'm a king of sorts, still there are those who would depose me if they could. They wouldn't take to you as kindly as I do, Khai Ibizin. You can thank your Khemish gods that your father was good to me!"

"He was good to everyone," Khai answered, turning his face away.

"Ah, yes," the Nubian rumbled more quietly. "I was forgetting." For a moment the two were silent and the black man put his arm about the boy's shoulders. "I, too, lost my father when I was your age," he finally said. "A stone turned over on the ramp and trapped him. He was worn out, slow-moving and dull-witted. The stone did him a favor."

Without another word, the black led the boy into the shadows, guiding him through a jagged gap in a wall and along a narrow alley toward a dimly burning oil lamp fixed over a hide-covered doorway. "I'm a Nubian," said Adonda Gomba, holding the hide cover to one side. "My ancestors always kept lamps burning outside their houses to light them home. As they did in Nubia, I also do in Asorbes," but he spat out the last word as if it were poison. "This is my house, Khai Ibizin. Not so grand as your own home, I'll grant you, but if nothing more it's a safe place to lie your head down for the night. Before that, though, I'd like you to tell me why you ran. And why do you call Pharaoh 'a monster'?"

"I'll tell you anything you wish to know," Khai answered, "but why are you interested?"

"I'm interested in all such things, Khai," the Nubian told him, ushering him in through the doorway and lifting down the lamp to bring it with him. By its light the boy saw a small room with a wooden table and three makeshift chairs. The ceiling was of stitched hides sagging from old beams, through which the night sky showed in several places. A second covered doorspace led on to the kitchen, from which came the smell of cooking and the rattle of wooden implements.

Adonda Gomba sat Khai down in one of the crude chairs and crossed to the curtained kitchen door. He parted the curtain and put his head through, saying something in lowered tones to whoever it was who worked by the glowing red light of a wood fire. "My wife, Nyooni," he told Khai as he rejoined him. "Most other slaves are asleep now for they need all the strength they can muster, but I no longer need so much sleep at nights. I only work when I want to, which is when the work suits me and carries small rewards. My masters trust me, do you see, Khai? It makes life easier and gives me time to make plans, for myself and for all of the others."

All of a sudden, the boy felt perfectly safe, and with this feeling of security came weariness. He was tired, drained—and he was starving. He sniffed at the air, savoring the odor that drifted to him from the unseen kitchen.

"Are you hungry, boy?" the black asked. "I thought so. You'll have some bread and a piece of lamb in a moment. One of Pharaoh's beasts," he grinned, "that got its head trapped in the hands of one of my men!" Finding Adonda Gomba's grin infectious, Khai attempted a wan smile.

"However," the black continued, "you'll have to pay me for your food. You'll pay with information. We slaves gather all sorts of information about Pharaoh—about his guards and the pyramid—against the day when we strike back!"

"When *you* strike? Slaves?"

"Oh, yes, indeed. That day will come, Khai, believe it. When the time is right, we'll rise up against Khasathut, and when we do, there'll be no holding us!" His voice had grown so grim that the youth could only believe him.

"But there," the black went on, "I've told you my secret, and now you must tell me yours. If you truly hate Pharaoh as much as I think you do, Khai, then you'll tell me all you can of him and his ways. Now then, what do you say?"

# part FIVE

# I

# ADHAN'S
# REVENGE

Now the night was far behind and already the
sun climbed half-way toward its zenith. Adonda
Gomba, weary but well pleased with himself, hurried through the streets of the slave quarters back
toward his poor house. He had made all of the
necessary arrangements to get Khai out of the city
in one piece, and now only one task remained: to
give the boy the latest information about his
brother and tell him how Adhan had taken his
revenge. It was not a task that Gomba relished,
but at least it would be repayment for those things
Khai had told him.

The huge black was more than satisfied with
the information he had gleaned from Khai. The
boy had been able to supply him with details of the
pyramid's internal structure hitherto unknown;
moreover, he had updated other information
which had been false or inaccurate. Gomba had
plans of all the pyramid's many rooms and passageways, but his drawings of the lower levels—
which had been designed and built all of three
generations ago—were very sketchy indeed and
subject to errors.

Not that Khai had physically been inside those
mysterious levels long enough to study them or gain
more than merely fleeting impressions, but over the
years for as long as he could remember he had been
allowed to pore over his father's drawings; and a
great deal of what he had seen had committed itself
to his memory. The black "king" of the slaves had

kept the boy at it all through the dark hours, tapping that memory, until Khai was quite literally exhausted.

He had questioned him not only with regard to the pyramid but also about Pharaoh himself; about his Vizier or so-called "high priest," Anulep; also about those dreadful occurrences which Khai had witnessed in the monstrous bridal chamber. Khai had found it strange indeed that Gomba accepted his version of that hideous ritual of blood without reservation—without even registering more than a flicker of surprise at the more grisly details—until the black explained that his story merely confirmed the slave community's worst suspicions, perhaps the suspicions of all Asorbes. Certainly a large majority of the city's more privileged citizens suspected that the Pharaoh was a monster (in mind if not in form) and they feared him desperately; but he was their king and a god omnipotent; and as all men know, the gods work in exceedingly strange ways.

What had surprised Gomba was Khai's account of Khasathut's *physical* abnormalities, for these had been a secret kept very closely guarded indeed. It explained, though, why the people had never been permitted to see Pharaoh's true form, why he had always hidden behind the great, larger-than-life, godlike exteriors constructed for him by his artists and carpenters. And of course those craftsmen were all members of Pharaoh's personal retinue, dwellers in the pyramid. If, indeed, they still lived!

These many thoughts passed through Gomba's mind as he neared the rude dwelling he called home. Now, in return for Khai's invaluable information, he must tell the boy what he had discovered of Adhan: how his brother had crawled home on all fours from the foot of the great ramp, making his way—bloody, delirious with horror and in hideous agony—to this father's now-empty house near the east wall.

And indeed the house had been empty. Only one of Harsin Ben Ibizin's paid retainers had remained there after the news had made it swiftly back to the house; the rest had looted the place of everything worth taking and had fled. Possibly they would soon flee the city itself. Better to be well out of it than to have been a member of the Ibizin household! At the last, soldiers had come for the slaves and they had been taken off to the city's slave quarters, where from now on they would serve only the Pharaoh.

Mellina the old cook had been the only one to stay, for she had nowhere else to go. And Mellina it was who cleaned Adhan's terrible wound and put him to bed. There he had remained, semi-conscious all through the late afternoon and evening, tossing in his fever and babbling of treachery and red revenge. Imthod Haphenid he named as the traitor, and swore that the junior architect would soon suffer the consequences of his devil's work—that he, Adhan, would be the author of an awful vengeance.

Sitting by his bedside, Old Mellina had awakened from an uneasy sleep some time after the midnight hour. She found the house empty and the door standing open. Leaving only a spattering of scarlet droplets to mark his trail, Adhan had gone out into the night. Mellina went into the dark streets after him, but she could not find him.

Indeed, Adhan's whereabouts were not discovered until mid-morning, when a messenger from the pyramid went to the house of Imthod Haphenid to bring the architect to Anulep. Haphenid was to be promoted to Harsin Ben Ibizin's former position, and Anulep was to present him with Khasathut's royal seal, proclaiming him Grand Architect of the Pyramid. Ah, but this was not to be! The messenger found Haphenid, most certainly, but he also found Adhan Ibizin.

By then Adhan was dead, seated stiffly in a chair in Haphenid's study, but the grim smile on his chalky face told of a revenge which had been grisly as it was sweet. Then, in a state of shock, Anulep's messenger stumbled about the house, and wherever he went he was met with pieces of the man he had come to find.

The traitor's hands were in the kitchen; nevermore would he use them to sabotage the plans of a better man. His tongue lay on the tiled floor of the hall; it would not lie again to gain Pharaoh's favor. His eyes were blindly staring nubs of jelly set neatly upon a small table in his bedroom; and they never again would glint green with envy at the marvelous works of a true master. As for his blood-less corpse: only the white feet of that stuck up from the seat in the tiny privy; and his blood filled the stone bowl in which Adhan's corpse bathed its feet!

Wondering how best to tell Khai all of this (a story which by now was the talk and terror of all Asorbes), Gomba slowed his pace as he drew closer to his house. Had there been observers to see him, they might well have wondered at the way his steps grew shorter with the lengthening of his face.

They might also have noted a slight bulge beneath his tatters which told of something concealed there: Khai's bow and quiver of arrows, cannily "lifted" from the now-deserted home of the once proud and flourishing Ibizins. When Khai fled the city, he would not go unarmed; Gomba had ensured that his favorite weapon would go with him. The huge black had a knife for him, too, but that was already hidden away. The penalty was death for any slave caught handling weapons, even a "king" of slaves, and Gomba risked his life in doing what he did for Khai.

There were no observers, however, only a handful of skinny, ragged urchins too young to be put to work. Except for these, the filthy streets were deserted, and Gomba's movements attracted no eyes other than those of a pair of furtive rats that chewed on some nameless morsel in the shadow of a crumbling wall. Kicking a pebble in the direction of the vermin, Gomba cursed himself for a fool that he was risking his neck this way—but then again, perhaps not. The boy's father had been good to him . . . and who could say? Perhaps the lad really would come back one day to send Pharaoh to hell.

The Nubian shuddered as he recalled the words of Aysha the witch-woman. He had left her hovel only a few short minutes ago and remembered her words most clearly:

"You have taken into your care a great redeemer," she had told him. "A righter of wrongs, a general, a killer! Ah, he is a rare one. Blond of hair and blue of eyes—a queer fish! And in caring for him you do well, Adonda Gomba, for he will free you in the end. He will free all of us, who have lived our lives as slaves! Mark well my words. . . ." And Gomba had marked them, for there was no way at all that Aysha could possibly have learned of his charge, except by that strange sixth sense of hers which told her far more than any pair of keen eyes ever could!

Old Aysha, yes. Blind and yet all-seeing. Black as old leather and yet bright as a new day. In Nubia she would be a *N'ganga* of great power. Here in Asorbes . . . she was lucky to be still alive. Ancient, withered, of no earthly use—but the slaves fed and protected her. Hers was the magic of the olden days, and her blind eyes invariably foresaw Pharaoh's downfall—which in itself was reason enough to keep her alive and well.

But now the picture of the witch-woman faded in Gomba's mind's eye as quickly as it had come. Despite his hesitancy, he now found himself at the door of his house. For a moment, he frowned, sighing deeply. Then a sterner look replaced the uncertainty on his face and his shoulders straightened. Life was hard enough without the addition of useless daydreams. He drew the hide that guarded the doorway to one side, stooped and stepped through into the cool gloom beyond.

"Khai," he barked, his voice rough and sharp-edged. "Hey, boy, wake up! There are things I have to tell you."

# II
# RAMANON'S VISIT

With Adonda Gomba's return, Khai began yet another day and night of terror. It started with the Nubian's story of Adhan's revenge which, while initially it left Khai pale, shaken and sick at heart, at the last filled him with a passionate pride and strengthened his already iron resolve: to follow in his brother's footsteps and seek vengeance, even on Pharaoh himself, no matter how long that might take. The terror only *began* with Gomba's story, however, for no sooner was the tale of Adhan's grisly revenge told than the Nubian received warning from one of his slave subjects—a crippled, one-armed Syran he used as a runner—that a certain captain of Khasathut's Corps of Intelligence, his secret police, was on his way to see him with a squad of bully-boys who were specialists in the twin arts of interrogation and torture.

Even the big black paled on receipt of this news, and he inwardly cursed himself for ever befriending Khai in the first place; but his plans were already too far gone for alterations, regrets or recriminations. To turn Khai in at this late hour would plainly be to disclose his own part in the boy's disappearance, which in turn would mean the end of Adonda Gomba. Before letting the crippled runner go, Gomba took Khai's knife from where he had hidden it and bundled it up with his bow, then tied the bundle to the man's side under his clothes. Finally, he gave the frightened Syran rapid instructions and ordered him on his way. When the man had gone, Gomba turned to Khai and explained:

"He will see to it that your weapons are smuggled out of the city and given to Mhyna."

"Mhyna?"

"You'll meet Mhyna soon enough, Khai, but right now we must get you hidden away."

He gave the boy a piece of dried meat, a large wedge of bread and a cup of water, then pried up a massive slab of stone from those surrounding it in the floor of his kitchen. In doing so, he revealed a shallow trench beneath which had once been part of the city's sewage system. Passing directly beneath Gomba's house, the hiding place was at once ideally and very dangerously situated. Ideal in that Khai could be hidden away without his leaving Gomba's dwelling in broad daylight, and dangerous in that if he should be discovered there, then the game would be well and truly up, not only for Khai but most certainly and conclusively for Adonda Gomba.

While no sewage had passed through this dried up bowel of a channel for many years, still the stench which instantly billowed out on removal of the slab was that of a charnel house. Gomba saw the way Khai was almost bowled over by the smell and remarked: "You'll get used to it soon enough, boy. The stink of a few dead rats can't harm you. It's the live ones who'll soon be visiting me that we have to worry about!" Then he had helped Khai to get down into the hole, somehow replaced the slab and covered the floor with the layer of dirt and dust which had previously been there. But if Khai had fancied that his hiding place would be as dark, lifeless, airless and silent as the tomb itself, then he had been wrong on all counts.

At first it was indeed dark, and so warm as to be stifling, but soon Khai became aware of a rotten luminescence that seemed to have its source in the baked brick walls themselves, almost as if the vile glow of putrescence remained after all these years of disuse. And of course it was by this intermittent and unearthly light that he first became aware of the rats. . . .

The rodents bothered him from the start, coming so close and in such numbers that he was sure they intended to attack him; but on each occasion, as soon as he made any threatening movement, they would disappear back to wherever they came from and leave him on his own. The mere fact that they were there, however, somewhere in the snaking sinus of the old sewer, was enough to fill him with a shuddering nausea.

Mercifully, the trench was not airless (though the warm drafts that passed along it were so redolent of rats both living and dead, not to mention the stenches of less easily recognizable refuse, that Khai almost wished it was), and it was far from silent. Instead it seemed to the boy that he had become trapped in the coils of some vast sounding shell—like those of the great snails which were often washed up on the Nile's banks—where every tiniest sound was magnified tenfold. The creaking of Adonda Gomba's ancient chair in the room adjacent to the kitchen sounded to him like the groanings of some mighty oak in a great wind, and the thunderous footfalls of the Nubian as he went from room to shabby room in the crumbling ruin overhead were almost deafening. One other sound—a monotonous, dull and apparently distant pounding, which try as he might he could not shut out—bothered him continuously and even had him grinding his teeth; until suddenly he realized that it was only the magnified pounding of his own blood in his ears!

But if Khai's predicament was unpleasant, Adonda Gomba's was surely worse. It would not be the first time Captain Ramanon had called on him and probably would not be the last, but each visit was invariably more nerve-wracking than the one before. And so, having put the boy out of sight, the Nubian covered his table with work details and lists of tools for replacement, with quarrying schedules and food quotas and many other matters concerning the administration of the slaves, then sat back and awaited Ramanon's arrival.

And sure enough, less than twenty minutes later, the captain and his escort of soldiers came to visit. Ramanon was Khemish by birth, though plainly it was the Arabban in him that came out in his swarthy features and bent beak of a nose. Adonda Gomba knew the captain's face well and he hated it, but he respected (as well he might in his position) the sharp mind behind it. On several past occasions he had pitted his wits against those of the chief of Pharaoh's "security" officers, and so far he had always managed to come out on the winning side. This time, however, he was less certain of himself.

For one thing, the boy was right here—within spitting distance if one could spit through a slab of stone—and for another, he was important. Aysha the witch-wife had first brought this fact to light with her predictions about Khai, and now Ramanon's visit only served to confirm the old woman's cryptic words. After all, why else should this powerful agent of Pharaoh find it necessary to come here in person? Why, as on those previous occasions, had he not been satisfied merely to send for Gomba? The answer was simple: this was not just a matter of a few missing sheep or the mysterious fall of a particularly hated overseer from the pyramid's face. No, the boy was very important to Pharaoh, and as such his immediate presence increased the danger to Gomba tenfold!

The captain's arrival was heralded by the sudden sound of soldiers halting in the dust of the alley outside. They had approached very quietly and Gomba would have had no warning other than the military thump of sandaled feet if his own intelligence system were not so finely tuned. As it was, he had time enough to compose himself, then to look up and assume an expression of surprise as the covering of his door was torn aside and the hawkish, red-robed figure of Ramanon appeared framed in the opening.

The captain grinned (a bad sign in itself) and entered the room in front of three of his lieutenants. Two of the latter looked like nothing so much as common thugs, while the third was a slimly effeminate creature wearing makeup applied as carefully as any woman's. Gomba recognized this last human anomaly as Nathebol Abizoth, the son of one of Pharaoh's most trusted overlords, and he inwardly shuddered.

Rumor had it that one of Abizoth's favorite methods of extracting information from an unwilling victim was to first extract his more readily removable parts, such as nails, testicles, eyeballs and skin, leaving the tongue, of course, to the last. And it was not on record that anyone had ever survived one of Abizoth's "examinations!"

"Master!" cried Adonda Gomba, springing up from his rickety table and flinging himself down on the dirt floor. "Illustrious Lord, I am honored!"

"Up, black dog," Ramanon quietly answered, but with no trace of malice in his voice. Hands on hips, he faced Gomba squarely as the black came to his feet. "There are one or two things you might like to tell me, my friend. At least I hope so, if you desire to remain my friend. . . ."

"Only say what I should tell you, Lord, and if I can—" Gomba began.

"*If* you can?" Abizoth cut in, his voice the hiss of a viper. "We come to you, black dog, because we *know* you can!" He snapped his woman's fingers and the two stony-faced thugs grabbed Gomba's arms and dragged him protesting out into the alley. As they came out into the open air, a squad of twelve spearsmen snapped to attention. Ignoring the soldiers, the thugs turned Gomba's face toward the pyramid whose peak rose massively over distant rooftops.

Ramanon and Abizoth came out of Gomba's house at a more leisurely pace and the captain stepped up close to the pinioned black. He stared into the Nubian's face. "Do you see Pharaoh's tomb, Adonda Gomba?"

"Yes, Lord," the Nubian stammered. "I see it, as I have seen it all my life, but—"

"Quiet!" Ramanon snarled. He picked at his fingernails for a moment, then once more peered close into the black man's fearful face. "Late last night a boy climbed out of a hole near the top of the pyramid. He slid down the south face—that face you see there—and we believe he came into the slave quarters. He is probably injured, badly burned from his slide, broken from the fall at slide's end. He could not get far without assistance. We want him, Gomba. We want him badly!"

"Lord, I know of no such—"

"Bring him back inside," Ramanon ordered, turning his back and re-entering the slave-king's house.

Gomba was bundled in through the doorway once more and Abizoth was quick to follow and pounce upon him. "Black dog," the pervert hissed, "where's your woman?"

"My woman, master? I have not had a woman for many months now," Gomba lied. He thanked all the Gods of Khem that he had sent his woman away that very morning. He had intuitively known that trouble was in the air, and so had sent Nyooni out of harm's way.

"Isn't it your duty to have a woman?" Abizoth insisted. "To produce a new generation of slaves for Pharaoh?"

"The woman I had was barren, master, for which reason she was sent to cook for the quarriers. I have not yet found another woman. My work is—"

"To hell with your work!" Ramanon's voice was low and dangerous. "Can you guess," he continued, "why my good friend Abizoth here wanted to see your woman, black dog?"

Gomba shook his head, his lower lip trembling in unfeigned terror.

"Then I'll tell you," Abizoth hissed. "In my experience, you'd soon speak up if your woman was yelping. But if you haven't got a woman—well, if I can't skin a black tit we'll have to see what I can do with a pair of black balls!"

Quickly, the heavily made-up eyes of the effeminate monster flickered about the room. "On the table," he snapped. "Strip him!"

The two thugs again grabbed Gomba, and one of them used his free arm to scatter the documents that littered his table. The crude papyrus sheets flew across the room and fluttered to the floor in crumpled disorder. Somehow the huge black broke free and hurled himself down on the dirt floor, scrabbling after his papers.

"Do what you will with me!" he cried. "But take care, masters, if you value your own skins. I control the slaves, and these documents are my schedules. Already Pharaoh grows impatient that his tomb should be finished—and where would he look for an answer if the work stopped altogether? Would you disrupt the God-king's plans for the sake of a mere boy? I do not know this boy; I have not seen him. Would I suffer for some runaway pup when I could gain favor by delivering him into my master's hands?"

"Hold!" Ramanon snarled. His men had already hauled the Nubian from the floor and half-stripped him. They were now holding him down on the table and Abizoth's long-nailed hands were reaching for him, twitching fitfully. Ramanon knew that his perverted junior was a near-madman, and that he would doubtless cripple the black slave-king if given the chance.

But what Gomba had said—about his own skin being more precious to him than that of any unknown boy—had rung absolutely true. And certainly Gomba's work as the internal administrator and co-ordinator of the vast slave workforce was all-important to Pharaoh. In actual fact, Khasathut probably did not even know of Gomba's existence—but he would soon track down the source of the trouble if the work on his pyramid were suddenly to show a dramatic decrease.

"Put your sharp woman's claws away, Abizoth," the captain commanded.

"Can't you see how you're troubling the slave-king? Why, I couldn't let any harm come to the good and honest Adonda Gomba! No, for he has been my friend for too many years and would not lie to me."

He turned to the thugs who still held Gomba. "Let him up. He knows nothing."

Released, the Nubian threw himself at Ramanon's feet, but the captain only kicked him away. "None of that, slave-king. Better gather your documents together and get back to work. For your threat cuts two ways, Adonda Gomba, and if work on the pyramid suffers from this time forward . . . well, I shan't have to look far for someone to blame."

"Meanwhile," Abizoth whispered, "you'd better keep your eyes and ears open, black dog, if you want to keep them at all. We're looking for a boy—a blue-eyed, fair-haired youth of fourteen or fifteen years—and when we find him. . . . If you've had anything to do with him since he fled the pyramid, then I'll be back. And next time the captain will let me come on my own!"

# III

## OUT OF THE CITY

With nightfall Adonda Gomba let Khai out of his hideaway. By that time, as the big black had expected, the boy was almost at his wits end. Twice he had fallen asleep, only to be shocked awake by rats scampering over him and nibbling at his crust of bread. In the end he had broken the bread into two pieces, throwing them as far as he could along the bend of the disused sewer before and behind him.

This action, while it doubled and redoubled the squeaking and scampering of the gray horde, had seemed nevertheless to satisfy them for a little while and had the desired effect of causing them to keep their distance—at least until the bread was gone. After that, they had grown more inquisitive than ever.

Once, galvanized into a sort of panic, Khai had actually thrown himself headlong at the rats, crawling frantically along the winding sinus after them until he came to a place where the ceiling had collapsed. While the rats could scamper on ahead without pause, disappearing into the tumbled debris, Khai himself could go no further; and so at last sanity returned. It was then that he had realized how quickly the already nebulous light was failing, and he had been lucky in the end to find his way back to his starting point. He had traveled a surprising distance along the track of the old sewer and there had been a number of junctions along the way, the entrances of which all looked alike in the near darkness; but at last he was back beneath Adonda Gomba's house.

There, under his breath, panting and trembling, he called himself several sorts of fool and coward, reflecting that the black slave above was risking his very life for him—and here he was afraid of a few rats! But for all that he was able to berate himself, still he longed to be out of the place. To stand in the cool, clean air of the world above, separated from him by only the thickness of a slab of stone that formed part of the floor in the Nubian's kitchen—which nevertheless seemed a million miles away. So that when at last he heard the thunderous approach of Gomba's feet, and then a hideous grating as the slab over his head began to move, causing a shower of sand and gritty debris to fall upon him, he almost cried out in joy.

It was plainly just as great a relief to the huge black man to be able to drag Khai out of the hole, and he hugged the trembling boy to him for long moments before pushing him away and holding him at arm's length. "Brave lad, Khai—you were quiet as a mouse down there!"

Khai shuddered. "Don't talk to me of mice—" he answered, "or of rats!"

"I know, I know," Gomba nodded, patting his shoulder. "But it's over now. I'm sorry I left you down there so long, lad, but it had to be. There have been squads of soldiers in the streets all day, poking about here and there, but they've more or less given up now. Now we can make you a bit more comfortable—but you'll still have to stay out of sight for the rest of the night. Tomorrow we'll move you."

"I'm to be moved?"

"Aye, out of Asorbes and upriver. Eventually out of Khem itself—but that'll be up to you. Don't worry, it's all been worked out for you. But Khai—"

"Yes?"

"There's one thing. If you are caught, I want you to remember something. My life will be in your hands. . . ."

"You've no need to worry on that score, Adonda Gomba," Khai answered at once. "I would never mention your name to any man of the Pharaoh. I might well be questioned, but I would not be harmed. They could threaten but never punish. Pharaoh has plans for me, yes, but they don't include torture just yet. No, first he would train me for . . . for other things." He shuddered and looked closely into the black man's eyes. "But I won't be caught, will I?"

"Not if I've anything to do with it," the Nubian gruffly answered. "But quickly now, let's get you hidden away again." He saw Khai's eyes go fearfully to the floor and added: "No, not in the sewer, lad, don't fret. You're going upward this time—" and he jerked a thumb at the low ceiling overhead.

Khai's eyes widened. "On the roof?"

"Under it," the Nubian grinned. "There's a small gap between the ceiling there and the roof above. It may get chilly before morning, but at least there are no rats. Once you're up there and comfortable on the rafters, then we can talk—provided we keep it quiet. I've a lot to tell you before you can sleep. And when you've heard me out, then you'll need to repeat my instructions over and over to yourself. There'll be no margin for error tomorrow. Now then, before we do anything else, tell me: can you swim?"

"Like a fish," Khai answered at once.

"Good! That's very important. You'll see why when you know the plan. But right now I'll show you how to climb up onto the rafters and hide under the roof. . . ."

Still memorizing Gomba's instructions, Khai eventually fell into a fitful sleep on a platform of rough boards placed across rafters above the sagging and cobwebby ceiling. Twice during the night he was disturbed when soldiers came to shake the Nubian awake and search the house; but on both of these occasions the black man grumbled so much about lack of sleep, unnecessary harassment and Pharaoh's displeasure if ever he should discover what was going on, that the soldiers quickly grew uncomfortable and left. Half-way toward morning, when it was much cooler, the youth did manage to fall into a deep sleep, which claimed him utterly until some hours later when he sensed furtive movements in the ruined apartments below.

"Are you awake, Khai?" came Gomba's urgent voice from the darkness beneath him. "Yes? Then come on down. Quickly, now. Our visitor has arrived." Easing the cramps in his muscles, Khai stiffly obeyed and lowered himself down between dusty rafters. As his feet swung in empty air, the big black caught him and lifted him down.

Gomba's visitor, a Kushite of about Khai's own age and size, was in the process of disrobing and wrapping himself about with a blanket. In the kitchen, a small oil lamp showed that the slab had been prized up again from the floor, exposing the old sewer beneath. As Khai dusted himself off and shook cobwebs from his hair, Gomba helped the other youth down into the claustrophobic hole under the floor. Before he could replace the slab Khai went over and kneeled at the edge of the hole. "Thank you," he said to the huddled figure in the sewer. Then the slab was moved back into place and dirt was scuffed over it, hiding the cracks in the floor.

Finally, as Gomba lit a second lamp, Khai began hurriedly to don the Kushite's rags. "Over the top of your own clothes, lad," the big black told him. "Quickly! You needn't have bothered to tidy yourself up, for now I've got to darken your face down a bit and sprinkle a little dirt over you. And here—" he produced a sliver of charcoal and expertly drew an *ankh* on Khai's forehead. "We mustn't forget your slave mark. There—and you can wrap this rag around your yellow hair. So—" He paused to cast a critical eye over his handiwork. "There we are, a slave if ever I saw one—if a little too well-fed! Right, let's be on our way."

"Did the soldiers stop the Kushite on his way here?" Khai asked as Gomba steered him out into the dark, dirty streets.

"They did, as I suspected they would. A couple of them have been watching the house all night, I think—probably the same ones who kept waking me up! They might even be watching us right now, but they're hardly likely to check us again. After all, they know now that you're just a Kushite youth come to waken me up so that I can get the rest of the lads moving!"

The "lads" Gomba talked about were one hundred male slaves detailed to work for a week in the quarries downriver. They would be transported by barge to a point above the second cataract, marched around the falls to a second barge below the white water, and so on down the river for another seventy miles or so to the quarries of the east bank. There would be ninety-nine of them in all, with Khai making the figure up to one hundred; but long before the slave-barge reached its mooring above the cataract Khai would have made his escape. That is, if all went according to plan.

It would not be the first time a slave had escaped, many had tried it at one time or another. Usually they only made their run when they were well away from the slave-city, when they could quickly head for open country or lose themselves in the forests and swamps. Sometimes they made it, but more often than not they were caught. When that happened the soldiers made examples of them, putting their heads on poles in the slave quarters to be picked into skulls by vultures. And of course there were other deterrents: the swamps were full of hungry crocodiles and there were many poisonous snakes in the grasslands. . . .

Now Khai and Adonda Gomba hurried through the deserted, garbage-littered streets, and as the first hint of daylight tinged the sky to the east, so the slave-king urgently banged on doors and shutters and called out the names of those slaves detailed for work in the quarries. In no time at all his ragged party was a hundred strong, and soon they crossed the perimeter of the slave quarters into the city proper where a small squad of six Khemish soldiers was waiting for them. Then, with the soldiers flanking them three to a side, they formed four ranks and tramped quietly through the still sleeping streets, marching through areas of Asorbes which grew ever more opulent, until at last they approached the looming city wall and the massive arch which contained and guarded the east gate.

This was one part of the plan which Khai had dreaded, when the guard commander himself would count heads against Gomba's list before ordering the gate opened. But to his surprise and relief the whole procedure went off without a hitch. Indeed, the sleepy-looking sergeant-of-the-guard hardly gave the slaves a second glance as he checked them off in bunches of ten. With the job quickly done, he ordered the gate opened and the slaves passed under the towering arch of the wall and out of the city.

"He can be forgiven his inefficiency," Gomba quietly explained to Khai out of the corner of his mouth. "He's been up all night, kept awake by reports of revellers, brawlers and other troublemakers in the streets between here and the slave quarters." He chuckled grimly. "Now I wonder who arranged that little lot for him, eh? Anyway, all he's interested in now is standing himself down from duty and getting home to his hot, fat little wife—who he probably suspects of having it off with his superior officer. Maybe she is and maybe she isn't, but that hardly matters to us. What does matter is that we're out of the city, right?"

# IV

## SLAVE SHIP

Outside and below the beetling walls of Asorbes, the party of slaves waited until their escorts were relieved by two dozen guardsmen from the gate, then began their march along the stone road toward the river. The soldiers, all weary from their night's duty, marched with a little less than their usual military precision, and their polyglot charges were not hard put to keep pace with them.

The slaves were not chained nor even roped, for there was little likelihood that anyone would be foolish enough to make a run for it so close to Asorbes. The land was all Khemish for hundreds of miles around, and of course each and every slave bore the telltale brand of the *ankh* on his forehead. Moreover, four of the guards were of Pharaoh's Corps of Archers and bore their weapons with them. A runaway slave would provide excellent target practice.

Now the air was a little brighter and the shadowy faces of the slaves were starting to take on a certain individuality, so that Khai was glad when at last they reached the palm-grown banks of the river. They moved out along a stone quay to where the wide-beamed slave barge lay low in milky mist that lapped almost to its gunwales. Without preamble, the slaves were herded aboard and made to sit on plank benches fixed in rows across the width of the reed decks. Then the vessel's captain came aboard.

Menon Phadal was a fat Khemite with a scowling face and small, piggish eyes. Quickly, those eyes now scanned his human cargo and he scowled all the more. Waddling to the door of his tiny cabin between the barge's twin masts, he turned and sat down heavily on his captain's bench. To Adonda Gomba he called out, "No girls, Gomba? No fun for Menon Phadal during his trip downriver?"

"Not this time, Lord Phadal," Gomba called back from the quay-side. "Next week, however—on that you have my word!" And under his breath he added: *"Aye, indeed you do, fat dog!"*

The slave-king was thinking of a Syran slave girl who had been forced by three Theraen embalmers one night more than a year ago. They had been drunk, entering the slave quarters in the dead of night and abducting the girl for their own vile purposes. When she had crawled back to her hovel the next morning, she was out of her mind and near dead.

Better, perhaps, that she had died, for upon recovering from her ordeal she was seen to have contracted the "Theraen Scab," and now she was riddled with it. It no longer showed so much outwardly, but inside she was crawling. Gomba was sure that Menon Phadal would notice nothing in the gloom of his little cabin, and a touch of syphilis would soon put a stop to his loathsome leching—especially when he gave it to his equally offensive wife! As for the girl herself: she only tittered and giggled and no longer cared much what happened to her.

"I'll hold you to that, Gomba!" the fat captain called out through the mist which was now beginning to shroud the boat.

Gomba grinned and nodded, "Aye, captain, I'm sure you will. You just leave it to me. . . ."

By now the soldiers had drawn lots for escort duty. Three of them were groaning and pulling faces as they clambered aboard and went to sit in the prow. Their swords were made dull by moisture where they laid them on their laps. Three guards for a hundred slaves, but that was enough; for each one of the hundred was now made to pick up and snap onto his wrist a manacle attached by a short bronze chain to a large stone. The stones sat between the feet of the slaves and weighed anything up to nine and ten pounds each. They were all big enough to drag any but the most powerful swimmer down, and no one but a madman would attempt to escape from the boat with one of these stones fastened to his wrist.

Now a bald, burly steersman passed among the slaves, looking to see that their manacles were fastened. In his belt, he carried a simple key designed to spring the mechanisms on all of the manacles, but he would not be using it until journey's end. Satisfied, he drew the captain's attention to the horizon of mist-wreathed trees on the east bank. A dull red rim showed its edge above a fringe of palms. The sun was up and it was time to get the barge underway.

"Cast us off, Gomba," cried the captain, and the Nubian obligingly loosened ropes and tossed them into the stern. The slaves seated by the port side reed gunwales were chivvied to their feet by the steersman who briefly, expertly cracked a long whip over the heads of those closest to him.

"Up lads," he bellowed, "you know the game. And watch you don't trip overboard, eh?" He laughed boomingly and cracked his whip again. The standing slaves took up long poles from where they lay along the gunwale and poled the barge slowly away from the quay. The steersman stood on a small platform in the stern and used his great steering-oar to guide the craft out into the river's current. All of the motive power would be supplied by the river itself and the vessel's sail would not be used until the return journey.

Khai, when he had found his seat by the starboard gunwale, (or rather, when he was jostled into that position by the slaves,) had been handed his stone, chain and manacle by a scar-faced young Nubian who closed one eye in a knowing wink. Most of these slaves had been to the quarries many times and knew every detail of the journey's routine—especially those details which one day might work in their favor. The manacle on Khai's stone was faulty— or it had better be if he was to have a chance.

When the steersman had moved back to his platform and while the barge was being poled out into the river, Khai unobtrusively tested his manacle and in a few moments discovered the secret of forcing it. It was simply a matter of flexing one's wrist and giving the manacle a sharp twist. He relaxed a little and began to breathe more easily. His stone was a large one and would take him straight to the bottom if he should fail to free himself in time. Nor could he simply jump overboard without it, for it must appear that he was drowned. Then, having freed himself, still he would have to make good his boast to Adonda Gomba that he could swim like a fish.

For the hundredth time, he went over the plan again in his mind. There would be three small bundles of broken reeds floating on the water. They would not move with the river, would in fact be tethered to the bottom by thin lines—except for the third bundle which would be in the form of a rough circle and anchored to the bottom with a rope. Khai would have to wait until the barge was level with this last marker before he leaped overboard. He would let the stone take him down into the water a little way, free himself and swim underwater to the ring of reeds. There, he could surface slowly until his head broke the surface within the ring where he would be hidden from the view of those on the boat.

And there he must stay, treading water until the arrival of Mhyna's barge. By then the slave ship would have drifted on down the river, leaving him for dead and gone to the bottom, freshly drowned and food for the crocs and fishes. He shuddered as a rapid swirling in the water just a few feet from the ship's side told of the passing of a large croc. The plan was not without its dangers. . . .

The mist had settled now to a milky layer that lay inches deep on the water and lapped in curling tendrils about the sides of the big barge. Caught in the midstream current, the craft moved a little less sluggishly and answered to the steersman's huge oar. Well astern, the quays of Asorbes slowly disappeared in thinly misted distance and the trees on the banks became grey ghosts that reared silently upward, as if they reached for the light of the new day.

And indeed that light was stronger now as the climbing orange ball of the sun probed the cool morning air with its heat. The prevalent wind from the north, little more than a breeze at the moment but strengthening with the sun's rising, would assist in dispersing the mist; but by then, Khai must be gone and fled into green deeps. So he sat there and watched the river, his eyes constantly scanning its surface between the east bank and the barge; and time and time again, he tensed the muscles of his legs, testing them for that lightning spring which would carry him over the gunwale and down into the water.

Dimly he was aware of the slaves talking in low voices, and the soldiers in the prow as they engaged in a noisy argument. He knew that Menon Phadal sat nodding in the doorway of his cabin, with his head sunk down onto his chest, and he could feel the slow surge of the river beneath the barge like the movement of a huge and ponderous living creature. It was only when his eyes began to water and twitch with the strain of staring into the floating, thinning mist that he took them off the river for a moment to glance once more at the steersman, and again at the boat's drowsing captain. He had little need to worry about the three soldiers for they were almost hidden by the mass of the central cabin. In fact, if he moved fast enough when the time came, he could be gone before anyone even—

And there his thoughts froze, for as he gazed again at the river suddenly he saw it: the first marker! A tangled bundle of broken reeds lying there in the water, rolling a little and bobbing gently but not drifting with the current.

Almost before he could recover from the shock of the sighting, the second reed mass drifted into view through milky swirlings of mist. This one was further away from the barge, perhaps forty or fifty feet, and Khai sat up straighter, almost got to his feet as he strained his eyes and craned his neck to search the river's surface for the third and final marker.

"You!" came the bass rumble of the steersman. "Sit down, man. What do you think you're doing?"

Khai half-turned, saw the steersman's puzzled eyes upon him. He turned back to the river and in the corner of his eye was aware that Menon Phadal was now awake, on his feet, pointing, shouting.

"He's going to jump! Grab him—you slaves, there—grab him!"

But then he spotted the third mass of floating reeds, seventy or eighty feet away, bobbing in breeze-eddied mist. The hands of the slaves flanking him reached clumsily for him and the voice of the scar-faced young Nubian whispered: "Jump, man—now!"

He snatched up his stone and leaped up onto the gunwale. Hands snatched at his legs, deliberately avoided clasping him. He jumped—

The water closed over his head and he sank; but already he cradled the stone between his thighs and sought to break the hold of the faulty manacle. The water was green and deep and the slow current tended to set him turning. He balanced himself, tried to maintain his sense of direction as he fought with the manacle, flexing his wrist again and again and jerking the wide metal band left and right until his wrist bled.

Then, as his feet struck bottom and sank in slime, at last the manacle snapped open. He kicked himself off in what he prayed was the right direction and struck out strongly with his legs. Already his lungs craved air, but for the moment he fought the urge to swim for the surface and headed across the bottom. By now, the slave ship would have drifted on downriver. How far, Khai wondered?

Now, with his lungs near-bursting, he angled his body for the surface and almost immediately saw stretched before him the rope which anchored the third marker to the bottom. He caught at it, followed its sinuous length hand over hand up out of the depths, until his head at last broke surface inside a bobbing tangle of papyrus leaves and stems. At its upper end the rope was tied to a leather bladder to give it buoyancy, and now Khai clung to this life-saving bubble as he trod water and scanned the surface of the river through a screen of reeds.

The slave ship was a mere shadow drifting away into a thin wall of rapidly dispersing mist. Figures moved on its deck and voices were blown back to Khai by the rising wind from downriver.

"Who was he? Why did he jump?" That was Menon Phadal. A lesser voice, almost inaudible and broken by the sound of wavelets lapping in the reeds, answered:

"He was just a lad ... no family ... acting strange lately ... out of his head ... drowned himself." But then the slave ship was gone and Khai heard no more.

# V

## ON MHYNA'S BARGE

Mhyna's barge was a curious affair, much like the slave ship in shape and construction, but very much smaller. Having the lines of a wide-beamed felucca with a shallow draught, the boat looked for all the world like a huge leaf which had started to curl up at the edges. And like a leaf, it was far more seaworthy than it looked. The port and starboard reed platforms were bound to a ribbed central keel formed of a single up-curving plank of great thickness, which supported a central mast with a scarlet lateen sail. From a large bronze ring at the top of the mast, a dozen taut ropes came down to the outer circumference of the barge's deck, where they were fastened to the tightly-bound reed gunwales. The barge was constructed in such a way that lading it with a cargo only served to compress its decks and make them more watertight.

Looking up through the network of ropes from where he lay on his back between bundles of crocodile skins and jars of oil and wild honey, Khai felt that he stared up at the center of some monstrous spider's web—except that the craft's mistress, Mhyna, could not by any stretch of the imagination be described as a monster! She was dusky, krinkly haired, with laughing slanted eyes and long, handsomely proportioned legs. Plainly, Mhyna was a child of several races; basically Khemish, there was also that of the East in her. Yes, and something of the jungle, too.

An expert sailor, Mhyna handled the vessel's

long-bladed, oarlike rudder with practiced ease as the prevalent wind from the north filled the barge's sail and drove it south against the river's flow. "Experts" of a later age would doubtless deny the existence of Mhyna's vessel—certainly of its sail—for their records would seem to show that sails were unknown on the Nile until shortly before the unification of Egypt under Menes. However that might be, Mhyna's ancestors had been plying the river under sail for more than four hundred years. . . .

"Are we clear of Asorbes yet?" Khai asked the girl, uttering the first words he had dared to speak to her since she had pulled him from the river something less than an hour ago. Lying as he was, with only his face uncovered and the rest of him under the freshly-tanned hide of a beast, he was unable to see that the massive-walled city now lay well in the wake of the craft.

Instead of answering him, Mhyna lashed her steering-oar in a neutral position and came amidships. Walking the central plank with the grace and agility of a cat, a few paces brought her to where she stood directly over her "stowaway." She loosened one of the ropes that controlled the angle of her small sail, then stood there with the rope wrapped round her arm, her legs braced and spread, her back to the mast, gazing down at Khai through brown eyes which were far from innocent.

He averted his own eyes a little, keeping his gaze from her legs where they were parted, from the narrow strip of linen that passed between them and only just concealed the darkly bulging triangle of hair beneath. It was not that the girl was indecently or even immodestly dressed (indeed, the ladies of Asorbes seemed almost to vie with one another to see who could leave the most flesh uncovered!), but it was the angle at which she leaned against the mast and the way her short skirt rose up when she braced her sun-browned legs against the barge's slow sway.

In contrast to many of Khem's women, Mhyna kept both breasts covered. A wide scarf looped over her shoulders from the back of her neck, crossed over her breasts and passed behind her back where its ends were tied. Upon her brow she wore a scarlet headband which looked to be of the same coarse material as the sail, and in her ears were rings of gold that caught the morning sun. Her feet were bare, with toenails painted a bright red.

She looked, Khai thought, like some female pirate from the Great Sea. Certainly the glint in her eyes was piratical—or at least mischievous—as she shielded them with a hand to scan the banks of the river. And at last, as Khai began to move his cramped body and relieve the ache of lying so still, she spoke:

"Best stay quiet for now, little friend, for while we've left Asorbes behind, still there are plenty of soldiers on the banks. They seem to be searching the reeds for something—perhaps for you!"

Again she scanned the riverbanks, then stood up straight to wave gaily at someone unseen. "If you keep them amused," she explained, "they don't bother you." But a moment later, when Khai began carefully to raise himself up on one elbow to have a look for himself, she put a foot on his chest and pushed him back. "No," she said, "you must keep your head *down*! We'd both be in for it if you were seen."

Khai could not know it, but Mhyna was playing a game with him. The banks were almost deserted, with no single soldier in sight. In a field of cropped grass on the west bank, a shepherd boy paused for a moment to wonder who the girl was that waved to him from her barge, then went back to tending his sheep.

"Why are you helping me?" Khai asked after a little while.

Again she stared down at him, spreading her legs wider yet and squirming her hips, ostensibly to scratch her backside on the mast. Finally, she shrugged. "I have two brothers doing time on Khasathut's pyramid. When I come up the river from Wad-Gahar, the slaves of Asorbes bring me word of them— just as they brought me your bow and your knife last night. The slaves help me, and so I help them."

"Your brothers are criminals?"

"No—" she began, then continued: "yes, I suppose they must be. At any rate, they were accused of getting a town official's daughter with child."

"Both of them?" Khai's raised eyebrows showed his own innocence and lack of knowledge regards the ways of the world.

Mhyna shrugged. "The stupid girl didn't know which one was the father," she answered. "And so, since neither one would marry her, both were sent to prison. Then they were transferred to Asorbes. And there they'll stay—for another three months at least. Or perhaps they'll get time off for good behavior!" She laughed. "Hah! little chance of that. No, for the children of Eddis Jhirra are a lusty lot and wicked."

"Eddis Jhirra?" Khai queried.

"My father," she told him with a grin. "We all take after him—if you know what I mean."

"No," said Khai truthfully, "I don't."

"Oh?" she cocked her head on one side. "Well, I have four brothers and two sisters—that I know of. All of them are older than me. My sisters are married with lots of kids of their own. As for my brothers—" Again, she shrugged. "Two in Asorbes building the Pharaoh's tomb; the other two seeking out his enemies west of the river. But if I know those soldier boys, they'll be more interested in the village girls than fighting off Kushite marauders!"

"So two of your brothers are Khasathut's men?"

"Pressed by his recruiters, aye—stolen out of their apprenticeship four years ago and soldiers ever since. Why do you think my father puts his barge in my care, eh?"

Khai stirred a little, and once more Mhyna cautioned him: "Lie still, little man. Don't forget the soldiers on the banks. My, but they're out in force!"

"If I can just turn on my side a bit," Khai grunted. "There's a spelk or something sticking in my back. Uh!—there, that's better," and he collapsed back again with a sigh.

"I can't understand why you're so uncomfortable," she said. "Is it too cool for you in the shade of that hide? Are you still wet?" And she reached out a toe, hooked it under the soft leather and flipped it to one side. "There, let the sun warm you for a bit."

She looked at Khai's body and pouted, arching her back against the mast and pretending to locate an itch between her shoulder blades. "Such a pale little boy," she commented huskily, "but I like your eyes. They're so strange and blue!"

Suddenly, Khai felt annoyed. The girl was getting under his skin with her references to his youth. "Little man" and "little friend," and now he was a "pale little boy!" Why, she couldn't be more than eighteen or nineteen years old herself! And certainly he was an inch or two taller than she was.

"Oh? And are you angry with me?" she asked, seeing the narrowing of his eyes and the stubborn set of his jaw. "Did I say something, my young friend?"

That was the last straw. "I'm not so young!" Khai burst out. "And I'm certainly not your friend. As for being a little boy: I escaped from the pyramid, didn't I? And I've vowed to go back to Asorbes one day and kill the Pharaoh himself. Let me tell you something, Mhyna: there's no one in Khem shoots a straighter arrow than I do and no one *ever* slid down the side of a pyramid before—and lived to talk about it, at any rate!"

"My!" she said. "Such a lot of credits! And won't your girlfriends miss you, Khai the Archer? And won't they cry for you while you're away, Khai-Who-Slid-Down-the-Pyramid?"

He immediately reddened. "My girlfriends?"

"Surely you have girlfriends?" she said. "Why, you must be all of, oh, fifteen years old—maybe even sixteen?"

"I'm seventeen!" Khai lied. "And of course I've had girlfriends."

"Well," she answered, squirming again and using her toe to toy with the hem of his simple kirtle. "I suppose you *could* be seventeen. You're quite tall." She lay her head on one side and squinted at him. "Hmm—your legs are very sturdy—and I can see that you think mine are, too." She laughed at his expression, knowing that he couldn't keep his eyes from the spot where that thin linen strip had finally worked itself into her body, so that the center now barely showed through a glistening bush of tightly curled hair. The muscles in her legs and buttocks tightened as she deliberately flexed them, and all the anger ebbed out of Khai as he began to react to her sexuality, her taunts.

With her toe stroking his thigh, suddenly she froze. "Don't move," she said, "not an inch! There's a great boat coming down the river—with soldiers on board. They seem to be steering toward us. . . ." She crouched down, laid a hand on his thigh, threw the soft hide back over him, this time covering his face as well as his body. "Don't move now," she whispered. "Stay perfectly still."

Khai froze—not only his body, but his mind, too—his senses so alert for exterior occurrences that he was almost oblivious to matters closer to home. Almost—but not quite. For Mhyna's hand was furtively moving on his thigh, cunningly seeking him out! As she took hold of him, he started violently, cracking his head on a jar of oil.

"Stay still, Khai," she giggled. "The soldiers—"

For a moment longer, he suffered the exquisite torment of her languidly moving, gently squeezing hand—but then could stand it no longer. He reached down spastically to trap her hand in his own, and in so doing uncovered his face. He stared up in half-amazed astonishment at the girl where she crouched beside him, her large brown eyes half-shuttered with silken lashes. "The soldiers," she whispered again—but by now he knew that there were no soldiers.

Trembling in every limb, he began to raise himself up onto one elbow, his free hand tracing the curve of Mhyna's inner thigh. Every nerve of his body seemed tinglingly afire, about to burst into flames; and sure enough, before his hand could reach its silky objective, suddenly a tide of sweet agony washed over him. He gave a low cry and fell back, spending himself in long bursts.

"Oh!" Mhyna said, a surprised expression growing on her face. She stood up and wiped her hand on her skirt. "So you *are* a virgin after all, are you?" And she laughed delightedly.

Still trembling, Khai pulled the hide back over his exposed body and turned his face to one side. "Oh, no, no, Khai!" she cried, kneeling beside him and taking his face in her hands. "I'm not scolding you. I've always wanted to know what it would be like with a virgin—yes, and now I shall! You'll see, for you'll be ready again in a little while."

She steered the barge toward several large clumps of papyrus reeds where they grew beneath overhanging willows on small islands which lay twenty or so yards out in the water from the east bank. There, where fringing branches leaned down and the nodding reeds grew tall, she moored her craft so that it could not be seen and drew up the sail.

Cool in the shade of the trees, Khai watched her movements as she finished with her camouflaging of the boat. He was unashamed now that the sun was out of his eyes and all the tension gone from his body. Mhyna came and stood over him once more. She looked down at him and smiled, her face and body dappled by beams of sunlight glancing through the overhanging branches. Then, as he started to sit up, she tut-tutted.

"My, but you're the one for fidgeting," she told him. "Lie still and be good."

Instead of obeying her, he kneeled, pulled half a dozen soft hides from where they were piled at one side of the boat and formed them into a comfortable nest where he had been lying. Then he took off his clothes and lay down again, his hands behind his head.

Mhyna's eyes had narrowed until they were slits—the eyes of a cat—and lithe as a cat she was as she threw off her own clothes. Then she took a jar of oil and liberally splashed herself, rubbing the sweet liquid into her body until her skin gleamed. When she was done she looked down at the boy again, laughing low and huskily at what she saw. "There," she said. "I told you you'd soon be ready again."

As his arms came up to reach for her she stepped over him, crouched down with a sigh until she sat astride him with her knees gripping his middle. In another moment, his hands had found her breasts and she leaned forward so that he could kiss them. He was aware that she had removed her headband and that her hair now formed a tent of tresses about his face, but beyond that he could not think. All else was lost in the sweet heat of her body and the languid rocking of the boat. . . .

# VI

# THE PARTING OF THE WAYS

It was noon before Mhyna once more let down the sail and steered her barge out from its hiding place. During the intervening hours, Khai had learned many things (chiefly that he was not inexhaustible!), for his teacher was extremely well-versed in the amorous arts.

Looking down on him where he slept, Mhyna thought: "What an *odd* boy. And his eyes: so blue, so strange! And his body: so sweet. And strong, too, for all that he now sleeps."

Thinking back on their coupling, she stretched with pleasure. Khai had been more relaxed, less eager to please, more restrained the second time. She had shown him how to mount her from behind; bracing his feet against the boat's ribs, his arms encircling her, his hands fondling her oiled breasts where they hung soft and ripe. Finally, though by then he had been ready for sleep, she had taken him with her mouth. And when at the last moment he had tried to draw away from her, then she had fought off his hands and gripped him tight, plying him with her tongue until there was nothing left of him but a whimper of pleasure.

Now he was asleep and the river stretched ahead, and Mhyna wondered what would become of him when she put him ashore on the Nile's bank in just a few hours' time. That would be before she reached Phemor, a small town on the east bank. Phemor was rapidly growing into a garrison and Mhyna's wares were bound for the town's shops and markets, but Khai must be off the barge twenty miles earlier than that. She would put him ashore where marshland merged quickly into forest.

She dared not approach Phemor closer than that, not with Khai aboard. The town was certain to be crawling with recruiters and other troops, and the youth's unusual appearance would be bound to attract attention. Recently, there had been a number of swift, savage attacks by Kushite raiders, and all the river's towns now contained heavy contingents of the Pharaoh's massive army. Those numbers of troops which Khai had seen at the parades in Asorbes had only comprised about one-third of the army's total strength; and if Pharaoh desired he could very quickly and effectively conscript every man, woman and child throughout all of Khem. It was not thought that this would ever come about, however, for none of the surrounding lands could possibly raise armies strong enough to cause him more than a perfunctory concern.

Kush, of course, was the odd man out, the only thorn in Khasathut's side. Kush with its hill-bred warriors and pony-riding rebels, who struck from their near-impregnable strongholds in the high passes and the looming plateaus of the Gilf Kebir. Rumor had it that even now Melembrin, the great war-chief of the Kushites, led a large force of raiders somewhere to the west of the river; and certainly there had been a spate of guerilla attacks on the forts of the western territories.

Many of Pharaoh's border patrols had been visited in the night and liquidated as the men slept or sat around their campfires; and this in areas where they had thought themselves perfectly secure. The outpost at Peh-il had been raided; the fort at Kurag on the verge of the western swamp had been besieged, starved, stormed and destroyed; and there had been constantly increasing harassment on the western routes out of Khem to Daraaf and Siwad—all of which must surely be the work of the Kushites.

That was why the ferries were even now working overtime at Phemor and Peh-il, conveying troops to the west bank—why reinforcements were on their way to the great forts at Tanos, Ghirra, Pethos and Afallah—why all of the river towns were choking with soldiers. And it was just as bad in the north, where entire regiments of men had been garrisoned at Mylah-Ton and Ohath; so that it was generally believed that this time the Pharaoh was poising his forces to deal Kush a crippling retaliatory blow—possibly one from which she would never recover.

Khai did not intend to head west, however (he feared the Kushites as any boy fears his country's enemies), but south-east. He would leave Mhyna's barge and strike out across country until he again met the river above the fourth cataract, where it flowed from east to west. Khai knew his local geography well, knew also that his plan would mean a journey of about two hundred miles through wild forests and jungles; but at the end of that trek, he should be able to cross the Nile into Nubia.

Although Nubia was still thought of as a satellite of Khem, the black king N'jakka was proving to be a stumbling block in the path of Pharaoh's dreams of total conquest and empire. N'jakka was young, strong and stubborn; he would not turn a blind eye to Khem's slave-taking in the manner of his now aged and ailing father. Nor would he allow too many of Khem's soldiers a foothold on his side of the river. Diplomatic intercourse seemed cordial enough—on the surface, at least—and all of the trading routes were open, but it was an uneasy situation at best and N'jakka knew that Khem's forces could overrun Nubia should Khasathut ever desire it. Even so, the God-king would not be given an easy time of it; the Nubian nation would resist him to a man.

Since Khem's influence was no longer completely overriding in Nubia, Adonda Gomba had given Khai a sign to take with him which would ensure his safe passage through Nubia and refuge in Abu-han, a jungle city where Gomba had many relatives. Abu-han was therefore Khai's destination. As to what he would do when he got there . . . only time would tell.

"Khai," Mhyna softly called, shaking his shoulder. He was already half awake, having felt the tremor through the boat's keel when she was run ashore on a sandbar of rough silt and soil. Opening his eyes from memories of strange, recurrent dreams which he had known as long as he could remember dreaming—dreams of flying, of soaring aloft like a bird on great silken wings over wild and craggy hills—Khai lifted his head to look over the barge's tilted gunwale.

Only a few yards upriver, the sandbar rose out of the water and formed a small island which was decked with willows and fringed with tall reeds. Just visible in a tangle of rotting foliage were the shapes of two badly waterlogged boats, fishermen's craft by their looks, deserted and left to drift down the river until the current had lodged their dead reed hulks in living papyrus. A smaller island—little more than a leaning tree whose roots stuck up grotesquely from the mud, surrounded by a densely-grown clump of reeds and bull-rushes—lay between the sandbar and the bank proper. The scene was so reminiscent of the place where Khai and Mhyna had earlier sated themselves that the youth's mind immediately flew back to their lovemaking.

He brushed sleep from the corners of his eyes and smiled at Mhyna, who seemed less superior now; more like a girl than the sophisticated woman of the world she had been earlier in the day. Sure of himself, he reached for her, his hand sliding easily along her inner thigh where she crouched beside him. Frowning, she slapped his hand aside.

"No, Khai, none of that. There have been boats down the river—several. There's a bend just up ahead. At any moment, there could be another boat. One with soldiers, perhaps—*real* soldiers! So get up now, quick as you can, and on your way."

He could hardly credit his ears. Was this the girl he had loved, who had given him her body so completely, this cold creature who now hastened him to be on his way? He propped himself up on one elbow.

"I may never see you again," he said, half-stumbling over the words.

Mhyna's face softened. She leaned over him and kissed him tenderly—but stopped his hands when they began to wander. "Khai, Khai!" she said shaking her head. "We know each other now—all there is to know, as much as any man and woman may know of each other in so short a time—so let it go at that. Don't you understand? You have to be on your way."

He turned his face away from her. Lines half-remembered and hidden in previously unexplored recesses of his mind suddenly floated to the surface. They were meant to be tender lines, but now Khai used them bitterly:

"'My beloved spake, and said unto me: rise up, my love, my fair one, and come away.'"

"Oh?" said Mhyna, twisting the hairs at the back of his neck and inhaling the smell of his skin with delicate little sniffs. "And are you a poet, too, sweet-smelling boy?"

Khai answered: "'A bundle of myrrh is my well-beloved unto me; he shall lie all night betwixt my breasts.'"

"Would that I could have you, my fine young man," she answered, "but I can't!" In one lithe movement, she stood up and stretched. "Where did you learn such poetry?"

"They are the words of a wise man, I think," he answered, "not a poem but a song."

"The Song of Khai," said Mhyna, smiling.

"No, of . . . of a king!" he answered.

"A king?"

Khai frowned, forcing himself to remember—but the memory was fading, clouding over in his mind. In another second it was gone, and with it went Khai's bitterness.

Suddenly, seeing the girl standing there against the mast, her young body proud and free, he felt that his heart was being strangled.

She was the last thread connecting him with Khem, the sole remaining symbol of an otherwise disordered universe. He got to his knees, threw himself at her and pinned her to the mast with his arms. Burying his face in her skirt, he kissed her belly through the coarse material.

"Will you not come with me, Mhyna? Flee Khem now and be mine in Nubia?"

She stroked his hair and looked down at his upturned face. The look in her eyes was one of surprise. "Do you love me, Khai?"

He made no answer.

She shook her head. "And what of my husband, and his child which I carry? Should I forsake the one and ask you to be father to the other? I think not."

"Husband?" he slowly stood up. "Child?" his eyes went to her belly.

"Oh, he's not showing yet, Khai—but he's there all the same." She patted her slightly rounded belly.

"Husband," he said again, shaking his head.

"He's an old man of—oh, thirty," she explained, "and he's good to me. Better than I am to him. He's my father's partner. . . ."

Khai said nothing but simply stared at her, his mouth half open.

She framed his face with cool hands. "Khai, I didn't intend you to love *me,* only my body. I only wanted to seduce you—not to break your heart."

He pulled sharply away from her. "My heart's not so easily broken, Mhyna." But there was a catch in his voice. He stooped and snatched up his bow and quiver of arrows, took two short paces along one of the boat's wooden ribs and leaped over the outer bulwark of reeds into water that was waist deep.

"Khai—" she began, then checked herself.

He waded ashore and climbed up onto a bank shaded with leafy branches. Only then did he pause to look back. Mhyna looked at him where he stood on the bank. "Will you remember me, Khai?"

His eyes were hot and angry, but he nevertheless nodded his answer.

Mhyna turned her sail into the wind and the barge began slowly to slide off the silt into deeper water. Khai wanted to wave, to call out to her, to wish her well. Instead he concentrated on the lump in his throat, which refused to be swallowed.

Then she was gone around the river's bend, and only the ripples on the river remained to say that she had ever been there at all.

# part
# SIX

# I

# THE SLAVERS

By mid-afternoon, Khai was unable to remember exactly what Mhyna had looked like. His nostrils could detect her perfume, the scent of her body, the pungency of the oil she had rubbed into her skin; but try as he might, he could not focus his mind's eye upon her face. Sensibly, he took this as a sign that he had not been and was not in love with her, and he put her to the back of his mind.

He must concentrate now on making good progress through the forest, and indeed he had made progress. He must have covered a good nine or ten miles since leaving Mhyna's barge. The forest was mainly still, shady, dappled with patches of sunlight and furtive with hidden animal eyes. Tiny creatures moved in the leaves and grasses; the occasional bird would rise up in a clatter of wings at his approach; more than one group of wild pigs had rushed off through the undergrowth as he came trotting through the trees.

Twice when he had paused to get his wind and check his direction of travel (he used the sun, which he kept at his back and on his right), he had noted an odd effect. It must surely be his eyes which were playing tricks with him in the gold-dappled gloom, but it sometimes seemed to him that he stood on a vast carpet of yellow sand, with huge dunes stretching away on every hand and lizards that moved underfoot instead of small rodents and leaf-mold beetles. Indeed, if he half-closed his eyes he could conjure the vision out of thin air, could draw the sand down from the sky and drown the entire forest in its mighty drifts. It frightened him a little, and he wondered if it could possibly be the harbinger of some fever contracted in Asorbes' slave quarter. Best to put it out of his mind, along with Mhyna and her forgotten face, and stop worrying about it. Still . . . he wondered if the forest's floor had ever actually been a desert, or if it ever would be—and then he wondered *why* he wondered.

When next he paused Khai heard a sound from somewhere not far ahead. At first, he thought it was the cry of a bird, but its paced regularity and rising, sobbing note was not the call of any creature he knew of. Moving carefully forward toward the source of the sound, he soon became aware that it was only one of a series, which as the distance between closed came more clearly to his ears. First there was a hissing, then a sharp crack followed immediately by the cry, and then the whole thing would repeat. And now Khai could make out that cry to be nothing less than a scream of agony. Someone was suffering a whipping!

Since the awful sounds were very close now, Khai proceeded with even greater caution. Presently, he came upon a natural clearing where, through a screen of ferns, he saw a scene of great cruelty. Inured as he had almost become to horrific sights, still the youth cringed at what he saw. From a slender tree near the center of the clearing hung the naked, lifeless body of a black man. A noose of rope was round his neck; his body was covered with blood from a dozen deep wounds; his sightless eyes hung out on his cheeks and the empty sockets were already full of flies. Khai shuddered unashamedly, knowing that the black had suffered hideously before he died.

There were six other blacks in the clearing, four males and two females, all naked. Five of them were bound and tied together with ropes, tethered to the same tree from which their former colleague now hung. They were slaves— or would be soon, when they had been sold in the slave-market in Asorbes— and their captors were Arabbans from across the Narrow Sea.

There were three hawk-faced, swarthy, turbaned Arabbans, one of whom wielded a vicious whip. At the moment, the three were gathered around a second tree to which was tied a bloodied, frizzle-headed thing which had been a man. Now he was a scarlet ruin whose upper torso was so badly flayed that Khai knew he must soon die. Blood flew as the slaver with the whip again used it on the black, but this time the *hiss* and *crack* of its delivery were not followed by a bubbling cry of agony. Instead, the Nubian's bowels suddenly opened and excrement spattered down his legs and onto the bole of the tree.

One of the Arabbans stepped forward with an exclamation of disgust, jerked up the black's limp head and stared into his face for a moment. Bulging, blood-flecked eyes were frozen in a blind stare. The slaver let the corpse's head fall forward and turned to his companions.

"Dead!" he pronounced. "And that only leaves us with five. Well, what do you think? Have they learned their lesson—or will they try to run off again?"

The smallest of the three—whose growth had obviously been arrested or had deviated before he matured, making him stocky, short-legged, long-armed and generally apish—laughed as he took the whip from the speaker. "Why don't we ask them?" he said, turning to the five remaining Nubians where they were bound to the other tree.

"Right, you lot," the freakish slaver cried. "You've seen what happened to the leaders of your little revolution, and now you know what'll happen to you if you make another run for it. We lost three days tracking you through the forest, but we caught you again in the end. We always will. By now our brothers have doubtless caught the rest of you, and we'll be meeting up with them in Phemor. Ah!—but there'll be faces you'll never see again, I guarantee it. After Phemor, we go by boat downriver to Asorbes, where you'll make all the work we've put in on you worthwhile."

He pointed the stock of his whip at the men. "You three bucks will go into the slave quarters to work on Pharaoh's pyramid. There's plenty of your sort there already, so you'll not feel out of it." He laughed coarsely and reached out callused hands to pull at the breasts of the two girls, black jewels of great beauty. "As for you two: you'll go to the highest bidder, whether it's a madame from the whore house or a fatbellied merchant who likes a bit of black!"

The Arabban stepped back and surveyed the captives through eyes which had narrowed now to mere slits. "So you see, you won't have such a hard time of it—if you're good. But if you're not—" He cracked his whip before the expressionless faces of the males, "then you'll be getting this, like he got it," and he pointed to the black and red thing tied to the other tree. "Or perhaps you'll end up swinging," and he used his shoulder to push against the dangling corpse, setting it slowly turning in mid-air.

"And you two—" he turned to the girls and parted his baggy breeches to produce a great log of a penis that flopped lazily into view. "Well, there'll be a lot more of this for you two—and you'll take it wherever it's offered!"

At last, Khai saw emotion on the faces of the bound Nubian males. Until now they had seemed impassive, completely unaware or uncaring of their predicament, but when the girls were threatened their attitudes changed dramatically. Their dark eyes glinted dangerously and their black muscles flexed. Their bodies, bound though they were, seemed to tense like an animal's before it springs on the back of its prey.

"Hah! You don't like that, do you my buckos?" the dwarvish Arabban slapped his thigh in glee. "Well, you'd better get used to the idea, for that's what these beauties are in for in Asorbes." By now, his two companions had joined him and stood grinning, arms akimbo, watching him at his play.

"Come to think of it," the freak continued, "it's been a long time since I had a bit myself, what with you lot running off and all." He moved close to one of the girls, stepping up to her until his face was between her naked breasts. His penis stirred sluggishly against her knee. And again the blacks tensed, their muscles straining against tough, tight ropes.

Khai had seen enough of rape and torture, and he had never liked the swarthy Arabbans with their questionable habits and appetites and naturally cruel natures. As he had peeped out upon the savage tableau in the clearing, it had seemed to him that he was back in his hiding-place in the pyramid, gazing in on Khasathut's "bridal chamber" and the horrors he had witnessed there. In the black figure dangling and turning in the air, he had seen the body of his father as it plummeted down the east face of the pyramid, flung like a rag doll by the God-king's Black Guard, and in the threat posed to the bound girls he had relived the terror of his own sister's ravishment atop the high, man-made plateau.

Now, as these red visions cleared from his head and he unconsciously found himself nocking an arrow, he saw that the three Arabbans were slowly and deliberately disrobing, and that already the two Nubian girls were wailing piteously and writhing in their bonds. He wasted no more time. The prisoners were Nubians, weren't they? And wasn't he hoping to start a new life in Nubia? Why not go there in triumph, as a hero?

The Arabbans, having stripped off their clothes and put aside their swords and belts, were now naked as the Nubians. Laughing, they converged on one of the quivering girls—

Khai's first arrow took the stunted man in the spine, knocking him down like a swatted fly. The second of the slavers, in the act of loosening the girl's ropes, saw the arrow strike home and instantly dropped into a defensive crouch, turning to face the wall of ferns. The third, hearing his colleague's cry of warning, also turned—in time to take Khai's second arrow in the breast. Coughing his amazement in a spray of scarlet, he fell to his knees and toppled forward onto his face, uncertain of what had happened even as he died.

The surviving slaver had had enough. Snatching up a sword and an armful of clothing, he went crashing through the ferns at the far side of the clearing and vanished into the forest, the sounds of his panic-flight rapidly growing fainter. Khai waited a moment longer, his third arrow nocked and ready, then slowly stood up and stepped out of the ferns into the glade.

He approached the astounded Nubians and looked at them for a second or two, then quickly took out his knife and set to work slicing at their bonds. As he worked, they began to fire a battery of questions at him in their own tongue, of which he understood only a few words. Then the eldest of the three, a barrel-chested man in his middle thirties, barked a word of command and the rest fell silent.

"Boy," the Nubian now addressed Khai in broken Khemish, "were they truly your arrows brought down these dogs?"

Khai nodded and finished off his work by severing the bonds of one of the girls where her hands were tied behind her. "I killed them, yes," he said, but he nevertheless kept his eyes averted from the bodies of the Arabbans where they lay.

*"Huh!"* The black nodded his appreciation. "Then you're a fine bowman, lad, and we owe you our thanks. But why?" He took Khai's shoulders in huge black hands and stared into his eyes. Then he frowned, saying: "Where are you from? You're not . . . Khemish?"

"I was," Khai answered truthfully, "but now I flee Khem. I flee the Pharaoh himself! I was befriended in Asorbes by Adonda Gomba, a Nubian slave—a king of slaves—and he gave me this." He produced a small piece of leather with Gomba's family sign branded into its center.

"Aye," said the black, tenderly feeling his raw wrists, "the Gombas are strong in Abu-han. Is that where you'll go, boy?"

"I would," Khai answered with fervor. "I'd go anywhere rather than return to the great pyramid in Asorbes. And I'd *do* anything rather than face Anulep again, the Pharaoh's Vizier—or worse still Khasathut himself!"

"And do you know the way to Nubia through the forests?"

"Of course! Don't you?"

The black shook his head. "No. We were blindfolded when we were taken and they kept us that way for three days and nights. Only today the slavers told us where we were headed, though we had already guessed it; but even knowing our destination, still we are lost. We know nothing of these lands south of the great river."

"Then let me lead you home!" cried Khai. "A Nubian befriended me in Asorbes, and should I not at least return the favour?"

The two younger blacks had taken up the curved bronze swords of the fallen Arabbans. Now they brandished them in the air and joined with the girls in a wild, whirling primitive dance about Khai, their blades glittering in the shafts of sunlight that lanced down through the surrounding trees. The dance finished as quickly as it had started and with a wild cry all of the Nubians, including the spokesman, flung themselves down at Khai's feet.

"What are you doing?" he asked.

"We honor you, young man!" cried their leader. "As all Nubia will honor you, if ever we can carry your story back there. What is your name?"

"I'm called Khai," he answered in bewilderment.

"Well, then, Khai, we honor you." The Nubian got to his feet and hugged the boy to him. "And you shall be called Khai of Khem—and they shall call you Khai the Killer!"

# II

# THE TRAP

As soon as the initial exuberance occasioned by their release wore off, the Nubians quickly quietened and turned to gaze at the horrific scene of torture and sudden death in the quiet forest glade.

Then they set about to bury their dead in a grief-stricken silence broken only by the quiet sobbing of the girls. One of these, the younger of the two—a beautiful girl who could not have been more than a year older than Khai at most—became so distraught that eventually she had to be lifted bodily from the grave of the man who had been hanged. Khai could only suppose that he had been her brother.

As for the bodies of the Arabbans: they were left to rot, or to be devoured by whichever scavengers might want them. And so, within an hour of Khai's timely intervention, the party struck out in that southwesterly direction which the Khemite youth knew must sooner or later bring them back to the river where it formed the border between Khem and Nubia.

Perhaps it was because they were all fugitives together, but a strong bond of comradeship—one which seemed actually to transcend the debt owed to Khai—quickly formed between the blacks and the white boy. Trotting through the forest, the three male Nubians spaced themselves into a protective arrowhead formation about him, with the girls bringing up the rear. Thus the six of them loped on

through the steadily lengthening shadows, and the forest grew more silent
and shady yet as the miles flew beneath their feet.

Every now and then, they would pause for a few minutes or at least slow
their pace to a walk, but never for very long. They could not forget that one of
the Arabbans had escaped Khai's arrows, and no one could say how long it
would be before more slavers came after them. During one of these comparatively short periods of walking, the Khemish-speaking black, Kindu, told
Khai how the Arabbans had come across the river in force to attack the river-
side villages of northern Nubia. The old people of the villages had been put to
the sword, the babies, too, but the young men and women had been rounded
up like so many head of cattle and made to build huge rafts.

Khai vividly remembered how, long ago, his father had drawn maps to
show him the routes used by slavers bringing blacks out of Nubia; and even
though he knew the rest of Kindu's story before he heard it, still he listened
to the tale in polite silence. As the black talked, Khai could see in his mind's
eye the massive rafts packed with prisoners, and he could follow the winding route they had taken down the river toward the third cataract in Khem
itself.

Since the Nubians were a simple people and knew little of the geography
of lands exterior to their own—and because the Arabbans had taken the additional precaution of blindfolding them—they would have been lost and confused long before the rafts were beached on the eastern bank upriver from the
cataract. Still blindfolded, they would then have been force-marched through
the forests in a northerly direction, skirting the cataract until they again met
the river on the approach route to Phemor. In Phemor, there would be great
Khemish barges waiting to float the slaves downriver to Asorbes, where
finally they would come to journey's end more than two hundred miles from
the land of their birth.

And of course all of this was in complete defiance of the black king,
N'jakka, and naturally Pharaoh would deny all knowledge of it. If ever
N'jakka dared to accuse Khem directly, then the blame would be laid
squarely upon the Arabbans, who must have crossed Khem from the east in
secrecy to strike at Nubia unbeknown to Pharaoh and certainly without his
consent. N'jakka could protest as much as he liked, but that would neither
change matters nor return his people to their burned and ravaged villages.

On this occasion, however, the slavers had overestimated their own
strength. They had taken so many prisoners that they soon found themselves
short-handed, and during the final leg of the march along the forest trails to
Phemor more than a hundred blacks had managed to free themselves and
make their escape. Since then, in groups large and small, they had been pursued by enraged slavers and many had been taken a second time. Kindu and

his friends had been recaptured only an hour or so before Khai had stumbled across them. . . .

After a while, breaking out of the forest and starting across a wide band of savannah, the blacks indicated their desire to call a halt for the night and Khai was only too glad to concur. The muscles of his calves already felt like water and he dreaded the thought of how they would feel the next day. Now the three male blacks went off in different directions and left Khai with the girls. In a little while, there sounded a series of whistles and birdcalls, and some moments later, the blacks returned. One of the young men had found a camp for the night—a patch of thorn bushes hidden in tall grasses less than a hundred yards away.

The Nubians used the swords of the Arabbans to cut a way into the otherwise impenetrable barrier of thorns. They cleared a *boma* big enough to use as a sleeping area. Then, as night set in and distant sounds of nocturnal predators began to fill the shadowy air, Khai's new-found friends beat the grass about until a small deer was startled into flight. Despite the poor light, Khai managed to bring the animal down with a single arrow.

By the time they had a fire going outside their thorn bush refuge, its smoke could not be seen against the darkening sky. Khai had not eaten since Myhna gave him a crust of bread aboard her barge, and as choice cuts of meat began to sizzle on the ends of pointed sticks his mouth watered with anticipatory relish. The only thing they were short of was water, but they decided against seeking a stream in the night. They must simply go thirsty until morning; then they would be able to drink their fill of dew from the broad, dish-shaped leaves of certain large plants, many of which grew in large patches on the savannah.

Beneath a sky full of stars and the soft glow of a rising moon, Khai drew straws for night-watch with the black males. He drew the shortest straw and so took first shift. Worn out, nevertheless he sat alone outside the clump of thorn bushes with a curved sword in his hand, and all he could think of in the star-bright night was sleep and how wonderful it would be when it was his turn to crawl under one of the large Arabban blankets scavenged along with the other possessions of the slavers. Soon, despite a firm resolution to stay awake, he nodded off to sleep where he sat; and slow but sure the pitted face of the moon slid across the sky.

An hour went by, and another, and intermittently Khai would start awake at the cry of some creature of the night; so that when Kindu gently shook his shoulder, he jerked upright with a small cry of alarm.

*"Shh!"* whispered the black. "All is well, Khai, and it is my turn to keep the watch. You can crawl under the first blanket beside Nundi, where I have left a warm space, or beneath the second blanket and warm a place for yourself. Sleep well."

A mist had drifted over the long grasses, wreathing them in slowly swirling tendrils that glowed silvery-gray in the moonlight. Moisture dripped from Khai's nose and his flesh felt cold and numb. Without a word, he handed Kindu his sword and crept through the gap in the thorns. He stepped around the first blanket, a dark lumpy mass on the bare ground, and got down on his knees beside the second. Whoever slept beneath it, more than sufficient blanket had been left over to accommodate Khai. With a sigh of relief he slipped under the rough weave, curled up and almost immediately began to fall asleep.

A moment later, in his final seconds of awareness, he felt a warm hand touch his cold arm, then the warmth of soft breasts against his back and rounded thighs against the back of his own thighs. And when his body was as warm as her own and his breath had slowed into sleep, then the girl carefully wrapped her arms round his neck and hugged him close in the cradle of the night. Sobbing quietly, she rocked him in her arms as if he were the young husband whose body the slavers had tortured and hung from a tree in the clearing where Khai first found them. . . .

Morning came with a golden glow low on the eastern horizon. With that, and with a warning of the terror to come.

Nundi, hearing an excited babble of human voices, the whining of dogs and breaking of branches in the forest close by, quickly woke up the others and breathlessly chivvied them into activity. With the sounds of pursuit moving closer, they left the patch of thorn bushes and headed out across the mile-wide strip of grassland toward the wall of forest on the other side.

Long before they could gain the cover of the trees, a cry went up behind them and they heard the high, nervous barking of *saluki* trackers. Looking back, Khai could make out not only the brightly colored garb of slavers as they burst from the forest wall in a long line, but also the dull yellow of Khemish soldiery. It fully appeared that the slavers had asked for military aid in rounding up the runaways, and that Arabban numbers had been heavily supplemented with troops out of Phemor.

Moreover, when he had looked back, Khai had been astonished to glimpse, at a distance of some three hundred yards along the grass-belt, a second party of Nubian slaves. There were at least a dozen of them and in all probability they, too, had spent the night in thorn-bush *bomas*. They had been sufficiently far away from Khai's party, however, that their presence had been unsuspected. Now, flushed into flight, they too raced for the green and protective wall of the forest.

As Khai bounded through the last of the long grass and plunged headlong into the shade of the trees, hot on the trail of his more fleet, completely panic-stricken companions, suddenly he found his mind working overtime. There had been something about the *shape* of that curved line of pursuers glimpsed at the far side of the grass-belt: a crescent-shaped formation closing like a net. He had seen it before: it was the formation used by beaters when they were beating up game for the hunting nobles of Khem. And Khai knew at once that he, his friends and the larger party of Nubians on their right flank were all being driven into a trap!

Actually, the trap had been set for the larger group of escapees, so that the smaller party was a bonus for the jubilant slavers, but Khai could not know that. He only knew that there was danger up ahead, and a cry of warning was already growing on his lips when disaster struck. He tripped on a root and flew forward, the side of his head glancing against the bole of a tree, his body thrown down on springy ground in a crumpled tangle. For a moment, his senses continued to function—if in a sort of slow-motion—and he stared dazedly into the heart of the forest, where the forms of his black friends were already disappearing into shrubs and undergrowth.

Kindu had seen him take his tumble, was heading back for him when two Arabbans sprang out from the bushes. The black gave a cry of fury and gutted one of the slavers with a single stroke of his sword, then smashed the hilt of his steaming weapon into the face of the other. But his efforts were useless and he could do nothing for Khai. As the bushes seemed suddenly to teem with slavers and soldiers coming on the scene from the flanks, so Kindu threw a last despairing look at the white boy where he lay, then turned and hurled himself after his black companions. That was the last Khai was to see of Kindu for almost four years. . . .

# III

# BACK TO THE RIVER

Khai regained consciousness to the sound of feet trampling leaves and grasses. He remembered enough of what had gone before to know that he must keep his eyes closed. There was a rocking motion and his body swayed in a sort of hammock, so that he soon came to realize he was being carried on a makeshift stretcher. When he finally did open his eyes a fraction, it was to squint up through high treetops to an evening sky. A breeze moved those high branches—a familiar wind from the north— and it brought to Khai a smell he had not expected to know again for some days: the smell of the Nile, which he recognized as surely as the lines in his own palm.

As he closed his eyes again the soldiers who carried him began to talk to each other, confirming the fact that indeed he had been transported many miles back toward his starting point. "Fifteen, sixteen miles at least," the man at the head of the stretcher complained. "Sixteen miles through the forest and the heat of the day—and for what?"

"Don't ask me," the one at the back grunted. "Those damned Arabbans get all the fun. We round up their runaways for them . . . *they* carry 'em off to Asorbes and sell 'em! What justice is there in that?"

"Not a lot, I'll agree," the first voice replied. "They get the black wenches and we get a white boy! And he gets, *uh!*—heavier with every mile, damn his hide!"

The one at the back stumbled a little and cursed,

then answered: "Aye, and I rather fancied a firm black tit to chew on. Huh! Some hope. . . . Who do you reckon the lad is?"

"Well, it's obvious he's no Nubian. A hostage, that's what he was—like Captain Pan-em said—or a prisoner, at any rate. Maybe there'll be something in this for us after all. I mean, we saved his life, didn't we? Took him off that bunch of blacks before they made off into the forest. The slavers got the main pack, but not that lot. There's no telling what sort of tortures those blacks would have worked on this poor lad but for us."

"This poor lad? You were complaining about how heavy he is a minute ago! And anyway, what was he doing with that bow of his—and the knife?"

"Look, he was running, wasn't he?" the man in front answered with a patient sigh, as if he were explaining to a small child. "We must have come on them just as he'd made his escape. My guess is that he was probably out hunting yesterday with his father or friends, and the runaways picked him up as a hostage on their way home. Pity we didn't get the black dogs!"

"*Your* guess—huh!" the other snorted. "You're just repeating what Captain Pan-em said before he sent us backtracking. 'Follow their trail backward,' he said, 'and you'll probably find the lad's father—or some friends of his at least—butchered!' he said."

"Well, and he was right, wasn't he?" the leading soldier snapped. "We did find something, didn't we? Those Arabban carcasses chewed up by lions, and the remains of those two slaves. A funny thing, that. What d'you suppose happened there?"

"Damned if I know. But since then there's been nothing and we're getting mighty close to the river. I can smell it."

They came to a halt and Khai heard a *saluki* bark in the near-distance. "Here comes Khon-arl and Taphan," said the man at the front.

"About time, too," remarked the other. "It's their turn to carry the boy. Here, let's put him down for a minute. My hands are a mass of blisters."

A moment later Khai felt his stretcher lowered to the forest's floor. The ground took shape beneath his body and gave it weight. Then he heard the soldiers move off a few paces through the undergrowth. "Here!" one of them yelled. "We're this way! Did you find anything?"

"Found the damn river, that's all!" came an answering cry from not too far away. "The dog must be crazy—took us right to the water's edge, he did. Seems to have his nose full of scents—birds, snakes, buffalo—anything but men! Crocodiles, too, I reckon. Why, if we'd let him, I'm sure he'd have gone for a swim!"

Now there came the sound of twigs and branches snapping and the swish of foliage shoved aside. Khai's stretcher-bearers moved toward these new sounds and one of them called: "What are you doing there?"

"The dog's in a bush now!" came the answer. "I reckon he's just playing around. He's putting us on, that's what. Needs a good kick in the arse!"

Khai rolled off his stretcher and got to his feet. His knife was still in his belt and his bow and quiver lay where one of the soldiers had thrown them. Bending low, he snatched up his weapons and crept into the shadowy undergrowth. Keeping as quiet as he could and taking care not to step on any twigs, he stole away between bushes and shrubs and put distance between himself and the soldiers.

His head ached horribly and he felt stiff and hungry, but clear in his mind's eyes he could see his new escape route. It lay across the river, through the forest belt to the savannah, then south down the edge of the grasslands into Nubia. The distance was half as far again as his first choice but the going should be easier and the land very sparsely populated. Better still, there'd be no chance of any dog following his scent across the river! As to how he would make the crossing: that would not be easy, but it would not be impossible. For one thing, the night was on his side and already the shadows were lengthening.

He was running now and the voices of the soldiers were rapidly receding. For a hundred, two hundred yards he ran through twilit underbrush, then turned through a sharp right angle and headed for the river. It all depended upon how accurately the *saluki* had retraced his steps. His scent could in no way have been fresh, and the way the soldiers had talked their tracker-dog was hardly dependable.

A few minutes later, coming out of the trees onto the grass of the riverbank, Khai's heart gave a great leap. The soldiers had been wrong about the dog! Less than one hundred yards upriver, he could see a nest of tiny islands which he recognized immediately. This was where Mhyna had put him ashore from her barge. Without pause, he moved through the willows and shrubs of the riverbank toward the nest of islands, and as he ran so there came to his ears a sudden uproar from the forest on his left flank.

His absence had been discovered. Now he heard the high-pitched barking of the frenzied *saluki,* and the steady cursing of the soldiers as they plunged after the dog along Khai's new trail.

The sun was low on the western horizon as Khai drew level with the tiny islands and made a clean dive into the water. In another moment, he was swimming for the southern point of the nearest island, and a few seconds later he had let the slow current drift him down behind the island and out of sight. Beyond this first small clump of reeds and water-lapped bushes, only a dozen or so yards away, lay the papyrus- and willow-grown sandbar of silt and boggy soil where Mhyna had grounded her barge to set him ashore. There, in the reeds, Khai remembered seeing a pair of waterlogged fishermen's boats. Using one of these, he would attempt to cross the river . . . tonight, if that were at all possible.

As the whining of the tracker-dog and the shouts of his handlers came closer along the riverbank, which was now separated from the fugitive by some twenty-five yards of fairly shallow water, so Khai swam through thickly-clumped reed stems until he found one of the two derelict boats lying low in the water. Making as little noise as possible, he pulled himself up onto the boat and stretched out in the damp hollow formed of its reed hull.

There, totally invisible from the riverbank, he lay low and watched through a curtain of foliage as the sun touched the treetops of the western bank. The crocodiles would be in the river now, but they would be sluggish with the cool of evening. He shuddered as he pictured the scaly brutes in his mind: their gaping jaws and voracious appetites. And still dwelling on visions of silently gliding monsters in the dark water, he started violently as close by a human voice said:

"What was that, Gon? That splashing, like a swimmer. . . ."

"*Shh!*" a second voice cautioned. "It *was* a swimmer, Athom, you fool! A croc, I should think, what else? You want to tell him we're here, invite him up onto the island? Or maybe I should stick my head out and take a peep at what he's doing, eh?"

"Oh, very fun—" the first voice started to say, only to be cut off by:

"*Shh!*" Quiet, you idiot! Listen—they've come back with that damn tracker of theirs!"

By this time Khai had traced the source of the voices to a clump of reeds on the island itself. They were Theraens by their accents, and they were obviously on the run—but from what? Khai was soon to find out.

There were two dogs whining on the riverbank now and a regular babble of voices that came drifting across to Khai where he lay barely afloat on the tiny derelict boat. He listened to the conversation and gradually began to understand what was going on. His own soldiers—those who had borne him through the forest all the way back to the river—had now joined up with a second party out of Phemor. The newcomers were tracking a pair of Theraen mercenaries who last night, after a long drinking session, had entered the house of a Phemor noblewoman and raped her. Typical of Theraens, when they were done with the woman, they had slit her throat; but her husband, coming home in the early hours, had seen them as they ran off. His description had been enough to start a manhunt which eventually led the soldiers to the river. Finally, their dog had tracked the Theraens to this spot on the riverbank.

Now there seemed to be something of an argument going on:

"I tell you we've seen no Theraens," one of Khai's soldiers was saying. "That dog of yours must be as crazy as ours! I mean, what man in his right mind—even a damned Theraen—would swim out to those islands, with the river alive with crocs and all? And even if they are out there, who's going to follow them? Not me—not tonight—that's for sure."

"Oh? And what do you suggest we do then?" asked an unknown voice. "There'll be the devil to pay if we all troop back into town empty-handed. And how will you explain this boy you've lost? Do you suppose he could be the boy from Asorbes—" (Khai's ears pricked up) "the one Pharaoh is looking for? You'll be in for it if he is!"

"Damned if I know," answered the fretful voice of one of Khai's bearers. "He could have been. . . . I suppose we could tell 'em he was delirious and ran off. Then that he fell in the river and a croc got him—perhaps?"

"Yes, well, that won't work for us," said someone else. "No, we'd best leave a couple of men here overnight with a dog. In the morning, we'll come down-river in a boat and give the islands a going over. Right then, all that remains now is to decide who'll stay. . . ."

As a fresh burst of arguing broke out, Khai noticed that the sun was almost completely sunken down behind a glowing western horizon. Then he sensed a stealthy movement in the reeds and in another moment, gliding across the thin ribbon of light cast on the water by the sun's rim, he saw a shape which at first he took to be that of a crocodile. No, not a croc, but the other boat! And flat along its near submerged deck lay two dark figures whose hands silently paddled the water. The boat moved into darkness, cutting into and drifting with the current, and was lost to sight. The unknown ex-mercenaries had made good their escape while their trackers argued on the riverbank.

Well, if the other boat was still buoyant enough to support two full-grown men, surely Khai's craft would carry him. Keeping the islands between himself and the voices of the soldiers, he guided his soggy craft out of the reeds and into open water, then used his hands to paddle for the other side.

The river was fairly wide here with a weak current, and the night wind from the north was quite strong. With a bit of luck, Khai should only drift a few miles downriver before reaching the far bank. After that. . . .

He would see what he would see.

# IV

# THE MERCENARIES

Two men drank water at the river's edge. Their reed boat, almost completely submerged now, lay hidden nearby in tall reeds. Exhausted by their flight and the river crossing, they had slept the night through in a tiny grove of palms, emerging in the early morning light to return to the river for food and water. Away upriver and on the far bank there had been some movement: doubtless soldiers come down by boat from Phemor to search the tiny islands where they had hidden. Well, they would find nothing there, for the fugitives had been careful to leave no evidence of their brief sojourn.

Originally, they were of a tribe of tomb-digging Theraens, expert fishermen with both net and spear and not averse to eating raw meat. This was just as well, for a fire would almost certainly attract unwanted attention—and not only from any Khemites who might still be searching for them in the forests of the east bank. During the night, coming to them on the wind from downriver, they had smelled cooking. Upon making cautious investigations they had spotted several Kushite sentries, and so knew that they were close to an encampment of those hill-bred warriors, possibly a fairly large guerilla raiding party. Since they had recently been mercenaries for Khem, the Theraens knew that the Kushites would make very short work of them if they were to fall into their hands.

The remains of a large fish, half-stripped of its flesh, lay on the grass of the riverbank where the men had thrown it when they had eaten their fill. Now they were ready to move off again, intending to head southwest across Daraaf territory to the half-mythical Mountains of Plenty beyond, where they knew they could outdistance their notoriety. Doubtless the raw flesh of the fish where it lay in the sun would soon attract one of the many small crocodiles which infested the river, and just as surely would any signs of their having passed this way be obliterated. . . .

It was the thought of crocodiles lurking in the reeds that caused Launie the handmaiden to run after the young Princess Ashtarta along the riverbank. Already the king's encampment was a mile to the rear, its tents low hummocks on a horizon of reeds and bullrushes, and only a moment or two ago, a sentry had sprung up out of nowhere to catch Launie's arm and pat her bottom, pointing the way the princess had gone and warning of brigands, swampy ground and crocodiles.

Crocodiles! Launie shuddered as she skipped nervously from grass tuft to grass tuft, her eyes on the lapping river's edge and among the close-grown reed stems that formed thick clusters where the ground was most swampy. Now and then, upstream, she would catch sight of a white flash, Ashtarta's short, shiftlike dress as the child played hide and seek with her among river foliage.

The trouble with Ashtarta was her wildness. She should have been born a boy, which would have suited her father well. Since she was a girl, however, and since there was no other heir to the throne of Kush and not likely to be one, Melembrin took her everywhere with him. The king was determined that she should learn all there was to know about war so that she might capably control her armies when he was gone. There were those among the king's advisers who wished he would take a second wife; Miriam had died giving birth to Ashtarta, and the king had looked at no other woman since that time. Miriam had been the love of his youth and in his eyes quite matchless. He was fifty now and the child only fourteen, but she was wild and wiry as any boy her age. Aye, and the tricks she played were often worthy of the most mischievous imps and demons.

Launie guessed that the princess was looking for a place to swim, for Ashtarta scorned the river's crocodiles as much as she loved the water. In Launie's eyes, this was neither the time nor the place for swimming. She was glad that they were striking camp today in preparation for the long trek back to the hills. Melembrin (or "The Fox," as Khem's soldiers knew him) had brought his army down out of Kush three months ago to strike Khem along a wide front. Using guerrilla tactics, he had harassed the Pharaoh's outposts and forts all along the western flank of Khem, until Khasathut had been obliged to deploy not only his existing forces but also several bands of mercenaries.

Now small encampments of the Pharaoh's soldiers were springing up like mushrooms all along the east bank, and soon they would cross the river in force to find . . . nothing. By then, Melembrin would have drawn all of his forces back to the hills and plateaus, leaving a massive and frustrated army far behind him. And if the Khemites dared to follow him back into the hills, then they would need all their many gods to protect them. There were fortified passes in the hills which could hold off entire armies, and others where those same armies might vanish in a moment beneath man-made avalanches.

Oh, Melembrin knew well enough that one day a Pharaoh would conquer all of the lands around Khem, and that then the Khemish army would inundate Kush like a vast river in flood, but until that time he would harass Khem as best he might and cause her rulers endless troubles and miseries. For this was no holy war Melembrin fought, but a war of the blood. In Asorbes, the Pharaoh Khasathut had enslaved and bred generations of Melembrin's people, children of Kush, to help build the mighty pyramid where the old Pharaoh was buried and where Khasathut would one day join him in a hidden tomb. There was only a handful of Kushites now in Asorbes, but nevertheless the warrior-king of Kush had vowed that he would ever fight to free them, even though they had been born to slavery and no longer knew any other life. For word was constantly reaching the king that the flame of life burned still among Pharaoh's slaves, and he was unwilling to see such a bright flame extinguished. For the time being, he would pull his armies back to the hills, yes, but there would be other days and other battles.

It was just as well, thought Launie, that Melembrin's command-post camp was to move back from the river today. At least there were no crocodiles in the hills, and Ashtarta would have to do her swimming in one of the pebbly pools formed of the mountain streams. She knew that Ashtarta was intent upon swimming because she had not bothered to don her underwear, merely the short dress she wore which was two sizes too small for her. Well, all the better to bring a hand across her bottom once she caught up with her.

Just as this pleasant thought occurred to her, Launie caught another glimpse of the girl darting out of a clump of tall reeds up ahead. The princess stopped, glanced back, and Launie saw her mischievous grin. Then—

With a thrill of pure horror the handmaiden saw a brown figure step out of the reeds behind Ashtarta and clamp a hand over her mouth. The child struggled wildly for a moment, was dragged viciously backward into the reeds and out of sight. Launie opened her mouth to scream and a sinewy, hairy forearm came over her shoulder and clamped across her face. She kicked backward, feeling her sandaled feet connecting with shins, then felt something else . . . the razor edge of metal at her throat!

# V

# RED RAPE!

In that same instant, the handmaiden knew she was done for, but even then she would have screamed a warning if she could. She could not, for her throat was full of blood and all of her strength was fast flowing out of her. Her last thoughts as she was released to flop to the soft earth of the riverbank were of the princess, and of Melembrin's grief when he found his daughter dead. If he found her.

Gon watched Launie's eyes glaze over and stood astride her until her body had stopped quivering. Then, wiping his blade clean on her skirt, he stared long and hard at her bare breasts and cursed the fates that had forced him to kill her. The woman had been big and strong and would have made a lively ride. Still, she had been about to voice a scream, and being as close as they were to the Kushite camp, that was out of the question. He bent from the waist to slap her breasts with caloused hands and grinned as they wobbled back into immobility. Then, hearing Athom's low curses from the clump of reeds where he had dragged the girl, Gon's eyes narrowed and the corners of his large mouth turned down.

The girl had been a young 'un, little more than a child. She would be much more easily handled than a full-blown hill woman. And anyway, young or old, large or small, they'd have to kill her afterwards.

Afterwards. . . .

Gon grunted and stepped over Launie's body.

Crouching low and using the cover of the river's greenery, he made for the clump of reeds where they shivered and rustled from the unequal struggle within. Perhaps he wouldn't go short of a ride after all.

Athom was having a hard time of it. He could have cut the girl's throat as Gon had done with the handmaiden. Or he could simply break her neck with a twist of his wrists. But no, he had decided that he needed a woman, and it just wasn't the same with dead ones. He had worked as a lad for old Tuthtor the embalmer in Therae, where even with his lusts the freshly dead had soon become unappetizing. No, a man might just as well stick it in a dead pig as a human corpse, no matter how lovely and vibrant the woman had been in life. Also, according to his old master, diseases proliferated in the dead like scum on a stagnant pool; and certainly the embalmer had spoken from experience. Old Tuthtor, with his syphilitic scabs and eyes full of pus. Worms had lived in the old ghoul for years before he himself was dead.

Yet again the girl bit his hand where it was clamped over her mouth, and again Athom cursed under his breath as he tried to pinion her hands with his free arm. Then Gon had crept into the clump and trapped the girl's legs. The grinning, big-mouthed lout forced himself between her knees and grabbed her thighs, pushing them outwards. The hem of her dress rode up as her legs parted, showing the Theraens her nakedness.

Now Athom used his free hand to grab the girl's throat, squeezing until she could no longer draw breath. Exhausted and suffocating, she began to black out. Releasing his grip, Athom tore a strip from the neck of her dress and quickly gagged her, then used a second strip to bind her hands behind her back. Finally, he slapped her face once or twice until she recovered her senses. With wide, darting black eyes, she stared fearfully at her captors.

The newcomer was the younger of the two, but even he was all of thirty years of age. Staring at him, Ashtarta thought: *"He's so hairy!"* And indeed, Gon was hairy. His bearded face, his chest, back, arms and legs, all were a mass of black hair. With his red eyes peering at her from beneath bushy eyebrows, he might well have been a demon called up by some black magician. The other man, who leaned over her and breathed his bad breath directly into her face, was some five years older than the other, much less hairy and burned brown by the sun. When he grinned, his rotten teeth showed full of raw fish.

"By all the gods!" whispered Gon hoarsely, staring between the girl's spread legs at her small tuft of pubic hair. "You'd think she'd known we were here and came out specially to entertain us. Naked as a whore under this rag!"

"A child," grunted the other, tearing Ashtarta's dress down the front and parting it to bare her small breasts. "Look, I've seen boys with bigger tits!"

"Oh?" Gon licked his lips and stroked the inside of the girl's thighs with both hands, then gripped the flesh there and forced his hands apart until an opening showed. "And did those boys have a sweet little hole like that?"

"Depends where you looked!"

Athom chuckled. The grin quickly slid off his face and he went on: "Well, are we to stay here all day then? Get on with it, man, since you're already on her." He grabbed Ashtarta's shoulders and pinned them to the ground so that her breasts stood up a little rounder.

Positioning himself so that his knees held Ashtarta's legs down and open, Gon quickly tugged his loincloth to one side until his penis sprang into view. Staring at the thing the girl was galvanized into one last desperate fight for freedom, which only resulted in a heavy cuff on the side of her head from Athom. Trembling in every limb, Ashtarta found herself hypnotized by Gon's penis. It reminded her of the small hill ponies of home when they were about to mount the mares. Except that this time, she was the mare!

She wriggled frantically one last time and heaved her bottom up off the ground—at which Athom immediately stuck his leg under her, forming an arch of her back. Now Gon started to lower himself onto her, grinning in her face as she felt him throbbing against her quivering leg. Tears began to wash her face and she squeezed her eyes shut.

Seeing her tears, Athom said: "Now, now, madam, don't cry. Why, if you think Gon's a big lad, just wait till it's my turn! All he'll do with that little thing of his is open you up a bit for—" abruptly he stopped his throaty whispering, gave a little cry, withdrew twitching hands from her shoulders.

Something warm splashed Ashtarta's face and she looked up to see Athom struggling to his feet and tugging at an arrow that transfixed his eye. Gon saw this too, and he was off Ashtarta in a flash, his knife seeming to grow in his hand as he turned in a crouch, snarling his shock and fear.

A figure stood not six feet away, just outside and partly obscured by the fringing reeds. As Athom fell at last on his back, his hands still gripping the shaft of the arrow in his eye, so Gon sprang straight at the intruder—and took a second arrow full in the chest. He fell to his knees, jumped up, staggered to and fro for a moment in complete silence, then toppled and crashed down among the reeds.

Unable to believe her good fortune, Ashtarta simply lay still and stared as her rescuer slowly pushed aside the fringe of greenery and stooped to enter her cave of reeds. He stared at her for a long moment, mainly at her naked-ness, until she began to struggle and kick, flashing her eyes at him in anger. Why, he was only a youth, albeit a very strange youth; a youth with a bow and a quiver of arrows. His skin was so fair, his hair too, and his eyes . . . they were blue! And now that she knew she was safe, those blue eyes of his irritated her inordinately—especially where they were looking.

She made an angry noise through her gag and finally the boy's eyes went to her face. Again she flashed her eyes at him, urgently, and tried to turn them down to look at her own mouth. At last he understood, creeping up beside her to loosen her gag. As soon as her mouth was free she turned her face to one side and spat on the ground. Then she looked at the boy again and said: "Who are you?"

"My name is Khai," he answered.

# VI

# THE COMING OF KHAI

"Well, Khai, my hands are tied behind my back," said Ashtarta. "You will untie them."

Now he frowned—then started violently as Athom's body twitched in a final spasm. Quickly, he checked the two corpses to ensure that they were well and truly dead.

"My hands," Ashtarta repeated, watching his movements. "Untie them—now!"

Khai turned on her with a snarl. "Don't you ever say please?"

"What?" her mouth fell open.

"I saved your life. They would have killed you—later."

"Listen, Khai—" her voice barely contained her rage. "Untie me right now or I'll have the skin whipped from your back! Who do you think you are anyway?" She frowned. "I've never seen you in the camp before, and you speak with a strange accent. Who—"

"I'm Khai," he told her again, kneeling beside her. "Khai of Khem," and after a moment he added: "Whom the Nubians call Khai the Killer."

Staring at him, slowly her eyes grew wide. "Khem? But then why did you—?"

"Save you? You're just a girl and they were . . . animals! And killing's a trade I have to learn, so that I might one day go back and kill the Pharaoh Khasathut. With such as these," he glanced at the two bodies, his nostrils wrinkling in disgust, "—it was easy."

He stood up, parted the reeds, narrowed his eyes and peered downriver. "Now I have to be going. I shouldn't think your guerrilla friends will bother to look too hard for just one man."

"Man?" she snorted. "You're only a boy. And you still haven't untied my hands!"

"Well, little harlot," he looked back at her. "And why should I?"

"Harlot?" she cried. "*Harlot?* I'm Ashtarta, Melembrin's daughter!"

Khai sneered scornfully. "Of course," he said, "yes! Certainly you're The Fox's daughter. *Huh!*" He glanced yet again at the lower, naked half of her body. "And he lets you run bareassed up and down the riverbank!"

"Why, you—"

"Good-bye."

"No, wait! Khai, listen. Untie my hands and—and I'll give you anything." It was not that she could not make her way back to camp alone, simply that she would not be disobeyed by a mere boy. Not even a boy with cheeky blue eyes who killed men as a killer born, then talked of "learning" the skill.

He came back and crouched over her. "And if I untie you, you'll run back to your camp and tell them I'm here, eh?"

"No, no, I promise I'll not tell," she gasped. "I'll give you—"

"Anything?"

"Yes."

"Roll over."

She complied and he took out a knife, slicing her bonds in a moment. She sat up, rubbed at her wrists and then, seeing that his eyes were back where they least belonged, pulled down the hem of her dress. As he grinned nervously yet again, she reached up and slapped him as hard as she could across the face. He jumped back in surprise, tripped and sat down with a thump on broken reeds. She laughed gleefully and wagged a finger at him.

"Oh, and is this how you Kushites pay your debts?" His eyes were scornful. "And you a king's daughter and all. Shame on you!"

"I *am* the Princess Ashtarta!" she cried. "And indeed I pay my debts."

"You promised me anything."

"Yes," she spat, gritting her perfect white teeth.

"Then give me that," he growled, "which these dead men would have stolen from you. . . ."

Her mouth formed an O and her hand went to her suddenly flushed cheek. "How dare—"

"Huh!" Khai grunted. "Just as I thought." But deep inside he was pleased. Plainly the girl was not just a little whore, though certainly there were prostitutes of her tender years in Asorbes. Also, he was not so sure that it would have been any good if she had agreed. A mere girl, she would not have Mhyna's expertise. Expertise? Why, she would know nothing at all!

"Virgin," he said, "I free you of your obligation." Then, turning his back on her, he pushed aside the reeds and stepped out into bright sunlight.

A massive hand caught him by the shoulder as he emerged from the reed-clump, spun him about until he stared at the sun. Off-guard and blind, Khai instinctively reached for his knife. In that same instant, he heard Ashtarta's voice shouting from behind him: "No, Ephrais, don't kill him. He helped me!"

Hearing her pleas, Ephrais the sentry turned his notched bronze scimitar and checked its weight, so that only the flat of the blade near the hilt struck Khai's temple, stunning him instantly. The boy's knife spun from his hand and fell with a splash into the river; but Khai was no longer aware of that, was aware of nothing. Before he could fall, Ephrais threw him across a broad shoulder. Then the big Kushite took Ashtarta's hand, saying:

"Come on, little princess. You'll have to explain to your father what happened here. I've seen those two brigands in there—Theraens by their looks. Are there any more of them about?"

"I don't think so," Ashtarta panted, running to keep up with the striding giant. She saw an ugly lump on Khai's temple. "Is he hurt bad? Have you killed him?"

"No, but I would have killed him if you hadn't stopped me."

"Even though he killed those two creatures who attacked me?"

"Yes, well, I didn't know that, did I? And anyway, when our enemies fight among themselves, does it make them any less our enemies?" Ephrais paused in his striding, then led Ashtarta away from the river. The girl looked back to see why the sentry was avoiding a certain spot on the riverbank, gasping when she saw the leg of the handmaiden sticking out of a clump of grass. She recognized Launie's leg by a red bangle round the ankle.

"Launie, she—"

"She's dead," Ephrais told her gruffly. "She followed you up the riverbank and I followed her. If you had not chosen to go running off, and if I had thought to follow more swiftly, perhaps the handmaiden would not be dead."

Ashtarta shuddered. "And if this Khemish boy had not helped me, I would surely be with her." She began to cry. "Oh, Launie."

"Too late for that now, girl," growled Ephrais. "If you must cry, do it for yourself. You'll have good reason after we report to your father. He'll have to decide what's to be done with the boy. Meanwhile, you can tell me what you know about him—what he told you—if he told you anything at all." He looked at her closely. "You seem very taken with him."

"He helped me and . . . I made him a promise."

"Oh? And what was that?"

"I promised him that—that he'd come to no harm," she lied. But to herself she said: *One day, Khai of Khem—you strange, blue-eyed boy—I might just pay that debt of mine. But not until I'm Queen of all Kush and you're a general in my army. . . ."*

And looking at her out of the corner of his eye, Ephrais wondered why the princess was blushing so furiously.

# part
# SEVEN

# I

# DEATHSPELL

As Khai entered the Kushite encampment slumped over the shoulder of Ephrais the sentry, downriver in Asorbes Anulep prostrated himself before Pharaoh in his pyramid audience chamber and suffered a tirade of threats and accusations.

"Gone!" Pharaoh whooshed from behind a smaller, more portable miniature of his ceremonial gown and mask. "The boy Khai, gone?" He sat on a small throne and his impatience and irritation were apparent in the way his robes twitched and shivered. "Missing for several days, you say—and yet I have learned of it only this morning? What sort of intrigue is this, Anulep? I have asked to see the boy—and you cannot produce him!"

"Run away, Omnipotent One," Anulep gabbled, his bald head close to the floor and his eyes fearfully upturned to gaze at the small but menacing figure of Khem's God-king. "On the night following the Royal Procession. Run away and fled upriver."

"But why was I not informed sooner?" Pharaoh whooshed.

"I had hoped to find him, fetch him back," the Vizier answered. "I would have punished him, made him repent, and the matter need never have concerned Your Most Perfect Being."

"But it does concern me!" cried Khasathut, "How *could* he flee? And where is he now? Call the Dark Heptad at once. They will tell me where he is."

"I have been to the Dark Heptad, master," Anulep crept fractionally closer. "I have been in constant consultation with them since the boy disappeared. Even they cannot say how he fled—but they do know where he is now."

"Ah!" Khasathut leaned forward, his octopus eyes boring through the slits of his gilt mask. "And where is he?"

Anulep trembled from head to toe. "He . . . he has met up with a band of Kushite raiders to the south. They have taken him. The Dark Ones saw it in their scrying, and—"

"Kushites!" Khasathut hissed. "Again the damned *Kushites!*" His good hand crept out from under his robe to grip the arm of his throne until the flesh of his fingers turned completely white.

"The Dark Ones say," Anulep gulped, "that Melembrin himself commands this party. As you know, Omnipotent One, the Kushite Fox has been raiding in Khem for months."

"Months? It seems like years!" came Pharaoh's answer in a *whoosh* of rage. "And what have we done to put an end to it? Nothing!"

"Master, the hour of reckoning is surely at hand for Melembrin," Anulep quavered.

"What? How so? Say on, Vizier, while I yet deign to listen."

"Why, you yourself have lately ordered troops westward, Son of Re!" Anulep answered, straightening his back a little as he gained confidence. "Those same troops you sent out to protect the forts and reinforce the border with Kush. And they close on Melembrin even now."

"And you say that Khai is with this Kushite king?"

"So the Dark Heptad tell me, master. The raiders have taken him within this very hour."

Khasathut sank slowly back into his chair and grew silent. "Kush," he finally mused, his voice a poisonous hiss. "Always Kush! Must every other word I hear be Kush?" He sat up again and his voice was loud once more. "Let there be an end to it. I want the tribes of Kush destroyed and scattered to the winds. Let my army work for its keep. Khem has suffered parasite neighbors long enough. Let war be waged. I don't care if it takes ten years and fifty thousand trained soldiers to do it, but Kush must be whelmed. Let Pharaoh's might be seen!"

"It shall be as you command, master," Anulep touched the floor with his forehead.

"Get up, high priest, and be about your work," Khasathut said. "Speak to one of my commanders and tell him what I want. We'll deal with this Kush once and for all, and after that—who can say? I do not like this black upstart N'jakka. Aye, and there's gold in Nubia, much gold for my pyramid."

"Master, I go," Anulep began to back away. "I go to hasten your word. I—"

"Back here, Vizier," Khasathut hissed. "On your knees."

Anulep approached, went down before the Pharaoh who placed his good hand upon his polished, shivering head. "Vizier," said Pharaoh softly, "if I thought for one moment that you were in any way instrumental in the boy's vanishment—that perhaps you feared for your own high station and thought to thwart my plans—then it would go very badly for you." He stuck his nails slowly and deliberately into Anulep's scalp.

"Master, I—"

"Very badly indeed." And Pharaoh drew the tips of his nails rakingly forward over Anulep's head, leaving four thin lines of blood to well slowly to the surface. Then he kicked his high priest away from him and shouted: "Now get out! Begone from me—and let my will be done!"

To go down into the chamber of the Dark Heptad of mages was to enter a pit of snakes, and for all that the Vizier had been there many times before, still he shuddered—even Anulep—and paused briefly before entering that room of bubbling vats, flickering shadows and mumbled incantations. The figures of the seven stirred as he entered and their mumblings ceased. One of them, in the voice of an asp, said:

"Are you come again to speak with us, Vizier? So soon?"

"I am come again, aye," Anulep answered, dabbing at his head with a square of linen.

"We are not doctors, Anulep," a second mage whispered. "We may not dress your wounds."

"Look to your own health, wizard!" Anulep snapped.

"Oh? And is something amiss, Vizier?"

"I'll not waste your time," Anulep answered. "The Pharaoh suspects that I have deceived him, which you may be sure I have—with your help!"

Almost as a man, the seven figures began to chuckle and titter. Finally, one of them said: "We have not aided you in any deception, Anulep. That would be a hard thing to prove."

"Oh? And what of the boy, Khai? You could have found him while he was still in Asorbes, if you had bothered to look for him!"

"We knew nothing of the boy!" a third mage whined. "Not until you told us. What interest have we in mere boys, we who serve the immemorial Gods!"

"But I would *say* that you knew of him," Anulep smiled his hideous smile, "if ever I believed you worked against me."

"You have threatened us before, Vizier," hissed the mage with a snake's voice, "we who have always served you well. We will not tell Pharaoh of your deceit."

"No," Anulep answered, "you will not, for I would be dead within the hour—and you would not last much longer! Even if Pharaoh let you live, still you would not be safe. It takes a powerful magic to sway a dart loosed in flight, or drain a draft of rare poison from an innocent cup of wine."

"More threats, Anulep?"

"Listen," the Vizier snarled. "Listen, all of you. I threaten because I am afraid. You see my head? Pharaoh himself did this! His anger is such that he might well be driven to kill. You know well enough the pleasure he takes in killing, but he rarely kills them that serve him. One word carelessly uttered, however, and—" He drew a finger across his throat.

"We understand, Vizier," said the one whose voice was a whisper, "and you have nothing to fear from us. We wish you a long life."

"Yes, I'm sure you do," Anulep sneered. He began to turn away, then paused.

"One other thing. I know you sometimes have the power to influence things to come. Well then, there is something you can do. Less than one hour ago, you told me that the boy Khai had fallen into the hands of the Kushites."

"That is so," the shrill-voiced mage answered, his skeletal face half in flickering shadow. "I myself saw it, and no other sees so clearly or so far."

"Good," Anulep nodded. "Now listen: Khasathut's soldiers may well take The Fox this time. If that happens, the boy must die. Do you understand me? Cast whatever spells are necessary—do what must be done—but ensure that Khai Ibizin is not brought back here to Asorbes."

"And if the raiders are not caught?" one of the seven asked.

"Then I am not interested. Doubtless, the Kushites will kill the boy themselves. I don't care, except that he shall not grow to manhood in Khem. I will not be replaced by the soft son of some soft architect."

"We understand," the Dark Heptad nodded as a man.

"Good, then understand this also: I plotted that Khai should escape. I told him this and showed him that which were designed to *make* him flee—and flee he did. Except . . . I had hoped he might die escaping. He did not die, and so I ordered officers of Pharaoh's Corps of Intelligence into the city's streets to find him. They were to return him to me and I would then have sought to kill him by another means. They did not find him. . . ."

"We could have found him," hissed the one with a snake's voice.

"Aye," Anulep answered, "and so discovered my plot. I did not want you to know of it. If you had been brought in, perhaps Pharaoh would have learned of my part in the matter. He might even have ordered you to protect the boy, which would be contrary to my plans. Now?" and he shrugged, "now it does not matter. Let me simply remind you that if my part in this thing is discovered, then that your own lives are forfeit. I have given orders to that effect."

"We can only repeat, Vizier, that you have nothing to fear from us," assured the whisperer.

Anulep slowly nodded. He dabbed again at his scarred head and peered at the mages one by one where their eyes regarded him strangely. Finally, apparently satisfied, he turned and left them.

Long moments after he had disappeared into gloom and his footsteps had faded into silence, the mage with a snake's voice hissed: "The Fox will not be taken—neither The Fox nor the boy Khai."

"True," answered another, silent until this moment. "And the boy will live."

"If we allow it," said a third with a voice which bubbled like the many vats sunken into the floor of the place.

"I do not think we could prevent it," added a fourth. "There is destiny in that boy. I feel it in my bones."

"That may well be," hissed the first, "but we had best be sure. I shall prepare a spell. Then, if the boy is taken back from the Kushites, he will not be taken alive."

"And is this a measure of your fear of Anulep?" asked the whisperer.

"It is," came a hiss in the darkness. "I fear him more than Pharaoh himself. Khasathut does the things he does because he is insane. Anulep is sane, wherefore he is far more dangerous. . . ."

When Anulep got back to his own sparsely-furnished apartments, he went straight to a secret nook and took out a small wooden box. Removing its lid, he gazed upon a set of polished bronze teeth. They had been made by a master craftsman three years earlier, after Anulep had suffered a severe beating at the hands of Khasathut. The craftsman had died soon after—very suddenly and mysteriously—and now only Anulep knew about his teeth.

He smiled as he slipped them carefully into his mouth. They fitted him perfectly and it was good to feel their cold metal against his shriveled gums. He had to be careful not to trap his tongue, for these were not ordinary teeth. Their biting edges were honed to a razor's edge!

For a moment or two, Anulep tenderly fingered his scarred head, then removed the teeth from his mouth and put them back in their box. They were for another day: that day when finally Pharaoh would decide to replace his Vizier with someone new. Anulep knew what such "replacement" meant. Ah, but Khasathut would have good reason to kill him. Indeed he would. Using his bronze teeth, Anulep himself would provide that reason.

He looked down at the awful teeth once again and smiled his monstrous smile, then carefully closed the box. . . .

# II

# KHAI . . . OF KUSH!

Khai had not regained consciousness until the Kushite raiding party set up its camp again in shrub- and grassland twenty miles west of the Nile. He had been bundled onto a travois-like framework amidst assorted supplies, to be dragged along behind a sturdy hill-pony and its bareback rider, and the bruises he discovered when he awoke resulted from a bumpy ride over fairly rough terrain. All of The Fox's supplies traveled the same way—his wounded, too, when he had any—for nothing so sophisticated as a wheel was yet known in the days when the Sahara was green.

When the new camp was operational, then Khai had sat himself up, rubbed the lump on his head and felt his aching bones; and the girl who called herself Ashtarta had been there to lead him staggering to the tent of the warrior king. Busy as they were with their work in and about the new camp, Melembrin's guerrilla warriors had taken little note of the Khemite youth as he was guided through their hustle and bustle. They had heard something of his coming and would learn the full story in due course, but for now there was work to be done and a watch to be set. And Melembrin had already mentioned his desire to seek out and destroy at least one more of Pharaoh's border patrols before making for the keep at Hortaph.

So Khai had followed Ashtarta into the presence of the mighty Melembrin, and from her obvious familiarity with the king he inferred that she was indeed his daughter. Remembering what had transpired on the riverbank and the way he had spoken to the girl, he was uncomfortably aware of her presence where she seated herself on a cushion to one side of the tent while her father questioned him. Now his story had been told in full and he stood as still as he could under The Fox's bushy-browed gaze.

The youth didn't look like much, Melembrin thought. A bit thin and pale for your average Kushite. In fact, he looked like nothing Melembrin had ever seen before; not with his blue eyes, fair skin and blond hair. He wasn't an albino, for a certainty, and his wiriness in no way suggested fragility. At the moment, he was probably underfed, and the bags under his eyes had doubtless resulted through lack of sleep before and during his flight from Asorbes. Actually, he was quite a handsome lad and would soon make a handsome man. His shoulders would broaden out soon enough and his forearms already had a width to them that the Kushite king liked.

He was intelligent, too, and his blue eyes had been full of blood and high-mountain ice when he'd spoken of Pharaoh and the way his entire family had been butchered in the slave city. There had been no tears, only a grim resolve, and Melembrin had liked that, also. This was no milksop, for all his soft looks, and if proof were needed of that, it probably still lay rotting in a certain clump of reeds back at the river's edge. In disposing of that pair of scummy runaway mercenary dogs, the boy had shown a natural killer instinct which completely belied the soft existence he must have known as the son of a great architect in Asorbes. More than that, without question he had saved the life of the next Candace of Kush!

Finally, Melembrin spoke: "These men you killed in the forest across the river. They weren't Khemish?"

"They were Arabbans. Slavers working for Khem—and for themselves," Khai answered.

"You must call my father 'Lord,'" Ashtarta reminded him for the tenth time from her cushion.

"And the mercenaries on the riverbank," Melembrin continued. "They were Theraens, right?"

"Yes," Khai nodded, and winced at the throbbing in his temples which the movement of his head produced.

"Yes, 'Lord,'" said Ashtarta, softly.

Khai immediately rounded on her. "And shall I call you parrot?" he cried. "I owe no allegiance to your father. If anything, he owes me!"

Ashtarta's mouth fell open at Khai's audacity and her eyes went wide. "Ephrais's clout has addled the boy's brains!" she gasped.

Melembrin's face was now black as thunder. "By all that's merciful!" he roared at his daughter. "You take a lot of interest in this fellow, Sh'tarra. Can't I talk to him in my own tent without your interference?"

"But he's only a boy," she protested, "an ill-mannered, stupid—"

"—And he saved your life, *girl!*" the king roared. "In my eyes, that makes him a man—and by the same token, it makes you an ungrateful little witch! Damn it all, I don't know whether to thank him for your life or curse him for it! And you—" he turned his wrathful eyes upon Khai. "Be more respectful or I'll knock your head off!"

Khai hardly heard him. His ears were still ringing to the sound of the pet name by which the king had addressed his daughter. Sh'tarra!

Sh'tarra . . . where had he heard that name before?

"Listen to me, Khai Ibizin, or whatever your name is," Melembrin continued. "There's room for marksmen in my army. Since you're fleeing from Pharaoh and we're heading for home—and since Nubia's a long way off and lots of dangers in between—I suggest that you forget Nubia and come along with us. That way you will eventually owe me some allegiance, and sooner or later you may even learn to call me 'Lord!' Well, what do you say? Haven't you been listening to me, lad?"

Dazedly, Khai shook his head, not in answer but as if to clear it. He staggered a little. His ears kept echoing to that name—*Sh'tarra!*—*Sh'tarra!*—*Sh'tarra!*—and each echo made his hair tingle at its roots. There was something important here, something he should know, something he should remember. But what?

He swayed again and put his hand to his head. Ashtarta was up off her cushion in a second, her face full of concern. She sprang to Khai's side, taking his arm and lowering him to the floor.

He pulled free of her and struggled to his feet. "It's all right," he said. "I was dizzy, that's all."

Melembrin, too, had climbed to his feet. "All right, lad, take it easy now," he said in softer tone. "You've taken a few clouts, sure enough; you've run too far and eaten too little. I reckon I can wait for your answer until you're feeling more yourself. Meanwhile, Sh'tarra will show you where you can rest."

"You can have my answer now . . . Lord," Khai answered. "And if you're worried that I can't kill Khemites as easily as I can kill Arabbans and Theraens, then you've no need to be. I can destroy anything that belongs to Pharaoh, *anything!* And I can kill anyone who works for him."

Hearing the sudden savagery in Khai's voice, a grim smile came to play about the mouth of the Kushite king. "I believe you, Khai," he said, "and we shall talk again—later. Until then—" he turned to his daughter. "Sh'tarra, take him away. Feed him and see he's well rested. When someone hates the Pharaoh as much as this one. . . . Well, that's the sort of hate we need to nurture!"

Khai slept through the rest of that day and did not awaken until late in the evening. His "tent" was a travois propped against a tree, forming a sloping shelter over his head, and he had been given a blanket to sleep on. At that, he considered himself lucky and was well satisfied. He had left Khem a fugitive, with only the clothes he wore, a bow, arrows and a knife. Now, in addition to these things, he had a job in the army of Melembrin, a blanket, and he seemed to have made a friend in the king himself. And so for the first time in a long while, Khai had managed to sleep a completely restful sleep.

Now, with the night creeping in, he found himself hungry. Since the sky was rapidly darkening over and smoke from the fires was unlikely to be seen, meat was already turning on spits and filling the air with its aroma. Khai drank deep of the evening air and got up. He stretched his limbs and felt good, then groaned as he heard a voice from the shadow of his tree:

"Khai? Are you awake?" Ashtarta stepped out from the darkness and came up to him. "There's meat for you and a seat by the fire. You can listen to the men talking and learn the ways of the camp. Tomorrow you'll have to start working for a living, and there's much you'll need to learn. The younger men are bound to bully you for a little while, but you'll have to put up with that."

"I can put up with a great deal," he retorted, "but not the prattling of a mere girl—even if she is a princess!"

*"You ungrateful—"* She stepped up close to him, her blue-shaded eyes flashing fire to match the blaze of the cooking-fires close by. And indeed she looked more like a princess now—a warrior princess! She wore black knee-length trousers of leather and a high-necked shirt of finest green linen tucked loosely in at the waist. Her hair fell in ropes almost to her waist, and in her hand, she carried a small, loosely-coiled whip. It was a horsewhip, whose dark color matched that of her roughly-stitched calf-length boots. Her ears were hung with golden disks and a third disk glowed in her forehead.

Now she thrust her face at Khai and stared at him through the darkness. "You drive my friendship too far, Khemite!"

"And you drive me too far, Princess!" and he spat out the last word as if it were poison. There was something about the girl that got right under his skin, making it impossible for him to treat her cordially. "Why don't you just leave me alone?" he asked.

Her jaw fell open. "How dare you!"

"No!" he cried. "How dare *you*! I save your life, and now I've dedicated my own life to the destruction of your father's enemies. All I ask in return is food for my stomach and a measure of privacy. Why, if necessary I'll even catch my own food, for the meat doesn't walk or fly that I can't bring down. But I'll not be pestered continually by a quarrelsome girl!"

Ashtarta couldn't believe her ears. "Why, I'll—"

"You'll what? You say I'm to suffer some bullying? Good! Better that than be followed around by a spoilt child of a princess with the temper of a crocodile and manners to match!"

"Temper?" she screamed. "Temper? You think you've seen the measure of my temper?" Tears flew from her eyes as she shook her head in rage. "I'll *show* you temper, you son of a Khemite bitch!" And before he could guess what she was about, her hand flicked back and forward and the metal tipped thong of her whip cracked across his cheek, stinging him but failing to fetch blood.

Off balance, Khai stumbled backward, tripped and fell, and Ashtarta moved to follow him. Again her arm drew back, but before she could use her whip a second time, he put his left foot behind her ankle and lifted his right to plant it firmly in her midriff. She was still coming forward and he took her full weight on his leg—then straightened that leg and drove her into the air with all the strength he could muster. She flew high and fell hard, flat on her back with all the wind knocked out of her.

By now their scuffling had attracted the attention of the men at the fire. A young man who was Khai's senior by at least two years got up and came over to them. Khai stayed where he was on the ground but the princess got her breath back and struggled to her feet. As she sprang at Khai, the young warrior caught her round the waist and put her behind him.

"Mind your business, Manek Thotak!" she cried. "I'll fight my own fights."

"What?" he said. "I should let you soil your hands on Khemish filth? No, Princess, your father would not thank me for that. If your little lash can't curb this cur, then we'll see how he answers to a real whip!" As he spoke, the young warrior took a coiled whip from his belt and shook it down like some fantastic snake on the ground. But Khai had not been idle.

He reached into the shadows beneath his travois to find his bow. Now, sitting up, he nocked an arrow and drew the bowstring taut against his cheek. Sighting his weapon almost point-blank at Manek Thotak's breast, he grated, "Would you like to wager, dog, that you can crack that whip of yours faster than I can loose my arrow?"

"Oh? And what's all this?" came the deep, gruff voice of the massive Ephrais as he came upon the tableau. "Put up your whip, young Manek. And you—" he addressed Khai, "put down your bow." He stepped between the two and narrowed his eyes on Ashtarta where she stood, arms akimbo, beside her would-be champion. "Ah! And is that you, Princess? And have you been baiting the boys again?"

She stepped forward, angry words forming on her lips, but before they could be uttered there came the drumming of naked hooves and the distressed snort of horses. A moment later, and three riders entered the clearing. They got down from their lathered mounts and asked for Melembrin. All were disheveled and looked winded through hard riding. Their ponies seemed near-dead on their feet.

"What's the hurry?" cried one of the men at the fire; and another called: "Are you pursued by devils, you three?"

"Worse than that," one of the riders panted. "There are thousands of Khemites north and south of here—columns from the forts at Afallah and Kurag, I think—marching through the night. They are closing in a huge pincer. I fear they may already have taken our lads to the north, and those to the south will be lucky if they make it home. As for us: we'd best be on our way tonight, now. Tomorrow will be much too late!"

# III

# RUN FOR THE HILLS!

In a matter of minutes, Melembrin received and interpreted the grim news. It only remained for him then to gather his men about him and give them their orders. This he did at the main fire, ringing himself about with warriors and explaining the situation to them in short, vivid sentences:

"Men," he began, "it appears we've stung the Pharaoh once too often. Normally, he doesn't much bother with this side of the river, certainly not this far from Asorbes, but this time he seems determined to have us. As you know, our little party here forms my command post; though we're also a fast-moving, highly mobile task-force in our own right when needs be. But mainly, this is where the brains are to be found which control our little forays against Khasathut's forts and border patrols—particularly here!"—and here he put a finger to his own broad forehead.

"Now then, there are only one hundred and ten of us here," he gazed around the small sea of faces that glowed in the firelight, "and we couldn't put up much of a fight if Pharaoh hit us with a big posse."

"We'd fight to the last man!" someone in the crowd gruffly protested.

Melembrin held up a hand. "Of course we would," he agreed, nodded his head. "To the very last man—and then we'd be overrun. That's why there are three hundred more of us to the north and another three hundred to the south. And it's also why they're the best Kush has to offer! I'm the brain and they're the fighting body, forming a buffer between us and any troops Khasathut may send against us—at least until now."

"Brave men all!" someone grunted.

"That they are," Melembrin agreed, "but against overwhelming odds even the bravest must fall eventually. . . ." He paused and there was complete silence.

"If Pharaoh has sent large numbers of his soldiers after us," the warrior king finally continued, "then they may already have met and clashed with our lads. If they have—" Again he stared around the sea of faces. "I gave orders that if ever Pharaoh should take after us in earnest, then that it would be every man for himself and full speed for high ground. There's no shame in flight if it means we live to fight another day."

"You think our men have fallen then, Melembrin?" this from a huge and glowering chief. "Or that they're already fled?"

"I didn't say that," the king answered, "though I'll admit it's not unlikely. Whichever, it means our flanks are now unguarded."

"Six hundred men—fled?" someone else grunted. "I can see so large a number fighting, but never fleeing!"

"My orders were clear," Melembrin answered. "If they have not fled, then they are now either dead or captive."

"Then it's up to us to pay Pharaoh's dogs back for their blood!" cried another voice, more passionately.

"Aye," the king agreed, "but not here. If they've come after us in such great numbers, it can only be that they intend to invade Kush herself. Pharaoh's been threatening that for years. Yes, and it's something we've planned for."

"That we have!" several rumbling voices agreed.

"But Melembrin, great king," a younger voice, full of unconscious bravado, called from the front ranks of the crowding warriors. "Are we really going to turn tail like cowards and hyenas? I hate the thought of showing my heels to any dog of Khem!"

"Ah, Manek Thotak!" Melembrin growled. "The voice of experience, eh? And what would you do, warrior? Stay and fight—and die? And who then would carry word of Pharaoh's invasion home? No, you are brave, but you are wrong! Should we kill a handful of Khemites here and die ourselves when we might run for home and live—and kill thousands of our enemies beneath the towering walls at Hortaph?"

"But—"

"But?" Melembrin raised his eyebrows. "But? When you are a captain or a general—which you will be one day, as your father before you—then you may 'but' me, Manek Thotak. But even then warily. As a whelp? *Do as you are told, boy!*" And Melembrin put the matter aside and turned to his men.

"We've wasted enough time and there's work to do. Pile everything in a heap—tents, travois, everything—then mount up. Before we leave, fire the tents and all. Let them burn. Let there be a blaze to draw Pharaoh's troops like moths. Take only your weapons with you, nothing else. We ride two-abreast, nose to tail, and we carry no torches. The moon will be up soon; the stars are bright; we move carefully, quietly, quickly—but with no panic. Hurry now, for we leave in minutes!"

Silently, swiftly as Melembrin turned away, his men moved to obey him. They took up sleeping pallets and travois, tore down tents large and small—even the king's command tent—bundled up blankets and skins and piled the lot close to the central fire. Then, almost before Khai could drag his own crude shelter over to the pile, the ponies were brought forward and the warriors mounted up. Someone took a brand from the fire and tossed it on the heap of flammable materials, and bright flames at once began to light up the night.

In another moment, ponies were being guided out of the camp area and directed toward the west, their riders armed to the teeth and sharp-eyed in the shadows. Suddenly panic-stricken, Khai found himself alone beside the bonfire which now roared up and hurled a pillar of sparks at the stars. In the leaping shadows around the campsite he saw the shapes of animals and men passing into the night, and he stumbled after them with his mouth open but too dry to utter any sound.

Then there came a pounding of hooves and a whinny of fear as a pony drew near and shied at the roaring flames. A grinning girl's face, all eyes and teeth in the firelight, looked down at him from the beast's back. "Ashtarta!" he gasped.

"Princess, to you!" she frowned, holding out a hand to him. "Come on, jump. Get up behind me—and hang on!"

While her pony continued to shy, Khai grasped the girl's hand and jumped, throwing himself onto the animal's back and almost unseating her. "Careful!" she cried. "Steady, there! Some horseman you, Khemite!"

"There are no horses in Asorbes," he angrily answered, his arms around her waist and his chin bumping on her shoulder.

"Aye, that's obvious," she told him. "Grip the pony's back with your knees and keep them bent. Grip his flanks with your feet. And watch where you put your hands—Khemite!" And she cantered her mount away from the fire and joined the column as it wound westward.

A moment later and the bulky shadow of the massive Ephrais drew alongside, pairing up with Ashtarta. "I see you remembered the lad, Princess," he said in a lowered voice. "I went back for him, but saw you pick him up. Your good-luck piece, is he?"

"He is not!" she answered hotly. "But a debt is a debt—and now it's paid in full!"

"I seem to remember it differently," Khai grated in her ear, just loud enough for her to hear. "The way I remember it—"

"You'd be well advised to *forget* it!" she hissed. She dug her left elbow viciously into his ribs and deliberately caused her mount to the rear. Khai hung on for dear life and his hand inadvertently clasped her breast. Her shoulder came up under his chin, rattling his teeth and caused him to bite his tongue. Hearing him utter a colorful Khemish curse, Ashtarta's anger left her in a moment and she chuckled as she drew her pony back into line.

Ephrais had already guided his mount to one side of the narrow trail and brought it to a halt, but he had seen something of the brief exchange between Khai and the princess. Now he watched the column pass him silently by until he was alone, then he too chuckled. Back along the trail at the deserted campsite, the bonfire's flames reared high, an open invitation to any of Pharaoh's soldiers who might be watching from afar. Ephrais stared for a moment longer at that fiery pillar and rubbed his chin.

"That's not the only fire I've seen set today," he told his mount. "It's going to be interesting when we get back home—if we're that lucky—to see how this lot works out. Our little Sh'tarra fancies the Khemite, of that you may be sure—and he fancies her, if I'm any judge. And as for Manek Thotak—"

Ephrais grinned again, turned his mount after the column and urged it into a trot. "Manek, my lad," he said, "it looks like you have a serious rival!"

Fifteen minutes later, the column began to climb through long grass and shrubs toward the humped horizon of a low ridge. Following the flashes of white paint on the hindquarters of the double-ranked animals ahead, Ashtarta craned her neck to see where the forward part of the column was already cresting the ridge.

"See," she told Khai. "If there are watchers, it will seem that the silhouette is of just two horses and their riders standing on the ridge. No one would suspect that we are over a hundred strong. And note how the ponies bear spots of white paint, so that we may all follow on like a snake in the dark."

"I see," said Khai, but his mind was not altogether on her words. So close to her, with her scent in his nostrils and her backside pressed against him—and the not unpleasant motion of the pony between his legs—he had discovered that his angry feelings toward the princess were melting away.

Suddenly he no longer minded the ache in his ribs where she had jabbed him, or the numbness of his tongue where he had bitten it. Instead, in his mind's eye, he was distracted by vivid pictures of Ashtarta as he had first seen her. Her little breasts, flat belly and firm legs. And the way she had fought the

Theraens. . . . With Ashtarta it would not be the same as with Mhyna. It would be more like fighting a Nile croc! Ah, but wouldn't *that* be a fight to win?

But now, aware of how he was beginning to react to Ashtarta's nearness and his own imagination, he relaxed his hold on the girl a little and gently drew back from her an inch or two.

"Hold tight to me," Ashtarta immediately hissed, "and sit close! If we have to make a sudden run for it, I'll lose you."

Obediently, but gritting his teeth and hoping she wouldn't notice, he inched closer. Impatiently, she tut-tutted and pushed her rump back against him. He groaned inwardly as he felt her body immediately stiffen. Beneath his hands the muscles of her stomach tightened, and he gritted his teeth as he waited for her outburst.

That outburst never came, for they had reached the crest of the ridge and the sight that opened to them as they stared across the nighted land ahead was one which shook both of them with an almost physical force.

Whatever it was that Ashtarta might have said or done, now she simply gasped: *"Look!"*

But Khai was already looking.

# IV

## MELEMBRIN RUNS
## THE GAUNTLET

Away to the west, at a distance of some two or
three miles as Khai judged it, a second line of low
hills formed an undulating horizon lit by the resid-
ual glow of a sunken sun. Directly in the path of
Melembrin's column, the hills were breached by a
deep gash which formed a pass to the west, and this
was obviously the war-chief's escape route. To
north and south, however, the hills leveled out until
they merged with the shadows and darkness of the
lower ground—except that it was not dark now but
burning with the light from thousands of torches!

Vast bodies of men were on the march, closing
in a massive pincer movement, and already the
points of that pincer had passed behind the dark
masses of the hills and were doubtless converging
upon a meeting place on the western flank—which
could only be the far end of the pass. Khai saw all
of this in an instant, and as Ashtarta dug her heels
in and urged her mount to greater speed, so his eyes
went again to the masses of moving lights where
they wound like rivers to north and south.

Why, he could almost hear—no, he *could* hear,
even at this distance—a faint blare of brazen trumpets and an even fainter chanting from thousands of
throats! The marching-chant of Pharaoh's army,
the war-chant of a disciplined military machine.
Quicker by far than Khai, Melembrin and his warriors had recognized their peril, and as the column
sharpened its pace so the chief fell back and hastened his men on, until eventually he spied Ashtarta

and brought his massive mount to a gallop alongside hers. Seated bareback astride his great horse—with his naked arms rippling with muscle, his leather-clad back straight and strong, and wearing his horned war-helmet like a metal skull—the Kushite now looked more like some great savage than a wise and respected king, and the flame-eyed beast between his legs must surely be a demon from the depths of blackest nightmare. Khai's flesh crept and he shrank from the vision; but Ashtarta, reaching out even on the gallop to grip Melembrin's jacket, merely cried:

"Father, did you *see* them? How many, do you think?"

"Too many, lass," he barked. "A mighty pride of lions if ever I saw one—and now we must outrun them. If they reach the far end of the pass before we're through it—" and he left the sentence unfinished.

"Father, I—" she began, but he quickly cut her off.

"Listen, Sh'tarra. Whatever else happens, you must get back to Kush. No heroics, girl—though I know you'd fight like a man if you had to—but you *must* make it home for two good reasons. One: someone has to warn Kush, and you've got the fleetest little animal under you that I ever saw. And two: you'll be Candace one day, and Kush will need you. Are you listening, Sh'-tarra?"

For answer, she nodded, leaning forward as her mount barely cleared a small shrub in its way. "I'll make it home, father—we all will."

"We'll see about that," he shouted. "We'll see. But you're certainly not going to get very far with the Khemite lad hanging on your neck. Give him here—" and he reached out a massive hand and took hold of Khai's arm near the shoulder. Khai let go of the girl and lifted up his legs, sliding clear of Ashtarta's mount and cocking a leg over the broad back of the king's animal. Then he wrapped his arms round Melembrin's waist and hung on for dear life.

"Cling like a leech, lad," the king grunted, "and old Thunder won't even notice he has an extra passenger. And don't worry if your teeth get rattled a bit. Believe me it's better than walking! Come on, Thunder—let's go, boy!" And away they went like the wind, flying up a rise to where the steep sides of the pass loomed like some great dark throat ahead.

Within those walls, which soon towered high on both sides, the pace of the column decreased and the riders began to bunch up. Up front, torches were hastily lit and the pace picked up again. Above, beyond jagged rims of rock that obscured the moon, the sky was a wide river of stars. Khai clung grimly to Melembrin's back and felt, to his amazement, a wild and savage joy rising inside him as the pounding of hooves became a rhythmic beat like the drums of war. In another moment Khai became one with the mighty rider whose back he hugged, one with the powerful beast beneath him, one with the night and the drumming of hooves.

Strange visions filled his head, of other places and times, of a lance under his arm, a high shield held against his breast and an armored opponent thundering toward him on a field of battle. He felt the curve of a leather saddle beneath him and the weight of the great lance as he tilted it to point at his opponent's shield. Then—

"There's the end of the pass up ahead, lad!" came Melembrin's cry, jolting him dizzily back to earth. "I see none of your countrymen there—but hang on anyway!" And lifting up his voice, the king bellowed: "Arrowhead, men, and the princess in the center. If it gets hot form two ranks, with sufficient room for her to make a run down the middle. Here we go—!"

With the echoes of that mighty cry still reverberating from flanking walls of rock, the column burst out of the pass to flow down onto an undulating plain of scrub and grass. Without pause, they took up an arrowhead formation, with the king in the lead and Ashtarta locked centrally behind three thundering walls of men and beasts.

Now, as those strange visions faded from Khai's mind—leaving him to wonder what mad recesses of his brain had spawned the idea of a seat for a horse's back and long spears on which riders might impale their enemies—he glanced off to the arrowhead's pounding, night-dark left flank and beyond it to the massed might of the Pharaoh's soldiery. It seemed that the land to north and south was awash with streams of fire—blazing with the light from thousands of torches—while up ahead, mere hundreds of yards away, the nets of flame were quickly closing.

The rapid emergence of Melembrin and his raiders from the gorge had momentarily surprised the Khemites, but they very quickly recovered. Now, along with the blare of brazen instruments, Khai could also hear the squealing and trumpeting of elephants. For the first time, the Pharaoh was using elephants as weapons of war.

The flaring torches that lit the darkness ahead were thinning out, stringing themselves into individual units that moved rapidly to close the gap and cut off the fleeing Kushites. Huge, lumbering shapes there were, too, and the sounds of shouted commands could be heard above the quickening beat of drums.

"Throw down your torches and run blind!" Melembrin roared. "And get your shields up—*now!*"

His warning came none too soon. No sooner were shields lifted than there came the concerted whistling of flight-arrows and their rattle and thud as they fell upon leather-covered bucklers. The gap ahead had closed now, but as yet only foot soldiers and archers blocked the way.

"Ride 'em down!" Melembrin roared as he sent his horse, Thunder, crashing into a pair of Khemites who loomed up like shadows and sprang at him from the darkness. In another moment Thunder shied sideways and Khai and

Melembrin were hurled from his back. Khai leaped to his feet amidst clouds of dust and flying shapes in time to see the war-chief's great knobbed club rise and fall once, twice, to an accompaniment of gurgling death-screams; then Thunder was pawing the ground and Melembrin leaping to his back, reaching down a hand to pull Khai up behind him.

The column had passed on and the dark ground all around was strewn with trampled Khemish corpses; but the war cries of warriors closing from the flanks were loud and the whistle of their arrows shrill and deadly. Digging in his heels, Melembrin sent Thunder galloping after his men, a dozen of whom waited to give him cover. Behind them as they fled, a squad of archers nocked long flight-arrows and aimed them into the night. A single sharp word of command was sufficient to fill the air with speeding shafts.

Pounding westward and slowly gaining on the rest of his men, suddenly Melembrin and his escort found themselves riding through a hail of arrows. Khai felt a heavy blow to his back and a sharp burning agony, and simultaneously saw a shaft appear over his right shoulder where it seemed to grow from the king's back. A number of horses and men went crashing down uttering their last cries, but Thunder merely reared up and snorted his alarm before continuing his run for the west.

Knowing he was hurt and feeling blood sticking his shirt to his back, Khai clung tenaciously to the wounded king and gritted his teeth. The other riders, wondering at Melembrin's slackened pace and closing with him, saw the shaft in his back and steadied him where he sat his great horse. Then they were over a low rise and the clatter and clash of Pharaoh's army was fading behind them. They had run the gantlet and there was no longer any way that the Khemites could catch them.

For ten more long miles Melembrin hung on, until he felt Khai's hands loosening where they gripped him and realized that the boy had had enough. Then, gentling his great horse to a halt, he allowed his men to lift the boy from him and slid himself down onto firm ground. As soon as he stood alone, however, he staggered and would have fallen. His men lit torches and lowered him to the ground.

"Get the arrow out of me," he snarled. "Quickly, for we can't stay here, and—" He paused as he saw Khai slumped on the ground close by, a second arrow sticking straight up from his back. Then the king's mouth fell open. "So that's why the lad was weakening! But for him, I'd have two shafts in my back. . . . Mattas!" he shouted. "Where are you? Where is the damn butcher? I must be mad to trust a doctor who'd rather be out breaking bones than stay at home and mend them! Khai—are you all right, boy?"

Slumped forward, with his wet face hanging down and his palms pushing against the earth, Khai managed to nod his head. By now, the rest of Melembrin's column had fallen back and dismounted, gathering in a circle about their wounded king. Pushing through their ranks came Ashtarta and the warrior-physician Mattas. Ashtarta flew to her father and kneeled beside him. He pushed her gently away.

"No, no, Sh'tarra. Better you cut the lad's shirt away while Mattas deals with me." He glared round about him at the encircling men. "Come on all of you—move! I want a litter made. And make sure Thunder is not used for its dragging. The litter's for me . . . aye, and for the youth there. Mattas, when you've done with me and the Khemite lad, then look to my horse. He, too, has an arrow in his shoulder. I tried to draw the thing but only succeeded in . . . *aahhh!*" And with that soft sigh of anguish, the King's voice fell silent as Mattas slit his leather jacket open and without ceremony drew the dart from his shoulder.

Khai saw all of this through a haze of wavering red shot with the yellow flames of sputtering torches; but then, as Mattas turned to him with a grim smile, he too fainted . . . .

# V

# THE KEEP AT HORTAPH

When Khai regained consciousness, it was to the sound of muffled sobbing. Opening one eye, he looked down the length of his raised pallet to where Ashtarta clung tightly to one of his projecting feet and sobbed into the fur which covered the rest of him. His body felt so stiff and bruised that for a moment or two he dared not move. The ache in his back was a slow-burning fire that threatened to blaze up if he so much as twitched, but he knew that eventually he must take that chance.

Still using one eye only, he experimentally turned his head to left and right and took in his surroundings. He lay on his pallet in a tiny, low-ceilinged cave which admitted light through a jagged hole in its roof. More light flooded from around a bend in the wall. Apart from a stone pitcher of water and a small pile of clothes, the cave was otherwise quite empty. Done with his inspection, Khai again turned his eye upon Ashtarta.

"Why don't you wake up? You ... you *Khemite!*" the girl snuffled into the fur. "If only to let me thank you for my father's life. For his and for my own. And how might I ever pay my debt to you if you insist upon dying?"

"Oh?" said Khai. "Then you admit there's a debt, do you?" His mouth was clammy and vile, so that he grimaced as he spoke.

Ashtarta started violently and let go his foot. Slowly she looked up, her mouth open, eyes wide and streaked with tears. An astonished smile quickly spread over her face, then gave way to a blush as she saw how keenly Khai's eye regarded her. She did not quite manage to disguise either her delight or her blushes as she answered:

"A debt, yes—but not the one you mean. I meant a debt of of . . . of blood! My father's blood and mine. You saved our lives, Khai, and that is the debt I meant."

"In that case," he answered, opening his other eye, "you can forget it. Both of you. All I expect is a place to live and some food to eat, I've told you that already. And as for saving your father's life: it wasn't of my own free will. Do you suppose I would have sat still on that horse if I had known an arrow was speeding for my back?"

"Nevertheless," she told him, "your back took the arrow which would have killed him."

Khai frowned. "It didn't kill me," he said.

"It very nearly did," Ashtarta answered. "It smashed the arrows in your quiver and they deflected it. It went in close to your spine, but not very deep. Since then you've been in a fever. Sometimes violent and babbling crazy things, other times so quiet we thought you must be dead."

"Oh," he said. "Well, anyway, I feel a lot better now. My back doesn't hurt too much and I'm hungry. Is that a good sign?"

"I'm sure it is! You'd like some meat, eh? Better than the slop I've been feeding you, when you'd take it. You got more down your front than you got in your mouth!" And she burst out laughing. Khai laughed, too, until his back began to hurt again.

"Where are we?" he eventually asked. "And why is it so quiet? You Kushites are supposed to be a noisy lot, and yet here—"

"Here it is quiet because we wish it to be so," she said. "We mourn those men of Kush who will never return, those brave men who guarded my father's northern flank and are lost."

"What of the others," Khai asked, "who guarded his southern flank?"

Her face brightened. "They are safe. Every one spared. We met up with them beneath the walls, and now it is the lull before the storm."

"Beneath which walls?" he asked. "And what storm do you speak of?"

"Now we are on the heights over Hortaph," she answered. "The Khemites followed us. We left a trail a blind man could follow. They are massed below, on the approaches to the keep. They'll attack soon—today, maybe."

"What?" cried Khai, struggling to sit up. "Hortaph? Isn't that in Kush? How long have I been here? I have to see what's happening. I—"

"No, Khai," she said, placing a restraining hand on his chest. "You can't get up. I've not spoon-fed you for a over a week to see you undo my work in minutes!"

He gritted his teeth, firmly moved her hand aside and finally sat up. The pain in his back did not noticeably increase, despite the fact that his head swam a little, and so he swung his feet out from under the pelt and onto the cool, dusty stone floor.

"You'll be weak as a kitten," Ashtarta protested, then shrugged and gave in. "Oh, come on then, but at least let me help you." She pulled his right arm over her shoulder and let him lean his weight on her as he stood up and stumbled on stiff legs. He was naked apart from a linen loincloth and a swathe of bandages tightly bound about his upper body. He leaned against the wall of the cave and shuffled his feet into a pair of sandals, then allowed Ashtarta to ease a shirt onto his back as he belted a kilt about his waist.

"If I had a stick to lean on, I could manage," he said.

She nodded. "You shall have a crutch . . . when Mattas says you're well enough to be up and about. As for now, you can make do with my shoulder to lean on." She tossed her ropes of hair. "Or is that too distasteful to you?"

He frowned at her for a moment, then shook his head and slowly smiled. "No, Princess, I don't mind—as long as you don't ask me to ride behind you on a horse again."

"Huh!" it was her turn to frown. "Well, at least I know *that* wasn't distasteful to you, you dirty-minded—"

"No, Princess," he held up the flats of his palms, "let's not fight. I suppose I should be grateful to you—honored, in fact—to have the next Candace of Kush fetching and carrying for me, as if I too were of royal blood."

"I only fed you!" she snapped. "Others saw to your other needs. And I wouldn't have fed you if The Fox hadn't ordered it."

"The Fox," he answered, remembering Melembrin's wound. "How is your father?"

"He has not youth on his side," she answered, her eyes clouding over. "Also, the dog who shot him dipped his dart in excrement. The Fox is not well—but he's on his feet. It was him I was shedding tears for when you awoke. . . ."

"Ah!" he nodded. "I had wondered about that. And where is he now?"

"You shall see him for yourself if you wish. But mind your tongue, Khai, for he holds you in high esteem. You can do well in his army. Indeed, he has asked after your health and will be glad to see you."

She half-carried him from the cave out onto a boulder-strewn wasteland of stone and sun-baked earth. A sudden and unusually chill wind blew dust in their faces and made sand devils at their feet. When the wind died down Khai blinked dust out of his eyes and gazed at horizons of sky. On every side there was only the wasteland, reaching away for hundreds of yards to enclosing walls of boulders where they had been piled high.

He looked at Ashtarta. She had said that they were "on the heights over Hortaph." It seemed more like the Roof of the World to Khai.

"This is the rim of the Gilf Kebir," she said, "a natural fortress mightier by far than the walls of Asorbes. Ten miles north the heights stretch, and ten south. Full of false passes and gorges. Hortaph is just such a canyon, carved by a stream when the world was young."

She led him to one side where the boulders were piled highest. If he had wondered where the Kushites were, he wondered no longer: they were crouched behind the heaped walls, looking down through gaps in the boulders. All of them were dressed alike, in brown jackets and kilts, so that they merged with the stones and rock formations of the plateau.

"Look down there," Ashtarta ordered as a Kushite warrior gave Khai access to an observation point. Khai looked—and grew dizzy at the sight that opened before and below him. He drew back, his head reeling. He had looked down almost vertically into a huge gorge where a rivulet wound its way out from the Gilf Kebir into the foothills to the east. On both sides of the stream, the valley was narrow and flat, grown with grasses and trees, splashed with the colors of flowers and dotted here and there with fallen boulders. From any other viewpoint, it might have looked most inviting.

"You do well to draw back, Khai," Ashtarta told him. "In many places, these cliffs overhang. But come, quick as you can. Everything is so quiet." She sniffed the air. "It smells funny to me. Perhaps the Khemites are readying themselves to attack."

"Here, wait," Khai answered, stumbling where he leaned on her shoulder. "That dry stick there, the one with the fork. Give it to me. Good! It's hardly a crutch, but . . . there, that's better. Now lead on. And by the way, I saw no Khemites."

"No, for you looked into the keep. The Khemites are outside in the foothills, keeping their heads down. What did you see when you looked down, Khai?"

Following her toward the east-facing wall of boulders, he answered: "Mainly, I saw how high it was!"

"What else?" she snorted.

"I saw stout gates standing open, and a pair of sentries sunning themselves on large boulders. I saw a shepherd tending sheep, and the smoke from cooking fires. Typical signs of a healthy settlement. I'd suspect that the ravine opens out deeper inside, and that there's a fair-sized village hidden in there."

"Good," she said. "That's what you're supposed to suspect, as will the Khemites. Except that Hortaph is not the name of a village but of the stream itself. There is no village. The canyon narrows to a defile which finally peters out where the cliffs rise sheer and unassailable. There are ladders, however, which can be drawn up to the top at a moment's notice. Come, this way."

As she led him along the base of the piled wall of boulders, past evenly spaced out watchers who all kept their heads down and out of sight, Khai noticed many logs where they were positioned over boulder fulcra. In his mind's eye, he pictured the devastation below when these avalanche traps were sprung, and he wondered how Melembrin would contrive to bring Pharaoh's troops close enough to spring them. This was soon to be explained.

One hundred yards south of the Hortaph canyon, they came upon Melembrin where he crouched with a handful of his men and peered out through gaps in the boulders. Khai immediately recognized the warrior king's tightly-curled beard and bushy eyebrows, and The Fox was not slow to know him.

"Young Khai!" grunted Melembrin in greeting. "Get down here—and keep your head low! I see you're all strapped up under that shirt? Aye, well that makes two of us. Damn Khemite archers! How do you feel?"

"Hungry, Lord, and a bit stiff in the joints."

"You're lucky, lad. They wouldn't let me rest at all! Still, it's as well I'm up and about. There was poison on that arrow and this way I may work it out of my system. Now then—look down there."

For a moment longer, Khai stared at Melembrin's face, at the puffy flesh about his eyes and the sickly yellow of their whites, before following the king's gaze out through the heaped boulders and dizzily down to where the foothills of the Gilf Kebir rolled eastward. The lower hills and the valleys between were quite thickly wooded and green with lush grass. The country seemed almost designed to give good cover—at ground level. But from up here?

Khai could plainly see his former countrymen, soldiers of Khem, where they camped in the woods beyond a low rise less than half a mile from the keep's gates. There were no fires and movement was controlled, no telltale gleam of sunlight struck fire from metal and no permanent works had been built that Khai could see—but simply by gauging the size of the encampment he could tell that there must be a least a thousand Khemites camped below. Even as he watched, he could pick out the covert movements of others through the trees they used for cover as they came out of the valleys to the east. Scanning left and right, he could see still more, at present distant from the massive walls of the Gilf Kebir, but creeping ever closer along a five or six mile front.

"A thousand, two thousand of them!" Khai finally gasped.

"More like three," Melembrin grunted, "but spread out along a wide front. Don't worry, lad, the entire wall is defended. We call the plateau's face a 'wall,' you see—a wall against Khem. This is the first time the Khemites have ventured so far in anger, and they're ignorant of this country of ours. But I tell you now that though our borders lie many miles to the east, there's not a single Kushite settlement between here and the Nile. No, for we pulled our peoples back into the Gilf Kebir and onto the western steppes years ago—against just such an eventuality as this."

"Then the plateau's front is uninhabited?" said Khai.

"Oh, there are some villages and small settlements—even a few big ones—but they all have their escape routes onto the heights, and they're all equally well-defended."

"Just as well," came the low voice of one of Melembrin's warriors, and Khai saw that it was Mattas the physician. "This is only the beginning. And if you're right, Melembrin, it's about to begin right now. For look—look there. Here comes our decoy!"

# VI

## RAIN OF DEATH

Down below, riding hard from the north along the crest of the low rise that separated the foot of the plateau from the wooded hollows and valleys lying to the east, came a dozen horsemen. Typical of a small raiding party, weighted down with weapons and bundles of loot, they looked for all the world as if just now returned from some successful foray into Khem. They rode arrogantly, shouting and laughing, totally ignorant—or so it seemed—of their peril. Less than fifty yards away from where they rode the crest, Khemish soldiers lay in their hundreds, waiting and watching, screened by trees and long grasses.

Khai could sense the bunched-muscle tension in those watchers and wondered at the audacity of the Kushite riders. He began to fidget as he felt excitement building in him, threatening to spill over. "Don't they know the soldiers are there?" he nervously, breathlessly whispered.

"Oh, they know, all right," Melembrin answered, equally breathless. "As Mattas said, they're a decoy. Until now, to the Khemites, the gorge of Hortaph has been simply a Kushite settlement—concealing a small village, perhaps, or a half-nomadic tribe. But now—now it can be seen that Hortaph is a base for guerrillas. Look—"

And now the horsemen wheeled to their right, rode down from the crest along a well-worn track toward the gates. They were greeted by the sentries sitting on their tall boulders just within the gates, and a pair of them brought their mounts to a halt and began to banter and laugh with these guardians of the keep. The others rode on into the valley, their cries echoing back from the looming walls as they headed deeper into the green gorge.

"See," said Melembrin. "That was what the Khemites were waiting for, proof positive that there's more to Hortaph than meets the eye. They weren't willing to use a boulder to crush a grape, do you see? But now—"

"Here they come!" cried Mattas.

The Khemites rose up in the grasses and trees, rank upon rank of them, and threw themselves up the slope of that final rise. They shouted and banged spears on shields as they came, and those on the flanks funneled themselves inward, crushing toward the gates of the keep. The sentries atop the boulders jumped nimbly down, slammed the gates shut, then leapt up onto the back of their friends' horses, which were immediately turned into the gorge to follow the path the others had taken. The lone shepherd likewise mounted a horse's back, and also disappeared along the winding trail of the stream. All of the riders had quickly outdistanced the pursuing Khemites, miraculously avoiding a cloud of arrows which had buzzed around them before they passed from sight into Hortaph's winding interior.

A moment later and the Khemites were storming the gates, knocking them flat in the sheer weight and crush of their charge. In less than two minutes, a thousand of them were in the keep, streaming deeper into the valley, and half as many again were forming into back-up parties beneath the beetling walls. That was when Melembrin sprang to his feet with a bellow like a bull elephant:

"All right, lads, *now!*—Let them have it!"

The Kushite warriors crouching behind their boulder walls now threw themselves on the bristling levers of protruding logs. Down below, the first two hundred yards of gorge were crammed with Khemites. They still rushed forward, deeper into Hortaph's cleft, seeking opposition and finding . . . death!

It was the earth-shaking rumble of avalanching boulders that first drew the attention of Pharaoh's soldiers to the heights, and in that same instant, their invasion of the keep became a mad rout of fleeing hundreds. They saw, turned and fled—but too late! There was nowhere to run. The entrance to the keep was jammed with their crowding colleagues; beyond the flattened gates, hundreds more pushed blindly forward, unaware as yet of the terror up ahead; and even those outside the gates were not safe. Not by any means.

Down came the boulders, thousands of tons of them raining from the heights, bringing huge sections of the very cliffs tumbling with them, falling on the Khemites where they milled in mindless confusion and horror. From both sides of the keep the boulders rained down, until the very ground heaved and bucked with the force of their impact. And still it was not at an end. Before the soldiers who crowded outside the keep could draw back, they too were caught in a rain of death, this time from the forward rim of the heights.

The fall of boulders was seemingly unending, and such was the cloud of dust that rose over everything that before very long no detail could be seen of what passed below. Nor did the frantically toiling Kushites on the heights pause until the last pebble had been dislodged and sent plummeting down into that roiling sea of dust.

Finally, Melembrin said: "It's done," and he caught Khai's shoulder in an iron grip. "Now we'll wait and see how successful our little trap has been, eh?" He looked down at Khai and frowned. "Did I feel a tremor in you there, boy? Is the killing a bit much for you after all?"

Khai shook his head. "My legs feel a bit rubbery, Lord, that's all. I've been on my back for over a week. As for killing: Pharaoh killed my mother, father, sister and brother. His entire army cannot compensate for that. Nothing can, except his own death and that of Anulep the Vizier. Yes, and the Black Guard, too. When they are dead, Lord, then I'll say an end to killing. . . ."

"Well said, lad," the king rumbled. "But look down there. That should compensate a little for your loss."

The dust was settling. The mouth of the gorge was choked to a depth of almost fifty feet with boulders and debris ripped from the faces of the cliffs. Away up the gorge, for more than two hundred yards, beyond which the stream turned a bend and passed into unseen canyons, the boulders lay deep and silent. Nothing living stirred down there, where already the stream formed a pool because its path was blocked. Along the front of the plateau, Pharaoh's forces dazedly drew back and shaped themselves into small formations, with their officers counting losses. Little more than half of the original force survived. Some thirteen or fourteen hundred men had been crushed and buried, never to be seen again.

And now, winding its way out along its old bed and gaining in strength even as Khai watched, having found a channel beneath all of those toppled tons of rock, the stream once more appeared. But Khai's face paled a little as he noted the color of the stream, which was red. It would stay that way for a day and a half. . . .

"Look there!" cried Ashtarta, drawing Khai's attention elsewhere. "There on that great boulder outside the gates. Father, do you see who it is?"

"Aye," Melembrin sourly grunted, "and I'd sooner we'd killed him than any hundred of the dead!"

"Who is it?" Khai asked, staring down from the now naked rim at the figure of a man who railed and roared and shook his fists at the massive, impenetrable wall which was the Gilf Kebir. Whoever he was he wore a scarlet turban and shirt, and black breeches of the type favored by Arabbans. His sword was Arabban, too, curving and vicious. He seemed to be in a veritable frenzy, screaming and threatening, and his voice reached almost to the heights.

"It's Red Zodba," Mattas answered for the king. "An Arabban slaver in Pharaoh's pay. He's the one who organizes the raids on Nubia, but recently he's spent a lot of time with Khasathut's border patrols. We know he's always had a greedy eye on the Gilf Kebir. He'd love to take slaves out of Kush— that's why he's here! And those threats he's making—they're not idle ones. If ever we do go under the yoke of Khem, be sure Red Zodba will be cracking Pharaoh's whip!"

"Do you want him dead?" Khai quietly asked.

"Are you deaf, lad?" Melembrin answered. "Haven't we just said so?"

"Then fetch me my bow and one good straight arrow."

"Eh?" Mattas laughed. "You'd shoot at him from up here? Are you daft? There's not an archer in all Kush could—"

"Nor in Khem," Khai cut him off, "not any more."

Ashtarta caught Khai's arm, stared deep into his blue eyes. They were cold as high mountain springs. "I'll get you your weapon," she said. "I know where it is." And she sped away across the roof of the plateau.

"You'll look a damn fool if you miss," said Melembrin.

"And if I don't miss . . . Lord?"

"Then I'll let you train my own archers. There's not a damn one of them worth his salt."

"Good," said Khai. "How high are we, Lord?"

Melembrin shook his great head. "Thirteen, fourteen hundred feet, perhaps. How can you hope to shoot an arrow that far?"

"Most of the way the arrow will be falling," Khai answered. "I have only to find the target—the world's pull will do the rest." He tested the air with a dampened finger. "Did you say you'd make me your Master of Archers, Lord?"

"Eh?" Melembrin frowned. "There's no such position."

"High time there was, Lord, if your bowmen are poor as you say they are. And what rank would a Master of Archers hold, I wonder?"

Melembrin joined in the game. "Captain, at least, I suppose."

Ashtarta was back. Breathlessly, she handed Khai his bow and a single arrow. He looked at her, smiled wryly, strung the bow, nocked the arrow, turned and sighted down the shaft at the red shirt of the figure on the rock far below. Then, standing firm and solid as the Gilf Kebir itself, he raised the bow a little and sighted out into empty air. In another moment, the bow was empty in his hand and the arrow was lost in a sigh of air, a blur that flew out from the clifftop and disappeared in sky and space.

All eyes were on the scarlet figure that capered and roared below like an enraged monkey. Again Zodba shook his fist at the looming cliffs—then seemed to freeze in that position. And slowly he toppled backward and fell from his boulder, then lay still in the grass and the dust. Seeing him fall, several soldiers ran to him. Khai's arrow transfixed his heart, with only its flight protruding from his breast.

Up on the heights, Khai turned to a voiceless Melembrin and said: "Thus will I serve you, Lord, who am your Master of Archers, your Captain of Bowmen."

Unashamedly, before her father could utter a single word in reply, Ashtarta grabbed Khai and hugged him to her breast.

Half an hour later when the Khemites had counted their losses, their commander came out and stood beneath the great cliffs near the boulder-blocked gorge of Hortaph. He saluted the watchers on the heights, then fell on his sword. This was obviously vastly preferable to returning to Khem and reporting his ignominious defeat to Pharaoh. His officers wrapped his body in his own standard and bore it away eastward, and for four years no more Khemites were seen beneath the looming walls of the Gilf Kebir. . . .

# part EIGHT

# I | KHAI'S PROGRESS

On those occasions in later life when Khai would be asked how he fared during his first years in Kush, his reactions would be varied. Despite the fact that he now held a definite position on Melembrin's staff of officers, still he was only a youth; and when he was not teaching his considerable skills as an archer he was subject, as are all strangers in strange lands, to the gibes and taunts and occasional cruelties of his hosts. One man in particular—albeit a young one, that same Manek Thotak who would have whipped him—was openly hostile, for a time at any rate. And since Manek was now a Captain of Horse and holding the same rank as Khai, there was little that the adopted Khemite could say or do about it.

Despite all odds, however, he soon formed a circle of firm friends, not least among them being the Princess Ashtarta herself, but he often felt lonely for all of that. He blamed his loneliness for the dreams—those inexplicable visions which came in the night to taunt him with half-remembered scenes of times and lands all but forgotten, or as yet unconceived—and began to spend a deal of time on his own, away from the camps and villages out on the free wild face of the steppes.

For following the crushing of Pharaoh's pursuit force at Hortaph, Melembrin had drawn back into the hinterland of Kush to convalesce. The sweet air and rolling green slopes to the east of the Gilf Kebir would be good for him, he had thought, and had retired to his birthplace in Nam-Khum. This was where he garrisoned his men, and from here they were allowed to filter back to their former homes and work, ready at a moment's notice for recall whenever Khem should pose her next threat. Surprisingly, that threat did not materialize; the lull turned into a period of real peace; and gradually Melembrin's guerrillas drifted back to their own tribes and became one with the fields, mountains and steppes which had spawned them.

Thus, as his duties declined, Khai found himself with much more time on his hands, which only sufficed to increase his loneliness and the incidence of peculiar dreams. The latter were no longer confined to the hours of darkness and of sleep but might come upon him as brief waking visions, and they were often so strange as to be frightening. He had always been prone to oddish nightmares even as a child, and some of his childhood dreams and fancies now repeated themselves: such as dreams of flying, or of riding at incredible speed in strange vehicles along black paths in an alien land. But if anything his newer nightmares were stranger by far than these earlier dreams. On awakening, he could never remember any real details of them, only the faintest shadows that remained to cloud his thoughts; but the waking visions—in the form of weird, intuitive flashes—were completely different and utterly bewildering.

It was at the half-yearly games at Nam-Khum that Khai first found some benefit from these peculiar visitations. He took part in the archery competition, of course, and easily won each of the four events. Manek Thotak equalled this achievement in the equestrian events, and he also took second place in whip-handling. Then came the wrestling.

This was more or less a free-for-all in which any young man who fancied his chances entered a great ring marked on the earth with pebbles. The idea was that the last man in the ring was the winner. The town's children had been playing at the game all morning and Khai had watched them. As he did so, a recurrent picture kept flitting over the surface of his mind, of small yellow men who bowed to one another and grinned with big teeth—before hurling themselves into hand-to-hand combat that was fast, furious and utterly ruthless!

As quick as they came the visions were gone, only to repeat after a minute or so until Khai shook his head in an attempt to clear it of their influence. For it seemed to him that he had fought with these yellow men. They had instructed him, made him a master of their arts. He knew it. Somewhere, somehow, it was so. His arms had been stronger then and his body heavily muscled, and his speed had been that of a striking snake. He had been a man, then—but how could he have been? Looking down at himself, at his body, his hands, he felt suddenly a stranger in this youthful flesh. But that, too, was a vision and soon vanished with the rest of them. Nevertheless, as he had watched the village children tumble and squirm, he had vowed that he, too, would try the wrestling.

Of all the young men who entered the ring of pebbles that day, Khai was easily the youngest. Tall and rangy, he had none of the breadth or muscle of the other contenders, but he did have . . . something. And no sooner had the game been opened then Khai became the center of attraction. Melembrin, near-crippled now and pale in his pain, sat on the judges' dais nearby and grunted his approval. Beside him, Ashtarta was astonished by a side of Khai she had never before seen, at which she could not possibly have guessed.

At first, the other contestants more or less ignored the fair-haired, blue-eyed youth out of Khem, but after he had very quickly thrown all of the lesser wrestlers out of the circle he was suddenly a very real threat. Three of the more experienced men, clad only in loincloths and gleaming with the sweat of their exertions, exchanged glances full of meaning. They turned on the Master of Archers in unison, and while one contrived to drive his elbow into Khai's mouth—totally against all of the rules, which did not allow striking as such—another tripped him from behind. As Khai sprawled and dabbed in astonishment at his bleeding mouth, the third man made a play of falling over him, his knees coming down on Khai's ribs. That was what should have happened. . . .

Instead it was as if a key had turned in the lock of Khai's mind. His reactions became those of someone else—he *was* someone else—and his speed and strength suddenly increased threefold. When those knees came down where his chest had been, Khai had already rolled aside, was springing to his feet, driving rigid knuckles in a stiff-armed jab that broke the nose of the largest of his attackers. At the same time, his head had turned, his eyes had seen the man who kneeled where he had lain, and his elbow had driven backward to strike him in the forehead with stunning force. The youth who had tripped him sprang at him from the rear, threw an arm around his neck and forced a knee into his back. His free hand he used to clout Khai on the side of the head.

A cry split the air then: of an enraged martial arts warrior under attack, turning his body to a fighting machine in a controlled frenzy of activity. Khai tore the man from his back and in a single motion hurled him headlong from the circle of pebbles. Then he was in among the remaining contestants, striking left and right, stretching them out almost as fast as the eye could follow his blows. By this time Melembrin was on his feet, shouting his encouragement, beside himself with savage pleasure.

"Sh'tarra, look at him! I was like that as a boy, daughter, since when I've never seen such fighting. The Khemite is a born killer!"

"But they're not wrestling," she answered. "They're really fighting! There's blood everywhere, and Khai's to blame for most of it."

"All of it—that I can see, girl. But they turned on him first. Hah! Like cubs snapping at a sleeping lion. Well, they've woken him up, and now they're paying the price!"

Now, seeing their danger and concerned that Khai had already bested so many of their friends, the remaining half-dozen Kushites threw themselves upon him in a last desperate attempt to get him out of the circle. He was a whirlwind among the six, sending them flying left and right, until at last he stood face to face with Manek Thotak. They tottered, both of them near-exhausted, at the very edge of the circle, glowering at each other with red-rimmed eyes. By now, however, Khai was feeling just as bewildered as the spectators. The mood was off him and his skill and speed were gone. When Manek mustered his last ounce of strength and charged at him, it was as much as he could do to turn the charge so that they flew out of the circle together.

"A draw!" cried Melembrin, on his feet again. "What say you, Sh'tarra?"

"A draw, father, yes. And look—do you suppose that they'll be friends now?"

The king looked and saw Manek and Khai staggering from the field of combat. Each had an arm around the other's neck, and their weary laughter came back to Melembrin where his eyes followed them. They limped, yes, but they also laughed.

"Friends?" he finally answered his daughter. "Yes, I should think so. I hope so, for they certainly can't afford to be enemies. And Kush can't afford to be divided."

As Khai became a man and moved into his third year with the Kushites, news began to filter back from Khem to the tribes of the mountains. War had flared up along the Nubia-Khem border—a confrontation over Pharaoh's continual and blatant slave-taking—and N'jakka had carried out punitive raids on Peh-il and Phemor. Pharaoh had begun to build forts all along the river between Peh-il and Subon; he had further cemented his friendship with the Arabbans beyond the Narrow Sea; and he was demanding vast tribute from Siwad and Syra to pay for a planned mobilization. Trouble was in the air, big trouble, and Kush began to feel the first vibrations of its coming.

Meanwhile Khai and Manek, with certain reservations, had become firm friends. For one thing, Manek never failed to let it be known that he considered Khai of inferior stock, a good Khemite but a Khemite for all that. And Khemish blood, as everyone knew, was degenerate, inferior. Oh, there could be little question of Khai's value to Kush, but he must really be looked upon as a mercenary rather than a true friend of the peoples of the Gilf Kebir and its hinterlands.

Both men were young colonels now and rising in stature with each passing day. Melembrin relied on their military judgement, took their advice and planned the rather sporadic training of his troops accordingly. The day was coming, he was certain, when Kush must once more protect herself against Pharaoh and his territorial avarice. The king was failing, however, and he knew it. The poison was spreading through his system at an ever-accelerating rate, and the end could not be too far away. As for Ashtarta: she was being groomed for her duties as the next Candace, and so had little time for anything else.

Khai's dreams no longer bothered him quite so much, but certain aspects of them had become more specific, more detailed, so that he could remember something of them on awakening. Now he dreamed of saddles, of wheels, and of dark metals in the earth; and there were names in his dreams which seemed synonymous with these strange symbols of his subconscious.

Then, toward the end of the third year, Melembrin died and Ashtarta became Candace. She went into mourning for a month, and when finally she took her seat on the throne of Kush, it could be seen that the transformation was complete. There had been a metamorphosis, and the tomboy princess was now an imperially beautiful, fully-fledged Queen. Without exception, the chiefs of the tribes accepted her and her administration.

# II

# THE COMING OF
# THE MAGES

It was at this time, too, that Khai first mentioned his dreams to the aged wizard, Imthra. Imthra had been Khai's friend for two years now, and the more he learned of the Khemite, the more fascinating he found him. It was not only Khai's blue eyes and fair hair—a combination of physical anomalies hitherto unknown to the peoples of the region—but also his ideas, his battle skills and now his dreams.

Khai had mentioned dreaming about a dark metal in the ground and had even given it a name: "iron." He had connected the metal with a name: Mer-ow-eh, which Ithra knew to be a town in jungled Nubia south of the Nile. Similarly, Khai spoke of "wheels" and had drawn a picture of a "chariot" for Imthra; and again he had a name to supplement these weird ideas. This time it was "Hyrksos," which Imthra knew to be the name of a people who lived some hundreds of miles to the west. And so it went.

Now Imthra, who was one of the wisest men in all Kush, soon came to realize that there was much more to his young friend than first met the eye. He spoke to others of his discovery, wise men from far and wide across the country, and gradually Khai's fame as a mystic, his recognition as a seer with access to as yet untapped powers, spread afar. Certainly the soldiers in his command already considered him as something magical. When Khai shot an arrow it invariably found its target, and when he wrestled . . . who could stand against him? Moreover, in this last year he had shot up like a sapling, putting on meat and muscle until he truly looked the young general which Ashtarta would soon make him. In Kush's army, the commanders were all young, for they must be where the fighting was thickest and their thinking must have the clarity, scope and vision of youth.

And this was the way things stood when, some months later, the seven mages came to Kush. They came from all the lands which enclosed Khem, some of them having traveled for thousands of miles to avoid that central country, and yet somehow all of them contrived to arrive on the same day, at the same hour, which was noon. Imthra had known that something of great importance was in the wind— he had seen seven shadows looming in his shewstone—but he had never dreamed that he would see this day, when the seven mages should all come together and visit him in his own humble dwelling in Nam-Khum on the steppes of Kush. Of the seven, he already knew Kush's own hermit-mage and had met him many times; the others he knew only by repute.

When formal introductions were done with and while Imthra took refreshment with his visitors, he asked the seven why they honored him with this visit to his humble house, why they had left their homelands and traveled so far to see him. The seven told Imthra that they did not wish to offend him, but they had merely called on him because he was Ashtarta's resident mage. In fact, they had come to Kush to offer their services to the Candace. Also, to give her their advice in a certain matter which would presently concern her people; and finally they had come to speak to the General Khai Ibizin, once of Khem.

"But Khai is not a general, not yet," Imthra had protested, only to be told:

"No, but he will be—tomorrow, after we have seen the Candace. . . ."

In the afternoon of the next day, at Ashtarta's palatial house, a meeting was held of all the chiefs or their representatives in Nam-Khum. This was the quarterly council meeting of the chiefs, presided over by Ashtarta; but on this occasion the agenda was to be other than the petty problems of tribes and far more important. All of Ashtarta's advisers were there, tribal elders in the main, and also fourteen chiefs or their representatives. In addition, there were six colonels—including Khai and Manek, the latter pair having returned that very morning from a hunting trip in the hills—and old Imthra, who was also Ashtarta's chief adviser.

The seven mages had seen the Candace in private earlier and had spent several hours with her. They had also seen Khai and had questioned him about his strange dreams and visions, and about his vow to return to Asorbes one day and destroy Pharaoh. They had not tried to explain Khai's dreams— indeed their entire audience with him had seemed designed purely to glean information *from* him—but upon leaving him they had all saluted him and called him General. Also, the Nubian mage had taken his hands, examining them minutely as if to satisfy himself of something. And upon Khai showing the black mage Adonda Gomba's sign, which he still carried with him wherever he went, then the ancient Nubian had addressed him as Khai the Killer.

At the meeting in the great hall of Ashtarta's house, the atmosphere was one of high tension. Obviously something massively important was happening, so that when Ashtarta finally stood and addressed the assembly her every word was eagerly seized upon.

"Chiefs, military men, councilors and friends," she began, "this will not be our usual meeting of tribal heads, but as you have doubtless guessed a most unusual meeting. Information of great moment has been brought to me by the seven wise men from all the lands around, whose word, I am assured, may only be ignored at the peril of all Kush. And this is the word: that even now Pharaoh poises his army like a great spear for a mighty thrust at Kush—one which will pierce the land through and through!"

As an excited babble broke out among the chiefs, Ashtarta held out her arms and spoke over their voices. "Make no plans, you chiefs, nor speak of battle and the ways of war. For every man you can muster Pharaoh has ten, and this time they won't fall into your traps so readily. No, and I am advised that . . . that Kush should not defend herself!"

"Not defend?" a gnarled old chief jumped to his feet. "Is this Melembrin's daughter who speaks to us? What then shall we do, O Candace? Give ourselves over into Pharaoh's tender care?"

"Advice such as I have received comes hard," Ashtarta answered him, "but its very source is such that I cannot refuse it. We will not make war with the Khemites nor even defend our lands against them—not yet. The world is far and wide, and our little land is but a small part. We shall go out into the world and leave Kush behind—for now."

"Leave Kush?" the chiefs cried as one man, their voices shocked.

"That was my word," Ashtarta answered sorrowfully. "Leave Kush—leave her ravished, burned, destroyed—so that the Khemites shall not benefit at all from holding her. Not a single animal, neither beast nor bird, nothing that lives shall they take. Burn the very ground, that is my word."

"And where shall we go, Queen?"

"That is a question you must ask of Khai," she answered them. "Of the General Khai, for thus I now appoint him. General Khai Ibizin, of Kush. And his brother general, Manek Thotak, also newly-promoted. Khai, what have you to say of the sundering of the tribes of Kush?"

Khai was astonished. He stood up, opened his mouth, said nothing.

"Huh!" snarled a belligerent chief. "See the Khemite, elevated to a general, little more than a youth and gasping like a fish out of water—or a man out of his depth!"

"Oh?" Khai found his tongue. "And would you put six of your best men in a ring of pebbles with this fish, Dori Antoshin? I think not. Only let me recover from the shock of this honor bestowed upon me, and I shall say where the sundered tribes must go."

He leaned his knuckles on the great table and frowned, then cautiously began. "Myself, I shall take fifty thousand men into Nubia. I have friends there and we shall fight Pharaoh's soldiers together, black and white side-by-side. Also, there is a metal in the ground, and I shall make weapons of it. The General Manek Thotak: he shall take a similar body of men into Siwad, and he too shall fight Pharaoh, for Kush and Nubia are not the only lands to suffer Khasathut's oppression. And in Siwad Manek will learn the arts of swamp-fighting, which will be useful when we return to Kush and attack Pharaoh in his house across the swamps. Moreover, the Siwadis are experts with fine and supple leathers, and there are things I desire to be made which Manek will bring back with him when that time comes." He paused for a moment and gazed at Ashtarta and Imthra at the head of the table.

"Our Queen and her mage, they shall go to the west, to the land of the Hyrksos peoples. The remainder of our warriors will go with her; the women and children, too. Pharaoh will not follow there, for that would be to advance his borders too far, and even he will not have the men for that—not with the Nubians and Siwadis worrying his flanks. The Hyrksos are a friendly people, for they have no enemies surrounding them and do not need to fight. But they are great craftsmen, and they have built travois which do not drag along the ground but ride over it by use of wheels. The Queen shall take many craftsmen and horse-soldiers out of Kush with her, and also designs which I shall give her; so that when she returns to Kush she may ride in a chariot of war!"

"Huh!" another chief, Genduhr Shebbithon, snorted his contempt. "The whole plan is a madness, based on the visions of wizards and the dreams of a foreigner come to power in Kush. 'Go here,' Khai says, and 'go there.' And 'do this,' or 'do that.' And are we supposed to obey? I challenge his authority, his right to command tribes, his very origins! Who is this Khai, blue-eyed and fair-haired, who holds such sway in Kush? And for that matter, who are these seven mages? Wizards, mummers and charlatans, say I. And if they are men of powers, what dark spells have they placed on Melembrin's daughter that now she would flee the Khemites? Now look—there sits Manek Thotak, also a general. What does he think of all this, who like his father before him has proved himself since a boy and loves Kush as a Kushite should?"

Manek immediately stood up. "I think we should all be quiet," be said. "You, too. Genduhr Shebbithon, until all is explained."

"But who *will* explain?" questioned yet another chief. "It is the right of the Candace to choose her generals as and when she will, but since when does Kush employ doubtful wizards for her guidance?"

"Now *hush*!" commanded Ashtarta, her face dark and angry. "You are all too eager to snap and snarl. And I will not suffer insults to our guests. Do you think I have not shared your doubts? Of course I have, who love Kush better than any of you. If it comes hard for you to give up your territories, how then for me, who must forsake a throne? Now I will say it one more time: Kush must be either sundered or overwhelmed, one or the other. You, Genduhr Shebbithon—you went raiding with The Fox in Khem. And now you compare me to my father and say I am bewitched! Well, and did not Melembrin himself—even The Fox—run from the Khemites when it suited his purpose to do so?"

"But, Candace—" two or three of the chiefs groaned in unison, for they knew she was hurt and would not have had it this way.

*"Hush!"* she cut them short, then bade the spokesman for the seven mages to rise. "You have heard me," she told her warrior chiefs, "and certainly I have heard enough of you. Very well, now listen to the words of men wiser by far than all of you gathered here. And having listened, then tell me I am wrong to accept their advice. . . ."

# III

# MESSAGE OF
# THE MAGES

No man knew the true names of the seven mages, for to let them be known would be to lessen their powers considerably. A name is a target at which an enemy may direct harmful spells. Thus it was that the spokesman for the seven, the yellow mage, was known simply as the Mage of Mentalism, and thus he introduced himself before he commenced the following narrative:

"Many years ago," he began, in a voice which, for all it was a whisper of dried leaves, still filled the hall, "Khasathut's father, who was then Pharaoh, drew seven evil men into his house. They were necromancers, wizards, users of dire magics. We, too, are mages—wizards, if you so desire to call us—and indeed there is a necromancer among us. But our magics are white and those of the Pharaoh Thanop'et's mages were black.

"He called them to him because he feared them, feared that they might work against him. Also, he was growing old and his son would need powerful allies when he claimed the throne. And Thanop'et set his Vizier over the Dark Heptad to keep them in their place, and they were put to work on mysteries for Pharaoh, who desired to be immortal. Thanop'et had acquired the skills of the Dark Heptad too late, however, and the task he had given them, to discover immortality for him, was too great. In time, he died and Khasathut came to the throne, last of his line, and later he appointed his own Vizier, Anulep, to council him and be his eyes and ears. And still the Dark Heptad worked their magics and saw to Pharaoh's needs; and for him, as for his father, they continued to seek out the secrets of immortality.

"Now this was all well and good, for in keeping the Dark Heptad busy, Pharaoh prevented them from working their own abominations, which had been a scourge on Khem and all the lands around for years uncounted. My brothers and I—" he indicated the six seated mages, "had long known of them and had long abhorred their interference with the ordered laws of nature. Now, with the Dark Heptad all together under one roof, as it were, we were relieved of the watch we must keep over them and could relax our guard a little; for we had long kept a wary eye on these evil wizards to know how they fared in their infernal work and how, if ever they should come too close to the blackest mysteries of all, their vile industry might be checked.

"Also, we knew that they could never discover immortality for Khasathut, for there was only one way that this might be achieved—which would mean such a blasphemy as never before was seen. It would be the unleashing of forces which must eventually destroy Khem, all the lands around, the world, the sun and the moon, and all the stars in the sky. So that even if the Dark Heptad should discover this road, still they would never go that way, for that would mean universal insanity. Not even the Dark Heptad would dare that . . . or so we thought. . . .

"But now this Pharaoh Khasathut, he nears the end of his span of years and his frustrations are many. His pyramid tomb towers in Asorbes, where in five more years it will be finished, but still Pharaoh is impatient with the work. His Dark Heptad promises him immortality, and gives him nothing. His Vizier plots and schemes and seeks more power, who already carries Pharaoh's might in his hands; and this also worries the God-king sorely. So sorely indeed that he has made plans for Anulep to go with him into his tomb when the last day is come, which is not at all to the high priest's liking. Also, Siwad and Nubia have risen up against Pharaoh, so that he must protect his borders; and he has learned that in Kush a certain man is grown up who has earned the respect of the Candace, who vows one day to return to Asorbes and destroy him who once destroyed all he held dear.

"And so Khasathut has made his plan, which is this:

"He will hold his borders with Nubia and Siwad, which will prove expensive in manpower but cheaper than waging outright war with the peoples of those lands. Next he will take Kush, against which he has a great grudge. To do this, his armies will surround the Gilf Kebir and slowly throttle the heartland. His warriors will strike from the hinterland, where no frowning walls of rock rise up to defy them. Thus will he drive the Kushites off the very edge of the Gilf Kebir, and those who might escape through clefts in the rock will find his soldiers waiting patiently in siege beneath the looming walls.

"Then, when Kush is fallen and its tribes overwhelmed, Pharaoh plans to split his army in two parts; one to strike south through Daraaf which is unprotected, and thus come into Nubia from the flank; the other to strike north, getting behind Siwad and crushing her from the rear. At the same time, he will mobilize all of Khem and reinforce his troops with fierce warriors out of Therae and Arabba. And these are the forces he will hurl against Nubia across the river, and against Siwad in the north. Thus will all be overwhelmed, and when it is done, Pharaoh will then rape the conquered lands of all precious things. . . ."

Here the yellow mage paused and the chief Dori Antoshin took the opportunity to ask: "And how do you mages know these things, who have been on your journeys for long and long?"

"How do you know when the sun shines?" the yellow mage countered.

Dori was taken aback. "Why!" he finally answered, "I see it with my eyes, feel it warm on my skin."

"Just so," nodded the yellow mage, "and we also have eyes that see and skin that feels, but you are just a man and we are the seven mages." Again he paused, but this time there was no interruption.

"Now, if the tribes of Kush go their separate ways according to the directions of the General Khai Ibizin, then when the Khemites get here, they will waste much time in the taking of a land which is undefended, for they will ever be on the lookout for the fierce men who are known to dwell here. And when at last the land is taken, then they will discover that it cannot support them, where there is no meat and even the grass is burned to dust. Also, by the time half of the army gets here, Nubia and Siwad will be fighting back all along their borders, and so Pharaoh will send no more men into Kush. Short of supplies and needed elsewhere, the Khemish invaders of Kush will fall back into Khem to reinforce the forts and camps to north and south. Eventually, though seasons and years must pass before it comes to be, only small garrisons will be left in Kush, and the rest of Pharaoh's armies will be fighting Nubia and Siwad across their borders.

"Ah! But the fighting will be bitter, with Siwad and Nubia bolstered up by men of Kush under the Generals Khai Ibizin and Manek Thotak. And soon Pharaoh will order all of his forces to those fronts to make an end of it. And now it will be the turn of Nubia and Siwad to hold the line. In Siwad, the Khemites will founder in mire; and to the south, where the Nile will be in flood, they will drown as they make the crossing into Nubia. Yes, and while this is happening the tribes of Kush will be reunited!

"Here in Kush, at this very spot, three-and-one-half years from today, the tribes shall come together, and now they will be armed with iron swords out of Nubia, leathers from Siwad, chariots from Hyrksos; and Khai shall bring an *impi* with him. Then shall Kush strike terror into the heart of Pharaoh, when the garrisons are overwhelmed and the war chariots thunder down out of Kush to strike the forts of the western marches and crush Khem even to the banks of the Nile and beyond. . . .

"Now this much we have seen, we who have access to dreams and visions, and we who hear the words of spirits of times gone and times still to come. But beyond this we cannot see, except to say that win or lose, Pharaoh will at the last cause his Dark Heptad to do that which will overwhelm the world. For he is mad and his madness waxes in him like moss on a damp stone, until it obscures the stone. So his madness grows, until Pharaoh will be no more and only the madness will remain.

"This is our concern, that an end be put to Pharaoh before he dooms the world, and to ensure this we pledge our services to the Candace Ashtarta of Kush. When the tribes of Kush separate and go their ways into the world, we also shall go where we may not be found, and when the tribes come together once more, we shall be here to work with them against Khem. . . .

"We have spoken."

For a long moment, there was silence. Then the chief Genduhr Shebbithon said: "How may we know that any of this will come to pass? Give us a sign."

"A sign?" the keen-eyed brown mage from Daraaf stood up. He was the Mage of Oneiromancy, an interpreter of dreams, and now his eyes were bright with sights unseen by the others. "Last night, I dreamed a rider would come from the Gilf Kebir," he said. "And the rider would say that word was come out of Khem of the gathering of Pharaoh's forces, that even now a great army marched on Kush."

"Oh?" said Genduhr Shebbithon uncertainly, "and where is this messenger?"

The brown mage gazed at him and smiled until his keen eyes twinkled like stars. "That is your sign, chief," he said, "for you spoke those very words in my dream last night. And I answered thus: 'Let the messenger speak for himself!'"

"Majesty!" an usher burst in through the great doors. "A rider has come from the east with a message."

Ashtarta smiled grimly at the suddenly wide eyes and stricken looks on the faces of her chiefs. "Send him in," she commanded. "We know what his message will be—but I should like certain of my chiefs to hear it for themselves. . . ."

# IV | PHARAOH'S FRENZY

It took all of five days for Ashtarta's message to get out to the tribes, but after that, her instructions were followed to the letter. All goods and chattels were bundled up for the journey or else hidden away in inaccessible places; beasts were either herded together ready for the drive out of Kush, or slaughtered where they stood; and as the first cohorts of Khem arrived at the foot of the Gilf Kebir, so the tribes of Kush departed, as it were, "by the back door."

After twelve weeks, when Pharaoh's forces encircled the Gilf's plateau-lands and got behind those frowning cliffs of near-impregnable rock, then it was discovered how sorely the departed Kushites had dealt with the land; when all about was seen the scorched earth and blackened houses, the choked wells and dams broken down so that streams ran to waste, the ravaged fields and stripped orchards. And when finally it dawned on the commanders of that expeditionary force that indeed the Kushites were fled, then they set up their camps, took stock of their meager supplies and sent word back to halt the advance of an even greater army which was clearly unnecessary and unsupportable.

At first Pharaoh greeted this news with a mad delight, for second only to a destroyed Kush was word of one in full flight or already utterly fled before his might; but as Nubia and Siwad began a new and savage offensive, his mood quickly turned to one of rage. And all came to pass as the seven mages had prophesied, with Pharaoh deploying the bulk of his men to north and south, intending to crush his resurgent neighbors in short order and so put an end to it. Here, however, he had reckoned without the advent of the Generals Khai Ibizin and Manek Thotak, without whose military skills and trained Kushite warriors it would have gone hard indeed for the Nubians and Siwadis. Also, the weather turned against Pharaoh and, in a deluge of completely unseasonable rain, the Nile became unnavigable, while the low-lying lands of Siwad turned into a vast and totally impassable morass.

Moreover, to the west of the Nile, the enemy's forces commenced a series of sly guerrilla raids on Khem's camps and forts, with parties of Nubians striking north through Daraaf and the Siwadis cutting south across Khem's own savannahs. And though month piled upon month, still the weather did not break, so that soon Khasathut became convinced that it would rain forever. Only then, after almost a year of battle, did the Dark Heptad approach Pharaoh through Anulep the high priest, with their interpretation of events; and only then did he begin to understand something of the truth of things: that much of the blame for what was amiss could be laid at the feet of seven mages who were the equal in powers, if not the peers, of his own seven wizards.

Now Khasathut had known of the seven mages for as long as he could remember, and he had often sought to find them and bring them together to work for him as his father had done with the Dark Heptad. Soldiers had been sent out more than once into the lands surrounding Khem (with the exception of Kush and Nubia) to bring back the seven dead or alive, but the mysterious mages had seemed like smoke to the grasp of his troops. Here today and gone tomorrow, they were as shadows that everyone saw but none could trace, whose owners were more wraithlike than the shadows themselves. Moreover, the peoples of their home- or host-countries could not be made to assist Pharaoh in their discovery; for the seven were as holy men and protected, so that Khasathut had never been able to take them.

Which was why, on learning that the seven had a hand in the business of the war—particularly in respect of the foul weather—Pharaoh flew into an evil temper and sent out chosen men yet again into Daraaf, Syra, Arabba and Therae to seek them out. Time passed and with the second summer the weather seemed to relent a little, and the seekers after the mages, some of them at least, began to return. Of the party sent into Daraaf, however, Pharaoh heard never a word and suspected that it had met with fatal troubles. The Theraen and Arabban parties did return, shamefacedly and empty-handed, but at least they carried home confirmation that the seven mages were indeed all gathered on the side of Kush and working against Pharaoh, which was to strengthen the warning of the God-king's Dark

Heptad. As for that party sent into Syra: they had not stopped there, but carried on eastward and were never seen or heard of again. For them the unknown east had more to offer than a return to their increasingly war-torn homeland.

Now, too, as if Khasathut's temper and nerves were not ground fine enough already, the Siwadis destroyed the fort at Tanos and slaughtered Khem's troops in their thousands to the west of the Nile; and the far-flung tribes of Daraaf also rose up to send guerrilla parties to the southwestern marches. It was not that Pharaoh was losing the battle—with his almost inexhaustible supply of manpower that would be unthinkable—but rather that he could not be seen to be winning it, and already the war was moving into its third year. Khem seemed hemmed in by mists, rains and swamps and surrounded by wraiths of warriors. And who may beat off the rain or smite a wraith?

And so now Pharaoh thought to change his tactics. For if the seven so-called "wise" and "good" mages had gone to bolster the Kushites where they fought like mercenary dogs for Siwad and Nubia, and if they were conjuring magic to control the very elements and thus contain Pharaoh's dreams of empire, why should he not answer in a like tongue? Thus he bade Anulep parade the Dark Heptad before him, along with his generals, administrators and all ambassadors and mercenary overlords in Khem, so that he could outline his new plans and issue his orders.

These were designed firstly to bring about a reversal of the weather which bogged down and foundered his troops; which task he placed squarely upon his Dark Heptad, with dire threats in the event of their failure. Secondly: he ordered that mobilization be effected on an unprecedented scale, and that any excess of troops be drawn down out of empty Kush to reinforce the forts and camps all along the western front. Thirdly: he offered fabulous enticements to Therae, Syra and Arabba for mercenary assistance in one vast and final push which he planned against Siwad, Nubia and now Daraaf. Kush he forgot entirely, for what was there now in Kush worth remembering?

He could not know of the strange red fires that burned in Nubia, or the metal that flowed into swords there. And he was equally ignorant that in far Hyrksos the wheels of war were even now turning against him, where Ashtarta built her chariots according to Khai's designs; where she tested them and built anew, and trained her warriors in their handling. And even if he could have known of the reins, leathers and saddles which the Siwadi craftsmen were producing in their thousands, still he would not have understood. For in Khem the horse was as yet a doubtful beast, fit only for the use of savages such as the Kushites, whose land was now empty except for a handful of Khemish cohorts—

—But for how long?

Almost three-and-a-half years had gone by since Pharaoh sent his occupying force into Kush. Things had gone badly for him since then, but now at last he was ready to deliver those hammer blows from which, if he were successful, the civilized world might never recover. Now, too, after almost three years of near-continuous rain, his Dark Heptad seemed to have turned the trick and the sun shone over Khem, drying out the mire and turning it to firm earth once more. It seemed to Pharaoh that there never would be a more opportune time—when the Nile's flooding was at an end and Nubia stood green and inviting across the river; when the swamps of Siwad steamed off their excess vapor and the mists lifted to reveal lands just waiting to be taken.

Moreover, Khem was full of soldiers—the entire Nile valley at arms—and thousands of fierce mercenaries choked the towns and villages and grew bored from lack of work. Even the border skirmishes seemed to have petered out, so that Pharaoh suspected his enemies of having lost their appetite for a war which ultimately they must lose. He waited no longer but hurled one hundred thousand mercenaries across the river into Nubia, and in the south ninety thousand more stormed the swamps to take the island villages of the pallid, morass-dwelling Siwadis. And in a little while, the first reports of these simultaneous assaults were carried home to Khasathut in Asorbes . . .

. . . Reports that drove him to the very rim of outright insanity, when his rage was such that Anulep himself fled from him and hid in the pyramid's most secret chambers, where he shook and trembled until at last Pharaoh's frenzy had burned itself out. Then, before seeking out his God-king where he lay exhausted and trembling upon the royal bed, the Vizier learned for himself the reasons for Pharaoh's fit. Not fifty of his Arabban mercenaries had come back across the river from Nubia, and those that did return told tales of formidable *impis,* trained to a razor's edge of fighting efficiency and armed with black swords which carved Khemish bronze as if it were green papyrus.

To further exacerbate matters, those mercenaries sent to invade Siwad had found nothing to invade; where for all their wading through crocodile- and leech-infested swamp, they had discovered Siwad empty of life, with the islands scorched and deserted. The Siwadis had forsaken their homeland in a pattern which Khasathut recognized all too well, and even now they were marauding along the border between Siwad and the rebuilt Tanos fort. Even so, the mercenaries had not returned empty-handed, no, for nine out of ten of them brought back the swamp's fevers which made them useless; and of the rest: they had lost all interest in Pharaoh's cause and dreamed now only of returning to their homelands. . . .

And Khasathut's troubles were only just beginning.

# V KUSH RESURGENT!

Manek Thotak and his army arrived on the steppes to the west of the Gilf Kebir some hours in advance of Ashtarta and Khai. His warriors, coming from Siwad, had split into two separate bodies to the north of the Gilf. One of these had curved round to the west, climbing onto the plateau-lands from the rear; the other had passed along the front of the Gilf below the looming cliffs. In the night, they had found two small Khemite garrisons, each of about one thousand strong, one on the heights and the other in a keep.

The high garrison had been taken at once, its sentries silenced by a small advance group before three thousand men of the main body rushed the Khemites, woke them, and drove them over the edge of the night-dark plateau. The taking of the garrison in the keep had been a little more difficult, had taken a little longer and had not been accomplished without cost—but only a very small cost. By contrast, not a man of the Khemites had been spared.

Then had the Kushite force down on the plain, all twenty-five thousand men of them, climbed up to the roof of the plateau along paths known of old; and before dawn, Manek Thotak's army had been on its way westward, completing the final stage of its journey home. On their way, Manek's men had been rounding up wild horses, offspring of many of their own animals set free three-and-a-half years ago. These would supplement that great herd of animals taken into Hyrksos by Ashtarta's horsemen, which now they would be herding back again.

It was noon when Manek arrived on the rolling plain overlooking Nam-Khum, and there he camped his army with the sun standing overhead and a warm wind rising from the west. He sniffed that wind suspiciously and smiled grimly. The *Khamsín,* that hell-wind which would scorch these green slopes brown before it flew down into the valley of the Nile, was on its way. It would be the first time for four years. . . .

Green fields. Manek smiled again. The last time he had seen these steppes, they had been black, crisped by his own people before they went into their self-imposed exile of war. Well, the fields were green enough now. These last few years, there had been enough rain to grow grass on solid rock!

These last few years. . . . How had Naomi fared, he wondered. Naomi Tyrass had been his girl when he was a boy, and he had loved her. Oh, he'd had his rivals—particularly Thon Emahl, the son of the chief of Naomi's village—but he had known that Naomi would one day be his. When he became a captain, however, and when Melembrin began grooming him as a commander, a general, then Manek had let Naomi go.

She had flown to Thon, who by then was a village chief in his own right, and on impulse she had married him. Now Thon was a chief under Manek, a colonel commanding his own regiment, which in effect was his own tribe. Today they were all home from the wars, for a little while, and Thon and Naomi would soon be reunited. Well, good luck to them. Life in a village with a pretty little wife was not for Manek. No, for he knew that the Candaces of Kush were obliged to seek husbands from their generals, and that narrowed down the field considerably.

Oh, there were other generals among the tribes of Kush, to be sure, but these were old men who no longer went to war but sat at home by the fire and told tales of the old days, when they were young. But Manek *was* young, and a general to boot, and who else could Ashtarta take for a husband? Khai Ibizin? Impossible, for he was of Khemish blood and it would be unheard of for any foreigner to sit upon the throne of Kush. No, Manek would be king one day, which was why he had let Naomi go. It was not that he loved Ashtarta, though certainly she was a beautiful woman, but rather that he did love Kush; so that his one ambition was to be ruler in the land, and his sons and daughters after him. . . .

Musing on thoughts such as these and chewing on dried meat where he sat in the shade of a sapling shrub bearing its first flowers, Manek heard the shouts of his lookout and rose to his feet. He ran up the hillside a little way to where the lookout stood. Beneath him, his men had been taking their rest or eating, but now he was aware that every eye was turned to the west. "There,

Lord Manek," said the lookout, a youth four years Manek's junior. He stabbed a finger westward. "That will be the Candace. See how she raises the dust!"

"Aye," Manek agreed, "dust from the hooves of horses. That will be Ashtarta, all right—but your eyes aren't as keen as they might be." He chuckled at the youth's expression. "See there, to the south, climbing the steppes in a long line like a thin, unending snake. Do you see? That'll be Khai Ibizin. Khai of Khem."

"I'm told he doesn't like that name, Lord."

Manek frowned. "A dog's a dog no matter his shape, color or size," he answered.

"It's just that I thought the General Khai was your friend, Lord," the younger man shrugged.

"So he is," the general grinned. "Damn me, I don't hold it against him that he's born of the Nile—just that he thinks himself equal to a Kushite, that's all! But enough—now I must go to meet them. . . . A pony," he shouted as he ran back down the hillside. "Get me a horse. The rest of you, stay here. Those of you with wives and sweethearts, don't worry. You'll be seeing them soon enough. But if I were you, I'd save my strength. It won't be long before you'll be needing it. Five or six days at most. . . ."

Manek and Ashtarta, both of them riding alone, came together on the rolling plain that leaned westward from Nam-Khum. They jumped from their mounts and clasped each other, their eyes full of questions, unwilling to speak or break the magic. For there was a magic in this, the reuniting of the tribes of Kush. Finally, the Candace stood back from Manek and fed her eyes on him. He was bearded, burly, a hawk. Every inch a general. Clad in leather trousers and jacket, whip at his side as usual, sword in his belt—he had gone away into Siwad a young man, and he had returned a giant.

"I've heard news of you," she said. "How you drowned the Khemites in Siwad and burned them at Tanos. My father was right when he said you'd make a mighty general. It's been hard to keep my own warriors back from joining you. They would have come to you in Siwad if I'd let them. To you, and to the General Khai."

Manek said nothing, but stood and grinned his pleasure through his beard.

"And did you bring back leathers as Khai bade you?" she asked more seriously. "The Hyrksos leather is not good stuff."

Now he frowned a little. "Leather? Oh, yes, piles of it, Candace. Saddles and reins and all, though I thought it was a great waste of time. Still, I could be wrong. Those of my lads who've tried these horse-seats say they're very impressed with them."

"I suspect that you are wrong, Manek," she told him, and her eyes were bright and twinkling like diamonds. "My own experience is that Khai knows what he's doing, and indeed I have marvelous things to show you." Forgetting herself for a moment, she clapped her hands in glee. . . . Then she calmed herself, tucked her shirt into her breeches and tossed her hair back out of her eyes.

"And where is the General Khai?" she asked. "A Nubian runner came to me last night where I was camped and said Khai would be here."

"He's coming," Manek answered. "I saw him from the hill. But he's coming more slowly. No horseman, the Khemite, Majesty."

"Yes, I remember," she answered. "Well, if he still can't ride bareback, we'll have to see how he sits a saddle, eh?" And again she laughed.

Now, while she scanned the low ridges to the south, shading her eyes from the sun's glare, Manek looked at this Queen of a Nation. He admired her legs clad in short, soft rabbit-skin breeches; her narrow waist; her firm body and pure, unblemished skin. She looked much more a woman than ever he remembered her, more a true queen than the tomboy princess he had known among Melembrin's guerrillas.

"There," she suddenly cried. "Look!"

Manek looked and saw something which caused him first to gape in astonishment, then to grin. Coming up over a low crest less than a mile away, eight massive Nubians bore an open litter. They chanted as they trotted, their limbs moving in perfect unison and providing a smooth ride for the man who sat the chair. It was Khai; and in four or five minutes the blacks reached the place where Ashtarta and Manek waited, put down the litter and fell on their faces.

As Khai stepped out of his chair, Ashtarta embraced him as she had done with Manek, and once again there was a silence as they looked at each other. Khai had grown massive of chest and broad of shoulder, and his eyes seemed bluer and his blond hair blonder than ever the Candace remembered them. Feeling a flush rising to her cheeks, she breathlessly asked:

"But who are these? And why do they not stand up?" She looked doubtfully at the prostrated Nubians.

"They are yours, Candace," he laughed, "and if they must stay there all day, they will not rise till you order it!"

"Then tell them to get up," she said.

"You must tell them," he answered, "for I no longer command them and they won't obey me. These eight are yours, Queen—but they know the rudiments of our tongue."

Uncertain, she turned to the eight. "Get up," she said, "at once." And as a single man, they sprang to their feet.

Ashtarta stepped back a pace from these giants who towered over her, all bright with dyes and fierce as lions, their bushy heads sprouting feathers. "Look, Manek," she turned to him. "See what Khai has brought home for me!"

"Aye," Manek admired the blacks and stepped forward to take Khai's hand, "a fine bodyguard indeed—but an inefficient way of getting about. I fancy you'd prefer your horse, Majesty." The two men laughed and hugged each other, then Manek added:

"And Khai isn't alone in his gift-bringing. Look—" From a pocket, he took out a fistful of massive gems. Of flashing colors, they were like fires in the general's fist. "The Siwadis have sent you a chestful!" he told the Candace. "These are but a few."

"Also," Manek continued after a moment, "I've brought your warriors home again—though four thousand of them shall never return." He nodded toward the great encampment higher on the slope.

"We've had our losses, too," Khai nodded, "but it hasn't all been a loss. Majesty, if you'd care to tell your guard to bring up their colleagues—"

"My guard?" She stared about with a puzzled look. "Their colleagues?"

With a nod of his head, Khai indicated the blacks.

"Oh!" she said, then did as he suggested.

The massive Nubians immediately put fingers to mouths and set up a shrill, beating whistling that echoed up and down the slopes and startled birds and deer to flight. As the echoes of that dinning note died away, there came other sounds: the pounding of feet, the rattle of assagais on shields of woven leather.

Rapidly the sounds grew to a roar that was deafening, and over the rise there suddenly poured such an *impi* that Ashtarta and Manek could only stand and stare. In two huge black squares of fifty men to a side, that regiment of Nubians came, halting less than a hundred yards away in a stamping of feet that shook the earth. Behind the squares, in military precision, twenty deep and stretching all along the fold of the hill, the warriors of Kush appeared, the whole forming a spectacle never before seen on the steppes of Kush.

When she could find her breath, finally Ashtarta turned to the west and waved a yellow handkerchief high over her head. In the distance, the tiny figure of a lookout raised an arm in answer. Then the Candace turned to her generals and said, "Oh? And did you think to shame your Queen, who alone seems to have come home empty-handed? Well, you are mistaken!"

For now there came the cry of horsemen and the sharp crack of whips; and Khai, at first dumbfounded but in another moment beside himself with savage joy, roared and laughed and shook his fists in the air as a thousand, two thousand chariots came speeding up out of the west, their spoked wheels a blur in the sunlight as they thundered in a tight, trained formation across the steppes.

But it was enough, too much for one day. Khai would not upstage Ashtarta but would wait until later before showing her his ten thousand swords of iron. Yes, later. . . . First, he would show them to the Candace, and then—then by all the devils of hell—*then* he would show them to Khasathut!

# VI

## KHAI AND THE CANDACE

Long into that night Ashtarta, her generals and chiefs, talked and planned around the old table in the great hall of her house. The seven mages were there too, having come out of the southwest together a little after the reuniting of the tribes. Shortly after midnight, when all plans were laid—at least in broad outline—when the meats were eaten and the wine jars half-emptied, then there came a wind from outside that found its way into and whined through the great hall. It set all the lamps sputtering, that wind, as well it might; for its breath was nearly as warm as that of the man-made fires. This was the *Khamsín,* the scorpion wind from the western deserts legended to lie beyond Hyrksos, which stirred the blood of men as other great winds stir oceans to their bidding.

At its coming, the seven mages nodded and smiled their knowing smiles, then muttered together where they sat apart, and Ashtarta saw them. Since all business was done and the chiefs were now content to growl, thump tables and mull over old times together, she made to leave the hall. On her way out and escorted at a discreet distance by her straight-faced, near awesome Nubians, whose weapons were long-handled hard-wood clubs of great weight and thickness, she paused by the seven mages and asked:

"And is the *Khamsín* your doing also? I think not, for this is its season—or have you merely hastened it by a day or two? And if so, for what reason?"

"We have not hastened it, Ashtarta, O Candace," the whispering yellow mage answered. "Though certainly it was a good idea and fits well with your proposals for war. Six days from now, when your warriors ride on Khem, the *Khamsín* will have left firm footing for them, where only the deepest and most persistent marshes shall bog them down. No, we have not done it—other hands have stirred the pot this time. . . ."

By now the sounds of boasting and tales of skill and battles bold were tumultuous in the hall as the chiefs and their aides set about to finish off the last of the wine. The hot wind no longer howled outside, had dropped its heat like a fiery blanket over Nam-Khum and seemed to be saving its breath for the bigger blow to come, when it would move east into the valley of the Nile. Ashtarta looked about her at the great hall, stripped bare of its furnishings three-and-a-half years gone and not yet put to rights, then returned her attention to the mages.

Unheard by the others in the room, she asked: "If not your hands, then whose?"

"Pharaoh's Dark Heptad, Majesty. Khasathut needs the *Khamsín* more than we do, who in the space of only fourteen days plans to hurl three hundred thousand of his finest soldiers into Siwad and Nubia!"

"But then he'll surely win!" she gasped. "For without the Generals Khai and Manek, how can—"

"No, O Candace," the yellow mage shook his head and smiled. "It will not come to that. Pharaoh merely poises his spear; he has not yet thrown it. Nor shall he, for before then the armies of Kush shall strike across the swamps and savannahs, and the forces of Khem will turn to face them, trapped between them and the nations they sought to destroy."

"You did not say this before," Ashtarta accused, "and it is not quite in accordance with the plans we made tonight."

"We did not know before, Majesty. It was the *Khamsín's* coming which told us, who have learned to commune with the elements. As for the plans: they were good and need not be altered."

"But three hundred thousand Khemish soldiers," she whispered, almost to herself.

"More than that, O Candace, for even now mercenaries pour into Khem in droves fresh from Therae and Arabba."

For a moment she was silent, then asked: "Can we win this war?"

"Yes, Majesty, we can," the yellow mage told her. "It is not the winning, however, but the time taken in the winning. We will use what powers we may in your aid, of course—but Pharaoh's Dark Heptad also have powers, and they work for him. If Kush is victorious, and when Pharaoh sees that he is beaten—he might yet call up forces which no man, not even a God-king, can control."

She looked at the seven and said, "You have not eased my mind."

"That would be easy, Ashtarta—but the truth is always harder."

As she turned to go, the yellow mage added: "It would be unwise to worry greatly, O Candace, for tomorrow and the next day and the days to follow, they shall come, no matter how you or I say or do."

She nodded and left, and her Nubians also nodded gravely as they followed her from the hall.

That night Ashtarta dreamed of Khai, as she had dreamed of him often enough, but this time the heat of the *Khamsín* was in her dream. When she awoke with a cry, a handmaiden was by her side, but when the Candace saw who it was—only a girl and not the figure of her dream—she sent her away with words which were unjustly harsh. She knew now, however, that it was time she paid her debt to the Khemite. With him so near, it was hard to concentrate on . . . on anything! Better to act shamelessly and put the matter behind her one way or the other, than to let it drag on.

If he would not come to her, then she must go to him, but it must be done carefully. She did not want the General Manek to know of her feelings for Khai, not before the fight with Khem. Something told her it could only cause bad blood between them. And so, though she hated it, she knew she must be secretive. She tossed in her bed a long time before returning to sleep, and though she could not know it, she was not alone in her restlessness. Khai, too, lay in a sweat and wide awake. But as for Manek Thotak: his was the sleep of a baby.

In the morning the *Khamsín* blew again, not furiously but with such heat that the very air burned the throats of them that breathed it, so that Ashtarta was glad to stay in the cool shade of her house. As for Khai and Manek: they were out on the steppes where, for all the *Khamsín's* furnace breath, they practiced the arts of the charioteer. In the afternoon, the wind died away and the heat seemed to lift a little, and Ashtarta went to find the General Manek, ostensibly to talk of the plans they had made the previous night and tell him of the words of the seven mages. In fact, she went to see him so that later she might see Khai.

She found Manek in his army's camp—half-deserted now that the married men had gone off with their wives to establish themselves once more in their villages and settlements, from which they must soon return to ready themselves for war—and spent an hour with him deep in conversation. It was a valiant effort on Ashtarta's part, but her heart was not in it. She could only think of Khai.

Finally, unable to keep up the pretext a moment longer and knowing that she must soon give herself away, she told Manek that she would now find Khai and tell him also of the words of the mages. Her Nubians sat her in her litter and took her straight to Khai's encampment, where she learned that he had gone off to bathe in a mountain pool. Now she knew where Khai was, for there was a favorite place where he had used to swim, where the water lay cool and deep over a bed of rounded pebbles.

She took the senior man of her eight with her and drove her chariot in a southwesterly direction for a distance of some four miles, until she came to the spot beneath a rocky outcrop where a spring filled the pool and fed a tinkling stream. Sure enough, there in the shade of the rocks, she found a chariot and pair, tethered where the ponies could crop lush grass. Dismounting, she told her man to go and tell Khai that she had come to speak with him, and that he should now robe himself to receive her. After a few minutes, the black returned and reported that the General Khai awaited her.

She found him seated on a flat boulder by the side of the pool. Trees grew over him and the sun, striking through their branches, dappled his face with its light. He rose as she approached, but she indicated that he should sit. She stepped up onto the rock beside him and threw down a square of linen, seating herself not too close and facing slightly away from him. After a little while, she said:

"Khai, I—"

"Yes, Majesty?"

"I—I want to tell you what the seven mages told me, about the *Khamsín*."

"It will dry out the land," Khai answered, almost unconsciously. "That's what Khasathut wants for his soldiers—but it's also what we want for our chariots. With the chariots and our iron swords, we'll cut them to pieces."

"That is what they say, yes," she breathlessly answered. "Also that we should first strike in the Siwadi- and Nubia-Khem borderlands. This will mean that—"

"That Pharaoh's troops, where they gather to hurl themselves against Nubia and Siwad, will turn to face us, trapping themselves between the—"

"Have the mages already spoken to you?" she suddenly snapped.

"No, Candace," he turned surprised eyes on her. "But it seems obvious to me that—"

"Oh, Khai," she cut him off again, the words sighing from her, almost pleading. "If you are so wise and if so many things are obvious to you, why is it you have not seen the most obvious thing of all?"

"Queen, I—" he looked puzzled, uncomprehending, and his slowness angered her.

She jumped to her feet and he rose with her. "I remember a time when there was fire in you," she snapped, stinging him with her words. "You were a man even as a boy, even as . . . as a Khemite!"

She made to step down from the rock, but her foot slipped and she would have fallen if he had not caught and steadied her. His hands were by no means as gentle as they might have been and she saw anger stamped on his face. His skin was tight with it and his eyes glittered like hard mountain ice.

"You forget yourself, Queen," he said, his voice harsh. "You can remember when there was fire in me, can you?" He nodded. "Well, and I remember when you were a spoiled brat, but now you are Candace of all Kush! How have I offended you?"

"Spoiled brat?" she raged. "Offended me? Let me go—let me go at once!"

"Damn it—" he said, astonished by her rapid mood changes, "I'm not holding you!" It was true, for he had released her as soon as she was steady. But now it was like one of his dreams of old. It had all happened before—or was yet to happen, he knew not which—but suddenly he knew what he must do, what he must say.

"I should strip you naked as the day I first saw you," he snarled, catching her hands so that she could not strike him. "I should throw you down on this rock and have you right here, now!"

"What?" she whispered, her eyes wide and amazed. "How dare—"

"What will you give me," he pressed on, half-afraid that his dream might betray him, "if I free you?"

But now she, too, was caught up in the dream. He *knew* what her next words would be, but even so breathed a sigh of relief when she voiced them:

"I'll give you . . . anything."

"Then give me that," he said, "which they would have stolen from you!"

In a voice which she no longer recognized as her own, she answered: "One day, you strange, blue-eyed boy, I might just keep that promise of mine—" And he let go of her hands as she threw them round his neck and sought his mouth with hers.

She could feel him against her, feel the core of him straining for her, and she gasped as their mouths filled with blood from the sheer ferocity of their kiss. His hands had slid down her back, were drawing her irresistibly to him. Her long nails went through the damp linen of his shirt and into his back. She tore his flesh and squirmed against him, unable to get close enough. Then—

"No!" she fought free of him. "No, Khai. Not here, not now."

"Last night," he gasped, holding out his arms to her, "I didn't sleep. To-night I won't even try! When, Ashtarta? When?"

"When?" she stepped down, almost fell from the rock. She was flushed, lost for words, and her limbs trembled like the wings of a trapped bird. She turned and ran back the way she had come.

"Sh'tarra!" he called after her, his voice a groan of desperation. "When?"

She looked back. "When we camp beneath the Gilf Kebir," she panted, "the night before you strike at Khem. Then and not before. You must not even see me. Will you come to me then, Khai, to my room of purple walls? Will you come, unseen in the night, like a thief, to the one who loves you?"

"Whenever," he moaned, his voice a rattle in his dust-dry throat. "Wherever. To the very gates of hell, if you call me. . . .

"Sh'tarra?" But she was gone.

# part
# NINE

# I

# THE IRON
# INVADERS

Time passed all too slowly for Khai from then onward, until at last the day arrived when the armies of Kush were camped below the looming escarpment of the Gilf Kebir. But all talking was done by then and all plans finally sealed and approved. The seven mages were gone up into the plateau-lands, but they had left this promise behind them: that in the battles to come, they would be close, and that when they were needed, then they would come. This had been the seven at their cryptic best, and while Ashtarta's generals had not understood their meaning—not then—still they had found some comfort in their words.

On the evening before the onslaught commenced, Khai found a quiet pool and washed away all of his worries and tensions as he swam in its cool depths. The *Khamsín* was gone now, flown down into Khem on furnace wings, but in its wake it had left a heat that came at you from all sides, down from the sky and up from the earth beneath, until the blood seemed to boil in your veins. Khai's blood boiled . . . but not alone from the heat. Not from any sort of heat which might be felt upon the skin or on the soles of the feet. . . .

By the time night was setting in he had returned to camp, and in his tent he found Imthra waiting for him. The old wizard had simply sought him out to speak with him of nothing important, for they were old friends now and there had been little enough time for talking since the reuniting of the tribes. So

Khai relaxed and they talked and drank a little wine, and the night grew very dark as stars began burning like diamonds in the sky. Then Imthra sensed Khai's impatience. Believing that the general desired his bed, the old man bade him good night and left him. Khai waited a few minutes more then slipped out under the rear wall of his tent and made his way in darkness to the outskirts of the camp.

He hurried through shrubs and tall grasses to where he knew Ashtarta's tent stood apart from the camp and backed onto the towering wall of the Gilf. Every sense alert—how had she put it? "Like a thief in the night,"—he approached her huge tent of poles and fine linens and made to slip between its rear wall and the face of the cliff behind it. Before he could take a single step into the gap, however, coming out of nowhere and pinning him to the wall of rock, a massive black fist caught hold of his neck. He sensed rather than saw the huge club held over his head and barely managed to choke out: "Hold, man—it's me, Khai!"

The grip on his throat relaxed and the huge black man lowered his face to Khai's own and sniffed at him. "The General Khai!" an amazed voice rumbled. "Why, I—"

"*Shh!*" hissed Khai, rubbing his throat. "Well done. I can see now how well you guard the Candace—only please be quiet!"

"The General sees poorly in the night," answered the black guardsman, "for the door to the tent of the Candace is on the other side. Come, Lord, and I will show you. . . ."

"No," Khai breathlessly answered, taking the other's huge arm in the darkness. "I . . . I do not wish to enter that way."

For a long moment, there was silence and the mighty Nubian guardsman peered closely at Khai. Then the starlight caught his teeth and framed them in a huge grin, and Khai frowned as he asked: "Oh, and do you laugh at Khai the Killer?"

"No, Lord," the black quit his grinning. "My thoughts were wandering— to when I courted the girls back home."

"Yes," said Khai sternly, "but I did not desire to be seen and you have seen me."

"Lord, I have not seen you," the guardsman turned away. "I have neither seen nor heard you. You are a shadow in the night."

"Good," said Khai. He turned back to the gap between the tent and the cliff, but again the Nubian caught him.

"Lord?"

"Yes?"

"Should I also be deaf and blind if my mistress calls out in the night?"

"She will not," answered Khai. "Now get to your duty." And in another moment the guardsman had melted with the shadows and was gone. But Khai could swear that he heard the man's chuckle. . . .

Then . . . it was Khai's dream all over again, that recurrent dream of his which seemed to have lasted through several lifetimes, except that this time there was no interruption. All else was exactly as it had been: the sandy floor (for the tent stood on the bed of an old stream which long ago had brought down centuries of sand from the heights), the chest of jewels (which Manek had brought out of Siwad, and which—if things did not go according to plan—Ashtarta would use as ransom money to buy the freedom of her commanders), even the color of the linen walls of the Queen's bedchamber, which was purple.

As for the Candace: she of course was unaware of Khai's dream; so that when the time came for her to open her body to him she could not understand the curse that escaped his lips, the gritting of his teeth, the way his face twisted in sudden agony—and his sigh of relief when he realized that the time had come and gone and still there had not been that sudden alarm, that nerve wrenching blast of sound which invariably destroyed the dream at this point.

For it was no longer a dream, it was real, and at last Khai felt that he was a whole, complete person. Time and space and the voids between had come together for him in the here and now. Dreams and fancies were suddenly one with reality, a huge puzzle snapping together, and the universe closed in on Khai and his Candace and took them to its bosom. . . .

. . . In the morning, as the sun came up and turned the eastern horizon to mist-haze, evaporating the last of the moisture from the land between Kush and Khem, the wheels of war began to turn against Pharaoh. Rumbling down from the foothills and onto the early morning savannahs, the chariots and carts and armored horsemen were splendid in their color, their eager ferocity, their relish of the battles to come.

Khai drove north—for Manek had not much cared to return to Siwad's borders, and likewise Khai had had more than enough of Nubia's jungles—and Manek drove south. The chief Genduhr Shebbithon, now a general in his own right, drove east for the Khemish fort at Pethos; and thus Ashtarta's army was split into three parts.

Khai took the forts in Kuragh and Ghira in his stride and rushed on north, skirting the edge of the western swamp and heading for Tanos and the forest-land which led to the Nile. Manek took the Afallah fort and wiped out a large body of Khemites west of Peh-il, then rushed into Nubia to reinforce N'jakka's black legions and slaughter Pharaoh's forces where once more they had crossed the river. In little more than a week, all of Khem's armies had turned from their preparations for full-scale assaults on Nubia and Siwad to form a front against Kush which reached from Mylah-Ton in the north to Subon in the south. West of the river, the Khemites camped in their thousands; and in Asorbes, where the Dark Heptad had now been ordered from their interminable task of seeking immortality for Khasathut to more pressing matters, Pharaoh pondered how best to employ them.

He knew now that his soldiers could not stand against the iron swords of Kush, and the chariots of the Kushites were terrible machines whose like had never before been seen in that ancient world. Sheer weight of numbers no longer mattered, for the new weapons of the Kushites made a mockery of all the old concepts of war. And this was where the Dark Heptad came into its own, for the Heptad's concepts of war were also radically different—as Kush was soon to discover.

Another week passed in which Ashtarta's armies consolidated their positions, took stock of the territories they had occupied, and deployed in regiments in the forests between the swamps and along the edge of the savannahs east of Daraaf. Nubia and Siwad were well in control of their own territories now and poised to strike when Kush struck; but Pharaoh had not been idle. Ferries had shifted thousands of mercenaries and hastily enlisted youths across the river along a vast front, and these now formed new regiments west of Asorbes, facing the distant camps of the Kushites.

But for all Khem's might (her armies still outnumbered those of Kush and her allies by more than three to one), Khasathut knew that the actual strengths of his own and Ashtarta's forces were evenly balanced, that Kush's weapons had robbed him of his advantage. Hence the hurried intervention of the Dark Heptad. The first weapon those devotees of darkness chose from their arsenal of occult devices was common enough along the banks of the Nile: it was the rat, whose numbers were greater than the armies of Kush and Khem put together.

# WIZARDS AT WAR

Pharaoh's black magicians worked quickly and surely, for their new task was more to their liking and well within their capability. "Destroy Kush!" Pharaoh had ordered: "Wipe the Kushites out— Nubia, too—and Siwad! Do what you must, but destroy them. Destroy their armies—and bring their leaders, any that survive, to me!"

If this had been Pharaoh's wish seven years earlier, then had it been carried out at once; but that would have been to deny him his source of slaves, the raw materials of his pyramid-building, the base upon which his empire was to be constructed. What use to be a ruler of empty lands? Now, however, it was far better to rule empty, destroyed lands than to relinquish sovereignty altogether. To relinquish life itself, before that life was fulfilled, before its ambitions were realized. Now the destruction of his enemies was necessary, essential to his own existence.

So the Dark Heptad invoked the Powers of Darkness and were advised, and accepting that advice, they recruited creatures of darkness to their cause. . . .

Khai had taken Tanos two days ago. Now his army camped in the forest between Tanos and Mylah-Ton, on the edge of swamps which were more desiccated than ever before they had been. The *Khamsín* lay over the Nile, where a great curtain of dust hung in the eastern sky and darkened the heavens, but the signs of its passing were right here in the forest: yellow grasses and shrubs, trees whose branches and leaves drooped and were utterly dry to the touch.

It was night and Khai lay in his small tent and slept, getting his rest as best he might. Tomorrow he planned to advance on Mylah-Ton, and the day after that he intended to take it. His sleep was restless, however, and not alone from the heat which found its way here from the heart of Khem. No, for a dream kept coming and going, formless as a wraith, so that Khai tossed on his rough bed and sweated in a darkness lighted only by a small hanging fire-pot. Eventually, as the dream took firmer hold on him, he submitted to its spell and so gave it form.

. . . He stood beneath the stars on a hill in Kush with the Mage of Oneiromancy—the keen-eyed brown mage from Daraaf—and with Genduhr Shebbithon and Manek Thotak. Together they stood and looked eastward, toward Khem.

"You fought me, Khai," said the brown mage, "with a will whose like I have rarely known. Did you not sense it was I, who not only read dreams but occasionally use them in other ways? No matter, for now you are here and I have a warning for you."

"A warning?" Khai repeated.

"Aye, and it is this: that Pharaoh's Dark Heptad have brought a monstrous ally against you, and that even now ten million feet race toward you in the night!"

"Ten million?" Khai gasped in his dream. "There are not so many fighting men in all Khem, Arabba and Therae together!"

"Men, no," answered the brown mage. "Rats, yes!"

"Rats?" Genduhr Shebbithon growled. "Rats?"

"Rats, yes—bearing a plague brought up from the depths of hell—for whomever these rats bite, he shall die on the spot, consumed, gone down in liquid corruption!"

"When, where will they strike, these rats?" Manek asked, hand on sword hilt.

"They come now," answered the mage, "from the Nile. You must get up at once, all of you, and build fires—a wall of fires from the north to south, wherever your men are camped—to drive the rats back whence they came."

"Fire?" Khai frowned. "But what of the wind? What little wind there is this night, it blows outward from Khem!"

"Faith, Khai," the brown mage answered with a smile. "Have faith. Trust in the Mage of Elementalism, who sends a wind even now from the hills of Kush."

Even as he spoke, the hill on which they all stood seemed to whirl beneath Khai's feet, to dwindle, shrink away; or else he himself was lifted up in a giant's hand and borne swiftly aloft . . . to be dumped down on his bed in a tent in the forest.

He awoke with a cry in the night, stumbled from his tent shouting hoarse-voiced orders, roused up his men in a frenzy as he rushed from tent to tent and sent other messengers to do his bidding. Then, east of the camp, he himself set the first fire, and as the forest began to blaze, so there came the first stirrings of a wind from the west, a mournful wind that played with the leaping flames and blew them north and south, set them jumping from tree to tree until Khai and his army drew back in fear. Then, as the wind strengthened, it hurled the fire eastward in a blaze that lighted up the land with a light bright as day.

And it was then that Khai saw the rats and knew that his actions had been just in time. The rats were there, in the fire, blazing as they came through the inferno, flashing into flame as they tried to breach the burning barrier and get at the men where they stood unharmed behind the fiery wall. Some did get through, driven on by the magic of the Dark Heptad, but very few. Bundles of smouldering fur they were, scampering and shrieking, and when they bit—

Khai stood near a man thus bitten, saw him crush the life from the smoking rat before he fell—then saw the flesh melt and slough from his body and the bones come through as all else turned to stinking rot!

"Kill them!" he roared then, snarling his fear and horror. "Kill any rats that break through, but don't let them bite you!"

The tale was retold in the hills west of Asorbes, where Genduhr Shebbithon sent fire roaring eastward to destroy the gray horde that rushed squealing out from the heart of Khem; and on the savannahs north of the Nubian forests where Manek was now camped; so that the morning sun rose on a scene of black, smouldering desolation. In the north, along a front eighty miles long, it was as if a mighty architect had drawn a straight line—to the east of which, even to the banks of the Nile, all was blackened earth. Likewise in the south, where morning found Manek Thotak gazing east across a wasteland of ashes. In Peh-il, the Khemites had seen the fire coming, had made fire-breaks and flooded irrigation ditches, and by some miracle, they had survived both the furnace and the surviving, fleeing rats; but all else was burned. West of Asorbes itself only the swamps had stopped the blaze, but even the swamps were now little more than vast beds of cracked and dried-out mud.

And so the seven mages overcame the black magic of Pharaoh's Dark Heptad . . . for the time being.

As Khai drove on Mylah-Ton—which only the surrounding swamps had saved from the inferno—and as his chariots and men cut a giant swathe through ashes of wasted forests all along the borders of dead swamps, so the

Siwadis crossed the river below the delta and headed east into Syra. The Syrans, themselves oppressed for generations without number, took up arms and joined them, pushing southeast for Arabba.

In the south, Manek Thotak took Peh-il and turned north along the river, while to the east of the Nile, N'jakka's *impis* marched on Phemor. The Theraens—in the main, a cowardly folk—had already retreated into their hills above the Narrow Sea, for they had sensed that Khem's days were numbered and they wanted no more of liaisons or friendships with Pharaoh. And eighty miles west of Asorbes, Genduhr Shebbithon camped his forces in a vast semicircle at the foot of the hills and gazed east in the direction of Khasathut's capital. There, like a great cat lying in wait, he licked his lips in dreadful anticipation.

Ohath fell to Khai and he crossed the river to take Bena, and wherever Khem's soldiers were found, they fell in their thousands; and those who did not desert Khem and flee before the iron invaders were driven back to their country's heart-land. Eight days after the Great Fires, Phemor fell to the Nubians and Pharaoh was now ringed in by the enemy's forces. Even then he could have fled east—but where to? The Narrow Sea would eventually stop him, and then he would be trapped between the water and the pursuing tribes of Kush. No, it would be a better plan to remain here and defend Asorbes, which was thought to be impregnable as the east-facing wall of the Gilf Kebir itself.

Moreover, there had been signs. Signs which told Khasathut he should remain at Asorbes. Shortly after the attack of the Kushites there had been green horizons at dawn and orange horizons at night, and the legends said that just such twilights had been seen before the advent of the God-peoples from the skies. Also, the Dark Heptad had warned that their supernatural experiments were taking them very close to the Great Source of all Knowledge, which was also the source of all evil. They might yet give Khasathut the immortality he so avidly desired, and in so doing, give him ultimate power over all men and creatures. The price, as he understood it, would be the Sanity of the Universe, but to Pharaoh that seemed a very small price indeed. . . .

And so, with Khasathut's blessing, the Dark Heptad continued with their occult experiments and plotted second and third terrors to hurl against the encroaching Kushites; and the more they worked their dark wonders, the easier it became to commune with the Powers of Evil, the closer those Powers drew to them in their gloomy chamber beneath the great pyramid.

As for Pharaoh: he was in a constant rage and continually issued threats against anyone who strayed too close to him. Anulep now spent all of his time placating, pleading and promising, and in hurrying about his master's business: either conveying Khasathut's commands or inquiries to his Dark Heptad or his military commanders, or carrying their answers or tremulous excuses back to the God-king.

And so things stood when, not thirty miles away, the General Khai Ibizin took Wad-Gahar above the cataract. . . .

# III

# THE WINGED LEGIONS

Wad-Gahar. . . .

The name struck a chord in Khai's memory, but the note was elusive and soon forgotten in the face of more important things. The taking of Wad-Gahar was easy, for Pharaoh's regular forces had been drawn back into a circle about Asorbes and they had left the protection of the town to ten thousand Theraen mercenaries. These had literally "occupied" the town, for being what they were Wad-Gahar's rightful inhabitants had been more at their mercy than under their protection.

Their "protection," indeed—the protection of Theraens!

Khai killed every last one of them, though that meant digging half of them out from their hiding-holes. And when the old people of the town (for there were only very old people and very young children left) saw that the Kushites would do them no harm, they very soon began to show the invaders just exactly where the mercenaries were hiding.

No treachery this, but vengeance! In the two days since the Khemish regiments had fallen back into defensive positions about Asorbes, the mercenaries had looted everything worth taking and raped even tiny children. Seeing their danger, the townspeople had kept them drunk most of the time, which accounted in large measure for the ease with which Wad-Gahar fell to Khai's warriors. Toward evening, it was all over and the general issued strict orders that the ordinary folk were not to suffer any further molestation at Kushite hands. There was little worth the taking in the ravished town and its people had already lost more than enough.

As Khai watched the townspeople building huge funeral pyres for the dead, his attention was called to evidence of several Theraen atrocities. One of these had been a local brothel, where the women had been beaten and raped repeatedly, even unto death. Arriving on the scene, he found a number of drunken Theraens asleep in various rooms where they were previously over-looked. Each of them he roughly awakened, then personally put to the sword.

Passing out of the place into evening air which already stank of burning flesh, he caught sight of a still mop of crinkly raven hair just inside the door. It was the head of a woman whose body lay with a number of other corpses, still and stiff. A tremble ran through Khai's massive frame then and he leaned weakly against the brothel's wall. Now he knew why the name of Wad-Gahar had struck that chord in his mind.

Kindu and Nundi were with him—those dear friends of his out of Nubia, whose very lives were his—and now Kindu said: "Lord, something ails you."

He nodded. "Aye, possibly. There is a woman in there. She is not black, not quite white, and her hair is much like yours. Bring her out here in the light, for I think I know her."

In a moment, the woman's body lay upon a blanket for Khai's inspection. Her eyes were closed forever now, but they were slanted and had known much laughter. Long-legged and dusky, she was that Mhyna whom Khai had known so long ago. Her own dagger protruded from her breast, with her own hand clenched tight about its hilt.

Khai washed her face and cradled her head and said nothing for a long time. His men left him sitting there and went about their work. As darkness crept in Khai looked up, his eyes dull with unspilled tears. His Nubian lieutenants fol-lowed him as he carried the woman down to the wharfside and laid her in the finest barge he could find. Then he poured oil on the reed decks and cast off the mooring rope. As the barge moved out into the river, he took a brand and tossed it aboard, then watched Mhyna's pyre pass down the river into the night.

That night, Khai camped just south of Wad-Gahar, and the next day saw him ferrying his army across to the west bank. This was not such a giant task as might be imagined, since less than half of his men had crossed with him at Ohath. Now, too, his carts and chariots were brought up and prepared for the final stages of the war—which were to be the siege and eventually the taking of Asorbes. It was late afternoon when the last barge came across, and in the final hour before twilight a hush fell over the river and its banks which was quite unlike anything Khai had ever known before.

There seemed to be a premature darkness to the sky, and not in the east but to the south. Yes, the sky over Asorbes was dark—and it was moving!

Khai was one of the first to note the phenomenon. Standing on the bank of the river and watching the darkly mobile mass of sky to the south, suddenly a dizziness came over him that caused him to stagger. Shading his eyes, he leaned against a palm and continued to watch the sky; and as he did so the giddiness came again and he would have fallen. Now, wrapping his arms round the bole of the palm to support himself, he closed his eyes tightly and felt his gorge rising. Then—

*"Khai,"* an echoing voice said in his head, *"do not be afraid, but listen to me. I am the Mage of Mentalism, whose powers were learned as a youth in Syra from an old magician out of the east. I have sought you out to bring you a second warning."*

Khai shook his head and looked wildly about. It was one thing to dream of warnings and such—even to know that such dreams were the work of the seven mages in Kush—but it was quite another to be visited in broad daylight! Shaking his head only made him feel more sick, however, so that he soon desisted and again closed his eyes; at which the voice in his head became much more insistent:

*"Do not fight me, Khai, for time is short. My message goes also to Manek Thotak and to Genduhr Shebbithon. Manek hears me and may save himself. Genduhr will not listen—and he is a dead man!"*

And now Khai recognized the urgency in the soundless voice and knew that this was no trick of his mind. "Very well," he said out loud, "say on."

*"Birds and bats and insects, Khai, flies and locusts and wasps. They will devour all that is green, everything that moves. And we seven mages have no power over these, which are not of the elements. The Dark Heptad makes dangerous magics indeed!"*

"Are you saying that we're doomed?" Khai asked, aghast.

*"All that is green—all that moves!"* the mage's voice repeated, more faintly, echoing as down a long, long tunnel. The giddiness passed and Khai opened his eyes. Now, too, the sounds of his men broke in on his consciousness, their cries of awe as they pointed south and skyward.

For the sky was alive with a great black blot of a cloud that shut out the light even as it descended like a mighty blanket out of heaven. The men began to panic; horses reared and stamped; the heaviness of the air became oppressive, and fear was a living thing which tittered and ran through Khai's warriors tapping each man lightly on the shoulder.

"Listen to me," Khai roared above the sudden moaning of his men. "Blindfold the horses. Do it now, and quickly! Let them see nothing. Then, when the horde descends, stand still. Remain still if it lasts all night. If you are stung, do not jump. If you are bitten, do not cry out. This is the word of the seven mages. If you would live—obey!"

His words spread like wildfire through the massed thousands. Blankets were brought out and thrown over hurriedly blindfolded horses; men covered themselves as best they might and sought shelter beneath carts or in the buckets of chariots; for minutes which sped by quick as seconds the army was a scurrying shouting mass of humanity. And the sky grew dark before its time and the air began to hum with a vast stirring of wings.

*"Don't move!"* Khai yelled one last time, and his cry was taken up and passed on echoingly in the leaden air. Then he crouched at the base of his palm and covered his head. Nundi, running up to him, threw a horse blanket over him and crouched down with him inside its folds. In another moment the roar of millions of wings blotted out all else and beneath the blanket it grew suddenly black as night.

*Things* landed on the blanket, many *things,* large and small, until their weight became intolerable. "Don't move," Khai hissed in Nundi's ear. "Not an inch!"

Then, after a matter of a few moments there came a sound like the trampling of feet, a crunching and sloshing as of an army marching over swampy ground. Amazed and horrified, Khai listened for a second or two, then said: "By all the many gods *they're eating!*"

Somewhere a horse screamed, a cry of dreadful fear, of agony. There was a commotion, a wild burst of animal movement, a frenzied whinnying and then another scream—but this time human! Nundi jerked in shock when he heard that hideous, fear-frenzied shriek, and jerked again and began to tremble violently when the scream subsided to a suffocated gabbling which was snuffed out beneath a vast whirring of wings and a more noisy *recommencement* of the feeding sound.

Khai's hand found Nundi's throat and he whispered: "Nundi—be quiet, keep still—or by your teeth you'll remember why I'm called Khai the Killer!" After that the Nubian grew silent and motionless.

For an hour or more, they crouched like that, until Khai was sure his joints were coming apart and his muscles liquifying. Throughout all of that time, the awful munching went on, and occasionally—sometimes close by, at other times more distant—there would be the screams of a stricken horse, or the nerve-wrenching shrieking of a man in mortal agony. And just as Khai was beginning to believe that he could endure it no longer, then the weight lifted from his blanket and in an instant the sound of millions of wings again filled the air. The intolerable whirring went on for a minute, two, then slowly receded and died away in the distance.

Many more minutes passed in total silence before Khai moved the blanket a fraction and breathed fresh night air through the gap he had made. With arms that creaked like those of an old man he pulled the blanket aside and peered at stars overhead. A thick white mist lay on the river. Silence lay everywhere.

"Get up!" Khai hoarsely shouted, clambering stiffly to his feet. "Light fires, many fires." His cry was taken up and passed on, and all about him the night stirred as his army came back to life. Nundi stamped about in darkness, pumping blood to legs which no longer had any feeling. There was a vast clearing of lungs, a drawing of air, a concerted sighing of utmost relief.

Close by, Khai found the skeleton of a horse, its bones dry and clean. The white bones of a man, his arm about the horse's neck, lay intermingled with those of the animal. Moonlight glittered on the remains in their stark whiteness. . . .

One of Khai's men, drawing close, grasped his elbow and made him jump. "Lord Khai," the man said in a whisper. "Of what shall we build the fires?"

"Of branches, fool!" Khai snapped, his nerves twanging.

"Branches, Lord?"

"Aye, branches and leaves and—" his words tailed off and he looked all about him into the night. And at that moment Khai knew himself for a very small thing in a very large and largely unknown universe.

"What branches, Lord?" inquired the man. . . .

# IV

## SIEGE ON ASORBES

In the morning, Khai saw the full extent of the horror: where for miles about not a leaf, not a blade of grass, nothing showed green at all, and only the largest branches, stripped even of their bark, remained attached and uneaten on the chewed and pitted trunks of the trees. He could see through the forest of naked, motionless timber for hundreds of yards; and the very soil beneath his feet, inches deep, was powdery, dry and void of life. No foliage showed on the banks of the Nile, no weeds, no fringing ferns or nodding papyrus reeds. A huge ribbon of water, unobstructed as far as the eye could see, the river curled away into the north; while in the south it rolled down silently, no longer green but gray, from mist-shrouded Asorbes.

Asorbes. . . .

Khai gritted his teeth with bitter rage as he thought of Asorbes, of Pharaoh, of Anulep and the Black Guard, and of Khasathut's Dark Heptad of necromancers. He wondered how Manek Thotak had fared: whether or not the plague of flying death had also found him in the twilight. And what of Genduhr Shebbithon?

Manek had received and reacted to the Syran mage's warning in much the same way as had Khai, and thus his losses were relatively few. Genduhr Shebbithon, on the other hand, had thought himself the victim of an encroaching madness. A simple man, however great a chief, his reaction had been violent and had taken the form of a fit. His men had seen him rushing to and fro with his sword, cutting at thin air, at phantoms! Those phantoms had become all too real all too soon, however—but far too late for Genduhr Shebbithon.

As fortune had it, ten thousand of his men were away from the main camp at the time, engaging a probing force of Khemites between Phemor and Asorbes. This had left twenty-five thousand warriors in the camp to face the twilight horror . . . which had caught them and Genduhr Shebbithon in the middle of his fit. The result was seen the next morning when ten thousand victorious Kushites returned to camp—to find a vast wasteland and an army of skeletal remains! Something less than two thousand horses had escaped the carnage, having fled out of the area of the aerial attack, but many of these had to be destroyed.

Of Genduhr's twenty-five thousand, however, only one man survived. He had been very drunk, wrapped in a blanket, asleep when the winged death descended. Now he was awake and sober, or as sober as his slobbering insanity would permit. A very young man, he simply sat among the tumult of bones and drooled, or occasionally laughed and shook his shock of pure white hair. . . .

Later that same day, riders arrived at the new camp of Genduhr's son, Gahad. They came from Generals Manek Thotak and Khai Ibizin, with orders to report back to their commanders with word of Genduhr's losses. Meanwhile, Khai had moved closer, poising his forces on the river less than five miles to the north of Asorbes, and Manek had deployed his army at a like distance to the south of the city. By mid-afternoon, the armies had taken up positions along a curving front which enclosed Asorbes in a huge semi-circle of iron, and Gahad Shebbithon's numbers had been supplemented by ten thousand of Khai's men and ten thousand more of Manek Thotak's. East of the river, having crossed the Nile north of Mer-ow-eh to cut through Khem's southern forests in a two-hundred mile push, N'jakka and five great *impis* lay in wait for any Khemites who might choose to flee to the east. And so at last, Asorbes lay under siege. . . .

It was as Manek Thotak went among his warriors where they were camped that he came across four huge Nubians known to him as one half of Ashtarta's eight-man guard, brought out of Nubia by Khai Ibizin. Ashtarta had kept the other four with her in Kush, but these men had begged to be allowed to go to war against Khem. Since Manek had been going into Nubia, the Candace had used the blacks as couriers to carry her pledge of friendship to N'jakka and to wish him well in the great war to come. Now Manek spoke to them, and when he would have passed on one of them followed after him and called:

"Lord Manek! Now that we are here in the heart of Khem, will your forces join with those of Khai the Killer?"

"In the final assault, aye," Manek answered. "Why do you ask?"

The huge black, a man of truly awesome dimensions, grinned his appreciation. "We have many friends among Khai's *impis*," he explained. "Soon we shall share with them stories of our battles."

"Aye," Manek grinned. "We Kushites do much the same thing."

*"Waugh!"* the black exclaimed. "The Lord Khai will have many marvelous tales to tell his children—when he is King of all Kush!"

The smile slipped from Manek's face in an instant. He took the Nubian's arm and stared at him. "Khai? King, did you say?"

"Ah! You need not pretend for my sake, Lord Manek," the black man whispered confidentially. "Since you are The Killer's brother-general, you must know well enough that he courts the Candace."

As best he could, Manek hid the sudden rage that threatened to suffuse his dark features. Somehow he managed to force a smile and answered: "Of course I know, certainly! But now . . . how do *you* know?"

"Why, have I not seen him myself, going to her tent in the night? Indeed I have—and not by the front door!"

"You saw him?" Manek continued to smile, his face frozen in a grin which was almost a grimace. "You saw him—and yet you did not stop him?"

"I guarded the Candace from her enemies, Lord," the black laughed, "but not from her lover!"

"Her lover. . . ." Manek slowly answered. "Yes, of course." Then he laughed a high, shaky laugh. "And I believed that I was Khai's only confidant. How mistaken I was! . . . But come, come you must tell me all about it," and he led the huge Nubian to a place where they could sit and talk in private. Which they did for quite a long time. . . .

Later that evening, the great gates of Asorbes opened and tens of thousands of Khemish troops and mercenaries moved out from the city for a mile or two and took up defensive positions within the greater circle of the besieging forces, which they outnumbered by at least two to one. Though the Kushite commanders kept a very wary eye upon them, the Khemites made no attempt to attack; so that it looked very much as though they were simply occupying the ground in order to retain it.

When all movement from the city had ceased and the gates were again closed, then the Dark Heptad brought their third occult device into use. This time it came without warning, and Khai was to learn much later why the seven mages had been unable to offer any assistance on this occasion: how the Dark Heptad had worked a spell to counter any possible intervention. As it happened, the new terror was not aimed directly at Khem's enemies, though certainly it must be effective in the long term.

At first it was thought that the *Khamsín* had returned, for a great draught of hot, bad air sprang up suddenly from the ground midway between the defending forces and Kush's encircling warriors and blew outwards in vile gusts that soon had strong men plugging their nostrils and retching horribly. After a little while, as evening drew on, the tomb-like fetor died away and the men in the Kushite lines breathed more easily and were less edgy. Then, just before twilight, the first effects of the Dark Heptad's injurious magic began to make themselves apparent.

As if the valley of the Nile had not already suffered more than enough, this latest terror seemed designed as one final, crippling blow at a once fertile land. It was a blight—but such a blight as never before had been dreamed of.

Slowly at first, but at an ever accelerating rate, the grasses, shrubs and trees where the foul wind had sprung up began to turn yellow and wither. The poison spread rapidly outward, so that the horses of the Kushites where they cropped green grass soon found themselves chewing on stuff which was dry and lifeless. Before nightfall, the trees were so desiccated that many began to snap off at their bases and topple into dust. Shrubs became powder at the merest touch and the very soil seemed turned to sand. As on both previous occasions, the total devastation could not be assessed until the following morning, but when at last the sun rose on Khem the next day—

A desolation of stumps, toppled boles and wind-blown weeds stretched farther than the eye could see, and the only remaining green land lay behind the Khemish positions and beneath the looming walls of the slave city. And not only the forests and grasslands had gone but the animals with them, so that Pharaoh's design was now clear as crystal. Working through the Dark Heptad of wizards, he had simply reversed the polarity of the siege!

Which is to say that *his* forces now occupied the only fit ground, and that the only decent supplies of food lay in Asorbes itself. His herds still grazed green pastures beneath the city's walls, and his soldiers still drank milk and ate meat and honey. But as for the Kushites: when their immediate supplies ran out, then they would have nothing!

It also meant that the siege could not go on as originally planned and that Asorbes must therefore be taken without delay. To this end, before noon, a horseman came and told Manek Thotak that the General Khai was coming to see him. Gahad Shebbithon would also be there, and they must all three make their new plans quickly and effect them without delay.

Manek had meanwhile done some planning of his own, and before Khai arrived, he went forward with a body of his men and called for a parley with the chief of the Khemish commanders. Long, earnestly—and privately— Manek and Pharaoh's general talked, in a small tent hastily erected on neutral ground, and when at last Manek returned to his own lines he found Khai waiting for him. Since Gahad Shebbithon had not yet arrived, Khai was alone when Manek went to his tent and found him there.

"Wasn't that a trifle dangerous?" Khai asked after they had clasped arms and exchanged greetings. "Your meeting with Pharaoh's general?"

"Dangerous? How so?" Manek returned. "There was an honorable Khemish commander, and there was me. We were not armed and I was bigger than he was. In what way dangerous?"

Khai shrugged. "It's just that you surprise me," he eventually answered. "Manek Thotak doing a little peaceful chatting with a 'damned Khemite'— and an 'honorable' one at that!"

Manek said to himself: *At least that one doesn't pretend to the throne of Kush,* but out loud he answered, "There's been enough innocent blood shed these past months."

Again, Khai seemed surprised. "Oh? And have you discovered a way to stop the bloodshed?"

"Aye," said Manek, "I believe so," and he paused.

"Well then," Khai prompted him, "say on."

"You may take exception to the scheme," Manek finally warned.

Khai was becoming impatient. "Get on with it, Manek, for you really are beginning to worry me."

"Well then, what would you say to this—" Manek began, and he quickly outlined all that had supposedly passed between himself and the Khemish commander. Except that every word of it was a lie—but the General Khai Ibizin had no way of knowing that. . . .

# V

# BLACK BARGAIN

"I find the thing incredible," Khai said when Manek was done.

"You say the Khemish soldiers are mutinous and that they demand a military takeover? And that when this is accomplished, they will open the gates and set free all of the slaves in Asorbes?"

Manek nodded. "Aye, that is part of it."

"And that then they will hand over Khasathut, Anulep, the Black Guard and the Dark Heptad to us?"

Again the other nodded.

"And what do they get out of all this?"

"They get their lives, and a better deal under their new ruler—Ashtarta!" Manek answered. "They get rid of Pharaoh, who they all fear desperately for his madness; and also of Anulep the Vizier, whose plotting has threatened all of them at one time or another. They see the end of the Dark Heptad of wizards, whose spells have reduced Khem— and for all we know of it Kush, too—to a wasteland! They will be spared the sack and destruction of their city, spared the inevitable slaughter of innocent thousands within Asorbes and they will once again rise to become a mighty nation—but under Ashtarta's rule, whose weapons shall make her new empire utterly unconquerable for all time to come. That is what they will get out of it. What more could they possibly ask?"

Khai frowned. "It all seems too good to be true. Are you sure they're not just playing for time while those damned necromancers of Pharaoh's work more hell's mischief?"

"Playing for time? No, for they desire to see you now, as soon as you are ready, to learn of your reactions to their plan. I can arrange a meeting in a moment, as easily as waving a yellow flag, which is the signal I've arranged. As you say, to waste time is simply to give the Dark Heptad an opportunity to make more magic. . . ."

"And you will come with me to speak to the Khemite commanders?" Khai asked, still uncertain.

"Of course."

*"Hah!"* Khai snorted. "And they will have us both together, caught like rats in a trap!"

The other sighed and Khai began to wonder if perhaps he was being over cautious. "My friend," Manek said, "even if that were so, still our armies can crush the Khemites without our assistance. There are chiefs enough, as you are well aware. What are we after all but two men? Besides, upon our acceptance to talk they have agreed to a withdrawal of their forces to the very walls of the city! We can ask no fairer than that."

For a long time, Khai was silent. He got up, went to the door of the tent and looked in the direction of the Khemish defenses. Night would be setting in soon and in an hour or so it would be dark. "If we agree to talk," Khai said, "when would this withdrawal take place?"

"It would begin at once. Also, Khai, we would go to the meeting-place in a chariot. In the event of any sort of treachery, why!—we'd be back among our own men before any Khemites could possibly reach us."

He went to stand beside Khai and gazed out upon the evening, unlovely now that the land all around looked like a corpse dead of some hideous plague. "Well, Khai," he said, "it seems to me we can have done with the thing at a stroke. What say you?"

"I say . . . that we wait until Gahad Shebbithon gets here before we drive out to this meeting-place. He should be here soon, for I spoke to him when I rode through his camp. Between now and then, let's see these Khemites draw back their lines, eh? Where's this flag you mentioned, this signal of acceptance?"

Half an hour later, Khai and Manek drove to a place forward of their front lines where the latter held up a spear draped with a large square of yellow linen. And there they waited as night came on, standing beside their chariot and watching the Khemites draw back under the walls of Asorbes. While they waited Gahad Shebbithon drove up, dismounted and greeted them. Gahad was a man of their own age, strong and capable, and they knew him well. They told him what was happening and instructed him, in the event of anything going wrong, what he must do: namely that he must call the chiefs together and consult with them, and thus decide the best way to deal with the situation.

As the first stars of night appeared, Khai and Manek then drove toward the ground so recently occupied by the Khemites. A lone tent stood just inside the circle of life which surrounded Asorbes, upon the only green grass untouched by the Dark Heptad's blight. Coming from the opposite direction, on foot, two figures in the garb of Khemish commanders arrived at the tent at the same time. Formal introductions were a little stiff, somewhat stilted, and Khai did not at all like the looks of these two generals of Pharaoh's army. Manek seemed eager to get on with it, however, and so all four of them entered the tent and seated themselves at a central table.

The tent was lighted by hanging lamps which gave a good, steady light, and Khai saw nothing to account for his steadily mounting feelings of apprehension and nervous distrust. As if sensing his unease, the Khemish commanders produced a stone jar of wine and four silver cups. One of them poured the wine and immediately drained his cup. His friend, Manek and Khai followed suit. As Khai put his cup to his lips, however, he noticed the sheen of sweat on Manek's brow, gleaming in the lamplight. The wine tasted bitter on his tongue and suddenly he knew that he could not be mistaken. The poison must have been in his cup before the wine was poured!

"'Ware, Manek!" he cried, starting up from the table. The eyes of the three were hard upon him where he swayed. Then Manek hung his head and looked away, but before he did Khai saw the sickness in his eyes.

The stricken man staggered from the table and slowly his world began to tilt. He fell, and falling saw large sods of grass tossed aside and Khemish soldiers where they emerged from holes in the earth; then there was a whirling and a rushing in his head and he saw no more. Before he passed out completely he heard parts of a conversation. Manek's voice said:

"Wait for a few more minutes until it's properly dark. Then you'll have to give me a good clout behind the ear to raise a bump that can plainly be seen. When I'm stretched out, one of your men should drive a sword through my shirt into the earth. I don't mind if it grazes me—all to the good—but no more than that. As for the General Khai: Pharaoh must let him live, but that's all. I'll not take Kush's future king home to the Candace, but the merest shell of a man. Is that understood?"

One of the Khemish commanders answered him: "And do you put yourself so completely in our hands, Manek Thotak? What if we choose to take you also into Asorbes?"

Manek laughed grimly. "And who then would quell the anger of the thousands come here to destroy you Khemites? And who would stay their hands? You'd not only have Kush and a few of her friends on your doorstep but all of Siwad, Nubia and Daraaf, too—and in less than a month, I promise you!

This way Pharaoh keeps Khem, what's left of it, and I get Kush. There is no other way."

This much Khai heard, but no more, not for a very long time. . . .

In the foothills of the Gilf Kebir, Ashtarta had gone wearily to the tent of her handmaidens where she had fallen fast asleep. It was now mid-morning, five days since Manek's treachery on the approaches to Asorbes. In the Queen's marquee Khai and Manek lay on their couches in attitudes of death. They had been left alone on the instructions of the seven mages, whose magical efforts for Khai's recovery had not been seen to work. The seven had seemed unperturbed, however, and had instructed that the generals should now be left alone in peace and quiet. Nothing more could be done. If Manek were successful in some future, as yet unborn world, then he would return with Khai eventually. But it must be soon, before life became truly extinct in the present bodies of the two men.

Thus, when color returned to the cheeks of the two and their eyelids began to flutter—as their chests rose and fell more steadily and with burgeoning strength, and their hearts beat more powerfully within them—none remained to see it. Some minutes passed in this manner and finally Khai awakened. His eyes opened and he stared up at the roof of the marquee above him.

For a mad, fleeting moment he was two men, with the memories of both. He was Khai of Kush—but, he was also Paul Arnott of London. Then, as a nightmare receding, his memories of Arnott dwindled and were gone. His Khai memories, on the other hand, were fresh and vivid in his mind—particularly those memories of Manek Thotak's treachery!

Khai sat bolt upright then, in time to see Manek awakening where he lay close by. For a moment, they stared into each other's eyes. Then the blond giant was off his couch in a flash, snarling his rage, dragging Manek by the throat until he had his back across his knee. He could have choked the life from him then, or simply snapped his spine, but he did neither of these things. Instead, he snarled: "Before you die, tell me why?"

"For Kush!" the helpless general managed to choke out.

"For Kush?" Khai released his grip on Manek's throat. "Are you mad?"

"No, not mad. I won't see a Khemite on the throne of Kush, that's all. Now get it over and done with. Kill me!"

"What do you mean?" Khai asked. "What are you getting at?"

"You're Ashtarta's lover, aren't you?"

Now Khai frowned his puzzlement. "Jealousy!" he finally said, his voice flat and disappointed.

"No!" Manek protested. "I'm not jealous. I want nothing of Ashtarta herself—only that when she marries, her husband should be a man born and bred of Kush."

"You fool!" Khai snarled, his face twisting. "You might very well have destroyed this Kush you love so much! Where are we now? Isn't this Ashtarta's tent? You'd better tell me all that's happened since you gave me over into the hands of those dogs. And you'd better tell me quickly, before I really do kill you."

He let Manek get up and they sat facing one another. Then Manek told all, haltingly at first but more hurriedly toward the end, eager to get it done with. When he had finished, they sat for some moments in silence.

Finally, Khai said, "Manek, our armies are waiting in Khem. They know nothing of all this. No one does, just we two. Will you come back now with me and lead your men against Asorbes, or do you prefer the one alternative?"

"What?" Manek was incredulous. "I don't need your mercy, Khai. What's the alternative?"

"Simply this," the other answered, "to stay here in Kush—a traitor!"

"I was never a traitor to Kush!" Manek protested.

"Tell that to the Candace—" Khai got to his feet. "Anyway, you will be a traitor if you don't return with me to Khem. Your army needs a leader and you're it. Whether you're worthy of their trust or not, they'd follow you to hell." He moved toward the marquee's door.

"Wait!" Manek also stood up. "And would you trust me, if I come with you?"

"It's your one chance to clear yourself," Khai grunted. "I would have to trust you."

Manek looked down at the white sand floor of the marquee and nodded his head. "It will be much more to my taste to double-cross Pharaoh," he finally said. "And in any case, he failed me miserably. You were supposed to be out of it, and look at you: there's more fight in you now than ever there was! Very well, Khai Ibizin, I'll come back with you." And they left the tent together.

# VI

## RED ARROWS

The first Ashtarta knew of the success of Manek's search down the centuries was when her handmaidens awakened her. By then, Khai and Manek had taken a chariot and pair and were already heading down across the foothills towards Khem. Tethered behind their vehicle, a second pair of horses galloped with them, reliefs for the two in front when they were tired. The men of Manek's escort had seen them leaving and were now shouting and rushing about the encampment, getting their horses, chariots and carts together so that they could follow their generals back the way they had come.

Within one chaotic quarter-hour, in total disarray, they had all left; and still Ashtarta was at a loss whether to laugh or cry. Imthra, too, had been awakened, and he also was both confused and delighted. Delighted that Khai was returned fit and well from what had seemed certain death, confused at his hurried departure, without a word to anyone.

But Khai had his reasons. By now his men must be growing short of food; certainly they would be edgy, spoiling for a fight, squabbling among themselves. And what of Pharaoh? What of his Dark Heptad? What new horrors would they be breeding in that dreadful vault of theirs beneath the great pyramid? To linger in Kush, even for minutes, would have been to waste precious time. There would have been questions to answer and lies to be told. Manek had been spared that much at least—if he deserved to be spared.

Still, he had been the one to come down the centuries searching for Khai, and so save his life—or at least one of them! The blond giant owed him that much at least.

Now Khai lashed his horses to yet more speed and lifted his voice above the rush of air and the rattle of the chariot.

"Manek," he cried, "what do you remember of that other world?"

"Very little," the other yelled back. "Only that I found you there. It seems like a dream now."

"A dream?" Khai repeated him. "Yes, I suppose it does. But I'll tell you something—from now on it's no dream. I have a feeling that as of right now it's going to be purest nightmare!"

Two days later, with the sun just beginning its downward glide, Khai and Manek reached the place where the latter's men were camped. By then Manek's escort was within sight but still had not quite managed to catch up with the two generals. Khai waited at Manek's camp long enough to see him take charge and begin issuing orders—which were for the organization of an immediate return to Asorbes—and then he drove off alone in the direction of his own camp. To get there he had to drive through Gahad Shebbithon's positions, and though the sight of him in his chariot drove Gahad's men into a frenzy of delight, still he did not break his drive. His reception at his own camp was similar to that accorded Manek by his men: a wildly excited melee of hoarsely shouting chiefs and cheering warriors, so that weary as he was from his journey, still he found himself uplifted and filled with a fierce pride. The uproar became louder still when he let it be known that he intended to take Asorbes the very next day.

Later, having rested for a few hours, he gave audience to a number of slaves recently escaped from Asorbes. There were six of them, young Nubians who wore their *ankh* scars not with shame but pride. Those marks burned in their foreheads were symbols of the oppression they had known in Asorbes; but they would paint them blazing red before they returned as soldiers of Kush, so that every Khemite soldier who saw them would know that these men would show no mercy. Khai applauded their savage determination, but he was more interested in the manner of their escape and asked them how they had managed it.

He was told that on the second day after Manek had taken him back to Kush, Khem's soldiers had once again come forward from the city to deploy in their former positions. With Manek's army out of the way, the Khemites had seen that they now held the upper hand. The Kushites were short two generals and one third of their warriors, and the balance had swung again in Khem's favor. Before they could join battle, however, Adonda Gomba—the old Nubian King of Slaves—had organized an uprising against those overseers and guards who still remained within the city's walls. To quell the rebellion, Pharaoh had been obliged to bring his troops back into the city. There they had remained until this very afternoon, and only now were they redeploying. The situation in Asorbes must therefore be well under Pharaoh's control once more.

As for Adonda Gomba: when his uprising failed, he had gone into hiding somewhere in the slave quarters; but during the course of that diversion and in the general melee, these six Nubians had managed to shin down a rope tossed from the north wall and so make their escape. There had been a dozen of them in all, but the others had been only halfway down the rope when a Khemish soldier parted it with his sword.

"So," said Khai when he heard this news, "the old slave-king is still alive, is he?—And creating mischief for the Khemites as of old." And his eyes narrowed in deep thought. For memories of Adonda Gomba had given him the inkling of an idea, and the more he considered it, the more it appealed to him. He called several of his men to him and told them to find him an artist, then tore three small squares of fine white linen from the door-flap of his tent. When the artist, a youth of one of the tribes appeared, Khai bade him draw the following symbols on each piece of linen in its turn:

First—Adonda Gomba's sign, which was a circle contained a triangle; next—a sketch of Asorbes with the north, south and west gates broken down; thirdly—a yellow sun rising over a green Nile; and finally Khai's signature, which was a pyramid with a twig figure sliding down its side. To ensure that there could be no mistake as to the author's identity, he had the artist sign the message yet again, this time with a blue eye. Then he quickly trimmed sections from the shafts of three red-flighted arrows and wrapped his messages about them, gumming them firmly in place.

All done, he called forward one of his best charioteers and they set off at a gallop westward, curving around Asorbes and passing back through Gahad Shebbithon's camp, then turning eastward again and driving down onto that land which Manek Thotak's forces had held. The slave quarters of Asorbes lay on this side of the city, and in his mind's eye Khai clearly could see those dirty, vermin-ridden streets as he had known them so long ago. If he could put his arrows into the slave quarters, one of them was bound to find its way to Gomba. Then, when the armies of Kush drove against the city's gates at dawn of the next day, perhaps Gomba and his army of slaves would be there to help—and on the inside, where they would be of greatest assistance.

The first companies of Manek's army were just beginning to arrive and take up their old positions as Khai's chariot turned in toward Asorbes and sped directly for the slave city. The south gate was open and Khemish soldiers were hurrying out into the pastures beneath the walls. They had withdrawn when Manek took his army away, but now that he was returning they were preparing to defend the city as before. They saw Khai coming and many of them stopped to watch him, possibly in astonishment. Whoever he was, he was either a very brave man or utterly insane; for on he came, unswervingly toward the looming walls, as if he intended to take on the whole city single-handed.

A few moments more and Khai was within bowshot of those soldiers outside the gate, and still he came on. The Khemites began to shoot their arrows at him, but uselessly for the chariot was still a very small and awkward target. Then, close to the walls of the city, less than one hundred yards from Asorbes itself, Khai ordered the chariot turned and made his run parallel with the wall and in a westerly direction. As arrows began to fall about the thundering vehicle, he jammed himself firmly in position behind his driver and loosed his three arrows over the wall. He used his finest, most powerful bow and sped each shaft with every ounce of strength he could bring to bear; and all three were in the air together, flying up and over the wall and into Asorbes.

Many enemy arrows were falling now, singing as they buried themselves in earth or feathered the wooden car of the chariot. Khai held up a shield overhead, protecting himself and his driver, then ordered the man to make for Manek's lines. Moments later, they were out of range of the Khemish defenders and a few more minutes took them to where Manek was setting up his command tent. Khai told Manek his plan: how with the dawn they would take the city, and what must be done before then. He wasted few words but nevertheless left no detail to chance. When he was done, Manek immediately called his chiefs together around a fire, passing on Khai's instructions and issuing orders. Teams of men would work late this night.

Then Khai drove north to Gahad Shebbithon's camp where he repeated his instructions; and finally he hurried back to his own warriors where they camped on the northern approaches to the city. From there he sent his two Nubian lieutenants and a small body of men across the river to talk to N'jakka. By morning, having crossed the river during the night, two of N'jakka's *impis* would be camped on the west bank, ready to tackle any Khemites who might choose to flee Asorbes by the east gate. This would be the only gate Ashtarta's forces would not attack—but certainly it would be defended. Pharaoh might waste as many as one sixth of his forces defending that gate, which should make the going easier at the breaking of the other three.

By the time all was done, night had fallen and so Khai retired to his tent. There he sat for a while and drank red wine before lying himself down and trying to rest. His head was bursting, which was most unusual for he was not normally given to headaches. Before falling asleep the pains in his head lifted and it seemed to him that a small voice whispered to him, saying:

"Good, Khai, good! There has been much on your mind and your riding has wearied you. You have not been receptive. Now sleep, sleep and let the Mage of Oneiromancy speak to you in dreams. There are things you should know—things you must do. So sleep, Khai, sleep—and hearken well to your dreams this night, if you would live to dream again!"

# VII

## GREEN FIRE!

Khai slept for several hours before he once more found himself standing beneath the stars in Kush, this time on the rim of the Gilf Kebir with all the valley of the Nile beneath him, stretching away eastward toward a dark horizon of star-strewn, indigo night. The brown mage was with him, and the Mage of Elementalism, but on this occasion his fellow generals were absent.

As soon as he had greeted the mages, Khai inquired as to the whereabouts of Manek Thotak and Gahad Shebbithon: why were they not present to hear the words of the mages.

"We have no need of their presence, Khai," answered the Mage of Oneiromancy, "for if we were to tell them what we must tell you, it would make little difference. No, they sleep a dreamless sleep this night, and that is good, for tomorrow will be a day of great taxation. What will be will be, however, and there is no changing it."

"Your words are ominous," Khai answered, frowning.

"Aye, ominous—for we know that with the dawn, the Dark Heptad will send a fresh terror against you."

Khai's scalp prickled. "A fresh terror? What form will it take?"

The Master of Dreams shook his head; but now the spindly mage of Siwad spoke up. "I am the Mage of Elementalism, Khai, and while I am unsure as to the nature of tomorrow's terror, I believe it will be of the elements, which are Earth, Fire, Wind and Water. One of these, but which one I cannot say."

"Then tell me what I must do?" Khai said. "How may I avoid this elemental terror and take Asorbes?"

"You can do nothing, Khai," answered the Mage of Elementalism, "but I can do much. This is why we have brought you here, so that we might warn you. For until I know which power the Dark Heptad will use, I can do nothing. When I do know, however, then . . . no man is my master in elementalism. No seven men may best me, and I shall have the combined will of my colleagues behind me."

"Then all will be well?"

"Of this you may be certain: that whichever elemental power Pharaoh's necromancers use, I shall bend it to my will and send it back against them—to your great benefit!"

"That's good to know," Khai answered; but then, sensing that there was more, he asked: "And?"

"And there is another matter," the Master of Dreams told him. "A matter of great urgency."

"Say on," said Khai.

The brown mage nodded. "Very well. When you enter Asorbes, Khai, then you must find the Dark Heptad of necromancers and destroy them without delay. It must be your first priority. Their dark dabbling has brought them to the very portals of hell—portals which they would open! Indeed, they *will* commit the direst necromantic sin as soon as they know the slave city is doomed. Pharaoh has ordered it: universal insanity if Asorbes falls!"

Khai felt doubt gnawing at his insides. For the first time he was unsure of himself, of the seven mages. "How can you know these things?" he asked.

The mages smiled and nodded their great heads. "How can you doubt us, Khai, when you yourself have communed with the Mage of Mentalism in broad daylight?"

"The yellow mage?"

"Aye, and he has listened to the thoughts of the Dark Heptad, which are black as the pit. Have faith, Khai, and believe. But for now, sleep. Sleep and grow strong in mind, body and faith. The dawn is not far away, and this day shall be one of the most important days that ever men have known. . . ."

Rough hands shook him awake. He started up, gazed into the brown eyes of Kindu. "Lord, dawn will break within the half-hour," the Nubian told him. "The eastern sky has a bright edge to it, and Asorbes is waiting. The men are being roused and the horses paw the ground. Your battering rams are ready, and N'jakka's *impis* have come across the river in the night."

"What of the Khemites?" Khai asked.

"They are ready, Lord. Their armies on the ground outside the city are half as strong again as ours, and surely many more remain within. The gates are closed and heavily defended: and the Khemites mass beneath the east wall, too, perhaps fearing an attack from N'jakka. *Waugh!* And they are right to fear him. He is an excitable man and Pharaoh owes him a great deal. Perhaps he will decide not to wait but simply take what he is owed!"

Khai offered a grim smile. "I could not blame him," he answered.

He went outside into the cool pre-dawn and splashed a few drops of water onto his face. The crack of light glowed stronger in the east and the breeze from the north was gradually strengthening. Khai sniffed the air, lifted his head and stared through the dawn's half-light. It was strangely still. Dim figures moved as in a mist. Sounds were muffled, dull. Chill fingers seemed suddenly to tickle Khai's spine. He shuddered.

"It's coming. . . ." he half-whispered.

"What's coming, Lord?" Kindu's eyes were round.

Khai did not hear his Nubian lieutenant. He looked at the sky, at faint wisps of cloud which seemed to be revolving, spinning slowly in a vast aerial wheel above Asorbes. The silence deepened and all eyes followed Khai's skyward. The clouds thickened, turned an angry blue, then black. Their vast circular rush accelerated.

"Don't panic!" Khai's voice rose in the preternatural stillness. "Keep the horses calm. And when it comes—whatever it is—then look after your own skins. But whatever you do, whatever happens, *don't panic!* The seven mages are with us. Remember that: the seven mages are with us!"

His cry was passed on down the line, thrown from throat to throat, audible to tens of thousands of warriors. "The seven mages are with us! The seven mages are with us!" They shouted it . . . they *believed* it—and in this way, though unbeknown to Khai and his army, the strength of the seven mages was made stronger yet. . . .

Gahad and Manek saw the aerial harbinger of horror at the same time as did Khai, and while they knew less about it, still they recognized it as the Dark Heptad's work. For now the racing clouds were black as night, and bright green traceries of electrical fire stabbed here and there between arms of the spiraling mass. With the sun rising over Asorbes and setting the city ablaze beneath its own infernal halo, and the disk of cloud spinning madly above and glowing with its burgeoning energies, the scene was fantastic and awe-inspiring. And frightening—

Especially when the energies of the rushing cloud began to expend themselves downward!

And now Khai knew what elemental power the Dark Heptad had brought against him. It was fire . . . but not clean red roaring flame. No, for this was a darkly necromantic fire—a fire bred of hell's own breath—green lightning that lashed out of a throbbing sky and walked the earth on stacatto stilts of death!

Asorbes was enclosed behind a dancing screen of lashing bolts, forks of green fire that walked outwards from the city and advanced on the lines of the besieging armies. The front ranks drew back, their faces flashing green to the rhythm of the advancing bolts, their mouths open and gaping, screaming horror at the emerald inferno. Tree stumps burst into flame at the touch of the terror and steaming craters leapt open with each blinding stab. The ring of fire advanced, the green stilts lifted and came down in hissing, crackling fury; lifted and came down—

And came down among the massed ranks of Ashtarta's armies!

Three times the myriad bolts struck, rods of fire that fell in unison, tearing earth and men and horses and chariots, turning them to charred ruin. Three times and then—

Then they paused, withdrew, flickered back into the clouds like the tongues of startled snakes. The heavens became tumultuous, tossing and boiling in their anger, their indecision. And slow but sure, the spinning stopped, reversed itself, and the clouds began to turn in the opposite direction— against the will of the Dark Heptad!

"The seven mages are with us!" Khai sang out in sulphurous air. "They are with us!" And again his cry was taken up by a thousand, a hundred thousand throats.

Now the lightning walked again, and more purposefully—but now it walked back the way it had come, on forked stilts which strode devastatingly through the massed ranks of the Khemites. For minutes the slaughter went on, until Khai thought that he and his entire army with him must surely be deafened and blinded. Then, in one final burst of fire, the howling clouds expended the last of their energies on the gates of Asorbes themselves.

And the gates fell. In gouting ruin, they fell. Blown asunder and smashed flat, destroyed by that very power which the Dark Heptad had thought to hurl against Kush.

Khai turned his face to heavens which already were clearing even as he gazed. "Thank you, you seven mages!" he cried, his teeth white and wide in the glowing dawn. "Thank you. . . ."

He dragged a half-stunned driver into a chariot and handed him the reins. "Let's go," he yelled in the man's ear. "Now!"

And with a roar and a rumble only a little less loud than that of the now silenced lightning storm, the armies of Kush drove down on Asorbes.

# part
# TEN

# I

## "TAKE THE PYRAMID!"

Down into the riven pastures of Asorbes thundered the hordes of Kush, their iron swords invincible, their chariots devastating, their hearts bursting with the savage joy of meeting the foe here, now, face-to-face in his heartland, beneath the walls of Asorbes itself, whose name was now synonymous with that of the detestable Pharaoh and all that was evil. In streaming thousands, they cut through the remnants of the lightning-blasted defenders, flinging them down on the scorched earth in red and tattered ruin.

To give them their due, the Khemites fought back, but they were quite simply overwhelmed and swept under, as by some mighty wave. And when they were drowned, that wave did not pause but swept on—on and in through the shattered gates of the city.

Surprisingly, the rain of arrows from atop the walls was not as heavy as was expected. Later it became known that this was chiefly due to the activities of Adonda Gomba and his army of resurgent slaves. Though the slave king had received and understood Khai's message, he had known that he could not help in the matter of the gates: that in the hour of Asorbes' direst peril, his men simply would not be allowed anywhere near the gates. Therefore he had determined to help Khai in other ways.

One hour after receiving Khai's message, as night drew its dark cloak over the city, Pharaoh's elephants were poisoned in their pens. They would not be brought into action against the invaders. This was one way in which Adonda Gomba cut at the heart of Khem, but there were others. Since many slaves had been assigned re-supply tasks on the city's high, wide ramparts, the slave king had decided that this was where he must strike his heaviest blow for Kush. Thus, when Ashtarta's armies drove on Asorbes, the slaves working atop the walls had turned on the very Khemish archers they were supposed to support! And so the invaders' losses were minimal from what must otherwise have been a veritable rain of death.

Immediately inside the gates, all was scarlet chaos. Khemish reinforcements had massed there, had been torn to shreds when the green lightnings shattered the gates inwards. Khai saw this first, for his chariot was first under the massive arch of the north gate and so into the city. Close behind drove Kindu and Nundi, their vehicle leaping and jolting as it flew over shattered timbers and heaped bodies, while behind them ... behind them came the bulk of Khai's warriors, and leading them a sight to strike terror in even the bravest hearts.

For while the charioteers and horsemen had been busy mopping up the Khemites outside the walls, Khai's *impis* had ran—literally *ran!*—down across the scarred fields and into the city.

Some of those black giants bore clubs, others assagais, and all were painted like demons from men's blackest nightmares. Five thousand Nubians, huge men all, and each one of them trained to a peak of killing efficiency. Their shields went up together to meet whirring swarms of arrows; their voices chanted together as they advanced at the trot; and their message was one of grim and terrible resolution:

"*Waugh!* Kill for Khai!"

"*Waugh!* Kill for Khai the Killer!"

"We are N'jakka's strength. We are his mighty heart!"

"Khai is his white brother, and they are mighty above all men!"

"*Waugh!* Kill for N'jakka, in the name of Khai the Killer. In the name of Killer Khai!"

The wall of Khemites broke before them, broke and was trampled underfoot; and in through the gates poured the rest of the charioteers, the horsemen and warriors of Kush. By now the slaves of Asorbes were in uproar, arming themselves *en-masse* and turning on their overseers and guards, causing a hundred diversions in all quarters of the city. Many of them were starting fires, burning their old, verminous houses in the slave quarters; and others were climbing the stone stairways built into the walls, pouring onto the high ramparts and joining their brothers there, dealing with the Khemite archers wherever they found them.

All was a cataract of noise, a tumult of rushing, furiously brawling figures, of screaming, dying men and beasts. The streets were full of blood and crumpled figures, where bronze swords broke on iron swords and clubs rose and fell to the pounding rhythm of war-hammers. And through all of this Khai rode, his sword a scarlet wand which brought death in near-magical fashion to any Khemish soldier who strayed too close to his chariot; and close behind rode Kindu and Nundi, black and golden and red with blood as the sun rose over Asorbes.

With the majority of the action taking place in and around the gates, the center of the city was comparatively quiet. Breaking through the rear ranks of the defenders, Khai headed for the great ramp and followed the line of its base west toward the pyramid. He had not forgotten the dream-warning of the seven mages in Kush, and his priority now was to find the Dark Heptad and deal with them in short order. Racing parallel with his own chariot was that of his Nubian lieutenants, and a thousand of his most fierce horsemen rode behind.

Several bodies of Khemish troops broke and scattered before the charge of Khai's party, only to be picked off individually by the mounted swordsmen. The pyramid's largest body of defenders waited at the base of that vast monument itself, however, and there Khai spied them as he raced his vehicle beneath the sheer cliff of the great ramp. Ordering his driver to rein back a little, Khai gave his men time to draw level with him until they formed a solid front.

The ranks of crack Khemish infantry stood six deep at the base of the pyramid, with archers to the fore. Now, as the warriors and charioteers of Kush urged their mounts to the gallop, Pharaoh's archers lifted their bows and sent a concerted sleet of arrows leaping toward them. Khai knew how devastatingly effective those archers could be, for he himself had trained with them as a boy; but he also knew their limitations.

His timing was perfect as he roared: "Up shields!" And as bucklers were raised, so the long-shafted Khemish arrows struck home. Horses fell screaming and riders with them; chariots slewed and snapped their axles, flinging their drivers down to be trampled under razor hooves; men died scarcely realizing they were hit . . . but the rest thundered on without pause and seconds later struck the Khemites even as they lifted their bows a second time. Outnumbered the riders of Kush were, for the main body of Khai's force was still some hundreds of yards to his rear and diffusing through the city, but so ferocious were his warriors and so superior their weapons that Pharaoh's troops fell like grass before the scythe. It was no contest, but a slaughter, and in very few minutes, the Khemish defenders were bowled over and trampled down.

It was then that Khai's driver took an arrow in the eye, whose force was such it came out the back of his head and knocked him clean out of the chariot. Before Khai could grab the reins, the horses ran wild. Then one of them felt the razor edge of a bronze sword across its hamstrings. Down went the proud beast, tripping its fellow and tumbling the chariot in blood and dust. Khai leaped free of the broken vehicle and rolled, springing to his feet in the heart of the melee.

More Khemish troops had appeared, racing out in their hundreds from the many doors that led to the pyramid's lower levels, and Khai found himself hemmed in by furiously battling men who strove to bring him down. Chariots wheeled about him and horses reared over him; blood spattered his face and hair as his iron sword rose and fell inexorably; his breath rattled hoarsely as he gulped air to fuel his straining muscles. Then—

He could almost sense the shock wave that ran through the ranks of the Khemites facing him. He read horror in their eyes and saw it stamped on their faces as they fell back.

*"Waugh!"* came the roar of his *impis,* an explosion of sound made deafening by four thousand assagais and clubs rattled on shields; and *"Waugh!"* came that cry once more.

"We kill for Khai!" the Nubians roared as they ploughed forward, an invincible black mass. "For Khai the Killer—for Killer Khai! *Waugh! Waugh!"*

By now Kindu and Nundi were on foot, fighting alongside Khai, and the three of them snarled their savage fury through gritted teeth as they hacked a path through the pyramid's defenders. Others of Khai's warriors joined them from the flanks, and in a momentary lull a chief shouted: "What now, Khai?"

"Now?" he answered. "Why, now we take the pyramid! Into the hive, men," he roared. "Let's burn the vermin out!"

# II

# MAKERS OF
# MADNESS

The light in the lower levels of the pyramid was
as dim as Khai remembered it. Surging through
corridors which were still familiar to him despite
the intervening years, he and some fifty of his warriors engaged many small parties of Khemites in
those eerie, half-lighted tunnels and temples, but
their Nubian steel quickly conquered all.

"Clean the place out and then set it ablaze,"
Khai ordered, his voice echoing loudly over the
magnified tramp of feet and distant sounds of battle
from outside. "These wall hangings will carry the
flames, and the smoke will drive any scum in the
higher levels up through the pyramid to its top.
There's a fresh-air system, but it won't be able to
cope with that. Only don't set your fires until you've
searched these lower levels through and through. If
you come across anything that looks like a wizard—kill it! Kill all seven of them, if you find
them. Now go, scatter. Kindu and Nundi—you stay
with me. I know the whereabouts of the Dark Heptad's den. With luck, we'll find them at home."

Reaching a spot where steps descended steeply
into black bowels of rock, Khai snatched a torch
from its bracket and led his two lieutenants down
into dank and claustrophobic depths. He had been
this way before, with Pharaoh's Vizier, Anulep, and
he shuddered involuntarily as he recalled the terror
the place had held for him then. Even now, he felt a
strangling of his soul as he plumbed this pit beneath

the great pyramid. But he was driven by something greater than fear: a craving for red revenge!

These seven necromancers for whom he searched were responsible for the grisly end of far too many of Khai's friends and fellows, and if and when he found them they would pay the price in full. Except that they would die cleanly, not stripped to the bone by bats and insects, gnawed by plague-ridden rats or blasted in a holocaust of green lightnings. They would die by the sword, and steel was cold, sweet and swift.

The footsteps of the three echoed hollowly, and the sounds of their colleagues where they sought and slew above had grown very faint when the stone steps ended in a corridor whose roughly hewn walls and reeking atmosphere told Khai that he had reached his destination. This was that nethermost level where the Dark Heptad had its lair of bubbling vats; where they performed their black magics in accordance with Khasathut's schemes. Khai put a finger to his lips to indicate stealth, and then, sure-footed in the flickering light of his torch, he led his Nubians along the winding corridor. As they went, Kindu and Nundi pressed very close on his heels indeed.

Along the way, they passed an array of jars, boxes and containers of various shapes and sizes—the morbid chemicals and mordant liquids of the Dark Heptad's infernal work—all piled against the walls, and here the stench of nameless experiments filled the air to such a degree that even Khai's sputtering torch seemed to dim a little, as if from lack of good clean air. Then, faint at first, but rapidly growing louder, they heard the low mouthings of an interminably chanted invocation, and Khai's scalp prickled as he recognized the oft-repeated and monstrously evocative name of Nyarlathotep!

Nyarlathotep, the Crawling Chaos. The Howler in the Night. The Dark Messenger of Demon Gods trapped and chained in vaults of space and time since the earliest ages of Earth; master of all the world's imps of insanity, hatred and despair; and here the Dark Heptad called upon Him to come to their aid!

"This is it," Khai whispered to his friends as they approached a huge archway in the corridor's wall, from which issued a flicking blue glow. "And if that chanting is anything to go by, I'd say they're in!" And stepping forward, he thrust his torch before him into the room to light his way.

The oddly shimmering glow came from a large sunken vat situated centrally in the floor of this den of sorcerers, and as Khai's torch lit that awful cave, so the unnatural radiance seemed to dim a little. Seated cross-legged on the floor about the vat, hands touching, the Dark Heptad slowly turned their cowled heads to gaze at the intruders. In faces shaded beneath seven cowls, their eyes were luminous and poisonous as they stared. Then—

Before Khai and his Nubians could take a single step forward, the blue light sprang up like a shimmering wall and spread outward from the vat, pushing them back and out of the room! They fought against it, fought to win through that ethereal but seemingly solid wall of light, but to no avail. And all the time, the chanting of the Dark Heptad went on, gaining in volume and racing ever more rapidly from their lips as they hurried to bring it to a climax.

Now, narrowing his eyes to squint through the haze of blue shimmer into the den, Khai saw that the magic was working. Shapes were forming in that room, hovering over the vat, writhing and taking on substance. A kaleidoscope of wraithlike forms—and each one a little more solid than the one before—towering and leaping up from the vat like genies to sway over the hysterically chanting figures of the Dark Heptad. And they were shapes of purest evil!

All the horrors of universal insanity were there, the unclean spirits of Man's blackest nightmares, and Khai saw ghouls, afreets and ogres come and go in the ever-changing nimbus that rose over the vat. As for Kindu and Nundi: they saw their own demons, the night-things of the jungles and the leering familiars of witches and black *M'gangas*. And as each leering or frothing shape melted into the next, so it took on firmer form.

The chanting voices of the Dark Heptad were now reaching a crescendo. Khai knew that whatever was coming must come soon, and so he threw himself once more against the wall of blue light that filled the doorway and forbade him entry. Such was the energy he expended that his muscles corded and the veins stood out on his straining brow as he shoved against nothing; until his very mind grew numb with the effort. Only then, when the one thought in his head was an overriding determination to break through, did he hear that whispering voice in his mind, that voice he knew of old and which he had learned to trust.

It was the voice of the wind-carved, sun-scorched Syran mage—the Mage of Mentalism—and Khai fastened desperately upon it and forced himself to listen.

"*Good, Khai, Good!*" praised that voice, but it carried an ominously sad note. "*Now listen and understand. You may not break through this barrier, for it is a mindwall. Their wills are greater than yours, their minds stronger, and so you may not proceed. And this time we cannot help you, Khai, for we, too, are helpless against a mindwall. . . .*"

Khai looked again through the blue haze and saw a fresh shape writhing into view above the vat. And this time the shape was semi-solid, clearly discernible . . . and human! Human, and yet inhuman. For this could only be Nyarlathotep in His earthly avatar: a young man with the wickedly proud face of a fallen God, whose great black eyes contained a hideous humor. His mouth was cruel and yet langorous, and His lips had sipped of all the world's sin. Pschent-crowned, this tall sardonic Being reminded Khai of Pharaoh and of a great task as yet unfulfilled, and aloud he cried out to that dimly receding voice in his head:

"What may I do? What is this mindwall that resists me? Answer me—help me—but don't desert me now!"

Faint and fading came his answer: "*The mindwall is an illusion, Khai, it is not real. But since the barrier exists in your own mind, you may not cross it. No thinking creature may breach a mindwall. . . .*" And the voice of the Mage of Mentalism receded and was gone.

"But I must breach it!" Khai howled. "I must!" And again he hurled himself at the blue, impenetrable haze. In another moment, the hands of Kindu and Nundi were on his straining arms, dragging him from the doorway. Then, as he fought them off, his eyes lighted upon a row of large stone jars where they stood along the wall of the corridor.

He shook himself free of the Nubians. "Mindwall?" he gasped to himself. "An illusion!"

"Lord, what ails you?" Nundi asked. "Come, we must leave this place."

"No, no, wait," Khai answered, his forehead creasing in concentration. "*A mindwall!*" he said again, this time in a whisper, and his eyes went wide in sudden inspiration. "Aye, but since when has oil a mind of its own, eh?"

"Lord?"

"Never mind," he cried. "But quickly—help me!" And together they lifted the jars of oil and threw them against the blue glow where it issued from the door of the Dark Heptad's den. The jars passed through the glow without hindrance, smashing when they struck the floor within. Instantly thickly cloying, exotically scented fumes flooded from the sorcerers' den, and on instinct Khai swept his torch forward and sent it spinning into the room.

The searing heat from the holocaust of flame which then spilled out into the subterranean corridor drove Khai and his Nubians back as it scorched the walls. And as the fireball shrank, they heard the terrified shrieking of the Dark Heptad above the roar and crackle of flames. They heard *them* . . . and they heard something else, something much worse.

It was laughter—lunatic laughter that turned to a roar of outrage even as it dwindled and died. On the very threshold, Nyarlathotep had been sent back to those mental hells which spawned him. A moment more and two capering, flaming human torches leapt out into the corridor, beating at their blazing bodies in a vain attempt to smother the flames. While still they danced, the trio of invaders cut them down. Khai stepped over their crisped bodies and shielded his face as he stared at the inferno within the den. The heat was blistering and he knew nothing could possibly live in there.

Satisfied, he was turning to his companions when a movement farther down the corridor caught his eye. A tall, spectrally slender figure stared at him, then melted back into the flickering shadows—but Khai had seen him. He would recognize that figure anywhere: that black sheath of a robe and bald dome of a head.

"Anulep!" Khai snarled.

He made to run after the Vizier, but at that moment a fresh ball of fire shot out from the mouth of the wizard's den and drove him back. For precious seconds the flames licked the corridor, then died away.

Khai beckoned Kindu and Nundi forward and ran along the smoke-filled corridor toward the spot where the Vizier had lurked in the shadows, but scarce had he taken ten paces before he heard a sound which caused his flesh to creep and the short hairs at the back of his neck to stand up straight. It was a single, eerie, undulating note—and Khai knew that it had been blown on a tiny golden whistle. . . .

# III

# DEATH OF DEATHS

That single blast of Anulep's golden whistle almost brought Khai to a halt, for in his mind's eye, he now saw the sight which must surely meet him around the next bend in the corridor. He remembered the heavy metal gate in the wall, whose bars were thick and strong, and he remembered the *inhabitants* of that vault, how they had been brought to a moldering and murderous life by the Vizier's fiendish piping—that same warbling note whose echoes even now rang in his ears.

Khai's torch was gone, lost in the inferno he had wrought, and now the only light was that which glimmered from tiny lamps placed in wide-spaced niches along the walls. He slowed his run to a careful, crouching walk and spoke to his lieutenants in a voice which barely concealed his trepidation.

"Boys, around this bend will be something to freeze the blood in your veins—a sight you'll never forget, as I have never forgotten it—but we must not turn and flee. Anulep went this way, and we have to follow him."

Now Kindu best remembered Khai as the boy who saved his life those long years ago in the forest east of the river, and he was Khai's senior by almost twenty years, but still he did not mind Khai calling him "boy." He did object, however, to what he considered a slight on his own and his fellow Nubian's manliness.

"Flee, Khai?" he protested. "We would not think of—"

"No one doubts your bravery, man," Khai quickly cut him off. "I'm only trying to tell you that we—" but there he broke off as the horror abruptly lurched into view, coming around the bend toward them where they half-crouched in oppressive gloom.

"Zombies!" Nundi gasped.

"Dead men!" Kindu choked out the words. "But they walk!"

The corridor was full now of stumbling, shuffling corpses whose outlines were aglow with rotten luminescence. Their eyes were pits of balefire and fat, wriggling worms dropped from their crumbling flesh even as they moved silently on the trio of frozen intruders. There were perhaps two, three dozen of these terrible once-men, and the *smell* of their corruption beggared description.

For all that many of them were in the last stages of putrefaction, disintegrating even as they came, still the speed of their approach was terrifying. Before Khai and his Nubians could force their paralyzed limbs to mobility, the clawing, silently mouthing, greenly glowing horde of cadavers was on them. On the floor of the corridor legless trunks wriggled to trip them, and torsos without arms thrust forward mummied faces with open jaws and chomping teeth.

Khai was the first to pull himself together, and as he began to shout his instructions so his lieutenants started at the shock of his voice in the terror-laden silence. "They're only dead men," Khai cried. "Dead and rotting men whose souls scream in hell. They can't stand against us, so cut them down!"

Still Kindu and Nundi shrank back.

"Leather and bone and worms," Khai yelled. "Look—" and he swept his sword through two of the advancing creatures with one clean stroke. Down went the zombies, crumbling into dust and rot.

Now the Nubian warriors took heart, and Khai wondered if he himself would have recovered so swiftly had the roles been reversed. For he had prior knowledge of this blasphemy and should therefore be, in a measure, prepared for it. However that might be, now the trio stood shoulder to shoulder with their backs to the wall of rock, and as the undead horde pressed close so they hacked and hewed until at last they stood in a semicircle of heaped enemies.

Then, stomachs heaving as they gagged on poisonous air, they stepped gingerly through half-liquescent, half-powdery loathsomeness and went on shakily down the rock-cut tunnel. Khai paused at the first small lamp to lift it from its niche, turn and toss it back onto the pile of human debris that littered the floor. His action was one of instinct and not logic, for corpses are not so easy to burn. But these corpses had been treated with rare oils and chemicals, and sure enough they flared up in an instant with a bright and cleansing light.

And it was by that purifying light that the three men made their way along the tunnel to the next flight of stone stairs, which they gladly climbed to the saner levels above. There, where dimly cavernous temples and halls loomed beyond every stone arch, many of Kush's warriors impatiently prowled in the gloom and called Khai's name. Relieved to see him emerge from below, they now set about to burn every flammable thing in sight; and while some put torches to tapestries and curtains, others poured perfumed oil onto toppled statues of hybrid Khemish gods, or smashed rich chairs and tables into shattered fragments of kindling.

And so, retreating in the face of self-set fires, Khai's warriors moved out from the pyramid's center toward the clean air and the light of the outside world. It was then, as they hastened to join the battle which still raged in the streets of the city, that they heard high overhead a rumbling like that of long drawn out thunder. Khai paused in a corridor rapidly filling with fire to turn his eyes to the ceiling. He felt his flesh creep in sudden apprehension. Somewhere up above a great weight had shifted, a massive block of stone had pivoted. But for what purpose?

Khai believed he knew the answer to that question. He saw again his father's plans of the pyramid, remembering them from so long ago. Those sketches he had so admired as a boy, of gigantic mechanisms designed to operate at the touch of a lever—to spill thousands of tons of sand down into these lower levels. And worse: to seal the base of the pyramid off forever from the outside world!

"Move!" he shouted at once. "Out, quickly—or stay here forever!"

Even as he yelled his warning a stream of fine sand gushed down from an opening in the ceiling, quickly forming a mounting pile as it spilled upon the floor. And now there arose all around the whisper and rush and slither of sand; and yet again, from somewhere high overhead, there came a rumble of great weights in motion. Along all of the many corridors, jets of sand were now erupting from overhead apertures, similarly in the temples and halls, and already the floor was inches deep with fine grains which sifted deeper by the second as the flow of sand increased.

It was not the sand which bothered Khai as he ran, however, but the thought of something else. Even now, at this very moment, great slabs of stone were tilting in the mighty walls of the pyramid, pivoting beneath the weight of sand from above. Before the sand could begin to spill out through the many huge doorways which lined the four sides of the pyramid's base, these great stone "doors" would tilt into vertical positions and slam down, closing the lower regions off from the outside world for all time.

It was every man for himself now, for quite obviously to linger here would mean a monstrous, choking death. Khai raced with Kindu, Nundi and some fifteen others of his men along one of the square corridors leading to safety. Daylight showed ahead through a haze of yellow dust and flying sand, and

Khai urged his warriors on as he listened for a sound other than their cursing and the rushing hiss of sand.

And finally that sound came: of a massive weight slamming down like a hammer of the gods. The ground trembled briefly to the *thump* of that mighty blow, and Khai began to count as he ran. At a count of ten there came a second *thump* and shuddering of the earth, and now he knew the worst—that indeed the titan doors were closing, falling into their predetermined places.

Faster he ran, his feet dragging in sand, slipping and stumbling as he kicked at his men and urged them to greater effort. Daylight was a haze of light somewhere ahead, and close by there came a third great *thump* as another door fell. This time the solid rock beneath the shifting sand actually jumped, telling Khai that his time was almost up. The next door would be closer still, possibly the one which even now shifted above the doorway that loomed ahead. A doorway, yes—glaring white light seen through a mist of sand—but Khai hung back to send the last of his men scrambling and leaping out into the open air.

He made to follow, glanced upward once at the square base of a massive block that moved gratingly in the ceiling and poised itself, then closed his eyes and hurled himself forward. Full length in mid-air, Khai flew, willing himself across the deadly threshold and feeling the rush of air suddenly compressed by sheer bulk as that gigantic door fell.

And as he sprawled in the dust, so the earth jarred mightily beneath him and shuddered into immobility. Clouds of dust billowed up at once, obscuring everything, and when they settled Khai turned his head to look back. There, mere inches from his feet—where moments ago a huge doorway had gaped—now a massive wall of impenetrable rock stood solid and impassive.

In another moment—while yet he strove to convince himself that indeed he still lived and had escaped that horrible death of deaths—Kindu and Nundi were anxiously helping him to his feet. . . .

# IV

# A SPELL OF
# FASCINATION

While Khai and his body of men completed their task in the base of the pyramid and made their escape, the fighting in the city was furious and bloody. Ashtarta's warriors were winning inexorably through, however, and had closed in on Pharaoh's forces until the great majority of survivors were clustered in the streets close to the base of Khasathut's mighty monument. There they fought and died, hewn down by the iron swords of the invaders.

To any observer, the battle would have presented an awe-inspiring spectacle whose center was the great pyramid itself. From its base, which now gleamed yellow where patches of beaten gold overlaid the fine white skin, its sides rose steeply colossal to a now tiny summit. Its dizzy steps and hugely sloping ramp were splashed red with blood and obscured by a rising haze of sweat, dust and the steam of spilled entrails. Overlooking all, the sun, too, was shrouded, appearing as a bruised and bloodied orange eye.

But through all the chaos, it could plainly be seen that the war was over. Khem was the loser, her wizards and warriors defeated, her forts and now her fortress city brought down. Only the pyramid remained as refuge for those hundreds of desperate defenders who yet fought on, retreating ever higher up the steps and the great ramp as the invaders, swollen by thousands of blood-crazed slaves, poured after them in relentless waves.

Flanked by his Nubian lieutenants—gory with

blood-slimed sand—Khai ran from the base of the pyramid to join that thronging, victorious horde. Pausing at the foot of the steps, he sheathed an iron sword, cast about with worried eyes and sniffed at the reeking air. Then he grimaced, turned to his comrades and said:

"It's Khasathut I want. I won't rest until he's dead. He wasn't in the pyramid's lower quarters, which means that he must be somewhere up there—" and he pointed at the great ramp where it joined the sloping east face of the pyramid. "There will be soldiers in there, too, quite a few, I'd guess. But if our lads go in after them they'll be forced into the open sooner or later, and Pharaoh with them. Since the lower entrances are blocked, there's only one way in or out. Right there!" And again he pointed, this time at a dark square doorway high in the pyramid's face.

The entrance was at the very top of the ramp. Flanking it were wide steps cut into the face of the pyramid itself and rising to the flat summit. Even as the three gazed up at that dark doorway, suddenly there was movement in and about it. One, two of Pharaoh's Black Guards emerged—then four more, a dozen, and—

"Look!" Khai hissed through clenched teeth. He used a blood-streaked forearm to brush blond hair from his steely blue eyes. "Do you know what that is? That curtained chair they're carrying? It's Pharaoh's litter."

"And see," said Nundi, pointing. "There's the reason why the drones are fleeing their hive. Those fires we set are spreading."

As the last members of the Black Guard came pouring out of the high doorway, for all the world like angry bees or ants from a threatened nest, black clouds of smoke followed them, roiling out from the pyramid's single remaining doorway in ever-thickening ropes. Eight of the huge blacks struggled with the litter up the steps to the summit, somehow managing to keep the canopied chair on an even keel, while the rest, perhaps fifteen or sixteen of them, followed their laboring colleagues with curved swords drawn, forming a barrier against any attack from below.

"Khasathut's in that litter," Khai snapped, "and he's mine! And look—there's Anulep, the Pharaoh's Vizier, too. Tall and thin, like a praying mantis. He'll be the one who turned the sand on us. The two of them together. I don't know which one has the blackest heart, Anulep or his master. But it doesn't matter. All that matters is that I've got them.

"I've got them!" he roared, clenching his fists and shaking them over his head. "You there, out of my way," and he raced up the steps with Kindu and Nundi doing their best to keep pace with him. As they climbed higher, so the massed warriors made way for them; and Khai's orders—that Khasathut was not to be touched, that his cordon of blacks on the summit was not to be attacked—preceded him, were relayed ahead by the booming authoritative voices of his chiefs.

The fighting was almost over by the time the trio reached the ramp. Pockets of desperate resistance were still being encountered in the city's streets and squares and on its perimeter walls, but the desperation of the Khemite soldiers was born of the sure knowledge that they were finished. Khai and his lieutenants looked back once—gazed out over a city which already gouted flame and smoke from a myriad blazing fires, at streets overrun with rampaging slaves and warriors howling their victory as they hunted down the last remnants of Pharaoh's army—and then they made for the summit itself.

On their way up the center of the ramp—whose sides were lined with Kushites, Nubians, Siwadis and freed slaves alike, all cheering Khai and his companions on and forming a crowd behind them as they climbed ever higher—they hurdled bodies where they lay sprawled in death's poses and stepped over discarded, gore-slimed weapons. Never once did they accord this grisly debris a moment's consideration; their goal was to reach Pharaoh and his cordon of guardsmen on the summit, and nothing could distract them from it. Only upon climbing to the doorway, which still issued a little smoke, did they pause for a moment to gain strength for the final assault.

As the last few puffs of smoke belched out from the dark doorway and began to drift away over the city, Khai stared up at the two dozen or so remaining steps to the summit and stiffened. Seeing his look of disbelief, Kindu and Nundi peered upward through the rapidly dispersing screen of smoke. Khasathut's litter stood at the very rim of the flat summit, with its forward shafts projecting. Between the shafts, his head and shoulders hidden from view, Anulep kneeled with his back to the steps. Members of the Black Guard flanked the litter, spears at the slope in their right hands, curved swords at the ready in their left.

"What is it, Khai?" Kindu asked. "Why do you pause?"

For answer, Khai gazed once more out over the city, then turned his eyes upward yet again to the litter's shafts and the figure of the Vizier where he kneeled in seeming obeisance between them. The expression on the young general's face quickly changed from a look of disbelief to one of purest loathing. Shocking pictures flooded his mind, pictures of lovely girls skinned alive while Anulep brought the Pharaoh to a climax with his hideous mouth, and Khai *knew* what was happening even now beneath the gold-embroidered canopy of Khasathut's litter-throne.

It had been girls before—beautiful girls giving up their lives in agony and crimson horror to facilitate an orgasm in the hybrid monster called Khasathut—but now? *Now it was an entire city!*

Suddenly, while Khai still stood frozen in disbelief, there came a drawn-out shriek which rose to an almost painfully intense pitch before gurgling into gasped obscenities. At first, Khai thought that the cry signalled Pharaoh's climax, but as the cursing continued there came a sudden and frantic billowing of the litter's curtains. And now Anulep stood up and laughed long and loud—the laughter of a man made mad with terror—the baying of a crazed hound. The Vizier turned as he laughed, throwing his head back and his arms wide as he roared his lunatic mirth, and even Khai shrank back from the sight of the madman's face: his gaping, crimson jaws that dripped blood even as he laughed!

Confused, the cordon of guardsmen turned inward, made as if to leap upon the Vizier . . . but too late. Pharaoh himself tore aside the canopy of his litter to stand naked, twisted and deformed behind Anulep, a curved dagger gleaming in his one good hand. With a downward sweep of his arm, he cut short the Vizier's laughter and sent his skeletal, black-sheathed figure stumbling and staggering down the steps toward Khai. The high priest almost made it, but at the last moment, he tripped over his own spastically lurching feet and crashed down on his face. Pharaoh's dagger was lodged deep in the top of his spine. He flopped on the steps for a second or two and flailed his limbs, then somehow turned over onto his back, snapping off the dagger's handle and driving its blade deeper yet.

His face was full of blood, and as his death rattle sounded so his scarlet mouth fell open and released a pair of hinged bronze teeth which clattered onto the stone steps. Then he lay still. Khai still did not understand all of it— would never fully understand—but as finally he lifted his eyes from the body of the dead Vizier so he became conscious of a concerted gasping from his lieutenants and the warriors who crowded behind them. Again he turned his gaze toward the summit, and finally a glimmering of understanding came.

For there Khasathut stood, supported now by two members of his Black Guard, with blood flowing freely down his legs from his terrible wound. In that one region where once he might have claimed a certain kinship with men, he no longer laid claim to anything at all. And now Pharaoh saw Khai—saw him through those octopus eyes of his and knew him for the force which had guided Khem's enemies to victory. He threw off his guardsmen and somehow staggered to one side of his heavy litter, then indicated that the ornately-carved throne should be hurled from the summit.

In another moment, the litter came crashing down from above. Leaping to one side, Khai and his lieutenants somehow avoided its cartwheeling mass, but many of the warriors crowding behind them were not so lucky. Now, galvanized into action and snarling his hatred, the blond giant threw himself up the steps and as he went heard an almost hysterical command from above:

"Let him come!" screamed Pharaoh, his voice full of that remembered whooshing effect but higher pitched, like that of a breathless woman. "Let him come all the way. As for the rest: hold them back. Do not let them interfere before this thing is finished!"

Khai held his sword before him and made to defend himself against the Black Guard as they swarmed past him down the steps. One of them parried his thrust and lunged at him with a massive shoulder, sending him flying. He sprawled on the steps, losing his bow and quiver of arrows from his shoulder before he could regain his balance and spring to his feet. But the Nubians, obeying Khasathut's command, simply ignored him and formed a treble rank below him, defending the summit against any further incursions.

They were almost zombie-like, those blacks, glazed of eye and expressionless—but with no apparent loss of coordination or dexterity—so that Khai suspected them to be acting under some hypnotic spell or other. Counted against his own army, however, and despite their massive size and cold savagery, the Nubians could not hope to hold the summit for more than a minute or two at most.

Now, as Khai mounted the last few steps to the roof of the pyramid, Khasathut staggered backward away from him until he stood center of the summit. Naked, almost pitiful, stood the crooked figure of Pharaoh as the blond warrior advanced upon him high over ravaged Asorbes. Khai's blue eyes glared their message of loathing and red revenge, and his iron sword was half-lifted in a promise of swift, merciless death. But now Khasathut began to laugh, and the man who faced him was so astounded that he paused momentarily to listen to the lunatic's words.

"Once before I was told that you would not return to Khem, Khai Ibizin," said Khasathut. "That was when you fled me as a boy. But there's that about you which can't be stopped. So, when last I had you in my power, I did more than merely allow my Dark Seven to send your *ka* down the centuries. I suspected not even that would stop you. A stricture was placed upon you, Khai of Kush, a trance of fascination, that if you should return a second time, it would only be to obey my every command! You have seen such a trance working, for my Black Guard is similarly molded to my will. Even now they give up their lives for me, for how may they question the commands of their God-king?"

"You're no more a god than the stone blocks of your great tomb— *Pharaoh*," Khai spat out the last word as if it were poison. "Why, you're no longer a man—if ever you were one in the first place—let alone a god! As for 'molding me to your will': there are no more black magic spells you can cast over me. Now you die, Khasathut," and he lifted his sword up higher. "For my murdered family, for Khem, for an entire world which you would have destroyed. *Now . . . you die!*"

"Look!" the crippled monster whooshed with his gasping voice. "Look into my eyes, Khai, and then tell me you can split me with that sword."

Khai looked, and in that moment of contact between his own and the octopus eyes of Khasathut, it was as if chains had been wrapped around him from head to foot. He felt turned to stone, and was barely aware of the fact that his sword had fallen from suddenly nerveless fingers.

In the instant before their eyes met, however, he had seen something else. Something that glowed golden in the sky to the west and came silently closer by the second. Khai knew that shape—an impossible shape that should not, could not possibly fly—and even as he froze in the weave of Khasathut's spell, he knew the thrill of ultimate strangeness, the chill of the immense and awesome unknown.

For the spinning, glowing shape that pulsed ever closer in the sky was of a great, golden pyramid, which could only mean that Khasathut's own kind had at last returned from the stars!

# V

# OUT OF THE
# STARS

Now Khasathut's eyes seemed huge in his
young-ancient face, and with his elongated head he
looked more than ever like some great evil bird of
prey. Because he had his back to the wonder in the
sky, which even now began to climb higher as it
approached the titan-walled city, he was as yet
unaware of its presence. The warriors fighting their
way up the summit's steps also were ignorant of the
approaching marvel; they fought on and died seeking to cut a way through Khasathut's black defenders. Arrows could have brought the Nubians down,
but arrows were scarce now; and the approach to
the summit was narrow, treacherous with spilled
blood and littered with the stiffening corpses of
fallen warriors.

Several of Kush's mightiest men had struggled
their way up the ramp to the steps and the glassy-eyed
Nubians were by no means having it their own way.
One by one they were falling, and Kindu himself had
been responsible for cutting down three of them. He
and Nundi had known momentary qualms about
standing against fellow Nubians, but face-to-face
with them, they had seen that Khasathut's guardsmen
were utterly beyond redemption. They were no
longer Nubians—indeed, they were something less
than human. Nundi was out of the fight now, having
fallen back with a slashed sinew in his sword arm, but
Kindu battled on. That was the way things stood
when Manek Thotak arrived, bloodied and battle-
stained, to fling himself into this final fight.

He was opposed by a huge black, gutted him, then broke through the cordon and leapt for the top of the steps. The sight he saw as his eyes came up level with the pyramid's roof stopped him dead in his tracks. His mouth fell open as his eyes went from the scene on the summit to the colossal, silently spinning shape which even now reared its bulk over Asorbes until its shadow eclipsed the massive monument itself.

And as that shadow fell over Khasathut, so the Pharaoh turned his face to the sky and saw the golden pyramid for the first time. He, too, was stunned—but only for a moment. Then—

It was as if the sight of this fantastic aerial visitant had tapped some unknown reserve of strength within him. He no longer had need of the bellow-like amplifiers with which his bizarre, larger-than-life ceremonial effigies were equipped; and weak as he was from loss of blood, still he seemed to swell larger as the spinning of the gigantic craft high above him slowed and finally stopped. Now the thing hung motionless in the sky, its base a mighty square of gold even larger than the base of Khasathut's pyramid itself, and now too Pharaoh roared out his triumph to a city struck dumb with awe and terror.

"See!" he cried, pointing his one good hand at the incredible vessel poised impossibly in thin air. "In my hour of need, my ancestors have returned to succor me. You who have defiled my temples, my house, my tomb—all of you—" he had moved to stand at the south-east corner of the summit, from where he waved his arm imperiously over the city, *"you must pay!"*

His voice carried out over a city which, except for a low wind that whistled round the pyramid's summit and carried Khasathut's words afar, was suddenly quiet as a tomb. Only that eerie wind and the distant crackle of flames competed with the voice of the triumphant monster as he laughed his maniac glee and beckoned with his one good arm.

"And see," he roared again, "see what has become of your mightiest general! Did you think he would kill me? Come, Khai, show yourself. Let your warriors see how I have bent you to my will—the fate which they too must share, because they have defied me."

Khai stepped forward into view—shoulders slumped, arms and hands hanging limp, head low on his chest—Khasathut laughed again as the silence seemed positively to deepen. "Is this the great general?" Pharaoh roared. "Well, then, see how I break him—how you will all be broken." He pointed to the south and screamed: "Now, Khai—throw yourself down!"

Without protest, Khai took a lurching step closer to the rim of the steeply plunging south face. He stood on the very edge, rocking to and fro, threatening at any moment to fall.

"Jump, Khai, jump!" cried Pharaoh, and the blood-spattered warrior bent his legs until he half-crouched at the edge of eternity.

"*Stop!*" came the bull voice of Manek Thotak. He had recovered at last from the almost supernatural paralysis which still held the rest of the city in thrall, and he had snatched up Khai's bow and an arrow from his quiver. Now, drawing back the bowstring to its full, he aimed the shaft across the summit's small space and sighted it upon the two figures where they stood at the corner of the south-facing rim. Manek was aware of the vast mass hanging in the sky above him, so much so that its very shadow seemed to fall upon him like a physical weight. Without a doubt, Khasathut's own kind had returned from the stars, and it seemed equally certain that they were watching him even now.

"Jump!" cried Pharaoh again, rage written in his bulging eyes; and once again Khai tensed the muscles of his legs as if to spring from the rim. Manek's hands quivered as he traversed the bow from Khasathut's naked, pink and twisted form to the broad back of the young general: Khai—who was once Khai of Khem—who might yet be a king in Kush! Manek's lips drew back in a snarl. He gritted his strong teeth until beads of sweat stood out upon his forehead. But—

"*No!*" he cried then in self-denial, and in the next instant realigned the bow and released the arrow . . . which flew straight to its target and transfixed Pharaoh's shoulder, knocking him down dangerously close to the rim.

The shriek which Khasathut immediately vented seemed to break the spell hanging over the city. Brave warriors though they were, the victors could no longer face up to the powers of Beings capable of suspending a pyramid in mid-air. They began to flee the city in droves—rushing madly back down the great ramp in such a stampede that those unfortunate enough to be caught at its edges were sent screaming to their deaths—streaming like myriads of ants through the streets of Asorbes and out through its shattered gates—and as they fled so Manek ran to Khai and dragged him back from the rim, guiding him to the steps.

There Khai's control returned, and shaking his head as if to clear it of invisible, poisonous fumes, he stared after his fleeing army. Down below him stood the last of Pharaoh's zombie-like guardsmen, staggering to and fro as they, too, were released from the now broken trance of fascination. They bled from countless wounds and only the spell had kept them on their feet—until now. For even as Khai watched they slumped to the steps which they had defended to the last and the life went out of them.

"Come on, Khai," Manek shouted in the blond giant's ear. We have to get away from here!"

Khai followed him shakily down the first few steps and then paused. The last of his warriors were streaming down the ramp and the rout of fleeing humanity through the streets of Asorbes was now at its full. "Come on," Manek shouted again, taking his arm. "Why do you linger?"

Khai shook himself free of the other's hand. "You go," he told Manek. "I . . . I have to *know!*" He turned to stare at the summit's center where Khasathut now kneeled with his hideous face turned up to the golden, sky-floating pyramid.

"To know what?" Manek cried, lifting his voice against a wind that sprang up from nowhere to blow his hair in his face.

*"Go!"* Khai shouted, almost in anger. "I'll follow—when I can."

Manek argued no longer, but went bounding down the steps and followed the others where they fled. Khai, alone now, stepped up again onto the roof of the pyramid and turned his wide blue eyes up to gaze at the vast golden menace which hung cold and alien over Asorbes.

# VI

## A CITY DOOMED

"Strike him down!" screamed Khasathut, pointing at Khai where he stood. "Strike them all down and take me up, quickly, for I am surely dying. Take me up, my ancestors, for I am one of you and have suffered. Why do you wait? Do you not know me?"

Without warning, an area of the golden pyramid's base glowed brighter yet and Khai staggered and shielded his eyes as a beam of yellow light struck downward and fixed upon the lofty summit, trapping two lives within its perimeter and binding them like flies in honey. Khai would have fled then, if he could, but he could not. Through a haze of golden particles, he saw Khasathut—his mouth working in a sort of slow-motion, his octopus eyes bulging, pleading—but he could hear nothing at all through the screen of potent energies which now surrounded him.

It seemed to Khai that he floated in the void between golden suns, where a myriad motes of glittering gold dust blinded him and baffled his senses. The sensation lasted for a moment only, and then, out of the silence, a Great Voice seemed to speak— not to Khai but to Other Beings of equal potency.

He heard no words, neither saw nor yet felt anything at all, and yet somehow he was party to a conversation. There *were* Beings in that shape in the sky, certainly, and indeed They recognized Khasathut. But They saw him as an error—a failed experiment—that and nothing more. There was puzzlement, too, that such a creature could ever have come to power, could have caused to happen the earthshaking events whose reverberations had been detected at the very corners of space and time, calling Them down from far journeyings, from temporal and trans-dimensional investigations of times and spaces.

Then . . . a decision was made. Khai knew it, and so did Khasathut.

"No!" the naked monster's mouth formed silent words as the golden beam from above narrowed to enclose him and exclude Khai. "No, you can't! I'm one of yours. I'm one of—"

For a moment, the beam brightened to such an intensity that Khai threw up his hands before his face. Then that solid-seeming rod of golden light blinked out and the brightly glowing spot on the flying pyramid's base quickly dulled and faded into its soft yellow surroundings. The vast mass in the sky began slowly to revolve, rising straight up into thin air until it reached a certain altitude. There it paused and its revolutions ceased, and Khai took his hands from his eyes and craned his neck to gaze up at it. Then he looked at the small heap of yellow dust at the summit's center—dust which had recently been the Pharaoh Khasathut. . . .

The wind sprang up again, blowing Khasathut's last remains in Khai's face. He choked and covered his nose and mouth, then turned and stumbled down the steps, going back the way he had come as quickly as he could.

At the foot of the ramp, Manek waited with a commandeered chariot. He bundled Khai onto his vehicle's platform and lashed his horses to a gallop, and a few minutes later they clattered out through the west gate and raced for dried up mud flats which were once a swamp.

Eight miles from the city's walls, a low hill rose up from mud baked hard as brick. Recently it had been green, grown with trees, grasses and ferns, a paradise of living things. Now it was dead. A few blackened stumps littered the crest where Manek brought the chariot to a halt. Many warriors were already there—horsemen and charioteers, mainly—waiting for their generals; and for . . . something else.

The panic was largely over now. Between the city and the hill streams of chariots, horsemen and foot soldiers like ants on the march still hurried west, leaving the doomed city behind them, not looking back. The ordinary citizens of Asorbes were there, too, many thousands of them, loaded down with their belongings and fleeing from the ravages of war. Khai and Manek had driven through them, urging them on, but now they waited as the army caught up. In another half-hour, there would not be a single soldier of Ashtarta's forces within five miles of Asorbes—which was just as well, Khai thought, for something was surely going to happen. No one said anything, but everyone knew it. It was in the air, a tension, an electric feeling. And the eyes of each and every soldier on the hill were now locked on Asorbes and the golden shape that stood in the sky over the city like some silent sentinel.

After a long while, Khai said to Manek, "It will be soon now."

They stood side by side on the hill, amidst thousands of bloodied, battered warriors whose triumph was all but forgotten. All was unnaturally quiet. Even the clatter of late-arriving chariots, the whinnying of lathered horses, the moaning of wounded men and the low mutterings of chiefs and captains as they counted their losses seemed muted.

"What is it, Khai?" Manek asked, his eyes on the distant shape in the sky, a frown etched deep in his forehead. "What will it be?"

For answer, Khai shook his head, then stiffened as he focused his eyes on sudden motion about the vast vessel hovering over the deserted city. The golden pyramid seemed to be pulsating, glowing bright and pale in an ever quickening cycle. A shimmering yellow haze, similar to the beam Khai had experienced at first hand, but more diffuse and spreading out at a wider angle, fell like a diaphanous curtain from the pyramid's base over the entire city, covering it wall to wall. The pulsating continued, quickened, and the massive vessel began to lift into the sky. Amazingly, impossibly, most of Asorbes began to lift with it!

Caught in tractors of fantastic power, vast segments of the city's walls broke loose and shuddered into the sky; towers, buildings and temples became airborne; anything that was not deeply rooted in the bedrock of the earth itself was slowly, irresistibly drawn skyward. But most of the power was concentrated centrally, on Khasathut's tomb, on the pyramid itself. . . .

A vast sigh—a concerted gasp of awe and disbelief—went up from thousands of throats as finally that tremendous monument rocked and broke free of its base and millions of tons of stone were drawn bodily aloft. It seemed as if every man of Ashtarta's army held his breath then, as the city of Asorbes rose up and up. And as the golden pyramid exerted its incredible energy on the uprooted city, so that raw power was made visible in the lightnings that leapt between sky-floating stone and scarred and pitted earth.

Huge tongues of fire licked at the ground in electrical greed, and dust clouds like the dark breath of demons rose everywhere. A low rumble, rapidly growing louder, filled the air and clouds began to form in the sky, racing outward from the epicenter which was the shattered, elevated city.

Khai, Manek and their armies heard that rumble, felt it in the ground, in their bones, and knew that the end was near. Thus it was something of an anticlimax when suddenly, in an instant, the huge inverted funnel of golden haze blinked out—the beam and the golden pyramid, too, disappearing as if they had never existed—leaving the revenant fragments of Asorbes suspended in thin air. For a second it seemed as though those millions of tons were to remain frozen in the sky forever, but then they began to fall.

A city rained to earth, and the last trace of Khasathut's influence in the world was obliterated for all time.

The cloud of dust and smoke which then rose up in a mushroom-topped column heralded an earthquake that threw every watcher to the ground, thus saving them from the mad rush of winds that howled outward from the shattered, scattered debris of Asorbes. When it was over, Khai dusted himself down and turned his face to the west.

"Are you thinking, Khai, of the queen who waits for you in Kush?" Manek asked. "If so, you should know I won't oppose you."

"If you don't others will," Khai wryly answered. "No, a Khemite could never lord it over Kush, Manek. I think you've taught me that much. I'll return to Khem . . . eventually. To a new Khem. As for Kush—Kush is yours."

"Mine?" For a moment Manek showed his astonishment. He tried to speak several times, but could not find the words. Finally he said: "You do this for me, Khai? For me, a proven traitor? One who tried to destroy you?"

"Who else knows it?" Khai asked. "I know it, and already it is forgotten. Yes, you tried to destroy me, but since then you've twice saved my life. And are you really such a traitor? A traitor betrays his own country, Manek, and you only wanted to keep yours safe and free. No, because of what you tried to do, I have been made to see that I could never stay in Kush. It's Khem for me, and Ashtarta will be my Queen here. It might take some time to convince her, and there will be many things to do, but. . . .

"But what of you? Will you take a Queen, Manek?"

"A Queen?" Manek looked surprised, then showed his teeth in a grin. "That I will! She lives in the village of Thon Emahl, in Kush. She's Thon's widow, though I knew her before he did. I gave her up for . . . for the throne of Kush!"

"Well," Khai answered, nodding, "now you shall have both." He clasped the other's arm. "Now we shall both have our hearts' desires. Isn't it enough, Manek?"

"More than enough!" Manek laughed. "Well, come on. What are we waiting for? If we make good time, we can be home in three days!"

"Two!" Khai answered, and he also laughed. And in his mind, he pictured Ashtarta's marquee and a certain chamber within it where the walls were of purple linen. But what use to dwell on memories when the real thing waited for him at the end of a chariot ride?

The two men climbed aboard their vehicle's platform and Khai took the reins. He wheeled his horses round and aimed them westward, then shook the reins and laughed again as he gave the animals their head. . . .

# epilogue

Wilfred Sommers watched the *Egypt-Air* jet take off and climb into the sun. He watched it until it was little more than a silver sliver in the sky, then turned and made his way from the airport lounge, through the crowded foyer and out to the car park. As he drove back to the museum, he managed to get his thoughts sorted out a little, so that by the time he climbed the museum's stairs to the second floor he believed he finally understood something of what had happened. More than that he could not, dared not admit to believing. But the whole thing had impressed him deeply and it was not something he would soon forget.

For the tenth time, he pictured the meeting between Paul Arnott and Omar Dassam as he had seen it less than a week ago. They had met; Dassam had given Arnott a ring which he had slipped onto his finger; then—

Sommers shook his head as he made his way along aisles of relics toward his father's private rooms. The transformation had been amazing, frightening. There had been recognition in the eyes of the two men, real recognition, and something else. That other something had seemed to span untold centuries of time, had reached out from the past to bind both men in an unbreakable spell. Sommers and his father had felt nothing physical, nothing really . . . tangible. And yet there had been—yes, something.

Arnott had finally broken the spell, when in an

instant he changed from a civilized man into—into what? Whatever, his totally unexpected attack on Dassam had been like greased lightning. The other man had not known what hit him, and yet at the same time, he seemed somehow to expect it. Arnott struck two blows, so that his victim was already unconscious and falling when he was snatched up and hurled headlong through the old hardwood paneling of the study into the next room. And still not satisfied, Arnott had been after him with a bound—doubtless to finish the job—when his hang-gliding injury caught up with him. Then he had collapsed against the wall, crumpling in a moment, and all of that primal power had seemed to drain out of him. Just as well, for Sommers and his father had known that he was intent upon killing the other man, the stranger from Egypt.

And what of that exchange between them, before Arnott's attack? There had been recognition in that, too. They had spoken, nothing in the English tongue, words in a language dead and gone for thousands of years. That was Sir George's guess, at any rate, and it was that chiefly which had determined the elder Sommers perspective of the thing, his explanation of what he thought had happened. His son had more or less come to agree with his theory, though when first he heard it, he could not help but compare it to Paul Arnott's own wild fancies. And yet how else could any of it be explained?

But for all the Sommers's talk of race-memory—of Arnott's instinctive fear of Egypt, despite his fascination with the subject; of his being a throwback to some forgotten race of men whose homeland had been in or near the Nile Valley—still their concept could only remain one of purest conjecture. Never in a million years could they have guessed how close they were to the truth of things.

Dassam had not been seriously injured by Arnott's attack and had recovered a few minutes later when Wilfred Sommers applied smelling salts. Arnott, on the other hand, had been taken back into hospital. He, too, as it worked out, was lucky. He had done himself no permanent damage; indeed something seemed to have clicked back into place, so that within a few days, he was out of hospital permanently and free at last of his "concrete breastplate."

Moreover, there had been . . . changes.

Changes in both men, inexplicable alterations in memory, character and mood. The one, Dassam, seemed to have lost something: the element of instinctive *drive* visible in him before was no longer there. He was no longer searching. He could not explain his coming to England, his purpose in approaching the elder Sommers with his find, that prehistoric funerary mask from the foothills of the Gilf Kebir. Indeed, he seemed horrified that he had dared smuggle the thing out of his country and into England in the first place, and he couldn't wait to take it back and hand it over to the rightful authorities.

Sir George could only agree with Dassam's sentiments in this matter, and he further agreed to say nothing of the affair, but simply pretend that it had never happened.

As for Paul Arnott: paradoxically, he seemed to have both lost *and* found something. He was much less restless, had lost all of his old moodiness, was no longer continually bothered by dim dreams of far, fabulous places and half-remembered occurrences in a world which existed in an age when saber-tooths still prowled England and the last mammoths still wandered the Siberian plains. On the other hand, he now seemed to know where he was going and what he was doing. He had . . . direction.

He had been shocked when he was reminded of his attack upon Dassam, for apparently he could not recall it, knew nothing at all of it, would not accept that it had ever happened—until Wilfred Sommers visited him in the hospital and brought the Egyptian with him, and he saw Dassam's face: the badly bruised jaw and blackened eye. And even then he had difficulty accepting the fact that he was to blame.

Finally, there was the matter of the two rings which Dassam had found with the golden mask. When Sir George had asked the Egyptian if he intended to hand them over also, he had declared that that was not his intention. One of the rings belonged to him—the other belonged to "Khai." Afterwards he had not known why he had called Arnott by that name, and he never used it again. . . .

Now Sommers had reached the door to his father's study and he knocked before entering. Sir George was pacing the floor, deep in thought. After a while, he stopped his pacing and looked up. The two faced each other and each knew what the other was thinking. Then Sir George smiled and his son joined him.

"Did everything go all right?" the elder Sommers asked.

"Oh, yes, the plane got off OK," Wilfred answered.

"And Omar is sure he can smuggle the mask back in again?"

"He thinks so, yes."

For a moment, the older man was silent, then he said: "It has all been very strange, but now it's over."

"Is it?" His son seemed doubtful.

"You think there's something else?"

"I don't think we've seen the last of Paul, no."

"Ah!" his father thought he understood. "You think he'll make some great discovery up there in the Gilf Kebir, do you? You believe that he and Omar will have a successful dig, is that it?"

"Oh, that's possible, but it's not what I meant. I think he's gone out there to search for something, yes, but not for anything he'll find buried in the ground."

"Ah!" his father said again. "Perhaps you're right. The face on the mask, eh?"

The other nodded. "If there ever was a Sh'tarra—if there is now—where better to find her?"

"And do you think he will find her?"

To which there was really no answer. . . .